Land of the Morning Calm

Land of the Morning Calm

A Novel

Harry Bryce

iUniverse, Inc.

New York Lincoln Shanghai

Land of the Morning Calm

iUniverse books may be ordered through booksellers or by contacting:

iUniverse
2021 Pine Lake Road, Suite 100
Lincoln, NE 68512
www.iuniverse.com
1-800-Authors (1-800-288-4677)

Because of the dynamic nature of the Internet, any Web addresses or links contained in this book may have changed since publication and may no longer be valid.

This is a work of fiction. All of the characters, names, incidents, organizations, and dialogue in this novel are either the products of the author's imagination or are used fictitiously.

ISBN: 978-0-595-46939-0 (pbk)
ISBN: 978-0-595-70929-8 (cloth)
ISBN: 978-0-595-91223-0 (ebk)

Printed in the United States of America

To my wonderful wife, Hedy, who inspired me to tell this story and to my good friend, Ross, the smartest man I know, who guided me through the writing process.

Contents

Old Army Riddle

"What's the difference between a Fairy Tale and a War Story?"

<u>The Answer</u>

"Well, one starts with, 'Once upon a time'
The other starts with, 'This ain't no shit'
But after that they're pretty much the same."

Unknown Soldier

So for those of you who want to know if every word of what you're about to read is really one-hundred percent true ... Well ...

"This Ain't No Shit!"

1

1965 Prologue

I was a typical product of the sixties, just a big kid having great fun in high school. By my senior year, I'd reached six foot three and 210 pounds of mostly muscle. I played football, which I became fairly good at it, defense mostly. Because I lacked fine motor skills, our coach didn't want me to ever touch the ball; he knew it would end up an almost guaranteed fumble. So, I played defense; as a Middle Linebacker, all I had to do was knock people down and I got pretty good at it, plus, I liked it a lot.

To the best of my knowledge, street drugs hadn't been invented yet, at least not in the North Kingstown, Rhode Island of 1961. I guess it must have been around somewhere, but I never saw or even heard of any. To my Class of '61, these were truly the *Happy Days*. I now often joke, saying I went to school with *Richie Cunningham & the Fonz*.

The Korean War ended eight years earlier and all I really knew about it was that it happened a long time ago, when I was just a little kid. My Dad went and flew carrier-based combat missions for the Navy.

North Kingstown was a *Navy Town*. Quonset Point Navel Air Station and the Davisville Seabee Base were the town's biggest employers; so, there was a very strong military influence. Two aircraft carriers were even based at Quonset. The Naval War College and a bunch of Navy destroyers were also just across the Narragansett Bay, at Newport.

Vietnam may have been going on in some way back then, but my guess is most Rhode Islanders hadn't even heard the name and wouldn't be able to find it on a map. To us, Vietnam was this obscure, little *Backwater* skirmish somewhere in south-east Asia, way over on the other side of the globe. It must not have been very newsworthy either because I don't really remember hearing much about it until probably after the 22nd of November, 1963. That's the terrible day President Kennedy was assassinated and Vice President Johnson assumed the Presidency. In the late 50s and early 60s, America was more worried about happenings

90 miles off the Florida coast in Cuba. A revolutionary Communist by the name of Fidel Castro had come into power down there. We still had yet to endure the humiliation of the ill-fated CIA/Cuban "Bay of Pigs" invasion and to get scared out of our wits by the Soviets during the "Cuban Missile Crisis" in October of '62.

I personally place President Kennedy's death as the official end of the *Happy Days*. That smack of harsh reality ended ten years of glorious fun between the end of the Korean War and the beginning of the Johnson Administration's escalation of America's intervention in the Vietnam. I feel really fortunate to have come of age during those fun times of early Rock n' Roll, tail fins, hotrods, A&W root beer stands and drive-in movies. My only worries, back then, were gas money for my '41 Chevy convertible (19.5 cents a gallon) and deciding whether to take Beth or Linda to the Saturday dance. They played Betty and Veronica to my Archie Andrews throughout my high school years. After high school I went on to college, first at Roger Williams and then to the University of Rhode Island.

It was now late summer 1965 and, being a product of the sixties, my life followed a pattern familiar to so many young men of my era:

- I got out of school in '64.

- I landed a great job with an electrical manufacturing company as a design draftsman.

- I helped in the design of a better and cheaper way to get plastic parts out of hot molds by using compressed air instead of knock-out pins.

- As a reward for all this, I got a promotion, a pay raise and a bonus—cool!

- I took the bonus and blew it on a bright-red, Chevy, Corvair Monza coupe—pretty damned cool!

- Then, Uncle Sam drafted my young ass into the US Army.

I remember that day vividly; it was August 15th, my birthday. I had just gotten home from work. At that time I was paying rent but still living with my folks. First on the evening's agenda was birthday dinner with my parents and then off for an evening of dancing with Linda (*Veronica*) at a new little dance place I'd recently found. I was getting pretty serious about Linda and was even contemplating popping the big question around Christmas. Now that I was beginning to earn real money, I could visualize a career progression. I picked my mail up off the bookcase just inside the front door; only this time there was an official-looking envelope from the US Government. In 1965 all young men had to register for the "Draft" and we all got these official-looking envelopes fairly regularly. The Government made sure they kept in touch with all us draft age males. These letters didn't bother me too much, because I had nothing to worry about. I'd swapped in my student draft rating for a 1-Y classification. The 1-Y was because I had a medical condition which precluded me from being drafted. I zipped open the envelope and stared at it dumbfounded. It read something like:

Greeting: You are hereby selected for induction into the Armed Forces of the United States of America, etc., etc.

The rest of the letter just gave the particulars of when I was to report for my pre-induction physical and my ultimate induction. The dates were 4 September for the physical & 15 September for induction. That was exactly one month from my birthday. Needless to say, the rest of the evening had a pall cast over it. I tried to convince myself there was some big mistake. Hadn't I had the chance to join the Rhode Island National Guard as a way of beating the draft? Didn't my Dad even have a well-placed Guard Colonel friend who said I didn't have anything to worry about? He said, "Don't worry about joining the Guard, Herb; you have a 1-Y classification. You'd only be drafted if there's a 'National Emergency'. Heck, women and children will be drafted before they come after you!"

Alongside dozens of other worried looking young men, I showed up at the East Greenwich Armory for my physical. Unlike the others, I had this air of confidence about me and my 1-Y classification papers in hand. When it was my turn, I proudly announced to the doctor, "Excuse me, Doctor, but as you can see from this medical report dated just last April, there's been a big mistake. I have this Pilonidal Cyst thing at the tip of my spine and a 1-Y classification." He looked up from his desk and reached out for the papers as he asked, "Let me see it please?" He pulled the curtain around our tiny examination area while I dropped my drawers and bent over the gurney. The doctor studied my terrible medical problem up close and personal. "Umm Hum, Umm Hum." he then stood up, snapped off a rubber glove and announced, "Nope! No problem here; we can fix that thing when you get to Basic Training." He confiscated my prized medical documents and presented me with new ones, after taking out his big rubber stamp and "Bang!" stamping it with a big red "1-A" *Available for Military Service.* Son of a bitch! I'd been drafted into the Army kicking and screaming from my Mother! Those Bastards!

I got sworn in on 15 September along with a bunch of other scared looking boys and we all climbed aboard a *Greyhound* bus in Providence, Rhode Island bound for Fort Dix, New Jersey. I waved goodbye to my parents and my darling Linda.

I did to Linda what a lot of young men do in situations such as mine; I declared my intentions by giving her an engagement ring. Several months later, with no explanation, she sent it back to me in an envelope with no note. I was crushed at the time, but when you sit down and really analyze it, a guy giving his girl a ring then going off on his big Army adventure is really a pretty selfish thing to do. What you're actually saying to her is, *"Put your life on hold for me, Baby!"* The ring ends up just a "symbolic placeholder" intended to keep her in check until you get back. It's really not a fair or even nice thing to do to someone; so, I never really held long-term ill-feelings toward Linda. She went on with her life while I had mine forced upon me by my good old Uncle Sam.

My story now jumps forward about two years. I've been through all my training, including, Infantry Officer Candidate School. It's now January, 1967, but I'm gravitating towards my first overseas assignment, a short tour, remote assignment in Korea. This was a pivotal time because so much happened; my life and the world changed in so many ways in just one year. So, let me take you back and tell you about my thirteen month long year in *The Land of the Morning Calm*. And, let me tell you once again, "This ain't no shit!"

2

Ain't I Supposed To Be in Nam?

I graduated from Infantry OCS (Officer Candidate School) at Fort Benning, Georgia that chilly, 11th day of January, 1967. My Mom and Dad drove all the way down from Rhode Island for the ceremony. Dad, a retired, enlisted, naval aviator, was so proud of me standing there in my brand new dress greens and shiny, new, gold, Second Lieutenant's bars. As this bear of a man stood in front of me, with tears in his eyes, I thought he was just going to burst with pride. He gave me my first salute and, in timeless Army tradition, I returned it and gave him a crisp, new, one dollar bill. Mom gave me a big hug, kissed me on the cheek and with a mother's pride, told me how handsome and fit I looked, as she unconsciously brushed away a speck of something from my lapel. I was fit too, more fit than I'd ever been. Dad pulled out the ancient Kodak, snapped a few pictures of Mom and I out in front of Infantry Hall by the *Iron Mike* statue and that was that. It was one of those special moments and I was truly proud of my accomplishment. Only ninety-seven of the original 225 who started out last July, on this OCS odyssey, were still standing here six months later to enjoy this day. The others had academically flunked out, dropped out for various reasons, or were simply asked to leave. Up to this point in my life, this was the most difficult thing I'd ever done and, to this day, I'm still damned proud of it.

Like every other brand new *Butter Bar,* Second Lieutenant, I thought the instant those little gold bars were pinned on my shoulders I would magically be whisked away to the steaming jungles of Vietnam. After all, wasn't that the purpose of being drafted in the first place? Everyone knew Infantry OCS Second Lieutenants were nothing but cannon fodder for the war. We were designed, built and trained just to lead infantry platoons in combat. Unfortunately, Infantry Lieutenants also have a very high propensity for getting their asses killed. *"Follow me men!"* Statistically, by percentage, more Infantry Second Lieutenants are killed or wounded in combat than any other rank in the Army. We'd even been given an extra week of special Vietnam training tacked onto the normal six month course. The Army hoped this information from our latest jungle returnees would help us stay alive a little longer. *"You better listen up if you don't want to die in Vietnam!"* Just a few nights ago, we Senior OCS Candidates were all crunching through quarter-inch thick Georgia swamp ice pretending we were sneaking up on a Vietcong encampment. The sound of an Infantry Platoon going **Crunch, Crunch, *Crunch*** through that thin ice crust would have woken the dead. All I was really concerned with was my freezing feet encased in those ice-cold, soggy socks and canvas jungle boots. I remembered my Great Uncle Fred telling me World War One stories about Trench Foot and amputations. Our Tactical Officer then chimed in sadistically, "Pretend there's no ice here gentlemen. This is just warm, leach infested, Vietnamese swamp water". *"Pretend my ass!"* The sound was deafening that freezing, January night down by the Chattahoochee River. I whispered to the guy next to me, "Right, and let's hope *Charlie* is fuckin' deaf!"

Anyway, I didn't go straight to Vietnam and I don't know why, unless, maybe it's because I branch transferred into the Military Police Corps while sill in Infantry OCS. Branch transferring was not an easy or comfortable thing to do, but I did it anyway, because I'd already discovered the Infantry was not my cup of tea. My defection in our 18th week of training singled me out for a lotta' extra special attention by the 73rd OC Company Tactical Officers. From the instant I was accepted into the MPs, until graduation day, my life was made a living hell. Translation: I did about a million push-ups plus every other dirty detail the cadre's sadistic little minds could dream up to try and break me. Instead of breaking, I just got stronger. I must've been consuming 5000 calories a day, and yet, I was still losing weight.

I've often pondered why I didn't go to Nam, but now I'm pretty sure it was God's work. No, I'm not a religious nut or anything like that, but there's a reason for my feeling this way. I'll tell you about it later on and you can decide.

So, I didn't go in 1967; that adventure was to be reserved for a bit later. In between graduation day and Vietnam, a lot happened. I spent my first two weeks as a commissioned officer at Fort Rucker, Alabama *"The Home of Army Aviation."* Then, I was off to ten weeks of Military Police Officer's Basic training at Fort Gordon in Augusta, Georgia. Compared to Infantry OCS, MP Officer Basic was a vacation. After that, I was sent back to Fort Rucker, where, as a Second Lieutenant, I took over command of 141st Military Police Company from a newly promoted Major who, in just a few days, was leaving for Vietnam. With the buildup going on over there, it seemed like everyone was headed that way.

So much emphasis was being placed on the Vietnam War that the rest of the Army was sort of left languishing in the shadows. That's why I, as a very, very junior Second Lieutenant (2LT), ended up in a Captain's command position. To add insult to injury, they assigned Jimmy Crowell, another MP 2LT, just two weeks junior grade to me, as my XO (Executive Officer). To round out the bad joke, they assigned a *Shake & Bake* E-6 Staff Sergeant as my acting First Sergeant. Heck, Sergeant Trumbull had even less time in the Army than Jimmy and I did. Ours was truly a case of "*The blind leading the blind*".

For some strange reason, after just a few weeks in command, I received assignment orders for Ranger training right back at Fort Benning. This came as a big shock because I knew one had to volunteer for the Rangers and I never had! Again, because of Vietnam, Ranger School was expanding and opening up training to other than just the Infantry, Armor and Artillery branches or what the Army refers to as the *Combat Arms*.

When I came down on orders I called Military Police Branch, in the Pentagon, inquiring about their obvious screw up. They said, "No mistake!" Seems the MP Corps received their first-ever allocations, two of them, and were looking for two Infantry OCS trained MP Lieutenants to fill the slots. They selected me, *Royce*, and another of my classmates, 2LT *Don Cherry*. The party line was they had scoured dozens of records of recent Infantry OCS grads who'd branch transferred into the MPs. The assignments guy said MP Branch knew we'd be in shape to meet the physical rigors of Ranger training. He said they'd carefully selected Cherry and I because our records indicated we were "The best of the best." Now, I pretty much know BS when I hear it, and this crap was knee deep. It didn't take me long to figure it all out. After listening to this Headquarters asshole for five minutes my best guess was that late some Pentagon, Friday afternoon, this lazy bastard went alphabetically through the most recent Infantry OCS graduation rosters he could find. He picked the first two Infantry School trained MPs he saw, hence the "C" for Cherry and the "R" for Royce. After that ordeal, including a bunch of stitches at Martin Army Hospital, I went back to Fort Rucker for about seven more months as an MP company commander; then I came down on orders for Korea!

3

The FNG

I was assigned to the 5th US Missile Command, Camp Page, Chunchon, Korea. After a very long Northwest Orient *Red Tail* plane ride, which started in Boston, I arrived at Kimpo Airbase in Seoul. When I stepped off the plane and momentarily stood at the top of the roll-a-way stairs, I encountered my first impression of Korea. To be polite, let's just say I had never smelled a smell like that smell in my life and I will remember it to my dying day. It smelled so *bad* I couldn't think of anything to compare it to.

Once inside the terminal, actually a big Korean War era airplane hanger, I lined up with all the other "Newbies" for my Gamma Globulin shot. These were really big shots and they really hurt. They gave them to you in the butt and for about a week just casually sitting isn't an option. The teenage medic said, "Drop your drawers and take the weight off your left leg Lieutenant." The second I complied, he stabbed me in the left cheek with this three inch long, hollow, ten penny nail and injected about two shot glasses full of a maple syrup-thick, brown fluid. I suppressed a scream and fought back tears as my eyes welled up. "Just massage the lump, Lieutenant, and it will gradually go down." I really wanted to let out a scream and maybe cry like I did when I was a little kid, but in 1967 we were still into manly ways because Oprah and Dr. Phil didn't exist yet. This Gamma Globulin stuff was an experiment the Army hoped would protect us from contracting Hemorrhagic Fever, whatever the hell that is. To this day, I'm still not totally sure what it really is. All I was told was, it's in Korea, it can kill your ass, and the Army says you got no choice; you will get the damned "GG" shot!

I watched as everybody from my flight was either met by NCOs (Non-Commissioned Officers) or Officers from their new units. Others just limped onto military buses headed for the 8th Army Personnel Replacement Depot at Yongsan Compound in Seoul. After a short while, everyone had left; everyone except me! I ended up being the last Newbie in this huge, quiet, dimly lit, old hanger. I sat there on my duffel bag for about an hour, feeling very lonely and a bit like the last puppy in the pet shop window, when a Korean man in a flight suit approached. He was slim, tall for a Korean, and looked like he should be the leading man in one of those epic Chinese movies. He walked up to me and asked, *"Are rue Roo-tenant Roy-cee?"* I jumped to my feet. Back at Fort Rucker, the Army had given me a two-week crash course in Korean language and culture and it was time to try and cash in. Part of the training included learning what the various ROK (Republic of Korea) military rank insignias looked like. I replied loudly, **"Yes, Captain!"** I even popped one of my best Infantry OCS salutes on him. He looked a little startled, then amused and humored me with a far less dramatic salute in return. "I am Captain Song. *Preese* you come *rith* me. I *fry* you to Camp *Pa-gee.*" I grabbed my gear and followed, hoping *Camp Pay-gee* was the same place as Camp Page.

In the fading rays of evening light, we walked out of the hanger and onto the tarmac towards what I recognized as an old Dehavilland "Beaver". Living most of my childhood on naval air stations, I became a minor expert in aircraft recognition. It was OD (olive drab) green with yellow U.S. Army markings and appeared to have a lot of ware and tare on it. This plane probably was made in the early 50s. It was a single engine prop job with a straight parasol wing and came from the tail dragger era. I was motioned up front to the right seat next to Captain Song and I buckled myself in. A few smoky coughs and sputters and the old radial engine caught and roared to life. With very little fanfare, we lazily accelerated down the runway, the blue airfield marker lights passing my side window at an ever faster pace. I felt the Beaver's tail wheel rise off the ground as we leveled for a brief moment, then slowly we rose off the runway and we were *frying*!

As the old Beaver droned on into the ever darkening sky, I kept glancing at the radium face of my watch. We'd been airborne for over half an hour and the cockpit compass had hardly moved off "North-East" the whole time. *"North was where North Korea was, right?"* We were mostly flying up river-valleys at less than a thousand feet above the ground. A lot of strange thoughts went racing through my sleep deprived brain. The Captain was silently piloting the plane and didn't seem to want to talk much. In the silence, I was trying to calculate distance and our location based on airspeed, time and compass heading. I knew Beavers were slow, but it was now getting very dark outside. I looked again at the insignia on the shoulder of Captain Song's flight suit. In the dim red glow of the cockpit instruments, I scrunched up my eyes trying to see more clearly. *"Was his insignia South or North Korean? Shouldn't we be there by now?"* I knew North Korea was not that far from Seoul because I'd been looking at Korean maps for weeks now. All this was whirling around in my tired head when the silent Captain Song banked the sturdy Beaver over to the right, pointed towards the ground and finally spoke, *"Rook,* Camp *Pay-Gee dare!"* Even in the inky darkness, I could still make out neat rows of Quonset Huts and street lights below. There was also a reflection off a river to the west.

The blue airstrip landing lights suddenly popped on and gave dimension to this rather small base. As we descended, I could now make out the perimeter fence lights outlining the camps shape. I silently thanked God I hadn't been captured by North Koreans while feeling a bit foolish all at the same time. I decided I really liked Captain Song; he was a cool guy and my very first Korean. I hoped I would get to know him better. He cranked the flaps down and the Beaver slowed to near stall. We floated down onto the runway in a perfect two point landing. The tail wheel finally settled to the ground with just the slightest bump. Captain Song expertly taxied the Beaver up to the control tower and shut down the engine. Well, I was finally here, twenty-five hours and fifty-one minutes out of Boston. Must be a world's record! For a Walter Mitty moment, I fantasized about how Lindbergh must have felt landing in Paris after his historic Atlantic crossing. The *Spirit of St. Louis* didn't look a whole hell of a lot different from this old Beaver and it undoubtedly flew faster.

It was now close to midnight. I saluted and thanked Captain Song for the lift. I grabbed my duffel and was escorted by the Staff Duty NCO to my *Hooch* which ended up being a small part of the Quonset hut labyrinth I saw from the air. Light green Quonsets of various sizes made up just about ninety-five percent of the buildings on Camp Page. Quonset huts in winter, *hummm*; this was going to be interesting. Let's see; corrugated metal outsides and quarter inch thick *Masonite* walls inside with zero insulation in between, how cozy! The NCO led me down a long, narrow, hallway and stopped outside room 103. "This is it Lieutenant. This is the room you've been assigned to." The sergeant departed; I twisted the brass knob and the door creaked open. The small bulb in the hall gave me just enough light, through the half opened door, for a quick glimpse around my new digs. A sleepy voice came out of a darkened corner, "Hey Buddy, close the damned door and kill the light; some of us are trying to sleep in here!" I eased the door closed and let my eyes slowly adjusted to the darkness. A nearby pole light helped by allowing just enough illumination through a window so I could make out the lay of the room. These accommodations were set up for junior officers, four guys to a room, with a bunk in each corner. I found an empty bunk to the left of the door, flopped down in total exhaustion, pulled up an Army blanket I found neatly folded on the bare mattress and almost instantly fell fast asleep, uniform, shoes and all.

My roommates, whom I wouldn't actually meet until the next morning, were Second Lieutenant David Ross and First Lieutenant Paul Gleason, the senior officer in the room. A strange little southern, Second Lieutenant by the name Ab Abercrombie would arrive one day after I did to round out our foursome. Ab was short for Abner.

My first Korean morning, I awoke shivering in my compact quarter of this un-insulated tin can of a room. *"Christ, it was cold!"* The early morning light streaming through our two, basement-sized windows, revealed some sort of stone-cold heating device in the center of the room. This thing later became known to me as a *Cannon heater*. It was a very rudimentary looking device. First of all, it was sitting in a four by four foot, shallow, metal box. The main fire box was nothing more than a 55 gallon oil drum surrounded by a slightly larger metal, cylinder shaped cage. I guess the cage was there so you only got second-degree burns, instead of the first-degree variety, if you accidentally touched it. Halfway up the side of this thing was a small door about eight inches square. Hanging on a bracket, high up on the side of the thing, was a standard five-gallon Jerry Can just like the ones strapped to the back of Army Jeeps. There was some sort of pump fitted into the mouth of the Jerry Can. A red handle protruded to prime the line between the Jerry Can and the oil drum type heater box. This let diesel oil (I could smell it.) drip to the bottom of the heater's fire box. To light this thing, and I'm not kidding, you opened the little door and threw a small burning piece of oil dipped rag into the fire box. There was a red knob connected to the line that somehow metered the dripping of the diesel into bottom of the drum. On top of this Rube Goldberg device sat a *Maxwell House* coffee can full of water to put moisture back into the air.

I later discovered the main problem with this contraption was, when lit at bedtime, it would always run out of fuel in the wee hours and someone had to get up to change fuel cans and re-light the thing. If not, everyone in the room was at risk of freezing to death in their sleep. Of course, no one was awake to tell me this and none of my roommates cared about it running out of fuel. They had bought electric blankets from the PX (Post Exchange store) so they wouldn't have to get up.

So there I was, shivering convulsively, trying to figure out how to fire-up the damned thing before I fell victim to hypothermia. Paul Gleason grumped at me, "Hey, watcha' doin'? Don't touch that!" Giving me a silent, *You dumb shit!* glare, Gleason grudgingly emerged from his warm bed, brushed his blond hair away from his eyes as he fumbled for his black horn-rimmed glasses. He expertly changed Jerry Cans and got the silly looking thing fired up. He scolded me not to touch the damned heater until I attended a training class and got my "Space Heater Operator's License." (I'm not kidding; I still have it to this very day.) Gleason warned that these Cannon Heaters were dangerous as hell and had already caused a few really bad fires in the enlisted barracks and the BOQs (Bachelor Officers' Quarters). After sufficiently chastising me, he flopped back into his bunk and pulled his *GE* electric blanket up around his ears.

Having already served as both an enlisted man and as an officer, I always found it strange enlisted men lived in *barracks* while officers resided in *quarters*, even when the accommodations were identical. At Camp Page they really were exactly the same. All officers below the rank of Captain lived four to a room, same as the enlisted men and Junior NCOs.

I explored my way down the rabbit warren of hallways, to a wonderfully warm latrine (bathroom), where I showered, shaved and got ready to start this new and exotic chapter in my life. A guy shaving in the sink next to me glanced over and asked, "You the FNG?" I said, "What?"

"The **F-N-G**—you the Fucking New Guy MP?"

"Oh, yeah, that's me; I'm the FNG, I flew in last night ... late. My name's Herb Royce."

Carefully trimming his moustache, he asked, "You meet the Screaming Eagle yet, Herb?"

"Sorry, haven't had the pleasure."

Finishing up, he made eye contact and said, "You're in for a real treat Lieutenant and it won't be no fucking pleasure." He stuck out his hand and said, "Welcome to the asylum; I'm Chief of Personnel, Jim Dunkerly, but everybody calls me Dad!" I sort of laughed while shaking his hand and was hoping this was just an icebreaker intro. We finished shaving about the same time and then departed the wonderfully warm latrine. After going down a few wrong hallways, I finally found myself back at my strange, curved walled BOQ room 103.

Now that I was dressed, I stepped outside, the crisp early November wind had a definite bite to it, but it felt good. Coming from LA—that's *Lower Alabama*—I was probably feeling the change more than most. Paul Gleason walked part of the way with me then pointed me towards the Provost Marshal's Office before he veered off towards his workplace.

There I stood, outside another light green Quonset hut, reading a suspended sign gently swinging in the breeze over the door. "5th USMC PMO—United States Marine Corps?" I must have been thinking out loud because a big MP Sergeant, with the name "Kelser" on his uniform, came up behind and said, "5th United States Missile Command, Lieutenant, and P-M-O stands for Provost

Marshal's Office." I knew the second acronym, but didn't make a big deal of it. I returned the Sergeant's salute and thanked him. I stood there for a minute thinking to myself, *"Here I am, a Second Lieutenant for less than a year and I've already been an MP Company Commander, and now, I'm about to become the Provost Marshal (chief of police) for a major command and about 10,000 square miles of northeastern, South Korea. How in the hell did all this happen so fast?"* I didn't know it then, but North Korea was plotting an interesting, not to mention scary as hell, welcome for me.

I walked through the main PMO door and was now standing in front of a raised Military Police Desk. Every MP Desk I'd seen so far was raised up so the Desk Sergeant had the "high ground" and a commanding view over the rest of the room. It also made it difficult for a drunk, or anyone else, to come over the top of the desk and attack the Desk Sergeant.

The room was full of MPs, about a dozen or so. Somebody yelled "Tench-Hut!" and the room visually and audibly snapped to attention. It's Army custom, when a superior officer enters a room, the senior most military person in the room calls everyone to attention. I always had two reactions to this. First, it scared the hell out of me, and second, I always instantly thought, *"Is it for me or is there a General standing behind me?"* Protocol dictates I immediately yell back either; *At Ease, As You Were* or *Carry On.* This time I chose *"At Ease!"* and hoped there was no General.

I met and shook hands with everyone in the room. Each wanted to impress me with their firm handshake. After the bones in my right hand had been sufficiently rearranged, I was shown to my office. Then, in the best of Army FNG traditions, I received a series of briefings on the mission, the current status of things, the unit's personnel and our area of operations. I was formally introduced to each NCO and enlisted man who, in turn, told me what their job was. There was something definitely wrong in that room, but I couldn't quite put my finger on it.

I also was introduced to my Korean staff. There were five of them. First, was Mr. Chong, or as all the MPs called him, "Cop Chong". Cop wasn't his first name and I never thought to try and find out what it really was. He was my KNP (Korean National Police) liaison man. Cop Chong was short, about regular Korean size, probably pushing fifty, powerfully built and he had this great gold-toothed grin. I guessed I was going to have to get used to this bowing thing because they all did it when meeting you. It didn't take me long before I became quite proficient and at ease with this formality.

Next, was another Mr. Chong. This Mr. Chong everybody called "Big Chong." So, I had two Chongs. Well at least I wouldn't get their names mixed up. One was a cop and the other just big. Big Chong had to be over six foot because he looked me dead level in the eye, while shaking my hand, and I'm six foot three. He had these heavy black framed glasses that looked like they were stolen from Buddy Holly. Big Chong, I was told, usually stayed inside the MP Station, behind the desk, during days and was the interpreter-translator for the MP Desk Sergeant or anyone else in the PMO who needed his services.

Next was Captain Ye. He commanded my Korean security guard unit. In addition to my MPs, I discovered I also had a one-hundred man strong Koran Security Guard company that patrolled the Camp Page perimeter and manned other static security posts. One of these guards could be found about every hundred yards along the fence line 24 hours a day, 365 days a year. Captain Ye was also a very big Korean, even taller than Big Chong. The one thing I later found funny about Captain Ye was his voice. When speaking to me in English, he had this very deep, booming voice, but when outside giving commands to his troops, in Korean, he had a high pitched, squeaky, girly-voice. It never ceased to just crack me up.

Mr. Su was a very handsome Asian gentleman and the best dresser of the lot. He sort of looked like he just stepped out of the Korean version of "GQ Magazine." Mr. Su had the same MP Desk job as Big Chong, only he did it during the night shift.

Last, but certainly not least, was Mr. Shin. He was this very small, slightly built man standing, unobtrusively, in silence, almost in the shadows. Mr. Shin was introduced as my personal interpreter-translator. I bowed and said, "Hello Mr. Shin, it's a pleasure to meet you;" and extended my hand to this shy little man. Mr. Shin bowed, took my hand in the both of his and gave me a firm hand shake and a warm smile. I took an instant liking to Mr. Shin. From my two weeks crash course in Korean, I knew using two hands during a hand shake meant great respect. He and I would be spending a lot of time together during my thirteen month year in South Korea.

The rest of the day was spent doing those million and half things every soldier has to do every time they're transferred into a new Army unit. This meant dropping off my assignment orders as well as my personnel, finance and medical records. At the clinic, they checked my records to ensure my shots were all up to date. They weren't, somehow they never are, and I had to get a few more pokes. Next, I went to Central Supply and picked up uniforms, special cold-weather clothing and my personal military equipment. Lastly, the Arms Room Clerk handed me my .45 pistol and made me sign for it. After that, I received the standard 8th Army "Newcomers" briefing on a thousand different things, most of which would be forgotten in just a few days. I did remember them talking about North Korean infiltrators, curfew, VD, off-limits areas, on-limits clubs and the two local national beers Army soldiers are allowed to drink, "OB" and "Crown." A universal truth about soldiers is they always pay attention when anyone talks about beer.

It was now after 1700 hours and I was exhausted after a long day, a short night and half a world's worth of jet-lag. I think Korea is just about twelve hour's difference from our U.S. Eastern Standard Time Zone. I got back to my tin can room about the same time as Gleason and he said, "Come on, I'll show you to the Officers' Mess and introduce you around." He guided me through the narrow connecting corridors to our Officers' Club. The O-Club was just a series of bigger Quonset huts all hooked together. Inside it looked amazingly nice. To the left of the entrance was a very small Class VI (Booze) Store. To the right was a large game room with several pool, ping pong and card tables. There was no TV because there were no English speaking TV stations up where we were. Straight ahead was a nice enough bar and beyond that, with a dog leg turn to the left, was the main dining area, with enough tables and chairs to seat about a 150 people. I was impressed, and soon realized this place had to be nice, because it was one of the few places you could be on cold, Korean winter nights at Camp Page. The others were: the Post Chapel, the movie theater, the craft shop, the gym and the library. These facilities had to entertain 110 officers and about 800 enlisted men for thirteen months of their life.

In the bar I noticed a hundred or so highly shined brass plates displaying the blue, yellow and red 5th USMC insignia. Each had a rank and last name engraved at the bottom of the plate. They were all lined up in a neat row all along the wall near the ceiling and went almost all the way around the room. Gleason saw me looking at them and explained, "Each plate has the name of an officer assigned here. A new plate goes up each time a new officer arrives. When the officer is about to leave, his plate is taken down and presented to him at our monthly Hail & Farewell dinner, right here in the club. You can figure who's about to leave by where their plate is on the wall. Your plate will probably be here this week and will be hung on the wall at the beginning of the line over there." Paul pointed towards the club entrance. "You can watch your plate progress around the room for your thirteen months here. You'll know when it's about time to start packing your bags, because you'll see your plate approaching the end of the line over there, at the end of the bar." Dave Ross and our new FNG, Ab Abercrombie, came through the door behind us and we all went into dinner together.

The Officers' Mess reminded me of a really nice Chinese restaurant. I guess it was because I was not yet versed in the subtle nuances between Korean and Chinese decor. The place looked great, the food was wonderful and the service even better. Korean women of varying ages made up the serving staff. Their names depended on ease of pronunciation to the western tongue. I don't remember all their names, but there was Miss Woo. She was a bit older and sort of a den mother for the rest of them. After just a few minutes of watching, it was obvious she was the head *Honcho* in charge of the dining room staff. Mehay was a beautiful girl in her late teens or maybe early twenties. She looked just like a porcelain, oriental doll, absolutely perfect in every detail. Everyone noticed Mehay, but if the younger officers noticed her too much, Miss Woo would come up, hands on hips, and say things like, "Hey GI, what's-a-matta-you! I not good looking as her?" Everyone would laugh at Miss Woo's theatrical indignation, but the point was well made, and everyone would put their eyes back in their heads. Miss Woo kept a close eye on Mehay. I was just about at the end of my tour before I discovered the beautiful Mehay was really Miss Woo's daughter. Waitresses, with unpronounceable Korean names, were just given American first names. Sandy, Donna and Suzy are three names I remember. Waitresses with pronounceable Korean names simply had "Miss" placed front of it. No explanation of this naming system was ever given; it's just the way it was.

After dinner, the four of us sort of drifted back into the bar. In my fledgling days of drinking, I drank rum and cokes. That night, I also found out one of my roommate's additional duties. Dave Ross was assigned as the *Class VI* Officer. This meant he was in charge of the oversized closet serving as our liquor store. Every night after dinner, Dave, or his designee, would swing open the upper half of the Dutch door to the closet sized room and our Class VI would be open for business. There was a large fixed glass window next to the door where customers could view the stock of booze, beer and cigarettes all neatly arranged on shelving. This was a very popular place indeed.

The drink in my hand tasted so good, I decided to make my first booze purchase in Korea. It was a fifth of dark *Bacardi*, and it only cost me 70 cents! GI booze, overseas, was not only tax free; part of the price was even subsidized by the Army. Back in the 1960's drinking was not discouraged; it was a big part of being an Army Officer and you were actually expected to drink! The Friday, after work, *"Happy Hour"* ritual was something you were both encouraged and expected to attend, as were the monthly *"Hail & Farewells."*

Although very cheap, Army booze and cigarettes were rationed. All of us were issued our 8ᵗʰ Army Ration Cards. This wallet sized fold out document authorized GIs and Department of Army Civilians to buy American booze, beer and cigarettes in the Class VI stores. The card had a bunch of tiny squares divided up into months and categories of rationed items for a whole year. If you bought two bottles of booze and a carton of cigarettes, you had three of your tiny squares paper punched for the month of purchase. It was very liberal system and had far more items in each category than anyone could reasonably consume in a month's time without falling down dead. It was something like, eight cartons of cigarettes, eight bottles of booze and eight cases of beer per month. If you consumed all the allotted month's supply per individual, every day, you'd be drinking a third of a bottle of booze, about seven beers and smoking almost three packs of cigarettes. Yet, somehow, there were a lot of guys who were able to fully deplete their ration cards each and every month. The idea that rationing would, somehow, help control the Black Market in Korea was looked upon pretty much as a joke.

While in the club, I decided to have a second drink. As I approached the bar, one of the hugest and most physically fit human beings I've ever seen came up off a barstool, leered menacingly down at me and growled. "Who are you?" I looked up at this giant, with the furrowed brow and said, while extending a hand with trepidation, "Hi, I'm Herb Royce; I flew in last night." The Goliath's eyes narrowed, his eyebrows lowered and his face contorted into an evil grin. It was obvious he'd already had a few too many. In a thick, slurred, southern accent he loudly demanded, "Where bouts you all from?" His immense size and broad shoulders made me sense my answer might affect my personal wellbeing; so, I rattled on quickly, "My Dad was in the Navy and I sort of grew up around the world but I was born in Norfolk, Virginia." *Bingo, right answer!* The big man grabbed my still outstretched hand, swallowed it in his, crushed it completely and proclaimed, "Hell, you alright!" He plopped back down on his perch at the bar to concentrate on his drinking. I found out later, he was First Lieutenant, Bill Block, one of our Engineer officers. Two years earlier, he was starting, senior, left tackle at the University of Alabama. I was very glad not to have said, "Rhode Island!" I'd lived there longer than any place else and that's where I attended high school and college. But this was not the night to be counted as a Yankee.

On the way out of the bar I looked into the game room again. Over by the outside exit door was a Second Lieutenant sitting alone at a table. I noticed it was the same guy I saw sitting there nearly two hours earlier when we came in. A waitress was delivering a fresh beer and a hamburger to his little table. I turned to Paul and asked, "Who's the Lieutenant over by the exit door?" Paul smiled, "He's this evenings 'Lookout'. His job is to eat and drink free of charge and yell 'Screaming Eagle on the way' or 'Incoming' if he sees Colonel Weatherspoon leave his hooch and head this way. Our Colonel is a real boozer and a nasty, nasty-ass drunk. When the Lookout yells 'Incoming', everybody gets the hell out of here. Better that than get screamed at by the Screaming Eagle." I must have had a disbelieving look on my face because Paul continued, "It really is that freakin' bad Herb! The guy totally loses it!"

We made it back to the room. I turned in early, still suffering from a massive headache and the mother of all jet lags. Tomorrow was going to be a big day. I was going to meet my House Boy and my KATUSA (Korean Augmentation to The US Army) MPs. I also had to finish in-processing then venture out into the City of Chunchon, for the first time, to see another part of my job. However, the most important thing about tomorrow was, I was going to attend a class to get my "Space Heater Operator's License".

4

The Dragon Lady

It was now my second day in country and the first item on the agenda was to take a tour of the City of Chunchon, or *The Ville*, as most GIs called it. You have to remember, the Korean War, at least the main shooting part of it, was over in 1953 and it was now November 1967. When you think about it, 13–14 years really isn't all that long. South Korea was not the booming industrial giant and high-tech dynamo it is today. They were just starting to really recover from decades of invasions and enemy occupations.

Chunchon, on this crisp November day, was so incredibly different from anything I'd ever seen. It looked to me like a really dirty Chinatown. Everything was coated with a thin patina of fine gray-black dust. There was even a taste to it when you took in a breath of air. The whole town looked like it could use a good scrub down.

Mr. Shin and I climbed out of our Jeep in the center of town near the main traffic circle. There was a Korean National Policeman (KNP) standing in the middle of the circle on what looked like half a 55 gallon oil drum, painted white. On this tiny pedestal, he was putting on this amazing, choreographed, Whirling Dervish performance, as he addressed traffic coming into this hub from six directions. There he was, blue cap, blue uniform, shiny black combat boots with white boot laces and white, *Mickey Mouse* gloves whizzing through the air. Clenched between his teeth, he had this glistening, brass whistle which was continuously blowing, but somehow, the drivers instinctively knew pretty much what he wanted them to do. He also had an old .30 caliber, M-2 carbine slung over his back and I thought this was an odd weapon for a traffic cop.

We got out of the Jeep and Mr. Shin motioned for me to follow him into a dingy looking building. The sign over the door read, *Starlight Club*. Once inside, it was explained this was one of six nightclubs in Chunchon that were on-limits to American GIs. The place wasn't much to look at, some tables, chairs, a small dance floor and a mirrored bar with a small stereo and speakers on a shelf behind it. They served *OB (Oriental Brewery)* beer, Korean whisky and, of course, *Coke*. They had a tub of ice behind the counter, but I was told GIs were warned not to ask for it. I was then informed what this club and five other similar establishments really were, and why this was to be of interest to me.

Mr. Shin explained, "This is *Working Girl* club. GIs come here to find girls for comfort, you know, sex." That Navy training film I saw didn't lie! There really are some nasty strains of VD in this part of the world, some of which have no known cures. Uncle Sam, in a strange but well meaning way, had come up with a system to help protect the health of our young, brave and horny soldiers. In theory, eighteen and nineteen year old American males, no matter what, are going to find something to screw, because that's what eighteen and nineteen year old American males are designed to do. Good old *Peggy Sue* may be over 5,000 miles away, but Korean Street Women are available … for a small price. Problem was, a lot of them had various kinds of VD. So, the question ended up being: What's a young American boy going to do? Answer: Despite all medical warnings, after a couple of beers, he's gonna' risk it!

So, the 8th Army Medical Officer and Camp Page Clinic came up with a solution. They put most of the City of Chunchon off-limits except for the main streets and shopping areas where there were no whores or whorehouses. Next, in conjunction with selected Korean club owners, the Camp Page Commander allowed six clubs, in one general area, to be on-limits. This was done with the stipulation that club owners would follow some very strict rules. They were required to have all the girls working in their clubs come to the Camp Page clinic, where they would be routinely tested for Gonorrhea and Syphilis. The working girls had to agree they would work exclusively in just one of the sanctioned clubs and only turn *tricks* for American GIs. Each of these girls was issued an official *8th US Army VD Card*. The card contained the prostitute's picture, her name and the name of the club where she worked. The card also contained the history of all her medical checks and the number of times she was treated for VD. This gave the horny GI an idea of what he was literally getting in to. To work in the clubs, the girls had to keep their VD Cards current. Weekly Gonorrhea checks and monthly Syphilis checks had to be duly recorded with the correct stamps and American medical staff signatures. If a girl was discovered to have VD, she was treated by Army doctors but could not work in the clubs again until she was cured. By Korean standards, Americans paid very well for sex; so, it behooved the girls to try and stay clean.

GIs went to these clubs to talk, dance and drink with the girls. But nobody was kidding anybody; the primary reason they frequented these establishments was to get laid. The soldiers would negotiate a price in the club, pay the girl, and then escort her up to the counter. The girl would give a good part of the money to the man behind the counter and, in return, he would hand over the girl's VD card. The girl and her "John" would then walk to the girl's nearby *Hooch,* normally just a room somewhere off a nearby courtyard. If the GI was interested in something *special,* the girl would normally ask for *"Extra"* money. There were also time limits involved. Prices were based on three time segments; Quick Time: (a Quickie), Long Time: (usually an hour) or All Night. All Night really only lasted until just before midnight because that's when Camp Page's curfew went into effect, and all GIs had to be back on base or they'd be in big trouble.

Mr. Shin told me part of my job was to frequently check these clubs to ensure only working girls, with valid and up-to-date Camp Page VD Cards, were plying their trade in these establishments. If there was an unregistered working girl present during our checks, she would be evicted and the club would be shut down for a specified period to punish the owners. To ensure the clubs were playing by the rules, these checks would have to be conducted, using the strictest secrecy. If not, any illegal activity or unchecked girls would just disappear into the night before the MPs arrived.

When we emerged from the dimly lit club into the bright sun and dusty streets, I was still trying to fully comprehend everything Mr. Shin had just told me. When my mind popped back into the now, and my eyes adjusted to the light, I noticed an immaculate, black, 1958 Mercedes Benz parked at the curb. The uniformed chauffer was dusting the car with some sort of soft brush. The right rear window was rolled down and I could see a woman seated inside smoking a cigarette. The driver immediately ceased his dusting, bolted over to her door and held it open. Out stepped a beautifully dressed, elegant, Asian woman. I estimated she was in her late 40s or possibly early 50s but I really couldn't tell. She was perfectly made up in every detail and had a wonderful smile displaying perfectly even, bright white teeth framed by crimson lips. The driver was now holding an umbrella over her. He was making sure not even the briefest ray of sun ever touched her alabaster skin.

A few words passed between this elegant lady and Mr. Shin. He then turned to me and made introductions. "Lieutenant Royce, this is Madam Kim." We shook hands and both did our little bowing thing. When I'd been introduced to Korean women on base I noticed they always cast their eyes towards the ground. Not Madam Kim, her eyes followed mine all the way through the brief bowing ritual. This lady was a beautiful piece of Korean art and I was somewhat fascinated by her. I then heard Mr. Shin's words, "Madam Kim owns the 'Starlight' and three of the other clubs." So, Madam Kim really is a *Madam*, and she owns two thirds of the on-limits clubs. I immediately wondered what this meeting was going to be all about.

A few more words were passed between the two then Mr. Shin again turned to me. "Madam Kim would like you to accompany her so she can show you her Korean gift of welcome." Mr. Shin was already getting to know my expressions and said, "You should at least go see what it is. If you don't go now, she will just keep asking. Best to do now." I noted something in his voice which I could not quite interpret, but for some reason, I knew he was concerned. Madam Kim gestured for me to join her in the Mercedes. I waived, "Oh no, no thank you, Mr. Shin and I will follow in our Jeep."

The city center of Chunchon was up hill, all the way, from Camp Page. From the traffic circle, in the center of town, it was a straight shot down the hill to the Camp's main gate. We followed Madam Kim up the hill, half way around the circle and then continued on a narrower side street twisting up what was either a big hill or a small mountain. I could never decide what to call it. To the citizens of Chunchon, it was a magnificent mountain. Off we went, but now on an even smaller dirt road and finally through an opening in a cement wall. What I saw made me blink and utter, "What the hell!"

It took me a second or two to get my bearings. We were now stopped in front of what looked like Ward and June Cleaver's house. There was a low, white picket fence around it. The lawn, although now brown, was neat as a pin. There was a cement walk leading up to a house that looked like it belonged in the suburbs of Cleveland or some other mid-west American city. The house itself was an American Ranch, one story, with a shingled roof, something I had not seen in this country. I got out of the Jeep, probably with my mouth open. Madam Kim smiled brightly at my dumbfounded expression and motioned for me to follow her.

As Madam Kim and I walked towards a very American looking front porch, the door suddenly opened. Standing there to greet us were two very beautiful, young, smiling women. One was dressed in traditional Korean *Kisaeng* style (Korean Geisha) while the other wore skin tight, black, Capri pants, an equally snug, black, long sleeved pullover and black high heels. Her deeply scooped neckline framed a single strand of rather large pearls as well as ample cleavage. Her clinging clothing also revealed her incredible, *Hollywood Perfect*, female form. Her shiny, raven hair was styled straight out of a recent issue of *Vogue* magazine. "*It was all there ever was in my dentist's office.*" At first, I thought the tall one in black was Caucasian, but as I drew closer to the door, a quick study revealed she too was Asian. It was the eye makeup that made her look western. A lot of artistry had gone into making her eyes appear rounder. Someone had done a great job. In the right light, she definitely would be mistaken for a Westerner.

The two girls standing in the door way were literally bouncing up and down with excitement. As we moved just inside the door, through Mr. Shin, Madam Kim made the introductions. First, she turned to the one dressed in a Korean *Arridong* ensemble, a traditional garment normally reserved for special occasions. "This is Miss Song." This living China Doll smiled warmly and gave me a longer than usual bow, which I simultaneously returned. Madam Kim now turned to the other of the doorway-duo, the one in the skin tight, black cat suit, "And this is Patty." Patty caught me totally off balance, literally. Anticipating the inevitable bow, I shifted my weight slightly to accomplish this maneuver. Instead, Patty jumped forward, threw her arms around my neck and gave be a big hug. I quickly adjusted my footing under the impact of her light but firm and athletic body. Along with the unexpected hug, Patty planted a big kiss on my right cheek. As surprising as this all was, there was more. After the kiss, she hung on to my neck and whispered in my ear, in perfect English, "I'm so glad you're finally here. We want to take care of you ... in every way."

I wish someone had photographed the look on my face as I have often wondered just how goofy I really looked at that moment. Patty slowly released her tender grip, smiled and slowly slid down my body until her high heels touched the floor. She maintained flirting eye contact, looking up at me with those amazing eyes. It was very hard for me to break eye contact with her. The spell was finally broken when Madam Kim, through Mr. Shin, told me this was a place for me to relax and to stay when I had the time. She then asked Patty to show me around the house. "*Oh, for a few moments, I'd forgotten there was a house.*"

Patty cut through formalities and went straight to work like a Vanna White showing off game show prizes. She was also showing herself off through various poses. "Herb, let me show you around your new home." "*Herb? My new home? What the hell?*" Patty continued, "This is our living room complete with TV, stereo with radio-record player combination. "*Our?*" "We also have a full bar with just about everything. Over here," she paused in her narrative, as I followed her over to the opposite side of the large living area, "is the game area. We have a new pool table, card table and three pin ball machines." "*Why does she keep saying 'We'?*"

Patty moved through a doorway in the back of the room and flicked on the florescent lighting. "And this is our American kitchen." And it was all American too! Gas stove, refrigerator, even a *Toastmaster* toaster and bread Box on the counter. The stainless steel double sink was just like my Mom's. I opened the fridge and there was nothing but American products in there. The freezer even had steaks in it. The packaging was all in English, *Land-O-Lakes* butter and *Schmuckers* strawberry jam. Where did all this stuff come from? I flipped open the bread box, *Wonder Bread.* The cupboards revealed American canned goods and even *Betty Crocker* cake mixes. I turned around from my brief look-see and Patty grabbed my hand, smiled and interjected, "I'm a good Korean and American cook too!"

Continuing on, Patty showed me into the bathroom. This place had an inside toilet, a true rarity in Chunchon. It looked just like a bathroom display at *Sears*, with one exception, the tub area. This tub was big, square and full of steaming hot water. Several candles were burning around the tub and there was a planter behind it with various tropical plants including a small palm tree. A bottle of wine and three glasses was sitting in the edge of it. *"Three glasses?"* The tub looked more like a very small swimming pool than a huge bathtub. Three or four people could easily be comfortable in there at the same time, *"Oh!"* It was then that I noticed Miss Song go over and sit on the edge of the tub and swish her hand in the warm water while looking at me. Patty grasped my hand and smiling that smile again said, "This is a very fun place!" I was too stunned to say anything other than "Uh huh!"

By my hand, she led me out a second bathroom door and into a dimly lit bedroom. *"Oh, my God, look at this place!"* There I was, standing in a very Oriental looking room. The overall color theme was crimson. The walls were covered in velvet-like wall paper covered with Eastern characters and scenes. The same held true for the crimson carpet. Mirrors and candles were everywhere. Soft, indirect lighting cast a red hue over the entire room. In the very center of the room was the biggest bed I'd ever seen. It was raised up and you had to ascend two steps to get to it. Above it was a ceiling mirror the same dimensions as the bed. You didn't need a woman; just this room could give a guy an erection. Although I knew the primary reason for the room was not sleeping, I was fascinated by how provocative it was yet still have this total lack of tackiness or sleaziness about it. This was one incredible room! I noticed both Miss Song and Patty were now sitting, *more like posing*, on the bed, both bathed in a red glow. The visual was very stimulating and intended to be so. I knew I had to get out of that room now, so I bolted for the bedroom door.

As I walked quickly towards the front door, Mr. Shin followed, practically running to keep up. I noticed one door I had not been through. The door was open only about six inches but it was enough that I could plainly see two Koran mattresses on the concrete floor, a small dressing table, a *young bok jun* (free standing Korean closet) and not much more. Somehow I knew this was the girl's living quarters when there were no house guests to entertain. It was absolutely shabby looking compared to rest of the place.

Everyone caught up with me at the front door. Madam Kim, through translation, said, "You have come a long way to defend our land. I just want to thank you by giving you someplace to make your job less stressful and more enjoyable while you are here. This is all yours to relax in any time you want to." I was thinking to myself, *"Madam Kim, you run one hell of a USO! Now how do I diplomatically tell you I can't?"*

So, I just blurted it out. "Madam Kim, I thank you very much for your concern for my comfort and wellbeing, but I cannot accept your generosity." For a moment, I saw a bit of panic in Madam Kim's eyes. She now spoke directly to me, in English. "Cannot accept! Why not? You no like these girls? I bring others over for your approval." Now Patty was looking like the interviewee who was just told she didn't land the job. For some strange reason, I was now feeling sorry for Patty and Miss Song as they were both way over qualified for their positions. "No, no!" I protested, "These ladies are very lovely. That's not what I meant." "Ooooh, so you maybe like boys?" Her smile was now quite wicked as she thought she'd discovered a chink in my armor. "We can do that too!"

"Oh No; hell No! That's not it!" I nearly shouted as I blurted it out. "I'm married, less than a month, and I don't think my bride would understand or approve of this arrangement." Madam Kim furrowed an uncomprehending brow and replied, "You over here, she over there, you no tell, we no tell, she no know, what the problem?"

"What you say may be true Madam Kim, but my problem is," I paused and looked at the beautiful, East-West girls, "I would know. Being with other women, no matter how beautiful or charming, is something I just cannot do." Mr. Shin started translating again and watched Madam Kim's befuddled expression. For the moment, she was lost for words. I took the time during the brief silence to speak to Patty. "I hope this will be okay for you and Miss Song." A teeny, tiny hint of smile crossed her eyes. She spoke very softly. "We be okay. You good man, Lieutenant." I think I blushed in front of this incredibly provocative woman. I bowed a few times to the ladies and swiftly beat a hasty retreat out the front door with Mr. Shin in tow.

5

I Think My Dick's Going to Fall Off!

Okay, right here, I feel I have to explain a few things before I'm branded as a liar or some sort of hormonal freak. Throughout my life, my moral compass has been guided by three things.

One: I would never do anything to dishonor, embarrass or cause my mother pain. My Mom was one of God's best creations. She contracted Cancer when I was in high school, but somehow survived and lived with it, in various forms, for nearly eighteen more years. She'd lick one Cancer, but a little later it would resurface, in a different form, some place else in her body. She would then muster all her physical and spiritual energy to fight yet another battle with *The Big C*. After battling this monster for so long, she just became too weak to continue on. So, I tended to stay on the "straight and narrow" because I always felt she had enough on her plate without me adding anything to it.

Two: I was twenty-five when I married. I believe in marriage, including the *"forsaking all others"* part. When you take vows to *"love and cherish"* they're supposed to mean something. I'm sorry, but I would never do anything to dishonor my wife. I would never do anything which might destroy the complete trust needed for a marriage to be a lasting success.

Three: I've always been afraid of my dick falling off!

These three forces, working in concert, made me bulletproof to anything any woman could try, no matter how beautiful or provocative she might be.

I have been afraid of my dick falling off, literally, just about all my life. When I was six, I moved from San Diego to the island of Guam. My Dad was in the Navy and we sailed there on the *USS Mitchell*, a converted troop transport. We were among the first Navy dependants allowed to make the trip. It was 1949 and WWII had only, officially, ended about four years earlier. There were still Jap snipers on the Island who had not surrendered. Sniper fire was not an unusual event and it was a constant source of conversation amongst the grownups. We even had armed Sailors or Marines on our school bus.

On Guam, the Navy was trying to make life for Navy dependants seem as normal as possible. Part of this was their attempt to give us kids an American tradition of that time, *The Saturday Afternoon Matinee Movie.* They would come around to our quarters every Saturday, pick us up in that same armed, gray bus they took us to school in, and drive us out to a sandbagged, underground bunker at Peti Point. The bunker wasn't really for our protection. Air conditioning hadn't really been invented yet and underground bunkers were nice, cool, dark places, ideally suited for a Saturday matinee.

The same two sailors who were on the bus would then hand out popcorn and candy and run the projector. Movies, back then, usually consisted of a few cartoons, two or three serials, a newsreel and a *Double Feature*, usually two cowboy movies. I loved cowboy movies and I still do. Cowboys, the good guys, were my role models and these films helped form much of my early concept of what's right and wrong. We were all supposed to be there for about three hours. Sometimes, one of the feature movies wouldn't arrive and the sailors would fill the time by showing a couple of Navy training films. *"Survival in a rubber raft"* and *"How to protect from frostbite"* were two I remember. I didn't understand the frostbite in tropics one but the sharks around the guy in the little rubber raft was really cool and scary. When the movies started rolling, the sailors would normally go outside for a smoke and to stand guard.

On one memorable Saturday, the sailors loaded the second reel and went outside. Only this time, it seems they made a big mistake. I know they did because we never saw those two sailors ever again. The Johnny Mack Brown western ended and a training film came on. It was about *"Venereal Diseases & Protection."* Sitting in that cool bunker, with eyes as big as saucers, I watched as eight to ten foot long festered pricks paraded across the big screen. This left a lasting impression on this first-grader. I knew my Dad had a big one because I'd seen him in the shower, but these were enormous and covered in disgusting, runny sores. At one point in the film, a doctor in a white lab coat proclaimed something like, *"We have seen untreated cases of VD in some parts of the Orient where the patient's penis actually rotted and fell off."* That was it for me! I was never ever going near a woman. I even took charge of my baths and no longer allowed my mother to help.

Throughout the rest of my life, there were reinforcing events reminding me how easily my dick could fall off. There were those *Sex Education* classes in high school given by Coach Del Veccio. "You guys keep screwing around with the little cock teasers around here and some day your dick's gonna' fall off." Three players had just come down with the *Clap*, all from the same girl, and our coach commented, "That little bitch's gonna' ruin this football team!"

My Mom forced my Dad into finally giving me *The Talk*. Dad was a highly decorated, fearless fighter pilot but he had been putting off *The Talk*. I was fifteen and the only kid my age, I knew of, who hadn't had *The Talk*. I eagerly anticipated learning "The Big Secret", the great mystery of life every boy must learn to earn his right of passage to manhood. Being a Navy Chief, he pulled no punches. *The Talk* I got was straight from the docks. He told me about *The Clap* and *The Siff*. He told me about whores, bad girls and sluts. He told me I always should carry protection just in case I just had to do it. He handed me three rubbers and told me not to go around screwing anything because that was just not right plus I stood a good chance of getting a disease, knocking a girl up or both. He said the rubbers were for when I'd been *swapping spit* (kissing, I think) with some girl and got her so *hot* there was nothing left to do but fuck her to calm her down. Until that moment, I hadn't realized girls got horny too and turned into rabid, bitch dogs. If you didn't screw em' to calm them down you might get all clawed up, or worse. He also told me if I needed more rubbers to come and see him and he'd be sure I got the good kind, the ones that don't break so easy. In later years, I wondered who the hell gave him his talk and what about my poor Mother? I left that room very confused and a confirmed celibate.

In Army basic training, at Fort Dix New Jersey, my First Sergeant further reinforced my paranoia about my dick falling off. After six weeks of hard training, we were going to be allowed off base, on Saturday, for the first time. At our noon formation, just before we would all be heading to beautiful downtown Wrightstown, New Jersey, he said, "Men, I know all of you are hot to trot and want to get some of that civilian *pussy* downtown. Well, I know some of you are gonna' be stupid enough to try. But, listen up! I want you all to know this: All civilian women is diseased! But, if you just can't help yourselves, at least wear some protection. If you're too damned dumb not to know what protection is, come see me before you get on the bus and I'll give you some. Remember; if you don't wear protection, your dick's probably gonna' fall off! *Dismissed!*"

Now, here I am, stationed in Korea, working with VD Cards, monthly and weekly VD checks, Madams, cat houses, club inspections and about 400 exotic, Asian prostitutes; and, it's all part of my new job. If there was one precise location on Planet Earth where you stood the greatest chance of your dick falling off, it was being in my job right here in Chunchon, probably the VD epicenter of the entire Universe in 1967.

6

A Canadian Nurse in Alabama

So now you know! Fear, love of wife and respect for my Mom were three, inter-laced forces working in concert governing my sexual decision making process and ensuring my fly stayed zipped up and padlocked in this strange land.

You may have also noticed, I said I was married. Let me catch you up on that minor, missing detail. I got married about two weeks before I shipped out for Korea.

When I took command of the 141st MP Company at Fort Rucker I simply could not believe it. Captains commanded companies! And, there I was, an almost brand new 2LT, and I'm taking command of the 141st from a recently promoted Major who's on his way to Nam. That's just how crazy things were in the Army in 1967.

So, as I told you, here I am with these 150 MPs, and I haven't got a clue about what to do with them. My Executive Officer is Jimmy Crowell, another 2LT, and he's just two weeks junior in grade to me. We don't even have a real First Sergeant. Our *Acting* First Sergeant is a "Shake & Bake", instant Staff Sergeant. The NCO (Non Commissioned Officer) ranks were also getting accelerated promotions due to the stress Vietnam was putting on the Army's personnel and rank system.

So, counting my almost two years enlisted time, before I got my officer's commission, I actually had more time in the Army than my acting First Sergeant! This was a bad thing! The three of us spent our days pretending to know what we were doing and our nights reading manuals about how to run an MP company. After about six weeks of our wandering through the wilderness, the Department of the Army showed some mercy and sent us a no shit, fire breathing, real deal First Sergeant.

I owe a lot to First Sergeant Billy James Robertson. He trained me the same way senior, American Army Sergeants have been training junior officers since colonial times and the birth of our nation. He was firm, but respectful towards me. My Dad was a senior Navy Chief; so, I was smart enough to listen to BJ. The first day we met, he commented on the Enlisted Good Conduct Ribbon on the chest of my khakis and I guess he took pity on me. He had no use for West Pointers and referred to them as "fancy college boys". Anyway, I owe a great debt to my first, First Sergeant.

My life was just sort of knocking around until one morning formation when I announced the Red Cross was at the service club collecting blood for the boys in Vietnam. I also announced that anyone volunteering to march down there with me and gave blood would get the rest of the day off. It was Friday morning and that translated into a three day weekend; so, 66 MPs took me up on it. We marched down to the service club and lined up to give blood. Leading by example, I was first in line.

The Italians call it *The Thunderbolt*. We Americans simply call it "Love at first sight". I think "Thunderbolt" describes it way better. This large room in the service club must have had eight or ten stations where nurses were all set up to take blood. Way in the back, in the right-side corner of the room, was this little, brunette nurse with this incredible smile. She was talking to a troop on a gurney. I watched her every move for about five minutes, then turned to my XO (Executive Officer), Jimmy Crowell, and said, "Jimmy, see that little nurse over there in the corner?" He acknowledged. "I'm gonna' marry her!" Jimmy's simple reply was, "You're shittin' me man!" But, there was a hint of believability in his voice. Fact is, seven months later I did marry that little nurse.

I maneuvered myself so I would be next in line for her station. She looked up, flashed that killer smile and said; "Next!" I stood there like a goof; so, she motioned me over to her table. With an exaggerated Dracula accent, she said, "Come over here Lieutenant, I need to suck your blood." As I walked towards that wonderful smile and those incredible blue eyes, my knees actually weakened. She became even more beautiful with each step I took. She was dressed all in white, such a bright white, that in the morning sunlight, it actually hurt my eyes. Her crisp, immaculate uniform and nurse's cap were heavily starched. She smelled like the combination of rubbing alcohol and "Ivory" soap, with just a hint of "White Shoulders" perfume. Now, I was never a *Casanova* type, but I was never really inept in social situations with the opposite sex either. Well, this freakin' morning I was totally tongue-tied and must have sounded like a blithering idiot. All I could really do was just stare at her. She probably sensed something, but was probably used to getting these kinds of reactions from other smitten soldiers. She was just so damned pretty!

I gave my blood, drank my orange juice and laid down for the specified amount of time. When I reluctantly got up, I just hung around her station while Jimmy kept sending my guys over to give blood. As long as it was my guys, as their commander, I had a legit reason to stay there. I tried to impress my little nurse by letting her know it was my company's men she was taking blood from and that there were 66 of us. I'm not sure exactly how I asked for or got her name and phone number, but I got it. She probably took pity on me, or just gave it to me to be free of my stammering, stuttering and staring.

I couldn't wait for evening to come. In my mind, I planned the exact time to call and ask for a date. *"Let's see; the blood drive would end at four, dinner time is usually at six, she'll need time to get home, then shower and change, the optimal time would have to be 5:35."* My company had a softball game against one of the aviation units at 2 PM the next day. I can't remember anything I said, or she said, but I ended up with an address and a Saturday afternoon softball date!

The next day, at the ballgame, I found out a lot about this woman I already knew I was going to marry. Joyce was Canadian and the daughter of the Canadian Liaison Officer to the US Army Aviation School. The other foreign, Liaison Officers at Rucker were the Brits, French and Germans. The US Navy, Marines and Coast Guard were also there in the same capacity. Joyce had recently finished nursing school in Ottawa and was just down here visiting her folks. Her Mom was active in the Officers' Wives Club and Joyce was at the blood drive just helping her out. Her Dad, Major Shackleton, a Canadian Army helicopter pilot, had only recently been assigned there. Joyce was the oldest of four girls; Jenny, Joanie and Zoo-Zoo, (real name Jonnie). Joyce didn't know how long she would be staying with her folks, but she wanted to get back to Ottawa soon to launch her nursing career. The last bit of news meant I'd have to work fast.

I asked her if she would like to go out this same evening for dinner and dancing at the Lake Tholocco Officers' Club. For some unknown reason, she said "Yes" and I don't know why. I was almost wooden that afternoon at the ballpark; I was so afraid I'd say or do something stupid and drive her away. Except for some of the small talk, she seemed almost bored to tears during with the game. She only perked up when I mentioned dancing. When I dropped her off, it was a little after four in the afternoon and I told her I'd pick her up about six. I rushed back to my BOQ to get ready.

She didn't know it yet, but I was getting ready to play my ace, early in the game. I had to; I was too afraid of losing her at the starting gate. Early in my teens, I learned the one universal truth about all female, women of the opposite sex. Most all of them love to dance! Thanks to my high school dance instructor,

Mr. Riccio, early in life, I learned to dance and dance well. It was actually part of our after school activities in North Kingstown, Rhode Island.

Every Wednesday evening, from the seventh through the twelfth grade, I took ballroom dancing lessons. I loved dancing and I seemed to have a knack for it. Play just about any music and I'll know what dance to do with it. I also knew how to lead, and once you've mastered leading you can make any girl look great on a dance floor, and that's what it's all about; all women love looking like Ginger Rogers.

Because of dancing, I got dates with girls I had no business getting dates with. Ask a girl to dinner, a movie, a sporting event or even to the beach and she may just politely say, "No!" Ask her if she'd like to go dancing and there's a ninety-nine percent chance she'll say, "Yes!" What can I tell you, it's in their DNA. Don't believe me; check out the romance novel section at any big bookstore. Half the covers of those trashy love stories have some damsel in the arms of some guy, and they're dancing. I also learned you can get away with stuff on a dance floor that you'd get slapped for anyplace else. In a private moment, Mr. Riccio once confided to a group of us guys: "Boys, dancing is the most fun you can have with a girl and still have your shoes on!"

I picked Joyce up at six and whisked her away in my brand new, baby-blue, '67 Volkswagen Beetle. The best things you could say about my Bug was it was new, clean and dependable. It cost me $1477.00 and my monthly payments were just a little over forty bucks a month, which I thought was pretty stiff at the time. When your take-home pay's not quite $200 a month, $40 is still a lot of money. It was also at a time in my life when all my worldly possessions would fit in the back of my Beetle with the back seat folded flat.

It was "Dollar Spaghetti Night" at the Lake Tholocco O-Club. We dined, we drank a little wine and we danced a lot. During the evening we also, somehow, emotionally connected. She smiled most of the time and we laughed a lot. We told each other about our lives, dreams and ambitions; most of what I told her was even true. She seemed completely at ease with me and was enjoying herself. In the light from that Chianti basket-bottle, with the candle stuck in it, I watched her every wonderful facial expression and imprinted every detail of that beautiful face to memory. I just loved listening to her talk. She was a good dancer too, and in an hour or so, we looked like we'd been dancing together for years. I just knew this had to work out. That night made me, more than ever, want her as my dance partner for life.

Over the ensuing weeks, romance slowly began to bloom, and bonds became stronger. Joyce decided to stay on in Alabama longer than she planned; so, she took a job working at the Enterprise General Hospital Emergency Room. Being a cop, I also spent a lot of time in emergency rooms. She was one hell of a nurse! If an ambulance ever got you to an emergency room, alive, this was definitely the nurse you'd want waiting for you. I don't know how they trained nurses in Ottawa, but it should be exported. A lot of our dating involved that emergency room. When she was working the graveyard shift and I was the Military Police Duty Officer, if things were quiet, I'd drive off-post to see her. Heck, I had a radio in my patrol car and her hospital was just outside Rucker's back gate! We would sit outside, in rocking chairs, in the evening breeze of those warm Alabama nights and just talk and talk.

If she worked the late shift on a Friday, I'd pick her up at eight Saturday morning. She would already have brought a change or two of clothes with her. We would drive those hundred miles from Enterprise, Alabama to Panama City Beach, Florida. I'd drive and she'd sleep. When we got to our destination, we'd put our blanket in the sand and she would sleep some more. My job was to ensure she stayed completely covered up, or in the shade, so she wouldn't burn. These were the days before sunscreen. I'd read a lot but I spent most of time just watching her sleep; even that kept me fascinated. Around two-ish, she would come alive. We'd swim, eat an early dinner and maybe dance at one of the local spots along the beach. Late in the evening, we'd climb back into my baby-blue V-Dub for that century mile trip back to the Fort, on what was now a very dark two lane black top.

After we'd been dating for around six weeks or so, she abruptly told me she had to go back to Ottawa. I didn't get it at the time, but there was something or someone drawing her back there. I asked if she was coming back and she said she didn't know. We bid a tearful farewell and I saw her off at the Dothan airport. After she left, I was not a happy camper; and much of my time was spent just going through the daily motions of living. About ten days later, she phoned me and asked when I was coming to see her. I started talking about seeing my commanding officer about some leave time and she started laughing. "I'm at my folk's house silly, I'm back!" When I saw her that evening, I didn't ask too many questions about why she went home, but I surmised it was either to tell some guy goodbye, maybe this doctor "Tom" guy I'd heard so much about, or to see him again before she made a final decision concerning who she wanted to be with. I asked some sort of stupid-ass question about why me over the other guy? She smiled warmly, gave me a big hug and whispered in my ear, "Because you're the better dancer!" "*Works for me! God bless you Mr. Riccio!*"

Shortly thereafter, I instituted a rather unusual ritual. At the completion of every date, usually at the side door, under the car port at her parent's quarters, I'd ask her to marry me. Dozens and dozens of times I'd ask, and an equal number of times she'd say "No." I'd dream up inventive ways to ask and she would try to top them with equally novel ways of saying "No." She once opened her compact and my question was written on the mirror. Later, I opened the front trunk of my VW to add gas and the word "No" would be taped to my gas cap; and so on it went. No matter how inventive I got, the answer always came back the same. One night, she said to me, "Marry you! You think I want to go around the rest of my life being called *Joyce Royce*? Are you nuts or something?" I had to admit she had a point.

When we'd been together for around four months, I came down on orders for Korea and the dynamic changed a little. It was about three months before I had to ship out, but I was still asking and Joyce was still "No-ing". However, we were having the long talks about waiting, letter writing, distance testing our love and all that stuff everyone, deep down, knows is pretty much crap. Hell, there were about 30,000 soldiers at Rucker. A huge number of them were officer pilots, higher ranking than me and all drawing flight pay. Hundreds of them even had Corvette convertibles. How was a poor, no-flight-pay, VW driving, MP Second Lieutenant going to compete with that from half a world away!

The part of me, deep inside, whose job it is to protect my emotional/mental health and well being was beginning to erect the "Toughness Wall". I was, subconsciously, rationalizing and resigning myself to the fact that, no matter what, when I came back a year later to wherever in the States I'd be assigned, there would be no Joyce waiting for me. It would be self-destructive to disillusion myself into thinking she was going to wait around for me for 13 months. Besides, with Linda, I already had some experience in that area! I even started weaning myself from the "Question & Answer Game". I'd still ask, but there were no more games. Now, it was just an almost automatic or routine thing in the car port, at the end of each date. The answer was still coming back a steady "No."

It happened about five weeks before I had to leave. I was taking spoken Korean classes and reading everything I could about this country I would be calling home for thirteen months. Joyce and I were returning from the base movie theater one evening and there we stood, once again, in that car port. I kissed her lightly, said goodnight and told her I would see her tomorrow to go for a drive. I turned to leave, and with hands on hips and in a deep, loud voice of indignation, she called after me, "Hey Soldier!" I turned. "You forgot to ask me to marry you!"

She was right, I had completely forgotten. Maybe it was that self-defense mechanism thing subconsciously kicking in again and telling me to give up the fight.

I smiled a tired smile, and slowly took the two or three steps back to her. I, dramatically, took her hand in both of mine, got down on one knee and with a weak smile robotically said, "Will you marry me, Joyce?" She jumped on me and hugged me around the neck so hard it hurt. "Yes, yes I'll marry you; all you had to do was ask, you big goof!" *Reality Check, Reality Check!* I questioned her and she assured me it was neither a trick nor a joke. Once before she had said "Yes" but phoned me the next morning at 4 AM in a panic and asked, "Did I say 'Yes' last night? Because, if I did, it was just that I had too much to drink and got caught up in the moment. The answer is still *'No'!*"

Okay, so now what? I'd seen those bride magazines a few years ago, before my sister got married. One of the topics was, *"What to do eight months before the wedding"*. The article then counted down what you needed to do by month, then weeks and finally, days. We were already at the lower end of the weeks part and Joyce wanted a big wedding. I was stepping on a plane to Korea in just five weeks. If there was to be a honeymoon—and I really wanted there to be a honeymoon—even if it meant I'd have to risk my dick falling off. We would have to get married in about three weeks to include a honeymoon. Don't panic! First thing I had to do was ask her Father, the really physically fit, tough as nails, Canadian, hockey player, Major for his daughter's hand.

The next night, I had dinner with the whole family at the Major's quarters. I was finally being allowed inside when he was home. This was a giant step in my relationship with the father. I already loved her Mother and really liked her sisters, but the Major was still pretty stiff and formal around me. I always called him *"Sir"* and he never corrected me; so, I assumed he wanted to keep it that way. Jenny and Joanie had been clued in by Joyce and were taking great pleasure in watching me sweat. The grand plan was: Right after dinner and dishes, the girls would grab Mom and leave me alone with the Major to do the ritual asking of the Father thing. As dinner was grinding to a close, the Major suddenly popped up and said, "Come on Katrina, if we're going to make that movie, we have to leave now." Mom jumped up, grabbed her purse and followed the Major out the door. The words, "You kids do the dishes." hung in the vortex of their speedy departure. As the emotional dust settled, we all just sat there looking at each other. The sisters were amused at my discomfort. Well, so much for *"best laid plans"* and all that stuff.

About twenty minutes later, the door burst open and the Major stormed back in with Mom close behind. The Major was highly pissed! "You can go to the god dammed officers' club wearing nothing but a jock strap and earmuffs and nobody says a god damned word! Show up at the god damned movies with sandals and the bastards won't let you in because you're not wearing god damned socks! Who the hell wears god dammed socks with sandals anyway besides queers and god damned Germans?" He snatched his pack of "*Rothmans*" cigarettes off the kitchen counter, put the leash on Sam the German Shepherd and notified us all he was taking the dog for a walk. He did an about face and disappeared into the night. My survival instincts told me it would be in my best interests to postpone *the question* for a minimum of twenty-four hours.

The next night I did. The major was in rare form. "You again Meathead? Don't you ever eat anywhere else? I wonder if I can declare you on my income tax." The name *"Meathead"* was not stolen from the old "Archie Bunker" TV show. It's a term, of not so much endearment, used in the Canadian Forces for their MPs.

I was beginning to wonder if this was going to be the right time either. Tonight was a little different, because Joyce had told Mom I was going to pop the question. I'm not totally sure, but I think the Major was still in the cold on this one. Right after dinner, all five women jumped up and cleared the table. Little Zoo-Zoo complained a bit, but Mom said she'd made a special dessert for her and she followed happily. Jenny appeared briefly with two cups of coffee and the Major's cigarettes. We heard the kitchen door opening and Mom saying, "We're all going for a walk and we're taking Sam. The screen door banged shut and there I was sitting across the table from the Major. He lit a *Rothman* and rhetorically asked, "What the hell do you suppose that was all about?" I figured the best thing to do was just come out with it and ask. He was going to kill me anyway, so why not just make it quick. "Sir, I want to ask you for your daughter's hand in marriage?" He paused, and looking at me over the rim of his coffee and inquired, "Which one?" I stammered as he continued, "I have four you know, but I'd prefer you not take the little one. So, which one of the three older ones do you want; the blonde, the brunette or the redhead?" I continued to be at a total loss for words as he continued, "You asked for her hand. Aren't you interested in the rest of her?" The only thing I could think of saying was, "Oh, yes Sir I, I…." he interrupted again,

"Have you asked her yet?"

"Yes, Sir, I have!"

"And what did she say?"

"She said '*Yes*', Sir!"

"Which one said yes?"

"Joyce said 'Yes', Sir!"

"Well, why didn't you tell me it was that one in the first place? We've been trying to get rid of that one for years."

I sat there, in shock, staring at him until I noticed a wicked grin beginning to appear from behind his coffee cup. He'd been having great fun at my expense.

"You know Herb, I know the signs, and I've seen this coming for months. I saw it in your eyes from just about the beginning. I'm a father, and that's why I decided I didn't like you much. I've also seen it in my daughter's eyes for quite a while too; so, I figured this day was inevitable. But, I do have a couple of father-type questions:

"Do you love her?"

"Yes Sir, I really do!"

"Next question: Do you promise to take care of her?"

"Yes Sir, I promise you I will."

"You do know I will personally hunt you down and kill you like a rat in the gutter if you ever so much as harm a single hair on her head don't you?"

There now was no smile below the coffee cup. I replied with his same stone cold expression.

"I have no doubt in my military mind that you will beat me to death if I ever harm your daughter, Sir!"

He nodded, got up and walked around the table. I came out of my chair at the same time. He stuck out this hand and I did the same. He gripped my hand powerfully then pulled me in for a big bear hug.

"Welcome to my dysfunctional family, Meathead!"

The women folk must have been watching through the dinning room window, because a loud cheer arose from the back yard when I got the big hug. Now, five women and a large dog came bouncing into the small dinning room, jumping up and down, shrieking, laughing, talking, barking and kissing all at the same time. It's a moment that's burned into my mind forever.

The next few weeks were a complete blur. Announcements, arrangements for a full blown, international, military wedding and all the other thousand and one things you have to do for such an occasion. I flew up to my folk's house in Rhode Island to get my meager finances in order and to buy Joyce a ring. My Mom was so happy. My two sisters, along with Joyce's three, were all to be in the wedding party. I helped my Mom buy a hat for the wedding and she helped me pick out a ring. I was as ready as I could ever be and, in one week, I flew back, officially gave Joyce the ring and we started the wedding countdown.

We were married on the 4th of November in a big, international, military wedding at the Fort Rucker Post Chapel with swords, dress uniforms from several services and countries plus all the storybook trimmings. My Executive Officer, and friend, Jimmy Crowell stood in as my Best Man.

An omen told me our marriage was meant to be. Joyce had helped her Mom pick out a hat for the wedding, same as I had. The mothers of both the bride and the groom showed up at the wedding wearing the same hat. The hats were purchased 1500 miles apart with no coordination. To me, these things don't just happen.

We drove off on our honeymoon in my little, blue VW Beetle. I really liked my Bug but was now wishing I had bought a real car, one that fit more than just me. Our honeymoon took in most of the East Coast. We drove to Key West in two days. After a few days there, we started north; with a two day stop at my grandparent's house in West Hollywood, FL. From there, we next stopped in the old city of Charleston, South Carolina. Our biggest adventure was in New York City, where we did all the touristy things, and even saw "Fiddler on the Roof" on Broadway, with a new performer, *Bette Midler*, whom we predicted would go far. From NYC we ended up at my folk's house in Rhode Island. We both knew I would have to leave for Korea at the end of the week and that sort of cast a pall over our last few days together.

In Rhode Island, Joyce hatched an idea which would end up being one of the great and defining moments in our lives. American wives were not allowed to be with their husbands in the part of Korea where I was going. This was what the Army calls an *Unaccompanied Tour*. Joyce decided, since she was Canadian, this rule didn't apply to her. She told me she was going to go through the Canadian government and see if she could get a Korean work visa and get a job in the city of Chunchon where she could be close to me.

Armed with this skeletal plan, saying goodbye was not totally oppressive. I had doubts it would ever come to pass, but then I did not know the tenacity and ingenuity of my new bride. On the 18th of November I put her on a plane in Providence, Rhode Island headed back to her folks in Alabama. The next day, I bid a tearful farewell to my Mom and Dad, and then began my long journey to Korea, *The Land of the Morning Calm*.

7

First Encounter with the Screaming Eagle

As we cleared the busy traffic circle, I returned a salute from the ROK Army *Hum Beung* (MP) directing traffic. It seems the ROK MPs and the KNP shared traffic control duties in Chunchon. As Mr. Shin and I drove through the smoky air, I could see the Camp Page Main Gate about half a mile straight down the gentle hill. Mr. Shin was grinning from ear to ear and making little happy noises under his breath. I asked him, "What gives Mr. Shin? What am I missing here?" He just kept on grinning, "You wait; you see." As we passed through the gate he said something in Korean to the KATUSA MPs. Now they too were grinning and visibly excited! We pulled up in front of the PMO and I jumped out of the Jeep. When I walked inside, with Mr. Shin following, to my surprise and a bit of concern, there were about a dozen or so MPs gathered in front of the MP desk. I thought for a moment something had gone terribly wrong and we were marshalling our forces in response. In my peripheral vision I half glimpsed Mr. Shin giving the thumbs up sign. To my amazement, the place exploded in cheers and applause. Evidently, I was the center of something I didn't understand. One of the men shouted to someone outside the door. "The new L-T just told the *Dragon Lady* to kiss his grits." There were more cheers coming from down the hall.

To the words of well wishing MPs shaking my hand and slapping me on the back, I was taken aside by Staff Sergeant Zack and Mr. Shin. It seems my predecessor *had* accepted the *Dragon Lady's* hospitality. I guess no one had told him his dick could fall off! Anyway, his off-post activity evidently had affected the Camp Page Military Police operation in many ways. In fact, the MP Investigations Section had been a department in name only for some time now and wasn't even fully staffed. The guy before me had even voluntarily extended his Korean tour of duty as Provost Marshal for an additional six months.

From what I was being told, the Dragon Lady was involved in just about everything illegal, immoral or fattening in Chunchon. This included: prostitution, gambling, black marketing, drugs, theft, loan sharking and just about everything in between. Let's be kind and just say that the previous Lieutenant didn't seem too interested in vigorously pursuing or investigating any activity in which Madam Kim might be a party to. Lack of interest in her operations had a huge effect on MP morale. Downtown, the MPs were seen as being totally ineffectual. I couldn't think of any way my predecessor could have pulled this off for so long unless someone above him in the chain of command was looking the other way. I hadn't met many of the senior officers, so I had no idea who that might be.

My first week in country was now coming to a close and I had yet to meet the Colonel, my boss and the same guy who would be writing my report card. I now knew he was the one also known as *The Screaming Eagle* and with a nickname like that, I really wasn't in all that much of a hurry to meet him.

My Provost Marshal's office (PMO) and the MP Desk were on the right end of the Quonset hut complex that served as Camp Page's headquarters building. Nobody's office was closer to the Main Gate than mine. The Personnel Section was at the extreme left end of the complex. Connecting the two ends was a long hallway nearly the length of a football field. Along this hall were the various staff offices. Precisely halfway down this long hallway was the Command Suite. This was nothing more than a really big Quonset with lots of plywood paneling stained in dark wood tones with a high-gloss, varnished finish. At least it was a change from the miles and miles of pale green painted walls found throughout the rest of the camp. If you came through the headquarters main door by the circular drive and the three flagpoles you would enter directly into this area. The Korean, American and NATO flags all flew over The 5th US Missile Command Headquarters.

Late that afternoon, I was still in my office unpacking and trying to make my pale green workplace look a little more personal, when one of my guys came in and told me Colonel Weatherspoon wanted to see me. That afternoon, I made the first of many walks down that long, pale green corridor to the Command Suite. I was motioned to a seat in the outer office by Lieutenant Huddleston, a sort of office manager for the Colonel. In the Army he's called an *Adjutant*. He was a senior First Lieutenant on the verge of making Captain. If he had been any paler and blonder he would probably have been considered an albino. He had this permanent sort of smug look that made me just want to slap him, for no particular reason.

As I cooled my heels in the Colonel's outer office, I watched the comings and goings of the rest of the Command Group. They were really an unusual crew. Other than the Colonel, Huddleston and an office clerk, there were three other Command Group inhabitants. They were; The Stupid Colonel Mixon, The Gorilla and Sergeant Major (Mealy) Mouth.

The Camp and 5th Missile XO (Executive Officer) was Lieutenant Colonel Mixon. None of the Koreans liked him because he always talked down to them. Mr. Shin was openly contemptuous and always referred to him as, "The Stupid Colonel Mixon". Mixon truly believed Koreans could only understand English if he followed Winston Churchill's advice, which was: "Anyone can understand English if it's spoken slow enough and loud enough." Churchill meant it as a joke! The Stupid Colonel Mixon thought it was a proven fact. I remember seeing Mixon passing information on to Mr. Shin, complete with wild hand gestures, mouthed airplane sounds and very loud and slow instructions. Everyone else knew Mr. Shin's English was probably better than 85% of the Americans on Camp Page. When the Colonel departed, Mr. Shin walked past me uttering, "What a flaming asshole!" Now there's one Korean with a really great command of the English language!

The *Gorilla* was actually Major Tyrone Monroe. Everyone; black, white or even yellow called him that, except to his face of course. *I have to make this perfectly clear. This was not an ethnic slur and was never intended to be.* It was just that this guy looked exactly like a gorilla right down to his short legs, big belly and knuckles that almost dragged on the ground. He had a sloping forehead, deep set eyes, two holes in his face instead of a proper nose and huge white teeth. To top off the image, he was probably the hairiest man I've ever seen. Except where he shaved his face, the rest of everything else was covered in dark-brown fur. He was also incredibly strong like a gorilla. He was 5th Missile's S-4 (the logistician). The Gorilla was a quiet, brooding man and he stayed to himself a lot. I don't think he liked the rest of the Command Group Team, which is probably why he spent just about every off-duty moment downtown with his *Moose* (Korean, live-in girl-friend).

A Moose is at the top of the working-girl food chain. A Moose is like your wife away from home. A lot of guys, single or married, had a Moose. Mooses kept neat and clean apartments or houses for their soldiers. For a significant monthly sum, they cooked, did laundry and did just about everything else a stay-at-home wife does for her husband. As a bonus, they also never got headaches and were always ready to party. Unlike many legitimate wives, a Moose only had sex with her man. It was "The code of the Moose". Women in the Moose business would grab onto a GI early in his tour and take care of him for the whole time he was in Korea. When the GI left, the Moose would take up with another newbie soldier. A lot of GIs ended up marrying their Moose and taking them back to the States. The Gorilla was shacked-up with the most beautiful Moose in all of Chunchon. Rumor has it; she was also the highest paid Moose in town.

Sergeant Major Mouth was probably the worse excuse for a Sergeant Major in the whole U.S. Army. I know this because just about every Camp Page NCO, at one time or another told me this. This was the Sergeant Major's last posting before retirement and he was just ineffectually cruising through it. No one expected anything from ole' "Mealy Mouth" and he never disappointed us.

So, basically, the camp had this dysfunctional family of leaders lead by a mean-spirited, alcoholic Colonel.

It was nearly three hours later, and too late for dinner at the O-Club, when the Colonel's clerk came into the room, apologized and told me I could leave. Seems the Colonel was just too busy to see me today. Evidently, something important had come up. I really didn't like the way this was all going, particularly later when Paul Gleason told me he'd seen the Colonel at dinner over an hour before while I was still cooling my heels in his outer office. A few days later, while exploring my surroundings, I noticed there was a back door to the Colonel's office. He could just sneak out any time he wished and no one inside would be the wiser. I didn't know it yet, but I would be meeting the Colonel, unofficially, later that evening.

I went back to my office to see if I had a candy bar or something in my desk. Some of the second shift MPs were making a run outside the gate to a sandwich shop and asked if I was hungry. The fried egg sandwich on lightly toasted rice bread was steaming hot and peppery. This was my first taste of Korean food and I really liked it. Seems these egg sandwiches were a staple for the guys after all the mess halls closed. You could buy ten of them for the equivalent of a buck's worth of Korean *Wan*. This had to be the best ten cent sandwich deal in the world.

Every BOQ room on the Camp had a house boy. Ours was Mr. Ahn. He was very quiet, shy and not really a boy. I never really knew his age but I guessed he was probably in his late thirties or maybe early forties. Each of us paid him the required equivalent *Won* fee of eight U.S. dollars a month for his incredible and diverse personal services. This guy did everything! He kept the room neat and clean. He washed, starched and ironed all our civilian clothing as well as our Army uniforms. He made up the beds every day and we always had fresh, clean, ironed sheets. He polished our brass and our boots till they gleamed but, most importantly, he would always put two full Jerry Cans for the Cannon Heater in our room before he left for the evening. He even did special favors for us such as getting our uniforms tailored or having all our military patches sewed on. I never knew if I should feel sorry for Mr. Ahn or not. We all made a pact, to tip him an extra two dollars each pay day so that meant he made forty bucks a month for the huge amount of work he did for us. We were told this was big bucks for a Korean and Mr. Ahn was doing okay. I never fully bought into that; so, above his protests, I'd tip him extra when he did special stuff above and beyond.

By this time, I'd given in and also purchased an electric blanket. So, now three of us were cozy-warm all night courtesy of the General Electric Corporation. We all bought the dual control models. The thinking was we could use them on double beds when we got back to the States. Actually they served another purpose. Not only did they keep us comfortable on these cold Korean nights, but we would hang the dual controls with their lighted dials on either side of our headboards. When working late, we could locate our beds in total darkness without disturbing our slumbering roommates. From time to time we'd mess around with the lights. Sometimes, when one of us was working late, the roommates would play around with the lighted controls. We'd move them around and the unsuspecting recipient of our prank, thinking his bed was between the two lights, would flop down in the darkness and miss it completely. You'd hear the crash then the inevitable cussing followed by muffled laughter from the other corners of the room.

Our Southern Gentleman from Alabama, Ab Abercrombie, refused to buy an electric blanket. He opted instead to spend his hard earned money on a Korean quilt. He said he'd use it to stay warm while in Korea then bring it home to his wife as a gift from this far-off, exotic land. He figured if it kept Koreans warm, it would keep him warm. It had been hand delivered to our room just this afternoon. When I arrived in the room, Ab and Mr. Ahn were discussing the quilt in ersatz sign language and a bunch of broken English and Korean. Neither understood the other. Mr. Ahn knew a little English but not the Alabama kind; Ab's southern drawl was unbelievable. The rest of us often didn't understand him either; so, we knew poor Mr. Ahn had to be totally lost. Ab wanted the quilt on the bed and Mr. Ahn was insisting it go on the floor. Reluctantly, Mr. Ahn gave in and placed it on the bed while shaking his head. It was beautiful brocade with Korean symbols and designs in an overall light blue color. Ab was quite proud of his find and was sure his Southern Belle, back home in Birmingham, was just going to love it. I walked over and hefted a corner and it seemed pretty darned heavy to me. I asked Ab if he was sure he was right and if it wasn't really some kind of Korean mattress or something as Mr. Ahn was insisting. He assured me it was, in fact, a quilt and he'd bought it at a place that exclusively sold expensive Korean quilts.

Around 2230 we all started to pack it in. Morning came early at Camp Page, about 0530. I was still hungry, having had just that one egg sandwich since breakfast, but now sleep was more on my mind. We were all settling in enjoying the warmth of setting No. 4 on our *GE* blankets. About thirty minutes after lights-out we heard this strained voice from Ab's darkened corner of the room. He was breathing deeply and speaking to us, in between deep, labored breaths, in that heavy Southern-Alabama accent of his. "Ya'll know *(Gasp)*, Ah nevah relized *(Gasp)*, jess how hev-a *(Gasp)*, these damned Korean quilts ah *(Gasp)*." We three started giggling uncontrollably. Ab slowly replied, "It ain't fuckin' funny guys *(Gasp)*." We three then exploded in unsympathetic, uproarious laughter.

About midnight we were all jolted out of our beds when the Fire-Watch kicked our door open and yelled **"FIRE!"** at the top of his lungs. We all grabbed our boots, pants, winter parkas and wallets and headed for the nearest fire exit. A strong, smoky smell hung in the frosty night air and we could see a reddish glow above the adjacent maze of Quonset huts. We all started running towards the fire and I could hear the approaching fire truck's siren and see the reflection of its flashing red lights in the BOQ windows.

The Camp Page fire department was almost one-hundred percent KATUSA (Korean Augmentation to the United States Army). KATUSAs were part of a quasi-Marshall Plan for helping Korea economically. It also kept down the cost of maintaining such a large U.S. military presence in that country. About twenty-five percent of the manpower total on Camp Page was KATUSA.

We all knew what fire meant, even me, the FNG. Since all our hooches were linked together by hallways, one totally out of control fire could potentially burn the whole damned place to the ground. When we arrived near the fire, the scene was chaotic and a lot of GIs were already helping the Korean firefighters. Someone shouted there were some troops overcome by smoke and we had to get them out. My MPs were now arriving and I hastily assembled a search team and put them to work. While the firefighters systematically worked the fire, we went room by room through the general area ensuring the wing was cleared.

I heard someone yelling in near panic, "We need that second damned team of fire fighters and more hoses *now*! Where the fuck are they?" The fire was now looking bigger and brighter. I took off down the hall toward the street where I'd last seen the second fire truck. Ahead of me in the narrow, dimly lit hall was a gaggle of Korean firefighters jammed up in a group with one tall, uniformed American blocking their way. As I ran through the smoke and up to where they were, I saw bewilderment mixed with fear in the Koreans' eyes. The tall American was rip-roaring drunk and yelling at the top of his lungs. "You fucking god-damned slope-headed bastards! You get the fuck out of my goddamned BOQ! I know you slant-eyed sons-a-bitches started this goddamned fire!"

I spun the drunken soldier around and slammed him into a corner with my forearm against his chest and yelled at the firefighters to get moving. Without hesitation they bolted past and hauled butt down the hallway towards the fire. As I knocked this man out of the way the glint off a silver rank insignia on his collar flashed in the reflected light. In that instant I realized it was a Silver Eagle. *"Oh, Jesus Christ!"* I thought, *"Tell me this can't be the commanding officer? This can't be Colonel Ralph K. Weatherspoon?"* As soon as I thought it, this drunken mess of a man screamed, "Get your fucking hands off me! Do you know who the fuck you're pushing around?" I instinctively whipped him into a police come-a-long hold with his face down and away from me; without saying a word, I pushed him outside into the cold, smoky darkness and walked him towards the O-Club. He was incoherent but cussing a blue streak. Halfway there we ran into Lieutenant Huddleston as he was running towards us to see what was going on. I asked him if he'd help the Colonel back to his hooch because I thought he was dizzy from inhaling way too much smoke while fighting the fire. As I turned back towards the fire I looked over my shoulder and noted Lieutenant Huddleston was holding him up and handling him quite well. I suspected this was not the first time he'd helped his drunken Colonel home.

The fire was now localized and gradually getting under control. It turned out a red hot, run-a-way Cannon Heater was the culprit. Thankfully, the fire was con-tained and only damaged four hooches. They were far enough away from our sec-tion of the tin labyrinth that we were allowed back in. We were lucky because a lot of other guys would be sleeping on Army cots in the gym tonight.

Exhausted, we dragged ourselves back to our room, showered and went back to bed to see if we could salvage a couple precious hours of sleep. Well, I now could say I'd finally met my new boss. How the hell was I ever to survive this shit for a whole year? I was so tired; I stopped caring and quickly drifted into a deep sleep.

In the morning, we awoke to the familiar sound of Cannon Heater priming and the muffled sounds of Ab cussing in that incredibly slow, Alabama accent while he fussed with getting the heater re-lit. "You piece of shitty Yankee ingenu-ity! There's a place hotter than normal hell for the northern bastard who invented this damned torture machine!"

The beautiful, new Korean "*mattress*" was folded neatly on the floor in Ab's corner of the room, never to be used or spoken of again. Shortly thereafter, the faint glow of electric blanket controls could now be seen in all four corners of our little tin hooch.

Other than fire-safety messages and meetings, the rest of the day was pretty uneventful. I kept waiting to be called on the carpet for manhandling our Camp Commander but nothing happened.

8

Lookin' for a Home!

Camp Page was one of about a dozen or so U.S. Army camps north of Seoul supporting either the 8th U.S. Army or the 1st ROK Army. Page was considered a *hardship post* because it was remote, had sub-standard facilities, was considered to be in a dangerous area and was a *non-accompanied assignment.* This meant wives or families were not allowed. Back in Alabama, Joyce was working on that particular aspect of the hardship.

I got eight letters from Joyce the very first day I started receiving mail. I was thrilled; I felt married and loved again! In one letter she said it looked like her plans to join me in Korea might just happen. Her Dad knew people in high places in the Ottawa government and he was calling in favors. The Korean Consulate in Ottawa had been contacted and people were working on Joyce's visa to come and work as a nurse at some hospital in Chunchon.

It also seems the Major had a lot more pull than his military rank would normally warrant. He had a long history of working with the U.S. Military. He'd been a Canadian Liaison Officer with the 5th US Marines during the Korean War in the early fifties; that was back before he became a helicopter pilot. Being on the team which formed "Canada One", the helicopter unit that flies the Canadian Prime Minister, probably didn't hurt either. I knew he wasn't thrilled at the prospect of his first born traveling to such a dangerous part of the world. However, he knew his headstrong eldest was going to do it, with or without his assistance; so, he decided it best to lend a hand and do it as safely as possible.

Now, I had the daunting task of finding a place for her, and hopefully us, to live. Second Lieutenants didn't make much money back then, but now I was being paid at the married rate and also receiving an extra $30 a month *separation pay* plus another $50 *remote assignment pay.* I wasn't going to get rich on it, but it sure as hell would buy a lot of Korean egg sandwiches. I was also going to have to get some sort of permission from the Screaming Eagle or this whole effort was going to turn into *"Mission Impossible"*. I was feeling a little blue as I realized my first overseas Thanksgiving was less than a week away.

About mid-morning the next day, a very loud horn went off and everybody started running around in circles. Still being an FNG I had no idea what this meant. I assumed it was some sort of alert so I ran to the MP Station where I was informed it was an attack drill and we MPs were the Camp's Quick Reaction Force. We were supposed to gather outside the PMO with our three Jeeps and weapons and be ready to take orders. A short time later, the big horn blew again and I watched all these armed soldiers climb out of rain ditches and saunter back to their unit areas to turn in their weapons and go back to life as usual. The whole event probably took no more than fifteen minutes.

After the drill, I asked some of my guys what sort of quick reaction missions we'd been tasked with and trained for. The answer was, "None!" Evidently, these drills were run just to meet the letter of some sort of 8th Army requirement. The horn goes off, everybody runs and jumps in a rain ditch, the horn goes off again and everybody goes back to work. "That's it?" Apparently it had been this way for as long as any of my guys could remember. Seems Colonel Weatherspoon was on his second tour extension and had already been in command at Camp Page for over a year and half. Weatherspoon was here first, so no one knew what it was like before him, except maybe the Koreans.

I now saw that I had a real job to do. I had to take my gaggle of twenty-eight MPs and give them "Battle Drills". I would set up a program of Infantry battle drill training and teach them to fight as six-man Infantry Fire Teams. If my Quick Reaction Force was not given specific missions, I guess it was going to be up to me to figure out what Camp Page's vulnerabilities were. Who were we worried about? What would they most likely attack? And, how would they do it? After I made my assessments, and based on the size of my team and weapons available to us, I'd try to determine the best ways to react to these various threats and situations. During the next few weeks, I read over the mission statements of the 5th USMC and its outlying "Hawk" sites. I then developed various reaction plans. We soon became the butt of a lot of jokes as we started doing our own "Alert Drills" two or three times a week. While training my men, I didn't realize we would all be battle tested sooner than anyone expected.

Meanwhile, back at Fort Rucker, my bride and the Major had been very busy. Joyce was now in possession a very important document, her Korean Work Visa. In this latest letter she was asking me to set a date for her arrival. Reading on, she gave me the name and address of the local hospital and Korean doctor she would be working for. She also said he had information on a house for us in Chunchon.

Further, this Doctor Han was asking to meet and show me the house. I sat in my room, stunned, as I stared at my curved, green walls. When we first talked of her coming to Korea, it seemed like such a long shot. It was one of those pipe-dreams lovers tell each other and themselves so parting won't be so painful. However, she and her Dad were now turning our lover's dream into a nightmare for me. Don't get me wrong, I wanted to be with Joyce in the worse possible way, but most of the work would have to come from her end and I just could not imagine it all getting done. At my end, all I had to do was find a house and get permission from the Screaming Eagle to live with her. Now, how the hell was I going to pull that off?

I had less than $1700 to my name and no idea what all this was going to cost. No American soldier in all of Camp Page had a wife with them, except those few who were married to local Korean women. What would house rent be? What about furniture? Lastly, and the biggest question: How do I get the Screaming Eagle, a man I had yet to officially meet, a man I had just roughed up in the night, give me special permission to live off base with my wife? Officially, there was a midnight curfew for all troops at Camp Page. If I had a house in Chunchon, I would have to be exempt from curfew or my bride would be sleeping alone every night in this not so safe city.

Paul Gleason, who was rapidly becoming my best friend at Camp Page, was the sounding board for many of my frustrations. "Paul, how in the hell am I going to afford furniture?" Paul brightened, "Furniture? You need furniture? Furniture's no problem; we can make it in the camp craft shop. The wood's cheap and I know my way around power tools. I'll help and I can teach you how to make furniture."

A lot of sawdust and a short time later I was proud owner of a huge linen chest and a *Young-boke-Jon* (armoire). Korean brass handles, hinges and decorative locks, purchased in the local markets, made our varnished plywood creations look quite professional. Now, all I had to do was find a place to put them in.

9

The Pig Doctor!

It was now Thanksgiving and all but essential personnel at Camp Page had the day off. I decided to use the morning to get something very important done. Mr. Shin had contacted Dr. Han for me. We took the Jeep and drove up to his hospital, *more like a clinic*. A Korean nurse told us Dr. Han was in the middle of an operation, she showed us to chairs in a covered atrium outside the operating room and then disappeared. After about five minutes, the sliding glass door and oriental screen in front of us slid wide open and out stepped Dr. Han. As I got to my feet, this horrifying sight of a man appeared. He was squat in stature, quite fat, and had what the Koreans call a *Moon Face* (*wide, flat, facial features*). He was dressed in white scrubs and over them was what used to be a white apron. His apron was generously smeared with blood. He walked the few steps over towards us while reaching up and pulling down his operating mask as he came. "Ah so! *Rue* are *Rootenant Roy-cee?*" He extended a rubber-gloved hand and I instinctively took a step backwards while starring down at it. He followed my eyes to where I was looking. Glancing down at his blood-covered hand he proclaimed, "Ah, I forget what doing." He then interlaced the fingers of both gory, rubber hands and rested them on top of his ample and equally blood covered belly. He started talking about the house he had available. "*Is nize new hozosa.*"

The doctor's words weren't registering with me because I was looking past him into the now wide open operating room. Some poor, dumb, bloody bastard on the table was obviously still under the knife. Two nurses, a male assistant and an anesthetist were just standing there around the bloody patient. Even with their surgical masks on, I could tell from their wide, stunned eyes they were as dumbfounded as I that Dr. Han had just walked out in mid-operation. I hastily asked Mr. Shin if he had the address, then I politely and quickly thanked Dr. Han, told him we were going to go look at the place. Dr. Han was left standing there outside his operating room as we beat a hasty retreat to the Jeep. I told Mr. Shin I was sorry for departing so quickly, but explained there was no way I was just going to stand there and chit-chat with the bloody doctor while his equally bloody patient bled to death on the operating table from lack of medical attention. Mr. Shin nodded and summed it up nicely. "Dr. Han is pig doctor. Nobody likes him. He only has medical practice here because there not many doctors in Chunchon." I wondered if I should write Joyce about him or just let her find out for herself after she arrived. Maybe he was a good doctor but just a bit eccentric, I doubted it, but what the heck did I know?

10

The House at Fourteen Oak Chong Dong

The house ended up belonging to Dr. Han's brother-in-law, or so we thought, and it was located on the upslope towards *Unnecessary Mountain* about 300 yards past the traffic circle in the center of town. It was just under a mile from Camp Page. If I had a sidewalk scooter, I literally could have stood on it and rolled all the way down hill to the camp's main gate.

I think the real name of the mountain, in Korean, is *Wee Bong,* but back during the Korean War GIs named it *Unnecessary Mountain* because it was small and stood there all alone in this valley surrounded, at a distance, by dozens of much more impressive peaks. With all these other mountains framing the valley, this little one in the middle seemed, well, *unnecessary.*

Standing in front of the place, on the dirt road, it looked huge. It was entirely made of cement smeared over concrete blocks and had a red barrel tile roof. The place was painted baby blue with horizontal, white racing stripe running the length of the front between the first and second floors. There were actually two levels. The ground level turned out to be a separate house. It was sort of a vertical Korean duplex. We met the man who occupied the ground level and discovered he was the actual owner, the brother-in-law. He had borrowed the money from Dr. Han to build it and he needed a tenant to help pay off his debt. He then showed us around the place.

There were two ways of entering. To the left of the house was a long set of incredibly steep, treacherous stone block stairs; thirty-two of them to be exact. They lead up to a solid double hinged iron gate with iron spikes on top. There was a small iron *Sally Port* door built into one side of the double gate. This is what one would normally use if they weren't trying to carry in something bulky. I could not imagine using these stairs under snow or ice conditions. The tread was only about eight inches deep and you sort of had to walk up sideways to keep your whole foot on the steps. The other way in was around back. If you drove up hill past the house and turned left you continued going uphill but now you curved behind the place. From this vantage point, the house now looked like a much smaller one-story. This side of the house was enclosed by a seven foot tall cement wall with broken glass cemented in the top to discourage thieves. There was an equally strong iron gate with spikes in the back. The place was built like a mini Fort Knox and I liked that aspect!

Once inside the small rear courtyard, the house looked even smaller. I did note, with some trepidation, that there was a cement block and stucco outhouse in the courtyard. Inside the house there were five rooms, including the walk-in kitchen pantry, and a sort of bathroom. There was just this small, deep, cement tub with just one cold water faucet in the bathroom. There seemed to be enough space for a toilet but there was none. Our walk-through revealed a very small kitchen with a small stone and tile sink, and again, only a cold water tap. The kitchen floor was just plain old cement. The master bedroom was the largest room in the place. I don't think it was supposed to be the bedroom but that's what we were going to use it for. To round it out there was another small bed room and a small living room with a sliding glass door which emptied out onto a cement-walled balcony overlooking the street two stories below. From my high-ground perch, I had a commanding view of half the city rooftops and purple-hued mountains way off to the east. This place was close to the camp, strongly built, securable and had a great view. There were drawbacks, which included: no inside toilet, no hot water and no visible means of heating the place. Other than that, it was fine!

Mr. Shin negotiated with the owner about the price. Seems the concept of rent was not the preferred method of payment in 1967. The Koreans had this system called *Key Money*. Interest rates were so high at the time that putting a lump sum of American Dollars in a Korean bank would generate a lot more money for the landlord then just getting monthly rent in Korean currency. The owner wanted $1500 American up front. He told me that at the end of my tour of duty in Korea he would simply give me my $1500 back. I asked Mr. Shin if this was true and he said "Yes!" Evidently, it was a common way of renting homes to foreigners. I would still have to figure out the hot water, toilet and heating situation on my own, but the place was brand new and I was eager to make a deal.

I asked Mr. Shin if it would be okay to think about this for a few days or would we run the risk of losing the place. Mr. Shin looked at me and smiled, "Nobody in Chunchon have $1500 American dollars, you be safe." Mr. Shin told the landlord we would get back to him in one week; we did all the requisite bowing and hand shaking, then left.

11

Turkey Day

Thanksgiving afternoon, we all got ready for the *Mandatory Good Times* dinner event at the Officers' Mess/Club. It was a dress blue uniform affair and all 110 of us officers were expected to be there along with several invited guests. I was actually looking forward to it. Ab, Dave, Paul and I walked through the warren together and into the Mess. I hadn't worn my dress blues since the wedding and I was feeling quite spiffy. Ab was commenting about the color of his dress uniform in his thick Alabameeze. *"Ma Granddaddy, a cavalry Colonel during the second battle of Manassas,* ah might add, *would not like the Yankee blue color of this uniform. There should at least be some gray in he-ah somewhere out of respect for the South."* We all groaned while pushing and jostling Ab. We could never figure out if Ab was serious or just always pulling our leg. "Get over it Johnny Reb, and let's just go eat us some turkey and forget about the 'War of Northern Aggression'."

It amazed me just how festive the club staff could make this big old Quonset hut look. The whole place smelled of turkey, stuffing and fresh baked pies. It was all wonderfully familiar; I don't know how they did it, but somehow I felt happy and a little like I was at home. I'd skipped both breakfast and lunch and I was ready to do some serious turkey damage.

First thing I noticed was that my brass plate had finally started to move. There were now three plates in line behind mine. It had been a couple of weeks since my arrival and I was beginning to know people. Most importantly, I was no longer the FNG!

Dad Dunkerly, our CW4 (Chief Warrant) Personnel Officer, was perched on his designated stool at the very end of the bar with his signature glass of Jack Daniels neat. Dad was a veteran of World War II, the Korean War and Vietnam. Up to this point in my fledgling military career, Dad had more ribbons on his chest than any Army guy I'd seen. He just about had his thirty years in and was nearing retirement. His main claim to fame at Camp Page was that he was the only officer who wasn't afraid of the Screaming Eagle when he was rip-roaring drunk. When Weatherspoon was "on a tare" everyone would clear out of the mess and find someplace to hide, everyone that is except ole' Dad Dunkerly. He would just sit there at the end of bar sipping his *Black Jack* and chain-smoking his unfiltered *Camels*. When Weatherspoon would come over and try to mess with him, Dad would just lock eyeballs with the "Old Man" and say something like, "goddammit' Colonel, sit the hell down, have a drink, and stop making such a damned fool out of yourself. It's embarrassing to us old farts!" Invariably, Weatherspoon would quiet down, sit with him and have that drink. As much as I can remember, Dad was the only guy I ever saw who could actually calm the Colonel down when he had a snoot full.

I never got a chance to know Dad all that well, but I always wanted to. I wanted to talk to him about his chest full of medals; he just about had them all. From all his combat and valor ribbons, I guessed he hadn't always been in the Adjutant General Corps. He walked with a limp and I just knew there was a story there too. Some of the other guys told me they heard Dad went ashore at Omaha Beach on D-Day and was also one of the heroes of the Korean War. Like most *real* "War Horses" I'd meet over the years, Dad never talked much about his war exploits. You just looked at that stack of ribbons, that craggy old face and those deep-set, dark, sinister eyes and you knew you were in the presence of a real, no shit, warrior. Time may have done its damage to this old man, but those hawk eyes and that chest full of ribbons silently spoke volumes.

For me, this was a Thanksgiving to remember. The club staff had done everything to make us feel as close to home as possible. It was a neat trick too since most of us were half a world away from our families. The food was great and everything else was equally wonderful. Even the Colonel was delightful. He came into the club in his dress blues and looked every inch an American, Artillery Colonel. His uniform was impeccable. He worked the room like a polished politician seeking reelection. Everywhere he went there were smiles, short exchanges of words and laughter—a lot of laughter. This guy was fucking charming when he wanted to be. I now had a glimpse into the controlled Colonel Weatherspoon. This was the Colonel of Thanksgivings past. This was not the drunken bum I ran into the other night at the fire. I turned to Paul and said, "What gives? This guy is great."

Paul looked at me, "Just watch him; everybody in this room knows what's going to happen. We're just enjoying the nice twin while it lasts. Most of us are already planning our escapes after his seventh or eighth drink. Some of us even count his drinks and make our plans accordingly. Problem is, we don't know how many he's had before he got here. Tonight my friend, I guarantee you will see a true Dr. Jeckel and Mr. Hyde performance." Paul continued, "Did you know Dave Ross, our indispensable Class VI Officer here, is a Mormon?" I looked at Dave and he nodded his head in confirmation. "Dave got the Class VI job because he doesn't need his ration card cause he doesn't drink or smoke." Dave, sipping on his cranberry juice and soda, nodded again, "But I do sin a bit; I drink coffee." Paul continued, "The Colonel goes through his own ration card in less than two weeks. When the Colonel's ration card is all punched out, Dave covers him by punching out the squares on his own card. This guy drinks at least half a bottle of booze and ten to twelve beers a day. That's just in his hooch and don't even count what he drinks here in the club. Our boss, that great looking Colonel over there, the guy in charge of this Missile Command and all our rockets, missiles and warheads is a gold plated alkie. Frankly, it scares the shit out of me." Dave again nodded in agreement and continued nursing his cranberry juice cocktail.

Paul then brightened, "You got that request to live off post with your wife ready?" I replied it was back in our room. "Well go get it, because by my drink count and calculations *Super Trooper* over there turns into *Sloppy Drunk, Abusive, Colonel Guy* in one drink and about 15 minutes from now. Check it out; some of the guys in the back of the room are already starting to slide towards the door. Quick, go get the request now!" I slid out of my chair as stealthily as I could, exited the club and sprinted down the hall; I retrieved the request form and tore back to the club. I noted a few officers were already carefully sneaking out of the Mess. I got back to our table and asked, "Now what?" Paul grinned, "Okay, its show time! Just think up some bull shit, go over there and give it your best shot. He's not thinking so good right now; so, this might be your only chance"

I walked towards the head table, paper down at my side. The Colonel was talking to the newly promoted Captain Huddleston about picking him up a bottle of Johnny Walker Black at the Class VI because he was getting ready to leave. Huddleston turned to depart on the errand and the Colonel did an abrupt about face and there we were practically nose to nose. He gave me his broad, patented smile, "Well hello, Lieutenant, Happy Thanksgiving!" I stuck out my hand, "Happy Thanksgiving to you too, Sir. Wonderful meal, Sir! Sir … I'm doing some work in town for the homeless. They won't have a proper place to live if I don't get involved in fixing a place up for them. I'm in the process of making all the arrangements and will be spending a lot of my own time and money on this project. But to make this all work, I may have to be off post past curfew some nights when I'm not scheduled for duty here. I assure you, Sir, I won't let any of this endeavor affect my official duties, Sir." The Colonel smiled again but this time he seemed a little confused and I thought I detected the hint of a slur in his words. "*Thish* is great, Lieutenant! I'm glad to see one of my men getting involved in the Korean *kammoonity*. These slope-headed bastards need all the help they can get, right? *Thish* also looks good for my command." I brought the request form up from my side into the Colonel's view. "Would you please sign this for me, Sir, so I can get on with my work downtown?" The Colonel's brow furrowed and a look of disorientation crept across his face, "What's *thish* about again, Lieutenant?" I suppressed panic and blurted out, "It's for the homeless, Sir, please sign here, Sir." To my utter amazement, he plopped right down in his chair, whipped out a pen and signed the paper right where my finger was pointing. As soon as his pen rose a millimeter above the document, I whisked it away and into my inside breast pocket. "Thank you, Sir, and again, Sir, Happy Thanksgiving, Sir!"

I did a perfect Army drill and ceremonies one-eighty and walked at a hurried pace back to Paul. Without changing pace Paul and Dave joined me and together we strode towards the door. Behind us, it was starting. "Which one of you god-damned idiot, slope-headed, waitress bitches took my fucking scotch? I wasn't through with it. Bring me another fucking scotch *now!*" The door closed behind us and I showed Paul the five sheet manifold set of forms with the Colonel's signature on it. Paul grinned, "Perfect, freaking perfect! I know Dad Dunkerly really well; he'll put a copy in your official personnel folder in the S-1 (Personnel) office to make it all official. Right now, my friend; you are authorized to live off-post." Paul put an arm around my shoulder and we walked back to the hooch smiling and laughing. Before I turned in, I wrote Joyce a long letter.

That same night I got my first real dose of the fabled Screaming Eagle in all his drunken glory. We had a few more drinks in our room and played several hand of Hearts, then we four all turned in around ten. Shortly after midnight our door opened and one of my MPs flashed his light around the room until he found me. "Sir, we need you down at the MP Desk, Weatherspoon's there raising Holy hell!"

My whole life I've been and *instant on* type person. No matter how short the sleep, I pop up out of bed ready for action. Over the years this has proven to be a trait which has served me well and probably saved my life once or twice. I came out of my bunk so fast it startled my guy. I mechanically dressed and asked him what was going on. "Weatherpoon's got everybody in the MP Station braced at attention and he's screaming at the top of his lungs."

The two of us took off through the labyrinth as fast as we could go emerging outside just about twenty-five yards from the back of the MP Station. Why the hell couldn't they have built just one more section of connector tunnel to my office area? If I wasn't fully awake, that blast of ice cold, late November, Korean mountain air made my nose hairs go stiff when I sucked in my first breath. It was like hitting some kind of thermal wall. Growing up in Wickford, Rhode Island, I can remember the Channel 10, WJAR weatherman talk about winter cold fronts moving down from Canada. Just before I went to bed tonight the AFKN (American Forces Korean Network) weather guy, on the radio, said a cold front was moving down from Manchuria. As we jogged towards the MP Station, I was thinking, "*Somehow, Manchuria just sounds a lot colder than Canada.*"

We pulled up to a walking pace just outside the MP Station. I gave a quick peek through the frosted window and saw everyone stiffly braced at attention while the Colonel was wildly waving his arms and yelling at the seven people in the room. I told the MP to stay outside as I entered the room. The Colonel was too drunk to notice my arrival. He was very wobbly and pointing at various individuals and indiscriminately spewing forth a string of loosely connected thoughts liberally sprinkled with racial slurs, profanity and blasphemy at nobody in particular. "You goddamned slope-head bastards are fucking up my command. And you, Sergeant, why is that slope-headed cunt in my MP Station after curfew?" He was pointing at a terrified, cowering Korean woman who had just brought food to the MP night shift. I knew Sergeant Oden was married to a Korean woman in and that they had a baby son. His wife also worked at the Camp's main Mess Hall; so, I guessed this woman he was screaming and pointing at was the wife of one of the NCOs under his command. Sergeant Oden's face was now turning purple and he was just about to come over the top of the desk to kill the Colonel.

Summoning up courage, I loudly blurted out, "Good evening, Sir, really cold out there tonight isn't it, Sir?" Sergeant Oden froze and Colonel Weatherspoon staggered a one-eighty and glared at me with hate in his eyes and spittle around his mouth. "Who the fuck are you, Lieutenant?" "Colonel, I'm your new Provost Marshal, Lieutenant Royce. I don't think we've formally met. Why don't we step outside and talk about this, Sir; these MPs have work to do." The sneering Colonel, not wanting to waist another minute before biting off a large piece of my ass, followed me outside. As I came through the door I motioned for the outside MP to take off. He was more than glad to do so and not encounter the Colonel's wrath.

I had on my winter parka, gloves, fir-lined cap and boots. However, the Colonel was still in his dress blues with low-quarter shoes and no hat. He had evidently come to the MP Station via some warmer inside route. But now he was outside, and even in his near drunken stupor, it only took him twenty or thirty seconds before realizing he was going to freeze to death if he didn't get back inside. My potential chewing out was short circuited by the sudden cold taking his breath away. He started to turn towards the door. I grabbed him by the arm and said, "Let me show you the fastest way back to your quarters, Sir." He slipped on the frozen ground and, in near panic, grabbed me by the arm and hung on tightly. I walked him around the corner where it was about a hundred yards to his hooch. We were also now walking into the wind. This area between the Quonsets formed a natural wind tunnel. He said nothing, but clutched my arm in a death grip as we walked slowly at his impaired pace. It was amazing how drunkenness combined with intense cold made him seem to forget everything. He just held on to me, trembling like a frightened child. I could feel him shuddering and shaking through his thin dress blue uniform. In some strange way I was even feeling sorry for him.

A few minutes later, we arrived at his door; he fumbled around with his keys then dropped them. I bent down and retrieved his key ring. Again he tried to operate the padlock but, after several failures, I took the keys from him, took off one glove and, with freezing but sober hands, opened the lock. The Colonel staggered inside, thanked me in a tiny voice and I closed his door to the frosty wind. This was the second of what would be my many encounters with our boozer Colonel. I guess you might say I won this round but I still had about a year to go and wondered how this would all have played out on a warm summer night. The fact that I had his signature on a document allowing me to live off base with my bride somehow made the freezing walk back to the MP Station seem a little warmer.

Things had calmed down quite a bit by the time I got back to the MP Desk area. Sergeant Oden explained, "Sir, every time the Colonel gets ripped, just about all the officers stream out the main gate like rats leaving the ship. Those that don't go to the Ville find some other place to hole up. Problem is, we're here on duty and we can't hide. The MP Desk and Main Gate are 24-7 operations. If he can't find somebody's ass to chew, he always comes in here for fresh meat and chews on us, and Sir ... we're pretty damned sick of it. Tonight was the very first time anyone's ever taken him on. We all want to thank you for that." I told them that from now on I wanted to be called anytime it even looked like the Colonel was headed our way. I realized my decision was probably going to set me on multiple collision paths with the Colonel. I did one last thing that night which would end up being very important. I asked everyone involved to write out a statement of what happened. The Desk Sergeant collected them, typed them up and then had everyone sign them. I placed these documents in my office field safe. Memories are short and I didn't want anyone to forget what happened this night.

That night, for some strange reason, I felt it my responsibility to apologize to Mrs. Oden for the Colonel's actions. I knew this idiot was out of it, and a mean-as-sin drunk to boot, but I've always had this almost uncontrollable need to apologize for Americans when they show their asses in foreign lands. It's like I'm some sort of unofficial representative of the United States in charge of smoothing the ruffled feathers of foreign nationals who've just encountered an ugly American. Several years later, a psychologist would tell me I possessed a "Caretaker" personality. I seems I have to try to fix things and help people. That would also help explain some of my six broken noses.

12

Let's Play Meet the Colonel

The next morning, after over two weeks in country, I finally had my first official meeting with the Colonel. Again, I was summoned to his office with almost no advanced warning. I thought it would be about my manhandling him back to his hooch. During the short time I was in his office he neither mentioned it nor did he give any indication he even remembered it.

But, before I actually made it into his office, once again, I had to cool my heals in his outer office. I sat there for just about three hours with the recently promoted *Captain* Huddleston looking down his nose at me with those pale, pale-blue eyes. Finally, I was ushered in. I strode up to the exact Army textbook position in front of the Colonel's desk and, with an audible heel click, I popped a perfect salute. "Sir, Lieutenant Royce reports!" The room fell silent. The Colonel never even looked up; he just kept shuffling papers and signing them. I stood there silently at attention, holding this perfect salute. Through months of OCS training, even my eyeballs were locked on some artificial horizon; you don't want to get caught "eyeballing" anything in the room. The only audible sound was paper shuffling and the scratching sound of the Colonel's fountain pen.

The proper procedure for me, as the junior officer, was to hold my salute until the Colonel returned it. Only problem was, the Colonel wasn't returning! The Army manual never said what to do in the event that ever happened. I wanted to drop it but was afraid it would give him a chance to chew me out. After what was probably about a minute, but seemed much longer, I assumed a *to-hell-with-it* attitude and snapped my hand sharply back to my side while still standing at attention. A few seconds later, head down and still signing papers, the Colonel spoke. "I've been in this Army for close to thirty years and in that whole time I've never met a Military Police Officer who was worth a shit!" The Colonel, again fell silent, and continued signing while still not making eye contact with me. My first thoughts were: "*This has to be some sort of a crazy test just to see how I'll react.*" I went along that and replied, "I assure you, Sir, I will do everything I can to change your opinion of MP Officers." There, I thought, that was a firm and positive statement. It also showed no sign of intimidation or fear; he should like my response. Without looking up, the Colonel ended our strange but brief little meeting with just three words. "You won't ... Dismissed!" Never once did he ever looked up at me, and the only physical hint he gave that I was even in the room was the little flicking motion he made with his left hand when he said, "Dismissed!" It was like he was shoeing a fly away from his desk.

Semi-stunned, I robotically snapped another sharp salute, held it for a long three count, and then quickly realizing it was not going to be returned, I dropped it, executed a sharp about face and strode out of his office. When I closed his door behind me, the wind just went out of my balloon. I could actually feel my shoulders drooping. Does this guy remember me from the fire, Thanksgiving night, or both? He makes no mention of it, yet he seems to dislike me immensely without even knowing me.

I was looking at my boots trying to think what to do next when I became conscious of Captain Huddleston. When I looked up, there he was at his desk, obviously enjoying my discomfort. "Didn't go well I presume, Lieutenant?" I glared back at him:

"No Captain, it did not go well!"

"That doesn't surprise me. Don't take it personal but ... he hates MPs ... all MPs"

"And just why might that be, Captain Huddleston?"

Captain Huddleston came around from behind his desk and walked over to a corner of the room. He pointed to a small, framed document with a brass plate affixed to it at the bottom. "He got this when he was working in the Pentagon, Military Personnel Center, Artillery section. He thinks this is the first of several career setbacks that's stopped him from being promoted to General." I walked across the room and looked at the little, framed document. *Holy shit!* It was an old Military Police traffic ticket issued for doing 50 in a 25 MPH zone and dated 26, September, 1946. This was a 21 year old speeding citation issued by the MPs in Washington DC. The engraved brass plate on the frame read, "ANOTHER REASON FOR MP FORCE REDUCTION." I looked at Captain Huddleston as he said, "The Colonel was a junior Captain in the Artillery Branch Assignments Office at MILPERCEN (Military Personnel Center) at the time. He got severely chewed out by his boss and the ticket was reflected in his annual Efficiency Report that year. He told me he hasn't had anything good to say about MPs since."

I nodded my understanding to the smirking but informative Captain Huddleston and walked out into the hall. So let's see if I got this straight ... I work for a habitual drunk who hates me just because I'm an MP. This is going to be a fun assignment!

13

Seoul '67

Later in the week, I got my first chance to drive to Seoul and visit 8th Army Headquarters at Yongsan Compound. I was going there to pay a courtesy call on Colonel William Condra, the 8th Army Provost Marshal. He was the *Top Cop* for all U.S. Army forces in Korea. I was also excited to finally see someplace other than Chunchon.

Two of my MPs were going with me, one who knew the way and could drive and the other who just wanted to go to the big, headquarters PX (Post Exchange). I stopped by the office and picked up a copy of my orders to present to Colonel Condra. When I came out, Specialist Krippies and Buck Sergeant Kelser were removing a newish-looking canvas top from the Jeep and replacing it with a rather ratty-looking, old top. The two turned towards me as I arrived at the Jeep. With a quizzical look, I asked, "What's with the tops?" In a matter-of-fact reply, Sergeant Kelser replied, "Slicky Boys, Sir!" I guess my expression silently solicited a more detailed answer. "Sir, every time we go to Seoul we seem to lose a top. Slicky Boys are all over Seoul, they sometimes travel in packs and just wait for you to stop somewhere and leave your vehicle unattended, even for a minute. They can steal a Jeep top faster than you can kiss a duck. Other times they zip open the canvas with razor-knifes and steal anything you have inside. Sometimes, they do it even if you're still in the Jeep. Sir, I'm from Detroit, Michigan, I know from crooks, and these guys are really pro. I'm not kidding, these guys are so good they can actually steal a radio and leave the music!" I could tell from the Sergeant's shit-eating grin he was stretching the truth a mile or two, but I got the point.

With the top changed, out the gate we went. Kelser drove, I was in the passenger seat and Krippies did as best he could in the back. Kelser told me he was driving because he was the taller of the two. Poor Krippies was just a mere six foot four inches and Sergeant Kelser had two inches on him.

I'd already made the observation that, at six foot three, I appeared to be one of the shortest men in my MP unit. So I asked, "Why are all the MPs here so freaking tall?" After some comic squabbling between the two, Sergeant Kelser stated he was the tallest in the unit and therefore he would answer the question. "Well Sir, it's like this. We work for you but we're also one of about three or four *Panmunjom, Freedom Bridge* feeder units. The Korean War started in June of 1950 and it never really ended. Sure, in July of 1953 there was this *Cease Fire* and most of our troops went home but, technically, the war's still going on. There's just this sort of uneasy truce that's been happening for the past fifteen years. So, we may not be shooting at each other near as much these days but we're still officially at war with the *Gooks* (GI slang for North Korean soldiers) up north. Panmunjom is where all the peace talks take place and, from time to time, they still do. The place is sort of the only neutral zone between North and South Korea. Every time there's an incident along the DMZ (Demilitarized Zone), the North and South get together there to talk it over."

"The North Koreans have their MPs up there and so do we. They and we are only allowed just so many MPs in the zone at a time. The Gooks are sneaky little bastards, and often slide in more MPs than they're supposed to. In the past they've ganged up on a few of our MPs when nobody's looking and beat the crap out of them. Official protests don't do much good so, Colonel "Wild Bill" Condra, the guy you're going to meet today, decided to send in nothing but monster MPs from then on. You have to be at least six foot three to patrol in the zone. Shorty back there barely made it." The comment evoked a quick kick in the back of the driver's seat by a size twelve combat boot. "We cover for them sometimes when the Freedom Bridge guys get sick or go on leave. When one of them rotates back home, we're sometimes asked if we want to volunteer to replace them. Going up there for a couple of weeks or so is fine, but that's just too much spit, polish and aggravation to put up with; so, nobody from Page has volunteered for a tour up there in a long time."

The ride to Seoul was pretty interesting, big trucks mixed in with severely overloaded little three-wheeled trucks and passenger-packed, brightly painted buses which were actually made out of recycled 55 gallon oil drums. I even saw an old Papa San struggling with an engine block on the back of his bicycle. The only consistent rule of the road in Korea seemed to be noise. Horns blew constantly and apparently for no particular reason.

There were reminders everywhere about the South's concern for North Korean infiltrators. NK raids had recently picked up and the South was pretty jittery about it. We passed through four ROK Army MP Checkpoints during our two-hour, sixty something mile drive to the South Korean capital. I noticed the large, black on white Military Police markings on our Jeep were drawing quite a bit of attention. At one point I was looking off at a ROK Army guard tower, maybe fifty or so yards in from the side of the road. The Korean soldier in the tower popped to attention and saluted our MP Jeep as we passed. I looked at Kelser, "What's with the long range saluting?" He smiled, "It's been fifteen years since the cease fire between the two Koreas but we still haven't signed a "Status of Forces Agreement" with the South Koran Government. We're still the law south of the 38th Parallel. In Korea, U.S. Army MPs are viewed as the big cops in this country. Theoretically, if we were mean bastards, our country would actually be in a position to make life and death decisions over these people. They salute to show respect and try stay on our good side, just in case we ever decide to exercise it. There's still a lot of loose ends left over from the war that don't make much sense to us now."

We drove through one of the great gates of Seoul with its huge carved stone lions that looked more like Chinese dragons or maybe even dogs to me. Kelser explained these were supposed to be *fire eating* lions posted at all the gates to protect the city. With millions of people packed into a place where most of the buildings are made of combustibles, fire is a real threat. Coal blocks and fire barrels were still the principal means of heating. Fire was still as big a concern in '67 as it was when those ancient stone lions were carved. A few hundred years ago Seoul had burned to the ground. The Lions were placed there to eat fire before it could harm anyone.

Like just about every other great city, Seoul had its slums. The ones I saw that day were down by the Han River. There were hundreds of shabby, wood and paper shacks with pieces of either corrugated tin or plastic for roofs. This vast area along the river seemed to create its own smoggy atmosphere. This city within a city was half-hidden by a smoky cloud fed by who knows how many burning coal blocks. From the horrific smell I could only assume the now frozen Han River served as the communal facility for everything from drinking water to toilets. From the back seat Krippies commented, "This is nothing, Lieutenant, you should smell this place in summer!"

All this squalor was clearly visible from the, still under-construction, modern six lane concrete expressway we were traveling on. Traffic was light and that was probably a good thing. Army trucks, Black Korean CIC (Counter Intelligence Corps) Jeeps, those oil drum buses, *Shinjin* taxis and the ubiquitous little three wheeled motor scooter/trucks all shared this expressway along with; bicycles, ox carts, and pedestrians. There was no posted minimum speed limit here. Everyone traveled at their own pace and everyone who had a horn was using it.

Most amazing of all were the men, and sometimes women who carried great loads on their backs in *A-Frames*. A-Frames are sort of like a great wooden backpack, often with a large basket made of woven twigs. The carrying straps were made of rope or woven grasses. I could only assume this was Korea's main means of carrying stuff before trucks and, probably even before the wheel was invented. The lower wooden legs of the A-Frame extended down two or three more feet from where the load was placed. The user would lean this device up against something and load the basket. They would then maneuver themselves under the load and slip on the shoulder straps. Most Koreans carried a stout wooden staff to aid them in their walking. Using their legs, and all the arm power they could exert on the wooden staff, they would raise themselves up into a hunched-over walking position, adjust themselves to handle the load and take off down the road.

I can only imagine, but many of these loads had to be at the edge of what human bones, tendons and muscles could endure without just snapping. As we were turning off what we dubbed "The Riverside Expressway" I saw this thin, gray-haired old man carrying a huge pig on his back in an A-Frame. The pig looked to be sleeping. Kelser laughed, "That pig doesn't know it yet, but he's on the menu for a bunch of people tonight. The reason he's not kicking up a fuss is because he's drunk on *Mokolli*; it's Korean booze, a kinda' rice wine I think. They mix it in with the pig's food to get 'em drunk so they can haul em to town without the pig objecting too much. You should see what happens when a pig like that sobers up before old Papa San there gets him to market. I saw it happen once, what a sight! Some of these farmers carry their livestock down here from miles and miles away. I just don't see how these old men can do it!" Before I could formulate a question in my mind, Kelser offered: "Mostly, the farmers out in the country are really poor. They can't even afford to truck in their livestock; the cost is too much for them. Selling prices are better in Seoul than anywhere else so they put themselves through all this for badly needed extra money. It's a hard life for most of these people, Sir." I silently nodded agreement as we passed the farmer. I could now clearly see his pained expression. He gave me a quick sideways glance and I could see and feel the pain deep inside his eyes. It was below freezing, but his exertion was causing steam to rise off his sweat soaked clothing. Every step was really hurting this guy down to his bones. For sure, his life was no garden party but as long as he had his strength, his farm and some livestock to raise and sell, he wasn't going to let himself and his family end up in one of those shacks down by the Han.

Even if we stopped and offered the farmer and his pig a lift, he wasn't going to take it. That's just the way it was. He was living in his world and we were living in ours. No matter, he wasn't going to understand our words or intentions and would probably think we were trying to steal his pig. I also noticed no Koreans were stopping to offer him a ride either. That's not something Koreans did in 1967. Most of them were just trying to eke out their own living and had little time or strength to help others.

That same helpless feeling came over me again. I would endure this feeling all my life. What could I do? There are millions and millions of people in conditions even worse than this old Papa San's. We Americans are blind as to just how blessed we are. We complain about the cable TV going out during a game. In comparison to most of the world, our problems are laughable.

14

The Slicky Boys

My meeting with Colonel Condra went well. I didn't mention any of our Camp Commander's unusual behaviors. For reasons still unknown to me, I've always had this loyalty streak that sometimes goes well beyond reason and often defies explanation. Over the years, I've stood behind and supported all my bosses, a few of them long after they ceased to deserve my loyalty. I guess with Colonel Weatherspoon, I somehow had it in the back of my mind that I was new and maybe this would all pass. He would, one day soon, sober up and we would enjoy this great professional relationship. Kind of silly, but I wasn't yet ready to give up on him. The question did come up from this grandfatherly Colonel I was now talking to, "Well, Lieutenant Royce, now that you've been at Camp Page for over a month, how's things going up there?" I smiled and lied. "Just fine Sir!" We small talked for about a half-hour then he abruptly rose, signifying our meeting was over. He shook my hand and said, "If you ever need my support for anything, anything at all, please call me … and I really mean that." I thanked him, saluted and departed his office. I filed his offer away in the back of my brain while wondering, at the same time, if it was just a meaningless, pleasantry or if he really meant it. I hoped I wouldn't ever have to test it to find out.

The three of us piled back into the cramped Jeep and made our way over to Yongsan's Big Post Exchange. Going to the PX in a foreign land is sort of a soldier's ritual. Whatever bases you traveled to, one of the things you just had to do before you left was check out their PX. This was done for two important reasons. First, you want to see if there's some little treasure that your PX doesn't have and the other is to rate your own PX against the ones you see along the way. Yongsan was widely accepted as the biggest and best PX in Korea. Army guys talk like this, "Did you make it to Yongsan and did you see their PX? Their stereo department's unbelievable ain't it?" Camp Page was a pretty small place and so was the PX. We were all pretty impressed with Yongsan. The 8th Army PX was gargantuan in comparison to ours and we just had to explore it.

In the '67, stereo was *the* hot, must-have item for young GIs. Just about every solder in Korea was trying to put together the best stereo setup he could afford and still have it fit into his corner of a barracks or room. This usually included a powerful AM-FM tuner/amplifier, a reel-to-reel tape deck, a turntable and four big speakers. I mean really big, honkin' speakers. Cassette players and graphic equalizers hadn't quite been perfected yet. We all bought something from the stereo department. I decided to start on my system with a rather unimpressive 120 watt *Sansui* tuner amp and a pair of stereo earphones. That way at least I could listen to the radio with the earphones until I could afford speakers. We stopped by the PX burger shop and consumed a few cheeseburgers apiece, grabbed three bottles of Coke to go and were now ready for the long trip back to Camp Page. Krippies arranged our treasures in the back of the Jeep and we were under way.

We'd spent way too long in the PX and it was now getting toward evening as we pulled out of Yongsan Compound right into Seoul's version of the evening rush hour. The traffic was horrendous! We'd poke along a little and then we'd speed up a little. We sort of had that whole accordion thing going on. No sooner did we speed up than we'd be back on the brakes. It sounded to me like every car horn in Seoul was now in constant use.

Kelser and Krippies were really *rubbernecking* and looking around. Kelser was intently watching his rear view mirrors. So I had to ask, "What are you looking for?" "Slicky Boys, Sir; they're all over the place starting at about this time. They aren't much trouble if you see them coming, but they will steal you blind if you're not paying attention to what's going on around you. On one run to Seoul they stole the five-gallon Jerry can off the back of my Jeep; another time they got my spare tire. If you noticed, we welded on brackets and now chain and padlock the cans and tires to the Jeep."

All of a sudden Kelser excitedly announced, "Heads up, Krippies, there's one running up behind the Jeep about twenty yards out. He must have been watching through the fence and saw us load our stuff in the Jeep. I'm going to keep us at about five miles per hour, so get ready." Krippies scrunched himself up, as small as his six foot four frame would let him, in the corner of the back seat and away from the soft, plastic rear window.

Our PX treasures were resting on the rear seat in clear view through the rear plastic window. Traffic to our front was now beginning to speed up and pull away a bit. Kelser announced, "He's right behind us now and I think I see a knife. I'm speeding up." Kelser brought the Jeep up to about 15 MPH and held it there for about fifty yards then dropped it back to about ten and then to five. The Slicky Boy had seen the goods through the back window and was now determined to get hold of them. Once again, Kelser gave us the situation report, "Just as I thought, he's got a buddy and this time both are coming up. They look pretty tuckered out, and wait … Yep, now I definitely saw light flash off a blade. Don't get too close to the canvas!" Krippies shifted his position giving himself about a foot between his body and the canvas. At the same time, he was doing all he could to make himself small and stay in the shadows of the back seat. It was quite comical watching such a big man try to contort himself into a tiny person. Again, Kelser advised, "Okay, this is it, here he comes and he definitely has a friend with him. These sons-a-bitches always seem to run in pairs or packs."

Just then, a shiny, razor-sharp, hook-blade effortlessly slashed open a huge "U" shaped cut in the back canvas and plastic window. Two hands darted in to scoop up our treasures. With precise choreography Kelser yelled, "*GET EM* Ray!" Krippies instantly clamped down on a greedy, intruding hand with both of his. At that same moment, Kelser stomped on the breaks with all he had. Slicky Boy Number One's ribs slammed into the spare tire, his knife flew into the back seat and clattered to the floor. With the wind knocked out of him, and empty-handed, he ricocheted off the spare and ended in the fetal position, gasping for air, in the middle of the road. As soon as Kelser felt the impact of Slicky Boy Number One against the back of the Jeep he down shifted and hit the accelerator hard. Slicky Boy Number Two's hand and arm were still firmly locked to the Jeep by Krippies' vice-like grip. Just past the speed where the trapped intruder's legs could no longer keep pace with the speed of the rapidly accelerating Jeep (25–30 mph), Kelser yelled again, "*DROP EM* Ray!" Krippies released his double handhold. Through the now flapping canvas I could see Slicky Boy Number Two bouncing and tumbling to a stop by the side of the road. Traffic was swerving around him as horns blew. I did see him struggle to his feet and limp to the curb. Looking at me, Kelser grinned wickedly and said, "And that, Lieutenant, is why we put the old tops on the Jeeps when we go to the big city! Maybe they'll think once or twice before screwing with the MPs or the U.S. Army again."

Both men seemed very pleased with themselves. I gathered from their conversation this was not the first time they'd worked this *Sting Operation* on the poor, unsuspecting street criminals of Seoul.

Out on the open road we stopped and fixed the ripped top as best we could with "100 MPH Tape". The ride back was mostly in the dark and I learned another valuable safety tip about driving in Korea. There were still some things about modern motorized transportation most Koreans just didn't get. For instance, their philosophy seemed to be, "If you don't use your headlights, they will last longer." A few dozen times during the ride back we'd be both dazzled and startled when out of the darkness, headlights would magically pop on from out of nowhere, sometimes less than a hundred feet in front of us. Most of the time headlights would just flip on right in the center of the two-lane road. With no headlights and uncertain road shoulders, I guess they figured the middle was the safest place to be. I was also told they don't put the windshield wipers on their cars until it starts to rain and they never leave them attached to their cars when parked. I understood the parked part because I'd already been introduced to the Slicky Boys.

We arrived back at Camp Page after the evening meal; so, I treated the dynamic crime-fighting duo and myself to a feast of toasted Korean egg sandwiches and cokes from the kiosk across the street from the Main Gate. Several of the men started gathering around the Jeep to witness the slashed top and hear the tale of how it all happened. As I walked towards my hooch, in the distance I heard Krippies starting the tale, "This ain't no shit guys...." I smiled and kept walking.

15

What's A Kuska?

Into probably everyone's life comes at least one unforgettable character. During mine I was blessed with meeting many, maybe too many. Fred Kuska was one of those kinds of people.

On this particular Friday night, I was working late in my office, going over some information needed for Joyce's travel. We'd finally decided upon her arrival date. It was going to be Sunday, January, 28th. Colonel Weatherspoon was scheduled to be on leave in the States and it should also be a normal day off for me. Kelser and Krippies already volunteered to drive and escort us back from Kimpo Airport in Seoul. I had already sent Joyce what money I had left for her flight over. She told me not to worry about it, that she had enough for the ticket, but I sent her $200 in postal money orders anyway. That was pretty close to a month's take-home pay for a married U.S. Army Second Lieutenant back in '67. It was also pretty much all I had because pretty soon I would be giving my new landlord his $1500 "Key Money." And, I still had to furnish the house with whatever I could make, buy or scrounge. End of month payday couldn't come fast enough.

I was working late in my office, near midnight, when I heard a tapping noise on my office doorframe. I looked up and there stood this person. As I recall, I had no reaction to him at all. I didn't really think about it at the time or for sometime afterwards, but he actually was a super-unique individual. It's difficult to describe him because he was totally devoid of any definable characteristics and therefore extracted no sort of emotion or reaction from me. Absolutely nothing about this man stood out. In other words, he was the most ordinary person I've ever encountered. He was like a soft clay statue before the artist decides to detail-in all the features.

"Good evening Sir, Staff Sergeant Fredrick Kuska reporting." He was still in the door, he hadn't saluted but then I hadn't asked him to come in either. "Please, please come in Sergeant Kuska, sorry, my mind's elsewhere." I came around my desk to shake his hand. "Where you coming from, Sergeant?" "Fort Riley, Kansas, Sir." He handed me a copy of his assignment orders. Looking back on it, even Fort Riley was one of those ordinary Army posts in the middle of a flat, square state on the corner of Nowhere and Who Cares. All I knew about Fort Riley was … no one wanted to be posted there. Unless you were born there and never traveled anywhere else, no offense, but Kansas is pretty darn unimpressive. The most exciting and only thing I can remember about Kansas is, years later I passed a water tower on Interstate 70 with the words "Home of Bob Dole" on it; but can't even tell you the name of the town.

I told Kuska his arrival was a surprise, as I hadn't been expecting any replacements. I also wondered why Dad Dunkerly hadn't told me I had a man transferring in. It was standard Army procedure to get a new solder's assignment orders well in advance of his arrival and assign him a sponsor. When I shook his hand there was still nothing to notice. I mean his grip was neither firm nor wishywashy. His hands were neither large nor small, hard nor soft and he wore no rings, bracelets or even a watch.

When he was speaking to me about his work in the stockade at Riley, I couldn't place any kind of regional or ethnic accent. He didn't have any speech impediments or quirks of any kind. His voice was neither gruff nor smooth and he spoke at a level, which was neither too loud nor too soft.

"Well, Sergeant Kuska, we don't have a stockade here. What else have you done or are you interested in?" "Well, Sir, I ran the Military Police Investigation section at Fort Bliss, Texas." I thought to myself, *Ouch! Didn't this guy ever get a good assignment: Hawaii, Germany, Colorado, California, Atlanta, something?* "I had another assignment in MPI (Military Police Investigations) at Fort Polk, Louisiana." I rolled my eyes. *Polk is widely agreed upon as the "Asshole" of all Army posts. If you were going to give the Army an enema, Polk is where you'd stick the tube.* I reacted, "Fort Polk, you poor guy!" Kuska replied, "I kind of liked it, Sir." "Well you're in luck Sergeant Kuska, we don't have much of an MPI section here but we do have one, currently only one person, but we're in bad need of an experienced NCO to come in and take charge. You'd be working with Buck Sergeant Boon. We've had a lot of larcenies around here but haven't had much success in solving very many of them. Would you be interested in that job?" "That would be just fine, Sir." We small talked a little while longer and then one of the MPs arrived to show our FNG to a room. Kuska saluted and left for the transient NCO billets for the night.

My Mom used to refer to certain people as a "Puddin' Face", meaning they had no pronounced facial features. Kuska was the first one of these I can recollect ever meeting. He was average height, build, and coloring and had light, mousey brown hair. Even his average-sized eyes were chameleon like, turning either brown, green or hazel depending on the light. I liked his average height because I would no longer be the shortest American in the unit.

I didn't realize it that night, but unsolved crimes were about to become a thing of the past at Camp Page. This unassuming, almost invisible man was about to work wonders. There was something else almost no one ever knew. It would be awhile before even I would learn that Kuska not only spoke fluent Korean, he was also flawless in Polish, Czech, German and Russian. This very average looking, unassuming man, recently from Kansas, was not what he appeared to be.

16

Honest John

To better understand my story, I have to give you a little more background. The 5th United States Missile Command at Camp Page wasn't just a pile of pale green Quonset huts down by some river. It had two very important missions. The first was to provide surface-to-air missile protection in our sector of South Korea. The Air Force was convinced, if there were ever a sneak air attack from the North, the Bad Guys would fly low between the mountains and along the river beds in an attempt to avoid radar detection on their way to surprise the U.S. airbases in the South. Our means of preventing this from happening, in our sector, involved four strategically placed *"Hawk"* radar guided, air defense missile batteries. These mountain-top installations were designated Alpha, Bravo, Charlie and Delta. One of the things making the Hawk missile so deadly was its *Look-Down-Shoot-Down* radar. Not only could Hawks knock down high flying enemy aircraft they could also pounce from above on sneaky, low-flyers. It was the best anti-aircraft weapon at the time for protecting the valley approaches to Seoul.

The other significant mission involved a weapon much less sophisticated than the Hawk but far more deadly. It was the *"Honest John"*, unguided, free flight rocket. In military terms *missiles* are guided and *rockets* are not. At the time, the Honest John was a twenty-five year old, World War II technology rocket which was fired off a launching rail attached to the back of a specially outfitted five ton truck. Oh, there's one other small but scary detail. These rockets could be fitted with either HE (high explosive) or nuclear warheads. The fact that we had an MSA (Maximum Security Area) storage site just a couple miles up the road from Camp Page at a KMAG (Korean Military Assistance Group) base should adequately cover the *official answer*. Back then, whenever our political or military leaders were asked, *"Do you have nuclear weapons in such 'n' such a country?"* The stock answer always was, *"It is not the policy of the United States of America to confirm or deny the presence of any such weapons."* I guess that was the best way to handle it because you didn't lie and you didn't just give up classified information either. It also sounded much better than, *"No comment!"* Reporters love to feed on that phrase.

Today, the only Honest Johns left are either static display monuments or in museums. It's also no secret that they were never expected to be used in anger with anything other than nuke warheads. The Army had artillery with more range and better accuracy. There was also close tactical air support from the Air Force; so, why resort to a less accurate, shorter range rocket unless there was something special about it? The special part was locked up tight and guarded in those special MSA bunkers.

To me, the most frightening thing about the Honest John was the free flight nuke part! Or as one Battery Commander said to me over a beer, "I shot a rocket into the air, it fell to ground I know not where." On top of that, the ones in the 5th USMC only had a range of maybe twenty-five miles or so. That would leave us pretty freakin' close to a really big bang, if we ever shot one off!

There were only about 50,000 American troops in Korea in '67, while Kim, our buddy up North, was bragging about his million man army. Don't know if he really had that many or not, but twenty to one odds are just way too lopsided for anybody's battle scenario. Sure, there was the ROK Army, but the U.S. felt it needed something to protect its troops and give us the edge if the "Nut From The North" ever decided to charge south across the 38th Parallel and raise hell.

The defense of the DMZ (Demilitarized Zone) was broken down into two major sectors, with the American 2nd and 7th Infantry Divisions in the Western Sector and the South Korean, 1st Republic of Korean Army (FROKA) along the Eastern Sector. The 5th USMC was, in actuality, the tactical Honest John support for FROKA in the Korean sector. We were joined at the hip to the 1st ROK Army to the point where we even wore both U.S. Army and FROKA shoulder patches on our uniforms.

To the rest of the industrialized western world, Korea was pretty much invisible in 1967–1968. The whole world seemed focused on the Vietnam War and all the war-protesting going on back in the States, the UK and Europe.

17

Military Intelligence Is An Oxymoron!

The evening after Kuska's arrival, I went to the Club early to find Dad and maybe engage him in conversation to see if he'd tell me about all those combat ribbons on his uniform. I sat at the bar waiting, but he never showed up. I did however get a chance to meet our resident MI (Military Intelligence) guy. I was sitting there, just people watching and nursing my drink. Now that I was spending more time in the Club, I'd become a much more sophisticated drinker. I'd graduated from Rum & Cokes to *Cuba Libras.* Okay, so the only difference between the two is just a twist of lime but it really sounded cool and grown-up when you ordered one.

This guy in a black civilian suit, white shirt, regimental tie and black wing tips walks up and sits down on the stool beside me. "Good evening, you are Lieutenant Royce the new Provost Marshal aren't you?" I nodded and he offered his hand. "My name's Prescott Smith." His voice dropped to a near whisper. "I am the SAC, Special Agent in Charge of the Military Intelligence unit here at Camp Page. I am responsible for all United States Army intelligence gathering activity in all of *Chang Won Do.*" It was the first time I'd heard this term, so I asked. "Chang Won what?" "Yes, the Korean province in which this Camp and the city of Chunchon are geographically located. Chang Won Do translates into Chang Won Province." I nodded understanding and wondered where all this was going and why this guy sounded like he was reading from an encyclopedia.

"Lieutenant Royce, you see me sitting here in civilian attire, but I am not what I seem to be." I'm thinking to myself *"A Dingleberry?"* He continued, "I'm actually an Army officer, not unlike like yourself. However, I am a Major! I just mention this so you will know you are not dealing with just some *Silly-Vilian.* The primary purpose of my seeking you out is to elicit your assistance in intelligence matters of great national importance." I was beginning to think to myself, *"Is this goof for real?"* when down low, out of the room's view, he flips open his MI credentials. No shit! This guy really is a Spook! "There are times when my three agents and myself have to be off-base, after curfew conducting important intelligence gathering operations." Now I was confused, "So, what's that got to do with me?" Smith glanced around, leaned in closer and softly said, "I need your assurance that your MPs will let us in and out the gate, any time of the day or night with no fan fair and no questions asked. Further, if you or your men encounter me, or my agents, downtown, including in the Off-Limits areas, you will ignore our presence and not acknowledge even seeing us. Because you patrol the town and the Off-Limits areas, I also need your assurance that a chance observation of any of our activities will never become a part of any of your official record keeping."

Even though Smith talked like a wooden recording, I assured him I would put the word out to my guys. He seemed visibly relieved and tried to assume the demeanor of a semi-normal person on his barstool. He smiled and said, "Thank you ever so much." He then turned his attention to the bartender and said, "Another Vodka Martini please, shaken not stirred." In mid-swallow, ice cold Cuba Libra shot out my nose. Coughing, I grabbed a hand full of bar napkins, excused myself and headed for the door.

Back at the MP Station I instructed that my newly acquired information be placed in the "Pass-On Book". My request elicited knowing looks, smiles and giggles. Buck Sergeant Eugene Godblood was the Desk Sergeant this night. I hadn't had the opportunity to really talk to him until now, but I'd heard he was quite the character. He had all the Korean KATUSA MPs calling him *Buck Sergeant God*. The other MP in the station was SP4 (Specialist 4th Class) Hank Jenson. Hank was from some part of coastal South Carolina where they spoke some sort of a rural, half English—half African, "Geechee" dialect and only those who'd worked with Hank, for awhile, could understand what the hell he was saying. Hank also had a nickname. Everyone called him *The Spaniard* because not many could understand a word he said. No one, that is, except Buck Sergeant God and a handful of others who worked closely with him.

Both men were smiling at me and at each other during my instructions about the MI guys. The giggles finally got to me. "Okay, what's so damned funny about what I just said?" Hank offered about two minutes of near unintelligible gibberish complete with hand gestures and various facial contortions. Totally befuddled, I turned and looked at Godblood. "Please allow me, Sir! Hank's a little hard to understand until you've been around him awhile. I'll use as many of Hank's words as I can, but I'll make it so as you can understand it. Hank said, *'Dat James*

Bond pretender Smif guy has you bamboozled and dat de only ting doze fools are *intelligencing is what every Korean ho, between here and da DMZ, looks like buck* *necked.'* He also wants you to know Smith and his bozos couldn't find a menstruating elephant in the snow if their lives depended on it. He says, *'Day lie and you* *shouldn't aughta' trust a word dat lyin' faker Smif sez.'* He also thinks, *'doze crackers* *are gonna' get dare asses kilt by some ho's Slicky Boy, pimp, boy-fren befoe it's all over.'* That's what Hank sez, Sir, and Hank don't lie."

I thanked Hank for his insight and he replied, *"Thaszokee, gldakahlp, Zah!"* It would take me awhile, but I would learn a little Spanish, detest Smith a lot and come to realize that Hank really don't lie. For a guy I could not yet understand, The Spaniard would prove to be very wise indeed. I took Hank's words under advisement and tucked them away in the back of my mind for future reference.

18

The First December

Somehow it finally became December and life seemed pretty good for now. Paul Gleason and I were becoming great friends and we went everywhere together after work. The Colonel, for some reason, was less visible these days and things were going well at work. The MP's were responding to the *Battle Drills* I was giving them; in fact they were actually enjoying this more active style of training. They were also beginning to develop a bit of a *"Rat Patrol"* like swagger, and when not on duty took to wearing special bush hats they had made up in the Ville. We'd taken our three M-151 gun Jeeps out to the Hawk Batteries, met the commanders and toured their facilities. We even worked out tactical plans and radio procedures so we could talk to them while in route to their sites, if they were ever attacked by North Korean infiltrators. That way, we'd have a better idea of what we were getting into before we got there and they could direct us to where we were needed most. The commanders' welcomed our interest. They told us they didn't know there was a Quick Reaction Force or that there was even anyone close by to back them up. We also discovered these poor slobs didn't even have a real PX. They would truck some of their troops down to Page on weekends to do their shopping. To them, *we* were the "The Big PX".

Under Kuska's guidance, the Investigations section was now humming along and beginning to uncover some pretty interesting stuff. For instance, the Provincial Governor's driver was now in KNP (Korean National Police) custody. Camp Page had the only airport around so, the Governor's plane used it to fly in and out of Chunchon from our landing strip. Coincidently, he also flew in a U-6 Beaver. His driver evidently had been in *cahoots* with a few of the KATUSA aviation mechanics and one U.S. Army aviation supply sergeant. Together, they had systematically been ordering, then diverting, replacement airplane parts and supplies and selling them on the Black Market.

Kuska had sharp ears and no one yet even slightly suspected his Korean was probably better than theirs. Somehow, he put it all together, watched it happen a few times from the shadows, then sprang his trap. We didn't know if the KNP would tip off the Governor's driver; so, Kuska arranged for the police to be invited to the airfield for another reason. He then sprung his trap while they were all on base.

The Governor was dropped off at the airfield for his flight. When his driver was about to exit the main gate, Kuska made it seem like searching the trunk of the Governor's car was a random thing and he was just demonstrating to the KNP how we searched vehicles. Of course, the trunk was full of stolen property and the driver was completely surprised. The police captain was thoroughly embarrassed. I never found out what happened to the Governor's driver; all I knew was the Governor now had a new one. The supply sergeant went to the U.S. military prison at Leavenworth and the KATUSA mechanics were escorted away by the KNP. The DeHaveland Airplane Company would now be sending a lot fewer airplane parts to Camp Page.

This incident caused some ruffled feathers downtown but stealing is stealing and there wasn't much anyone could really object to without looking foolish, crooked or both. From the looks I got from Colonel Weatherspoon, I knew he wished we hadn't uncovered this particular theft-ring. Politically, it strained relations between the city and the base a bit. Kuska said there were officials above the driver involved, but it would be to our political advantage not to expose them, at this time.

Kuska also told me he'd let the word out downtown that we had information on the others involved, but we would not reveal names unless we started missing airplane parts again. According to Kuska, in Korea, this was the only way to control these sorts of black market operations. If you didn't have more information to threaten them with, then the stealing would just start up again, but with different front men. How did Kuska know so much about Korean ways?

Mr. Shin made all the arrangements for me, and we finally transferred the *Key Money* over to Dr. Han's brother-in-law, and the house was now officially mine to play with. Mr. Shin contracted one of those little three wheeled truck guys to haul my hand made linen chest and wardrobe up the hill to the house. They looked great in the bedroom but it was obvious we would need more furniture and other stuff to make the place homier.

I took what money I had left plus some Paul loaned me and we headed for the Chunchon markets. Mr. Shin accompanied us on our house warming shopping spree. To a normal, healthy, newlywed male the most important piece of furniture is a bed, of course, and we found a beauty. The head and footboard were black lacquered wood with flower-like mother-of-pearl, inlayed designs. The mattress was covered in a black silk-like material with little multi-colored flowers woven all over it. Mattress, box spring, bed frame, head and footboard, all together, cost the "Won" equivalent of about fifty bucks ... what a steal! Later on, I found out the mattress was actually stuffed with straw, and slowly, night-by-night, it became more hammock than bed-like. But for now, this was where I dreamed my lovely bride and I would recline in sweet, marital bliss.

I'd read all the safety warnings and *Stars & Stripes* newspaper articles about anthracite coal fumes killing Koreans. It seemed to be happening somewhere almost every night in Korea. So, instead of using the heating system built into the house I opted out of that idea, even though my new landlord said our system was new and perfectly safe, *"number one."* In Korea, these coal blocks were really cheap and I guess that's why most Koreans risked the dangers. The blocks were made out of compressed coal dust, about the size of a big coffee can and provided heat for almost a full day. They'd stick them inside a little iron grated door in the foundation on the outside their hooch and light them. The warm smoke then draws through a serpentine tunnel under the floors and out a chimney on the far side of the house. The floors are very carefully installed and covered with this special kind of waxy-looking paper, which is sealed tight with some sort of brushed-on liquid glue. The floors stay really nice and warm and it's very pleasant. Problem is, if any cracks develop in the wax paper or cement flooring it can allow carbon monoxide fumes to leak in. Since most Koreans sit and sleep on the floor, they can be overcome by these fumes quite quickly.

So, I bought a brand new, Black Market, still in the crate, genuine U.S. Army Cannon Heater down in the Off-Limits area. More correctly stated, Mr. Shin said, "Gimme fifty bucks and I get you GI heater, they number one." *In Korea, number one is good and number ten is, bad.* Yes they could be dangerous too, but at least I now had a license to operate one and I'd not heard about any carbon monoxide problems with them ... just big fires. We hired some workmen to knock a hole in the bedroom wall for the heater's chimney-pipe, and, *voila,* we had heat. Mr. Shin made a connection with a Korean firm to deliver diesel to the house every few days. Occasionally, I did use the coal burning floor warmer, but only when it was very cold, and only during the day. The nights I did sleep there, I'd go outside and pull the coal block out of its little door before going to bed.

We measured windows and Mr. Shin helped me select some heavy brocade drapes for the house, red for the bedroom and gold for the living room. The windows already had these wood framed, sliding, opaque paper privacy screens, but it was not enough privacy, plus the heavy drapes would help with insulation. The Camp Page library was tossing out an old, green sofa and it yielded six thick green velour cushions. These were to serve as our chairs. These, combined with two low, Korean, folding-leg tables rounded out all the furniture we would need for our humble home.

Mr. Shin insisted on buying us a kitchen stove as his house-warming present. I thought this was too grandiose a gesture. I protested at first, but he insisted. I didn't feel nearly so self-conscious about it once Mr. Shin, grinning widely, ceremoniously presented me with what he proclaimed to be the very best Korean stove sold in Chunchon. Korean stoves are about one cubic foot square and run on kerosene. Our kitchen was made completely out of unpainted cement and had both a door to the outside and one to the inside of the house. When you're cooking, you close the inside door and crack the outside door to let smoke and cooking fumes out. The correct way for the cook to operate this foot tall, pink & white, enameled, metal piece of culinary equipment is to assume a position known to all GIs in Korea as the *Kimchi Squat*. You squat right there in front of this foot high stove and cook.

The Kimchi Squat is universal in Korea; it's a position which is easy for small children of any race, quite normal for most Koreans, but pretty difficult for all but the most flexible Americans to master. It's sort of like learning how to use chopsticks. It's hard until you master the trick of it all.

When Americans squat we normally end up on the balls of our feet. When doing a correct Korean Kimchi Squat, you remain flatfooted all the way down and up. You really have to stretch out the old Achilles' tendons to keep your heels in contact with the floor. To do it, you simply assume a comfortable standing position with your legs a normal distance apart, then lower yourself into this flat footed, squatting position with your butt just inches off the ground or floor. If you have an ample stomach, the untrained may just roll over backwards like a run-a-way beach ball. Unless all the tendons and ligaments in your legs are used to this stretch, it becomes quite painful, even after a very short squat. The trick is to get as much of your squatting weight directly above your feet. Koreans seem to be able to stay in this position for hours then get up without limping. You'll see grown men and women on the street squatting and engaged in eating, working or just lengthy conversations. We Americans would try it for maybe ten minutes then painfully rise and hobble away like ninety-year old cripples. It really is quite amazing to a Westerner. More amazing yet is that some of us who lived more like the Koreans than Americans actually did get to the point where we were sort of semi-comfortable with it.

Some funny things started happening along the DMZ. It was mainly just sporadic probing actions and a few brief artillery exchanges in the Korean zone. A few tunnels were discovered in the U.S. 2nd Infantry Division Sector. They lead from the North, under *No Man's Land* and terminated south of the "Z". This was quite remarkable when you consider the DMZ is 1.2 miles wide on either side of the line. The tunnels had to be over two and a half miles long. A few North Korean infiltrators from their special 124th Commando unit were discovered a few miles south of one of the tunnels. One blew himself up with his own hand grenade. Another one was severely wounded by gunfire and later died in a Seoul hospital. There were thought to be more, but no one seemed to know for sure. One disturbing finding was that they were all dressed in authentic looking ROK Army uniforms.

The tunnels were blown up by the Engineers and all forces, U.S. and South Korean, were ordered to increase patrolling south of the DMZ. A hunting frenzy commenced and everyone was looking for more tunnels. Camp Page went on some sort of half-assed, increased level of vigilance. However, things were so lax at Page it was hard to tell much of a difference from before. There were so many *"Stars & Stripes"* stories going around about the fabled North Korean Special Forces guys that everyone sensed they were being exaggerated just to keep us GIs alert and interested.

The North Koreans had also started seizing South Korean fishing boats in the East Sea of Japan. It seemed like they were doing just about everything they could think of to antagonize the South Koreans and the Americans. We didn't know it then, but we were just beginning to see the tip of the iceberg. Kim IL Sung, the megalomaniac leader to the North, had made a promise to re-unite the two Koreas under Communism before his 60th birthday, and he was running out of time. He was plotting to do everything in his power to make this happen.

Because Vietnam was such a hot button back home, reporters had virtually no interest in what was starting to happen in Korea. Even if it was reported, it was relegated to the back pages. The front pages were universally reserved for Vietnam stories or other important issues like President Johnson picking up his Beagles by their ears.

Unbeknownst to most of the free world, Kim had already engaged in secret talks with both Chairman Mao and President Brezhnev asking for their support in starting a parallel Vietnam-style insurgency operation in South Korea. Both the Chinese and the Soviets may have privately liked the idea, but diplomatically told Kim they were pretty much stretched to their limits supporting Ho Chi Minh and North Vietnam. Although officially turned down, Kim negotiated what he thought was an important concession from both. If the South Koreans and/or Americans attacked North Korea, they (the Russians and Red Chinese) would come to Kim's aid with money, equipment and manpower. Kim took this as a guarantee and his key to conquering the South. Now all he had to do was come up with something so outrageous, so infuriating, that surely the South would attack. He had already set the ball in motion. Secret tunnels under the DMZ and capturing South Korean fishing boats in international waters were just a warm up to what was soon to happen.

19

Prelude to a Korean Kristmas

As December arrived, we were all trying to come up with things to send home to our loved ones for Christmas. It was pretty easy for me, because I was about tapped out after spending nearly all my money on the house and various arrangements for Joyce's flight over. I just bought little Korean things like dolls and small hand-lacquered wood jewelry boxes for the girls on my list. For the guys, I picked up *Buck* pocket knives at the PX. That left me with only one more very important Christmas present to find.

I was quickly becoming fond of our House Boy, Mr. Ahn. This guy went out of his way to make sure all the *other* things in our lives were not a problem. All we had to do was wake up, go to work and save the World for democracy. Mr. Ahn would take care of everything else. As I said before; boots, uniforms, beds and room were always taken care of. If there was anything we needed from down town, Mr. Ahn would cheerfully take care of it too. Not only that, but often when his wife would make some Korean specialty food, Mr. Ahn would bring in a dish for us to sample. Some of it was a bit strange, but mostly, it was absolutely wonderful.

Mr. Ahn was a bit like a ghost. We all normally left for work before he arrived and most of the time he was gone before we got back in the evening. We would leave a mess and come back to a neat, clean and organized room. The only time you ever saw Mr. Ahn is if you happened to go back to the room during the day.

Well, the question arose about what to get Mr. Ahn for Christmas. Paul came to the rescue, "You hand him the 'Sears Roebuck Christmas Wish Book' and you let him pick out something for himself. He really likes stuff that comes directly from the States." I asked, "What if I can't afford what he picks out?" Paul assured me that just wasn't going to happen. I gave Mr. Ahn the catalogue; apparently, it was his favorite book, and he returned a wonderful smile. The next day, he was waiting for me when I got back from work and pointed out a green plaid *Pendle-*

ton, flannel shirt and gave me a big smile and bow. I returned the bow and said, "Okay."

Here I was worried he would pick out something really expensive and all this humble, hard-working man wanted was a nice warm, quality made, flannel shirt. I was so touched by this I sat down and ordered him his green shirt but also a red one to boot.

I was still spending just about all my free time trying to put the final touches on the *Love Nest*. I would just stand there in the middle of the room trying to figure out what was missing. I wanted the place to knock her socks off from the first moment she saw it. I also fully realized Joyce was going to do some nesting herself, to put in her own personal touches, things that would make her feel like it was her very own home. I guess I was trying to make a good looking skeletal frame which she could flesh out with her own personal tastes. This is not an easy thing for a guy to do!

While going over these sorts of matters in my head, nature called, and I took the few steps back outside to *Buckingham Palace*. Sight unseen, Joyce had named our outhouse after the privy in back of her grandfather's summer cottage on the Ottawa River. It was while I was seated inside this small, blue, concrete room that it suddenly hit me. I'd been in a lot of outside johns and, as far as privies go, this one was pretty darned nice. However, no matter how nice it was, my ass was still freezing this cold, early December morning. I also wished I had put on a jacket or something. Having one's bare butt pressed against an ice cold toilet seat tends to drain one's body warmth quite quickly.

The logistics and logic of having my brand new, western-type wife trotting out into freezing cold nights, even if she was Canadian, began to hit me. Now don't get me wrong, Joyce is a real trooper, most of the time, and probably wouldn't complain too much, but that didn't make me feel any better about it. I couldn't, with good conscience, let her venture out here in the dead of night by herself. I just knew I would be getting my warm ass out of bed to stand "Crapper Guard" every time she had to go. Enemy Commandos and Slicky Boys were minor concerns compared to the, big-as-a-cat, rat I saw in the courtyard just the night before. There was no maybe about it, I was going to have to find a western type flush john and somehow get it installed in the house before pooping was going to be a normal event at number 14 Oak Chong Dong, Chunchon, South Korea.

In the days following this revelation, I was having zero luck finding an inside commode. I had no less than twenty GIs and Korean Nationals assisting me in my toilet quest. None could be located, not even in the Black Market areas between Chunchon and Seoul. Where was Joyce's elusive John?

This would be my first-ever Christmas away from home, and as the days drew closer; I began to feel like Korea was on another planet with me light years removed from home, somewhere in deep space. Christmas has always been a special, magical time for me; so, I wished I had something other than toilet hunting to occupy my mind. Thanks to Kuska that wish came true early.

20

MPC

Koreans are an amazing and resourceful people and I have the highest respect for them. Problem is, Korean criminals are also highly resourceful and, therefore, a lot of their criminal activity is very difficult to detect. In Korea, the U.S. Army was going to great lengths to control Black Marketing. We not only had our 8th Army Ration Cards to control the amount of alcohol, cigarettes and coffee GIs could purchase from the Class IV and PX; we also had this "funny money" called MPC.

MPC is what we GIs called "Military Payment Certificates". It was this paper money we were paid in for use on all military bases in Korea. Soldiers weren't supposed to carry real American Dollars. Most of us always had a little of the green stuff, but everyone who got paid in cash got paid in MPC. We could use it in the PX, Commissary, Craft Shop, Class VI, movies and in the on-base clubs. If you had to send money home, the MPC was good for purchasing U.S. Dollar Postal Money Orders at the APO (Army Post Office) or for wiring money home through *Western Union*. The idea behind MPC was to help stabilize the fragile Korean economy. All GI transactions, off-base, were supposed to be made in Korean Won and you could exchange MPC for Won at any on-base finance office.

What our government never counted on was this Korean resourcefulness thing. MPC actually became the primary tool used by Korean Black Marketers to steal even more. It worked something like this:

- Prostitutes gave GIs the choice of paying for sex with Won or with MPC. Sex was much cheaper if the soldiers paid with MPC. To low-paid GIs, who were cheap as well as horny, it meant a lot of MPC was being placed in the hands of these working girls for services rendered.

- GIs, who were so inclined to seek out the sexual pleasures of these Korean working girls, mostly frequented the six, sanctioned on-limits clubs because it was safer, and your dick probably wasn't going to fall off. The

working girls would rather have the MPC because their cut of the pro-
ceeds for each "Trick" performed was significantly better. The club managers would give the girls twice the going rate in Korean Won if they
could get the GIs to pay in MPC.

- Now the question is: Why did club owners, like the Dragon Lady, want
  MPC? They wanted MPC because it gave them the correct form of payment to buy things from inside the American bases. A large number of
  Koreans worked on the U.S. bases, and in addition to those who were
  willing participants, the crooks could bribe, coerce or even threaten other
  Korean nationals into sneaking stuff off base. A lot of GIs got involved
  too, but they were in it mostly for the cheap or sometimes even free sex.

- In addition to MPC; Booze and cigarettes were also highly sought items
  on the local economy. It all worked something like this: A GI is given the
  promise of a free roll in the hay with any of the club's girls in exchange for
  two bottles of "Jim Beam" bourbon from the "Class VI Store". The GI
  buys the booze for less than a buck a bottle, takes it to the club and gives
  the two bottles of "Beam" to the manager. The GI then gets to ride the
  working girl of his choice for practically nothing and the Dragon Lady
  gets the two bottles of whisky. *Jim Beam* bourbon whiskey was highly
  prized downtown and pretty rare on the local Korean economy. The
  Dragon Lady then sells the whiskey on the "Black Market" for, easily,
  twenty plus bucks worth of won a bottle. She ends up making the equivalent of forty or more dollars for only a few minutes of one of her girl's
  time. Multiply this transaction by several hundred times a month and it
  results in thousands of dollars of Black Market activity.

- There was another way of making a lot more, but this included the
  involvement of PX employees. In this scam, drivers and managers from
  the larger PXs would be in collusion. The driver would maybe pick up
  twenty cases of booze and cigarettes for transshipment to a PX annex
  somewhere. The driver would off-load half of it at some off-post location,
  then bring the rest of it on to the PX annex. The annex manager would
  sign it in as all merchandise received. The driver would give the manager
  enough MPC to cover the missing half of the shipment. During the next
  week or two, the PX manager would add the Black Market MPC into the
  register through bogus sales. Whenever inventory was taken, there would
  be enough money to cover the part of the shipment diverted into the
  crooks' hands. Once all the illicit funds were back in the PX system, the
  theft was virtually invisible and near impossible to detect. The cigarettes
  and bourbon were then sold by the Korean crooks for a ton of money on
  the Black Market.

- All the MPC and merchandise used to make these lucrative Black Market transactions can be traced back to working girls turning tricks for MPC instead of Korean Won. And, that's just one of the ways Korean crooks were able to "steal the radio and leave the music".

In 1968, Korea was a really interesting country to be stationed in, but if you had any sort of weakness or flaw, the criminal element would quickly find it out and they always seemed to know exactly how to exploit it. Sex, booze, gambling and drugs were, literally, available everywhere. If you had a propensity for any of these, the crooks ended up owning you. The criminals also made it a point to find out who the homosexual GIs were and would even use that against them. They would threaten to tell wives about Korean girlfriends and they always had compromising photos to intimidate their victims. And they spent considerable effort in arranging girlfriends for lonely officers and NCOs. The bottom line was; if you had any kind of "handle" they would grab on to it and twist you in the direction they wanted you to go. That direction seemed to always involve Black Market activity.

On one of our stake-outs, Kuska told me all about this whole MPC/Black Market connection thing. So, armed with his information, I decided we should test it out. I had been out to the lettered Hawk Batteries a bunch of times. Each site had a sort of mini-PX, which was usually nothing more than a small room. It would be unlocked for business about two hours every weekday evening and half-a-day on Saturdays. Normally, all they carried were the essentials of a soldier's life: booze, beer, cigarettes, soft drinks, candy, snacks and condoms. But, the soldiers stationed on these mountain-top sites could special order things from a catalog and the items would be delivered out to them from the Camp Page PX.

I was pretty sure Mr. Lee, our PX Manager, was an honest man, however, I wasn't so sure about the short-haul driver who trucked merchandise from Camp Page out to the Hawk Sites in our store's van. Local shipments were not so closely scrutinized because nothing was ever reported missing and these PX annexes always had good inventory inspections. On the surface, everything seemed okay. I reviewed several of these inspections and monitored store sales. There were never any problems, but I did notice one thing that piqued my interest; these remote site soldiers seemed to be buying way more booze and cigarettes per capita than our Camp Page soldiers—and our soldiers bought a lot. At first, I wrote it off to the bourbon-for-sex trade, but I told Kuska we should check it out anyway.

It didn't take much investigating. I got Captain McCabe, one of our pilots, to take me up and trail our short haul PX van on its way to Charlie Battery. The truck pulled off into a Chunchon alley for a few minutes then continued on to

Charlie. I drove out there and checked in with the American sergeant in charge of their PX, and according to him, everything on the manifest was delivered. I didn't check the manifest I but I still had the feeling something was just not right; so, I kept a loose watch on the van's comings and goings.

A several days later, I happened to be driving past our PX and saw the van being loaded out back. Kuska was down in Seoul, but working on a hunch, I had a patrol drop Mr. Shin and I off near the same alley where I saw the van make its earlier stop. We went into the alley behind the street and stepped inside the back door of a little restaurant and waited. Mr. Shin told the owner we heard a bad GI was coming there to eat and we wanted to put the grab on him and throw him in the "Monkey House" (Jail). This seemed to placate the owner and he went about his business and ignored us.

To our amazing good luck, the PX van drove into the alley. We watched as the Korean driver unloaded beer, whisky and cigarettes. After he transferred several cases inside a back door across from us, we ran over towards him. I drew my .45 and thumbed the hammer to full cock. The driver was just receiving a fat, manila envelope from another man I recognized as Madam Kim's driver. Both men were totally surprised by our sudden appearance. The PX driver cowered and raised his hands over his head as Mr. Shin screamed out orders. Madam Kim's man broke and ran out the other way so fast I knew it was useless to pursue him. Mr. Shin asked, "You see other man?" "Yes, it was the Dragon Lady's driver!" We recovered the merchandise and the envelope and Mr. Shin drove us back to Camp Page while I kept an eye on our whimpering captive in the back of the PX van.

I knew what it was even before I opened it. It contained four hundred dollars worth of MPC in small denominations. We then drove out and apprehended the Army Sergeant who ran Charlie Battery's tiny PX and sweated the truth out of him. In the end, he confessed to falsifying PX, inventory records, signing that shipments were complete, and then, systematically, adding MPC back into the till to cover-up the crime. He also admitted he'd been doing this for more than nine months.

Cop Chong arrested the Dragon Lady's driver and got him to admit his part in this illegal operation. The driver said he was the one who masterminded the operation. He totally refused to implicate Madam Kim and, in the end, went to jail still protecting her. We knew the driver couldn't mastermind a trip to the bathroom let alone an operation like this, but there was nothing we could do. The Dragon Lady was so powerful, locally; the police did not feel like taking her on.

Black Marketing in MPC became so prevalent that 8th Army had to come up with a plan to, at least, interrupt it. We were all notified one week before payday that there was going to be an MPC exchange. Our Finance Office was given this, one short week to take back all the old MPC we had in our possession and exchange it for a new and different-colored MPC script. We were also told our end-of-month pay would be in the new MPC. After payday, any old style MPC was just going to be worthless paper.

There was a lot of grumbling because some of the more skillful GIs had a lot of the stuff they'd won at poker or dice and weren't too anxious to explain to Finance or their commanders how they came by having thousands of dollars worth of MPC in their possession. All in all, a currency exchange sort of lets everybody know what you're up to, who has a pile of money and who doesn't. This money exchange had a lot of GIs worried. There were a lot of deals going on that week. GIs with just about no MPC to exchange were being employed by GIs who were loaded with the stuff to help turn it in. Buddies were helping buddies while others were being paid to help in the exchanges. It was hard to unload ill-gotten gains because the Army Post Office and Western Union were restricted and not allowed to make transaction that were more than the GI monthly take-home pay.

Downtown, Koreans illegally holding large amounts of MPC were in total panic. Months and months of hoarding MPC to skillfully grease the gears of the Black Market system were being wiped out overnight. GI customers and boy-friends were exchanging MPC for the Club-Girls or their own girl friends. The problem was, there was just too much MPC downtown. Again, there was a limit to what GIs could exchange; anything over a certain amount would automatically give the suspect GI a chance to sit down with his commander or the Military Police and do some explaining. In other words, it was a big mess. We MPs thought it was great fun because a lot of the Koreans we knew were crooked were really squirming.

It actually got sort of scary as it got close to payday. There were even a few hundred Koreans outside the fence yelling and crying for help, trying to make any deal they could to get GIs to exchange their MPC. On payday, they ended up even throwing bags of MPC over the fence as the deadline loomed. We had to call the KNP to quell a near riot when some of them started to climb the fence. Afterward, we heard of Korean suicides and, even, two MPC-related murders. The morning after payday, tens of thousands of dollars worth of MPC was scattered all over the ground around the fence line. This MPC exchange wasn't going to stop Black Marketing, but for right now, it sure put a dent in it.

I didn't have too much time to dwell on the happenings of this MPC exchange because Kuska was uncovering further PX crime faster than we could investigate it.

21

The Big PX Caper

It was now only a few days into December and we had a really big mystery on our hands. We'd been experiencing thefts from our PX shipments but were completely befuddled as to how it was happening. Kuska had been working on it for a while but confided in me he had no ideas about solving it. When I first arrived in country, I remember Sergeant Kelser telling me that thievery in Korea had been developed into such an art form that experienced thieves could actually steal a radio and leave the music. I thought it was funny at the time, but now it seemed we were dealing with exactly that sort of a situation.

PX trucks manifested for Camp Page, and some other locations for that matter, were loaded with merchandise at the big, centralized, Yongsan PX distribution warehouse in Seoul. The various items ordered by PX managers, for all Korean Exchanges, were broken down by order and loaded onto tractor trailers at the Yongsan facility. Unlike the local PX van deliveries between our annexes, these trailers were locked, guarded and protected with numbered seals made of a hard to duplicate metal. Weekly, every Thursday, the trucks were dispatched to every camp's PX. When the trucks got to the sites, the PX seals were examined for tampering and the correct numbers before being cut off. The keys to these stout trailer padlocks were sealed in special, tamper-proof envelopes and kept in locked boxes inside the truck cabs. Even beginning truck mileage was recorded in Yongsan before the trucks ever turned a wheel. It was then checked again at the point of delivery by the camp PX managers. The drivers would unlock their in-cab lockboxes and hand the key envelopes over to the manager. The manager would inspect the envelope for tampering before opening. Then, and only then, the two would verify the number on the seal and open the trailers. The drivers were under threat of being fired and possible prosecution if they ever deviated, even as much as a mile, from the approved route to each PX.

Camp Page deliveries had only recently become a problem. Like everyone else, our deliveries came in every Thursday. The Camp Page shipments seemed to be coming up short more frequently now. It was usually things, such as, cameras or stereo equipment, but other stuff was always mixed in.

We'd been hit three times since my arrival and everyone was looking for answers. The top Yongsan, PACEX (Pacific Area Exchange), Depot Manager had his tail feathers all in a wad and was screaming that the thefts had to be the fault of crooked employees at the sites. This, of course, also reflected on the protection my MPs were providing at Page; so, I was more eager than most to get to the bottom of this mess.

The trucks always arrived perfectly secured at our PX; yet, Yongsan refused to believe the problem was not with us. They sent their PACEX investigators to look at our operation, but they found nothing which could explain the shortages. All seals, locks and keys were always exactly as they should be. The Yongsan central warehouse even made it a practice to completely stuff the trailer boxes. When you opened up a PX delivery trailer, the contents were always packed tight, right up against the doors, ceiling to floor and side to side. If there was anything missing, you could immediately tell because it would look like a jigsaw puzzle with some of the pieces missing. I knew it was a tough case because even *"Super Sleuth"* Kuska was stymied.

Kuska and I would be present every Thursday when the PX truck arrived at Camp Page. He and our Korean, PX Manager would go over the bill of lading with a fine-toothed comb then cross off everything as it came off the truck. Kuska would inspect the seals, locks and sealed key envelopes for tampering. All was always as it should be. Photographs of the condition of the load would be taken when the doors were opened. The load was always fully packed right up to the doors. Kuska could not figure out how the trucks could be so fully packed yet still be missing several dozen boxes on the shipments that were hit. He would copy down all the information, take out the "4X4 Speed Graphic" camera and take all kinds of pictures. A rather large file on the "Big PX Caper" was beginning to fill a corner in Kuska's office. He even tried to follow the trucks a few times but they were always okay.

Kuska contacted several other camps having similar shipment problems. He exchanged information with their MPs, to include, driver's names and key numbers. He studied his information for hours but his scowls indicated he was not making much progress. He even secretly tape measured the trailers. Then, it finally dawned on him.

I was working late in my office one night when he poked his head in. "Got a minute, Lieutenant?" I motioned him in. "What's up?" Kuska looked over his shoulder to ensure we were alone and in a hushed voice said, "I think I got at least part of it, Lieutenant. There are two sizes of trailers showing up here! I asked my buddy at Camp Red Cloud to secretly tape measure their delivery trailers too. They also have two sizes of trailers showing up. Problem is … the sizes just don't make sense. Usually, you'd have a significant difference in sizes, you know, like long, medium and short. The short trailers are only about twenty-four inches shorter than the long ones. Now, who the hell builds or buys them like that? I checked with Camp Red Cloud, and since we've been working on this together, their more recent thefts have been from the shorter trailers. I then snuck into Yongsan Depot, in the wee hours last night, and measured all the trailers in the yard. And, you know what? I shook my head as Kuska gave a little grin, "They only have long ones. So, I'm thinking, somebody's switching trailers. Unfortunately, I still got zero ideas how it's done."

I asked, "Okay, so what about the locks, numbered seals, keys and serial numbers on the trailers; how does that all work?" Kuska looked at me a little exasperated, "Lieutenant, I said I just had part of it! However, I got a couple more little pieces I'm working on." I looked interested and Kuska continued, "I checked all the driver's records, and in the past dozen or so thefts, there have only been four drivers involved. I don't believe in coincidence; so, these four drivers gotta' be in on it." I smiled at my chief investigator and asked the simple question, "Why don't we just fire the four drivers … case closed!" Kuska looked back at me in a fatherly way, "Nah, whoever is masterminding this would only threaten or bribe other drivers and start it up again; we gotta' nail these bastards! I'm also dying to see just how they do it. Oh, one last thing! The keys in the sealed envelops, the ones' that open the trailer locks, they have always been one of three key numbers. When the thefts happen, it always involves key 10805, 26646 or 05942. Now tell me if that don't sound strange?"

Kuska's voice got even lower, "I talked with Captain Mike McCabe this morning. He and I are going to trail our delivery truck day after tomorrow … by chopper." My eyes got big and I asked, "You got a helicopter? It took an act of God for me to get one just to fly around here locally for less than an hour. Only Colonel Weatherspoon authorizes the use of choppers." Kuska shrugged and grinned, "Yeah I know; and it's the Colonel's personal OH-13 'Gumball' we're taking. We're going down to Kimpo tomorrow afternoon. McCabe owes me one, plus, I told him we were going down for something else … something a little sexier. I'll tell him what we're really up to in the morning."

McCabe told the Colonel his bird needed routine aircraft maintenance. SP4 Cortez is going down ahead of us and poke around the PX motor pool pretending to be learning how to check truck manifests. I set that up last week with the

PACEX security people. He's going to find our load and keep an eye on it. Kimpo Airbase and the PX distribution center are practically in line of sight of each other. Cortez is going to radio us when our truck is about to leave the distribution point. He's tying a long red rag to the back of the rig when he's signing it out the gate. That way, from the helicopter, and through binoculars, we can visually track the truck all the way north."

I always hated overly detailed plans. There was just too much to go wrong, too many pieces. So I asked, "Are you sure this is all going to work?" Kuska gave a big shrug, "Shit Sir I'll be the most surprised one if it does! If it don't, we'll just think up something else. McCabe will be none the wiser. He's only taking me down on Wednesday because I told him I knew of this special place in Seoul. I talked it up all last week and promised to get him laid at the best damned cat house in all of Korea." I glared at Kuska, "You know where the best cat house in Korea is?" Kuska grinned, "No, but I'll find it Wednesday night. McCabe grew up on a Kansas farm. A few stiff drinks, some dim red lights, two good looking, experienced whores and in the morning that Jay Hawk will think he's just been to *the* best damned cat house in Korea. From talking to him, I don't think he's seen much to compare it to. I just got to make sure I get him back to Kimpo before eight and in shape to fly."

I didn't get much sleep that night. I wasn't counting sheep; I was counting all the ways Kuska's plan could mess up. In the morning; Cortez, Kuska, McCabe, the Colonel's chopper and an MP Jeep were all gone. The plan had been launched. As Sherlock Holms would term it, "The game is afoot"!

It took forever for Wednesday to turn into Thursday. I felt like a little kid wondering if Santa was going to actually visit, and if he did, what would he bring me? I'd been in an information blackout since I'd last talked to Kuska and the suspense was killing me. My irritation was taking its toll and I was barking at everyone. My guys knew I was in a bad mood so they stayed away from my office.

At 1102 hours I heard a noise, looked out the window and saw a big PX truck coming through the gate. I jumped to my feet and ran down the street to the PX. Just as I got there, the OH-13 passed really low overhead towards flight operations. I could make out two men inside the clear plastic bubble. Captain McCabe must be hung over to come in that low and wobbly across the camp. For a brief moment, everyone was startled by the chopper's noise and looked up. The PX manager was already checking paperwork, getting the cargo-box key and wondering what a long red rag was doing hanging from the trailer doors. I heard heavy breathing behind me; Kuska and Danny Cortez had just run the quarter mile up from the runway.

Kuska didn't appear to want to talk and went straight over to the PX manager where the two of them started their shipment checking routine. I turned to Cortez, and trying not to look too nervous, asked, "Well, how'd it go?" Cortez gave me a very worried look, "Excuse my English, but it was pretty fucked up, Sir! I'd rather have Kuska tell you all about it because he knows a lot more than me." It seemed to take forever for Kuska and the manager to go through the manifest and for the PX employees to unload the truck. In the end, there was about $6,000 worth of cameras, movie cameras and stereo equipment missing from the load.

Kuska called Cop Chong, and the two took the driver to our Interview & Interrogation Room back at the PMO. Mr. Shin and I joined them there. Kuska would question the driver in English, Mr. Shin would interpret and Cop would threaten him by yelling and making physical threats. The driver would just cower in his corner chair; he even cried at times. He stuck to his story, even under Cop's intense pressure. He swore he knew nothing, but he did insinuate the thefts must be happening back in Seoul. He said he was being set up and he was nothing but a poor truck driver just trying to feed his family. In the end, as before, we ended up just writing another report. Because there was no hard evidence that the trailer had been broken into or tampered with, the driver was turned loose to take his truck back to Seoul. We made all the appropriate phone calls and notifications and, of course, I would have to let Colonel Weatherspoon know right away.

The Colonel took great delight telling me, once again, how worthless he thought all MPs were and how the Army should save the taxpayers a bunch of money by just doing away with the Military Police Corps all together. He said *real* cops would have had this whole mess cleared up months ago and we were just incompetents farting around playing at cops and robbers. After enduring ten minutes or so of his berating MPs in general, and me in particular, I was thankfully dismissed.

I raced back to the PMO and into Kuska's office. We closed the door and I started in, "So, did we really come up empty again after all that?" Checking through a crack in the door, to ensure no one was outside, Kuska replied, "Not exactly, but I think we're definitely getting closer." I didn't understand, "And, just how might that be?" Kuska gave a little smile, "This trailer we just unloaded is two feet shorter than the one Cortez measured before it left Seoul!" My mouth must have dropped open a little, "What the hell did they do, shrink the damned thing!" Kuska raised a finger to his lips and cautioned, "Keep it down, Lieutenant, there are no secrets around here, these walls really do have ears. There's something else; the truck did make one stop. They pulled off the road at a long warehouse, in a little village, about twenty miles south of Chunchon. It's an old, beat up place only about fifty yards off the MSR (Main Supply Route). We lost visual on the truck for a few minutes but we didn't dare fly any closer. They were only there for five or six minutes tops, then the truck drove back onto the MSR and straight on to here. During interrogation, the driver flatly denied ever stopping anywhere, and I didn't tell Cop Chong he had. I wanted to take a look at that place before anyone knows we know. It might just be a gas station or something and the driver just had to take a leak. Problem is, I don't want to tip our hand just yet. I got to come up with a plan to sneak a peek. Something's going on in that place, but no way in hell can they pull off a theft like this in five minutes; it just can't be done"

I then asked Kuska, "How'd Captain McCabe do?" Kuska took in a deep breath, "Well, Sir, about Captain McCabe ..." It then dawned on me that Kuska and Cortez showed up together. "How'd you, McCabe and Cortez all fit inside that tiny flying Gumball Machine?" I didn't like Kuska's answer, "Well, Sir ... McCabe didn't exactly show up in time for the flight back. I went to wake him up and he was just nowhere to be found. I looked all over for him, Lieutenant, honestly. This morning, I really had no choice. So, I took a cab to Kimpo, then called Cortez on the chopper radio and told him I was going to land in back of the PX truck lot. I picked him up as soon as our truck pulled out of the compound. I needed Cortez with me because somebody had to use the binoculars and watch the truck through traffic while I flew the chopper." I had to ask! "While you flew the chopper? You know how to fly a helicopter?" Kuska shrugged, "Well, sort of ... I mean, I used to ... It was a long time ago, Sir. Captain McCabe actually let me fly it a little on the flight down; so, actually, I did get in a little stick time in before soloing the chopper back to camp."

I looked Kuska straight in the eye and demanded, "Where's McCabe?" He dropped his head, looked at the ground for a moment, then answered. "Sir, right now, I have no earthly idea where the hell he is. When I left him last night, he had two good looking hookers and a snoot full of booze. It was around 2200 hours and I watched the three of them go into his hotel room and lock the door. With the amount of booze he had in him, and those two cuddly young ladies, I thought he was good for the night." I had another question. "Is the chopper okay?" Kuska squirmed, "From what little I know about choppers, I think the damn thing's fine. I also don't think anybody saw us get out of the Gumball down at the airfield; so, maybe that part's gonna' be okay too." I glared back, "If something's happened to McCabe, nothing's going to be okay!"

The rest of the day seemed to just drag by. Kuska took off downtown to talk to his Korean Intelligence buddies about how to find McCabe in Seoul. I had a pile of paperwork to do and was glad because it took my mind off the missing pilot. Late that afternoon, one of the MPs called back to me, "Lieutenant, come quick, you gotta' see this!"

I jogged up to the desk and Buck Sergeant God pointed through the fence and across the street to the city bus stop, near the main gate. Standing there, by the open bus door, in all his glory, paying the driver, was none other than Captain Michael Quintus McCabe. He was decked out in a pair of Army fatigue pants, a Hawaiian flower shirt and he had several strings of those brightly colored, fake looking, paper flowers around his neck. He was barefoot, in December, and had this huge smile on his face. He strolled across the street as normal as pie, flashed his ID card to the KATUSA MP at the gate and sauntered up to me, humming as he came. From out of nowhere, a wildly grinning and out of breath Kuska joined us outside the PMO.

McCabe started in first, "Kuska, you sly old dog, I really gotta' thank you. That *was* the best damn night this ole Kansas boy's ever had. I mean, I never, ever, had my pipes cleaned like that before in my life, Woo-Wee! Those two little Korean cuties were something else. You didn't lie my friend; that just had to be the best damned whorehouse in all of Korea, hell, maybe in all the orient!" Kuska got to the question before I did. "Where the hell did you go, Captain? I went to pick you up this morning and you weren't in your room." McCabe came back with, "I know, I know, you told me to get some sleep, but those two little girls still wanted to party. They dragged me out of bed and into a cab to … hell, I don't know where the hell we ended up. All I know is, I was in a big ole steaming hot bath with six beautiful, naked, sexy Korean women and a ROK Army General. We laughed, we sang, we drank *Mokolli* and we had one hell of a time all night long. I woke up around noon today on satin sheets in a big old bed with three passed out women and the General. Wow-wee! That was one fun night! I just wish I could remember more of it." As I stood there listening to McCabe relate his tale, in the back of my mind I was asking myself, *"I wonder if his dick's going to fall off."*

Now with Captain McCabe back safe and sound, Kuska and I got back to the business of how we were going to try and bust this case wide open. Kuska had commandeered a Korean car, a shiny black *Shinjin*. Shinjins were nothing more than Toyota Coronas, assembled in Korea, with a different name, grill and chrome trim. Kuska's plan was, he and I, in civilian clothing, would go downtown, pick up the car and, after dark, drive it somewhere close to the warehouse.

Kuska would check the place out while I stayed with the car. A funny thing happened; this was the first time one of his plans actually went off exactly as it was supposed to. After waiting nearly a nerve wracking hour with my .45 pistol in my lap, Kuska came running up the dirt, side-road where we'd parked and jumped in. On the drive back, he told me what he'd seen.

"I found a window open and got in that way. I'm pretty sure no one saw me; it was so damned dark around the outside. Inside, there were just a few lights on and some men working. There *is* an empty PX trailer in there! I crawled up in the shadows and it has the same numbers on it as today's shipment. I didn't measure it but I know it's the short one! I went under it and saw the dime I wedged into the frame while it was at our PX. The driver must have dropped it off and picked up the longer trailer on the way back to Seoul. I brought my midget binoculars with me and it looks like they have a banding machine in there just like the one at the Yongsan PX Depot. I also saw a box of what I think are PX seals and another machine which, I'm betting, puts numbers on those blank seals. I think they drive in, open it up, and transfer the load, with the exception of the stuff they plan to steal. Then, they pack the short truck up tight, lock it and re-band it. Then, they just hit the road again." I reminded Kuska, "It still doesn't explain how they got the key out of the tamperproof envelope or how the hell they off and on loaded a whole shipment in five minutes. His reply was, "Well, we'll just have to raid them next time when the transfer is in progress."

Two weeks came and went. Captain McCabe checked out the Gumball Machine and found it none the worse for ware. He never even asked how the helicopter got back to Page and none of us ever told him. Most importantly, the Colonel never suspected nor found out about any of it. McCabe continued to tell stories of his sexual exploits in Seoul and it got wilder every time he told it. "This ain't no shit guys! This was the best ..."

Kuska and I used the time to plot and plan how we were going to solve our string of strange PX thefts. The trick now was: How do we come up with a plan that has everything we need without tipping our hand to the bad guys? The KNP were problematic; you never could be sure who was *"on the take"* or who the *"Straight Arrows"* were. I wanted to work with Cop Chong, Big Chong, Mr. Shin and Mr. Ye but Kuska said "When money like this is involved, you can't fully trust any of these people, even the ones we work closest with every day." I hated to leave my Korean staff out, but in the end, I did things Kuska's way. We ended up having to work with Cop Chong because he was our legitimate "in" with the Chunchon, KNP and it would look funny if we tried something of this size without him. Kuska's instincts had already brought us so much success in detecting long time, institutionalized theft at Camp Page that I had to rely on him being right this time too.

Kuska dreamed up this bogus plan which would energize Cop to go to his KNP Chief and get him to put together a task force of about twenty policemen. We would add ten MPs to this Raiding Party. Kuska told Cop there was this illegal drug lab some GIs and Koreans had set up, and we were going after it. This was supposed to be a traveling lab which sets up for a few weeks at a time then moves to a new location. Kuska tailored our cover story so there was no connection to our local police. Funny thing about most cops, straight or crooked, they all take it personally when criminals from outside their jurisdiction try to set up operations inside it. I guess it's because it gives even the crooked cops a chance to do real police work and an opportunity to feel good about themselves, even if it's just for a little while. Kuska picked out a location a few miles from the warehouse. It was a small, temporarily empty, manufacturing plant. Kuska designed a plan which would work at both the bogus and the real locations.

On Wednesday night, Kuska got word from his guy in Yongsan that our truck had just been loaded and locked up for the night in the depot yard. Key number 10805 went in our envelope, along with our bill of lading, and was locked in the office safe for the night.

Kuska poked his head in my room, before dawn, Thursday morning, "Lieutenant, its Showtime!" I grabbed all my stuff and was ready in no time. We rolled two Army Duce-and-a-halfs quietly out the gate, picked up our *Shinjin*, plus twenty Korean cops, and drove south through the early morning darkness. Two little cars and two big canvas covered trucks, doused their lights, and pulled off the MSR, out of sight from the empty factory. There were thirty-six of us in all. The plan was for Cop Chong, the KNP and the MPs to all get in defilade positions around the bogus target before daybreak. Kuska and I were going to go to another location where we could see the PX truck when it came up the road. We told Cop to keep his vehicles and police totally out of sight until we called for them. Within the hour, everyone was in position, hunkered down and holed up. It was now a little after 0500. We would all have to sit tight and not draw any attention to ourselves for the next five or six hours.

Without telling anyone what we were up to, Kuska and I drove south on the MSR to within a quarter mile of the mystery warehouse and took up position on a hill where we could see several miles down the road. There was a big bend in the road along the river and we could visually pick up vehicles moving on the MSR almost five miles away. That would give us a six or seven minutes head start. PX trucks were easy to spot because they were just about the biggest thing on the road. I got out the field glasses; Kuska smiled and brought out a welcome thermos of hot coffee. We were also in luck because, as the day dawned, it was un-typically clear and devoid of the normal early morning ground-fog. We had no way of communicating with Yongsan, so we wouldn't know exactly when our truck departed; we only had a good guess based on past deliveries and a key number associated with past thefts.

At 1031 I caught a glimpse of a big, American type rig through my powerful Artillery Binoculars. Kuska got Kelser on the radio. "Go to Cop and get everybody loaded up fast and start heading south on the MSR, we made a mistake on the location, the right place is further down river. We'll meet you in the road so don't run our asses over, now Go, Go, *Go!*" We scrambled down the hill, jumped in our Shinjin, drove it to where our dirt road met the MSR, and waited. Kuska turned to me, "You sure you got the right truck?" I was checking the two Winchester riot pump, twelve-gage shotguns just one more time to ensure each had a full eight rounds, one chambered and the safety on. "Whatcha' think? Of course it's the right freaking truck!" Now, damn it, he's got me doubting myself. I unholstered my .45 again and checked it, yep, full clip with an eighth round in the chamber, half cocked with the safety off. I was ready to rock and roll.

The KNP/MP convoy arrived behind us. Kuska was waving them down. I ran down the road to where I could see around the corner and I got there just in time to see the truck turn off the MSR towards the warehouse. I pumped my arm up and down several times. Kuska jumped in the Shinjin and rolled up to my position. He was closely followed by the Cop Chong's car and two truck-loads of cops. Cop Chong jumped out of the police car and ran up to me. I told him, "Same plan here, Cop!" He nodded and ran back to the convoy, yelling in Korean as he ran.

As we arrived at the warehouse, the big double doors were closed and the PX truck was nowhere in sight. Kuska and I drove around to the back of the warehouse and were followed by the truck carrying the MPs. Cop went to the front, followed by the other truck with the KNP main force. Everyone jumped out of the trucks, and we surrounded the warehouse. I tried the back door but it didn't budge. Kuska pushed past me and fired three quick blasts at the door hinges and the door just fell off into the dirt. Later, he told me his first three rounds were always "hinge busting" 12 gage slugs. The front door was also coming down as we entered. Cop Chong and his KNP crew were yelling commands at the top of their lungs and all of us had guns drawn. The first few seconds of any raid are the scariest because everyone's armed and pumped full of adrenalin; and, you don't know how the bad guys are going to react. In this case, it was pandemonium.

There were about sixty bad guys inside. Some hit the dirt when the KNP burst in, while others were madly trying their best to get away. Thankfully, none of them drew any firearms. One sprinted past me and out the back door. Sergeant Kelser was just outside the door and effortlessly snatched him off the ground by his belt as he zoomed by. The slightly built Korean was now being held off the ground by this very tall, very strong, *monster-sized*, American Army, MP Sergeant. Kelser lifted him up high with one powerful arm. The Korean struggled madly until his eyes met Kelser's, "And, just where do you think you're going, little man?" The fleeing crook went limp with resignation and was handed off to the KNP to be cuffed and stuffed.

It was all over in just a matter of minutes. Sixty-two bad guys were now sitting quietly in rows of ten. The KNP were threatening with their automatic carbines and yelling at the crooks not to even think about moving. It didn't take Cop Chong long to determine who the two ring leaders of this operation were and to separate them from the rest. He and Kuska took the two into a separate room and closed the door.

It couldn't have been more than a few minutes between the time the PX rig entered the warehouse and the time we busted in. I looked into the back of the two trailers. The original trailer was more than two thirds unloaded and the phony trailer was more than one third full already. About two pallets worth of electronic gear was neatly stacked out of the way to one side. The tractor had already been switched to the phony, shorter PX trailer. This had to be the fastest loading crew there could have ever been. They were NASCAR, Pit Crew fast.

On a table, between the two trailers, was a pile of photographs of what I guessed was the real PX trailer. The two were parked beside each other not ten feet apart. With a hand full of the photos I walked around both trailers. The trailers were as close to identical as could be. A new duplicate seal with identical numbers was also on the table. One of the photos was a macro shot of the seal. The last item on the table was a key bearing the number 10805. I looked around for the envelope but it was nowhere to be found. I climbed up and looked into the truck cab and noted the lock box was still locked. The driver's key ring was still in the ignition. There were two keys on the ring. I withdrew the keys from the ignition and with the smaller of the two I opened the Lock Box. Inside, I found the still sealed envelope. I felt around the envelope until I detected the shape of a key the size of the one I found on the table. *"Son-of-a-bitch!"* I whispered to myself. They somehow had gotten hold of a duplicate key! I guessed the same was true for the other two keys involved in the other PX thefts.

It had now been about two hours since we first burst in and things were well in hand and order had been made out of chaos. Most of the bad guys had already been transported back to the main police station in Chunchon. Kuska and Cop Chong were still behind closed doors talking to the ring leaders. Every once in a while you would hear a scream as Cop applied one of his tried and true interrogation techniques, Kelser and Buck Sergeant God were giving the Speed Graphic a workout and flash bulbs were popping all over the place as they took pictures of everything you could possibly take a picture of. The Camp Page PX manager had been called. In turn, he called the head guy in Yongsan and just about everyone was now beginning to descend on our little crime scene.

Kuska and Cop came out of the room with two very unhappy looking subjects in handcuffs. Kuska came up to me smiling, "I think we got it all or at least enough of it, Lieutenant. Cop used his unique ways and these two sang like birds this time. We should let Cop do all his interrogating off base. We've got the names of six more PX workers in Seoul who are in on it. There are also two dirty site PX managers, but thankfully, ours appears not to be one of them. Cop has notified the Seoul KNP and I had the PMO Desk Sergeant phone to the lead, Yongsan PX investigator. They were now rounding up those involved, down south. When Cop Chong saw what this was all about, he put two and two together really fast. He had to know this never started out as a drug bust. I could see his feelings were hurt because he thought we didn't trust him. So, I told him a little white lie. I said, we were instructed by the 8th Army Provost Marshal not to tell anyone and that's why he was left out. He seemed to brighten after that.

All that was left to do now was wait for the PX investigators to show up from Yongsan, do their thing, then let this load go on to Camp Page. The "Lookey-Loos" now began arriving to share in the "glory of the kill". The Chunchon Police Chief showed up and talked to Cop Chong. He came over to me smiled, shook my hand firmly and gave me a *"Josa Me Da!"* (Good job). *Stars & Stripes* and the local Korean paper were there too, as was, "The Stupid Colonel Mixon". When Lieutenant Colonel Mixon came in, I walked over, reported, and gave him a rundown on what had happened. Between the two of us, he said, "Great Job, Royce!" However, it wasn't five minutes later I overheard him talking to *Stars & Stripes*. "Yes, our Commander, at Camp Page, Colonel Weatherspoon, has been working closely with our Provost Marshal and Military Police on this for months. What you're seeing here is the culmination of all this planning between Colonel Weatherspoon and his Provost Marshal." I somehow was just able to contain myself. Neither of those idiots knew nor cared anything about the status of our investigation until five minutes ago. I, of course, briefed Lieutenant Colonel

Mixon, along with Colonel Weatherspoon, every time we had a theft. The only instructions I ever got from Mixon were, "You better fix this, Royce! If you can't figure out how to stop this damned thievery, the Colonel's going to have your ass on a platter!" The Colonel never said anything instructive. He just kept telling me how useless I was. The crazy thing about this investigation was, it wasn't even ours to solve. It really belonged to *Army & Air Force Exchange Service*. We actually broke the case for them.

As usual, we received no local recognition from our dear commander. We did, however, get a nice "Letter of Commendation" from the Army, Air Force Exchange Commander, thanking us for solving the thefts. I framed and hung it up on the wall in the MP Station for all to see. According to the cover sheet, Weatherspoon also received a copy, but if he did, he never so much as mentioned it to me. I did write Kuska up for an award but Colonel Weatherspoon wouldn't approve it. That was no surprise to any of us. The only thing I could do for Kuska, on my own, was write him a Letter of Commendation and have Dad place in his personnel file. Things settled down and went back to some level of normalcy, but just for a little while.

22

The Black CIC Jeep

Christmas was only a few days away now, but Mr. Shin thought it was high time I met my Korean Army Provost Marshal counterpart. His ROK Army compound was just south of Chunchon on the MSR (Main Supply Route) to Seoul. Mr. Shin made all the arrangements and a meeting was set up. About mid-morning, we arrived at the small Korean Army base near the recently completed *Soyang* Dam; there, we were shown to the Provost Marshal's office. A very fit looking, Korean Captain greeted us at the door and we exchanged salutes and smiles. "Welcome, Lieutenant Royce, I'm Captain Lee, I heard you had arrived and I have been looking forward to meeting you." He then flashed a brilliant smile, displaying perfectly straight and meticulously maintained, white teeth. I must have looked a little stunned because Captain Lee turned to Mr. Shin and said, "You didn't tell your Lieutenant I went to Princeton did you Mr. Shin?" It was apparent from the laughter that Mr. Shin was enjoying one of his little jokes. Not only had Captain Lee gone to Princeton, he had also attended the "Infantry Officer Advanced Course" at Fort Benning, Georgia and "Command and General Staff College" at Fort Leavenworth, Kansas. To top things off, he'd spent last year as Korean liaison officer to the 18th MP Brigade in Vietnam. In total, Captain Lee had spent over seven years in the States plus, another year with US Army forces in Nam. His English revealed only the slightest hint of a Korean accent.

He showed me around his compound and let me observe his MPs practicing unarmed combat. That was most impressive! I commented on their prowess and was told all Koreans, from an early, age take *Taekwondo* in school. He said his government believes all South Koreans had to be ready, at any time, for an invasion from the North. Part of their national readiness program was having every child schooled in martial arts and ready to fight—if the need ever came. Once in the army, all soldiers train until they become expert in Taekwondo.

Towards the end of my daylong visit, I accepted an invitation to meet Captain Lee at the Soyang Dam roadblock, the next evening, to observe how ROK MPs conduct roadside checks for infiltrators. I arrived at dusk and was instructed where to park my Jeep. I ended up standing next to Captain Lee, about thirty feet or so, off to the side from where his men were stopping and searching vehicles. There wasn't much I could learn from this, and after an hour or so and a couple dozen vehicle searches, I began dreaming up ways to politely get out of viewing this repetitive process. It was scheduled to go on until midnight. As I was mentally narrowing down my believable options to the one I thought most plausible, a black, Korean, CIC (Counter Intelligence Corps) Jeep came abruptly to a stop at the roadblock. All CIC Jeeps looked basically the same, shiny black with hard metal tops instead of the usual canvas kind. Once you knew what they looked like, you could spot one a mile away. The only other thing I knew about the CIC was, no Korean wanted to screw with them. They literally had the power of life and death over a large segment of the country's population. This included the ROK Army.

When the CIC Jeep came to a sliding stop, the driver's side door immediately flew open and the, obviously, irate driver and front seat passenger began yelling at the poor MP and ordering him around. By his body actions, I could tell the MP was intimidated. To me, it looked as if the MP was trying to explain to these important officials that he was simply following orders to stop all vehicles to be sure there were no infiltrators hiding inside. The CIC men were having none of this nonsense; they were CIC, and therefore above this kind of BS. The black Jeep lurched forward and, simultaneously, the driver's side door slammed shut.

Captain Lee had been talking to me about all the excitement surrounding the very first "Super Bowl" and wanted my opinion on whether I thought Green Bay or Kansas City would win. He'd been watching the CIC Jeep out of the corner of his eye. The split second the Jeep's door slammed shut; he yelled something to his MP and sprinted towards the black Jeep. I've never seen a human go from vertical to prone as fast as that MP did. But, even before the MP actually hit the dirt, Captain Lee had open fired with the old .45 Caliber "Tommy Gun" he was holding and unloaded a thirty round, stick magazine, into the Jeep. Every window was shot out as were two of the tires. The Jeep rapidly decelerated and, in a cloud of steam and dust, it jerked spasmodically, then bumped to a stop up against a boulder by the side of the road.

The instant the firing commenced, I hit the ground as fast as I could and tried to make myself as flat as possible just to get the hell out of the way. I had no idea what this crazy Korean was doing. Captain Lee was already at the Jeep before I was even able to start thinking about what was going on. When bullets fly, it's best to react first, then figure things out as fast as you can.

I lifted my head off the ground to see what was happening. Both doors had sprung wide open when the Jeep hit the rock. The driver had fallen out his door and looked like a rag doll tossed on the ground. Captain Lee had already drawn a pistol in mid-stride. The upper-half to the Captain's torso disappeared into the darkness inside the jeep. I saw movement through the Jeep's shattered rear window, then two bright flashes, accompanied by the sound of gunfire. I instinctively hugged the ground even tighter. It all then became very still and quiet.

I slowly got to my feet as other Korean MPs were doing the same. Captain Lee was now pulling things out of the back of the Jeep as fast as he could and cussing in Korean. *"Nimi ssipal nom … ah, ssipal jot-kkanne!"* I just stayed clear of this crazy man and then he pulled a Chi Com PPS 43 Sub-Gun and PPSH 41 Burp-Gun out of the back seat. He continued rummaging around in the back seat and recovered a couple dozen grenades, a crap load of ammo, plus other assorted military gear. After yanking out the bodies and searching them, he found maps and what he told me was North Korean propaganda materials.

Captain Lee's men began sorting through all the stuff he tossed out of the Jeep. The four dead bodies were lined up by the side of the road and illuminated by ROK MP Jeep headlights. Several other MPs were going through the dead men's clothing to see what else was there. Captain Lee got up from his searching and walked over to me,

"Sorry about that, Lieutenant, haven't seen this sort of thing in weeks."

"How the hell did you know they were North Korean?"

"Easy … Same way someone from Alabama knows a New Yorker when he hears one. These sons-a-bitches were definitely Northerners."

As we were talking, I noticed the roadside checks had started up again as if nothing had happened. I also couldn't help but notice that all the drivers were being extremely nice and cooperative with the MPs.

"Yeah, these Dick Heads are from that NK 124th Intelligence Battalion up there. They've been using every trick in the book to try and screw things up down here. Every one of those sons-a-bitches is at least a Second Lieutenant in the North Korean Army and there's supposed to be around 2,000 of them in this elite commando unit. To even be a member, they have to have been on at least one successful mission south of the DMZ and lived to return north. They sneak into my country, posing as anything they think will work. This is the first time I've seen them pretending to be CIC. They have to know our CIC guys are usually a bunch of pricks and most South Koreans are scared shitless of them." Captain Lee was still on an adrenaline high and talking a mile a minute. I just let him roll on and keep venting. "I couldn't see inside that fucking Jeep; so, I had to wait for the door to close before firing. I wanted to cause the least amount of danger to my men. I hit all four of them. The two in front were dead. I had to get over there fast because these bastards have the habit of blowing themselves up when cornered. One of the assholes in the back was going for a bag of grenades on the floor when I finished him and his buddy off. *Damn!*—I wish I could stop shaking!"

Captain Lee, eventually, began to calm down as his excess adrenaline began to wear off. Tonight, had been my introduction to real, no shit, military action and the first time I'd ever seen men killed in combat. Captain Lee taught me a valuable lesson that night. Never give the enemy even the slightest chance to get at you. Assess the situation quickly, then take swift, decisive and deadly action. Overkill is safer then under-kill. Combat, whether it be high intensity or low intensity—like it was now in Korea—is still deadly and you have to stay on your toes at all times to protect yourself and your men.

23

Ode to a Dutch Urn

Christmas day had finally arrived and it was a bizarre time for me in Chunchon. There were only a few Christmas trees around, but on the whole, even remnants of a Christian Christmas were really hard to find anywhere in town. Other than the few Oriental trinkets I'd purchased along the way, I hadn't collected anything notable to send home to her for Christmas. Joyce and I had mutually agreed; we would skip the present giving thing and celebrate our Christmas when she arrived. I was still looking for that one extra special present which would be just right. I needed something that would make her smile from ear to ear and be glad she came to Korea. No matter how hard I searched, absolutely nothing seemed to be *the* present.

There were these eighteen inch tall artificial Christmas trees at the PX; so, I bought one and had been keeping it in my BOQ room. At 0730 this Christmas morning, I had this incredible feeling of being all alone and I found myself carrying my little tree up the hill towards our house. My plan was to put it in the window, take a few pictures, and send them home to Joyce just to let her know I was thinking of her on Christmas day. I was sort of scuffing along the main drag and up the hill, brain in neutral, and thinking of home, when all of a sudden, there it was, in the middle of a shop window. I used my sleeve to wipe away some of the dust and window grime. I cupped my hands together, using them to shade my eyes from the widow reflections, as I peered in. God it was beautiful! It was truly the perfect Christmas present for Joyce. She even told me in her letters, if I ever found one, she wanted it more than anything. Up until now, no matter how hard I'd searched, I'd only seen one of them in all of Chunchon. In fact, I was almost completely resigned to the fact they hardly even existed at all in Korea. I stood there slack jawed, looking in that store window and wondering how many dozen times I'd passed by and not seen it. Maybe they just got it in! How much was this beauty going to cost? It didn't matter that I was nearly broke, all I knew was I had to have it. I was torn between running to find Mr. Shin or staying put until the shopkeeper showed up. I was that afraid of losing it to another customer. That wasn't going to happen ... I had "Squatter's Rights"; I was here and I was armed with my .45 pistol. This thing was now mine and I was willing to fight for it.

There it was, gleaming white, even on this dull, overcast, misty morning and even from outside the dirty window, it appeared to be in excellent shape. Amazingly, it looked as if all the parts were there too. It was unbelievable, but I wouldn't be able to tell its true condition until I could get in the store and examine it. From the dingy store window, even the wooden parts looked in great shape. At that very moment, it had to be the most beautiful inside flush toilet I'd ever seen. It was one of those 1930s classics with a wall tank above and a chromed stand pipe connecting the tank to the business end of the toilet. There was a silver pull chain hanging down from the tank with a porcelain pull-handle attached to the end of it.

My dilemma was over when I saw one of my MP Jeeps approaching. I flagged it down and ordered the driver to find Mr. Shin or one of the other interpreter/translators and get them to my location ASAP. An eternity later, a very tired looking, Mr. Shin arrived. When he saw the object of my urgency, he was both happy and dismayed. He was apologizing for not finding it himself. I had to assure him that nothing mattered except my obtaining this porcelain beauty. Mr. Shin disappeared, and in a few minutes, returned with the sleepy storekeeper.

I don't know what was said, but twenty minutes and twenty U.S. dollars later and a deal was made; the porcelain prize was on its way up the hill to 14 Oak Chong Dong in the back of an MP Jeep. On this wonderful Christmas day, I was now the proud owner of this marvelous piece of western comfort, sanitation and convenience. Upon closer inspection I ascertained it had been manufactured in Rotterdam, The Netherlands. I just could not imagine how it ended up in Chunchon but was ecstatic that it had.

24

The Crap Hits the Fan

Time was flying by. My Blue Christmas had, thankfully, come and gone and it was finally 1968. Mr. Ahn was sporting his new *Pendleton* flannel shirts. He would come to work every day and carefully place his new shirt on a hanger until he was ready to go home again. You would think he was caring for an expensive Italian suit. I can't remember ever giving anyone a present that was appreciated as much as those two flannel shirts.

On Thursday, the 11th of January, I was again summoned to Weatherspoon's lair. On the way down the hall I couldn't for the life of me figure out what this could be about. Lately, I'd been keeping my head down and I hadn't had any big run-ins with him. I walked into his outer office and the sycophant, Captain Huddleston, immediately opened the Colonel's office door and said, "Go right in *First* Lieutenant!" At that moment, it hit me. Because of Vietnam, there was this rapid promotion system going on. I was commissioned as a Second Lieutenant on 11 January, 1967. Today, it was exactly one year to the day and I was being promoted to 1st Lieutenant. I had forgotten all about it. Today, I'd be swapping in my little gold, *butter bars* in for silver ones. In the U.S. Military, and I never understood why, but it does, silver out-ranks gold.

So, now, I found myself standing at attention in front of the Weatherspoon's desk. He summoned me around to the side of his desk where the American flag was. I hadn't noticed before, but in the corner behind us was the camp photographer. Normally, promotions are a pretty big deal in the Army, but not today. My winter weight OG-44 uniform had a woven gold bar insignia sewn on one collar. The other collar had the matching crossed pistols insignia of the Military Police Corps.

Weatherspoon picked up a pin-on silver bar from his desk and walked around to my left side. In an impatient voice, he asked the photographer, "Are you ready?" The photographer said, "Yes, Sir!" and hustled around in front of us with his big, square camera. The Colonel stuck the silver bar right through the woven gold bar. The big camera flashed and clicked and the Colonel stepped away from me. Cocking his head to one side, he gazed down at my Military Police insignia, and then with a look of disgust said, "You MPs should not even be part of the Army's rank structure. You should all be Department of the Army, civilian security guards or something, but not U.S. Army Officers!" He then thrust some papers in my hand and went back around his desk, sat down and started shuffling papers. Copping an attitude, I didn't even attempt the formalities of a salute; I just strode out of his office. Under his breath the little Spec 4 photographer audibly whispered, *"Damn!"* as he quickly followed me out of the room. Once again, the Old Man was able to suck the air out of the room and any pleasure out of the event. It was plain to me; he intended to beat me down into … I don't know what.

The young reporter/photographer asked me some questions, took some notes and I filled out a *Home Town News Release Form* and that was the extent of my official Army Promotion Ceremony. So, I sort of just oozed into my new rank with no fanfare. Over the next week or so, word either got around or people just saw I was sporting silver bars. One by one, as it dawned on them, my fellow officers congratulated me.

Funny thing about Second and first Lieutenants, when you're a Second Lieutenant, nobody expects you to really know anything about anything. NCOs and Senior Officers just automatically help you along, with no questions asked. One year later, when you pin on those *magical* silver bars, they all expect you to know and be able to do just about everything. It's just amazing! I guess gold bars are looked upon like training wheels on your first bicycle. You're riding, but you're not expected to do it without help. When you get your silver bars, they take away your training wheels, and you peddle on alone, hoping not to crash.

1968 was not starting off very well back home either. The big story in our *Stars & Stripes* newspaper involved Dr. Benjamin Spock, the famous baby doctor. The old fool had gotten in cahoots with the Yale University chaplain, a novelist, a Harvard grad student and some peace activist by the name of Marcus Raskin. They were all being indicted by a grand jury in Boston for conspiracy to encourage draft law violations.

Time moved slowly on and I'd now been in country for just about ten weeks. It was the 21st of January, 1968, a Sunday, and I was up at the house aimlessly puttering around, trying to make our little love nest as perfect as I could. My Bride was scheduled to arrive in exactly one week and panic was beginning to set in. Would she love or hate the place I'd been putting together for us? I hadn't told her too much about it because, I wanted it to be this big, romantic surprise.

The biggest surprise, of course, would be the recently installed inside flush toilet. A crew of ROK Army engineers, friends of Big Chong, had installed it for ten bucks American. It was amazingly simple, except for the knocking a hole through the thick concrete floor part. They connected the toilet flush hole to an iron pipe and ran the pipe out at a downward angle through a freshly dug trench. The terminus of the pipe emptied out into the hole under the outhouse. So, no sewer system or septic tank, it was just an inside annex to the outhouse; but it worked fine and that's all that mattered.

I was beginning to understand some of the reasons why inside plumbing wasn't in vogue in Chunchon. The city's water pressure was somewhat suspect. Most of the time, the pressure just wasn't strong enough to fill the toilet holding tank high up on the bathroom wall. In fact, water only sporadically ran through our pipes. This miraculous event happened most mornings and then again, sometimes, for a short period, maybe just for an hour or so, in the evening. Using American ingenuity, I remedied the problem. I made it a practice to keep our cramped, deep, bathtub filled with water. With one foot on the edge of the tub and one on the toilet seat, via a little plastic bucket, I would transport water from the tub up to the holding tank. Five minutes of repetitive work and my labors were rewarded with enough water for one wonderful flush.

Once this system was placed into practice, unless there was dire need, Joyce and I could schedule a morning and evening flush to minimize the "Bucket Brigade". Since the male of the species has fewer problems with this sort of activity, as much as comfortably possible, I would still be using the "Buckingham Palace Throne Room" when taking care of routine business.

Big Chong and Mr. Ye bought us a brand new, Black-Market, U.S. Army, field phone as a wedding/house warming present. Big Chong's ROK Army, Signal Corps brother connected everything up by stringing WD-1 commo wire across the city's telephone poles from the MP Desk to the brand new field phone sitting on the headboard of our bed. I always suspected city officials never were asked if this would be okay. Nobody questions Korean Army guys when they're stringing commo wire; so, I guess no one was ever the wiser. All I had to do was pop in two D-Cell batteries and I had direct communication between the MP Desk and our house. I checked it out earlier in the morning, and it worked perfectly. Now if anything happened, I could be back on Camp Page before Weatherspoon even had time to ask my whereabouts.

I was polishing the headboard and thinking fond thoughts of Joyce when I heard a hand-cranked ring from the field phone. I picked up my first real call and said,

"Lieutenant Royce!"

"Sir, Godblood here, all hells broken loose down in Seoul; 8th Army just went on full alert."

"What the hell happened?"

"Some kinda' attack on the 'Blue House' in Seoul"

"Holy shit, is President Park okay?"

"We don't know yet, but I've got the Jeep on the way up to you now."

"I'll meet them at the bottom of the stairs." *click.*

By the time I got to Page, the streets of Chunchon were already being blocked off and gun toting KNP cops and ROK Army guys were everywhere.

Godblood had already been on the horn with the MP Station at Yongsan Compound and the Air Force APs (Air Police) at Osan Air Base. As best as anybody could figure out, it was a large raiding party of thirty or more North Korean commandos. The Intelligence guys were pretty sure they were from the "North's" 124th Special Forces Group. They were disguised as ROK soldiers and somehow managed to get within two blocks of the Blue House (South Korea's "White House") before being discovered. Once the attackers were confronted, a wild gunfight and grenade throwing orgy broke out on the downtown streets of Seoul. Twenty-eight North Korean commandos were killed and about thirty-seven ROK Army, KNP and South Korean civilians also died during the deadly melee. Dozens more South Koreans were wounded and taken to city hospitals. The fear was that this was just the beginning of something bigger. U.S. Army troops were now reinforcing the Marines at the U.S. Embassy in case it was also targeted. No one was sure how many infiltrators were actually involved in the raid or how many more were still out there. It was feared some of them had just melted away into the city and were now looking for other targets of opportunity.

Recently, several NK patrol boats had violated costal waters in the South and witnesses claimed to have seen invaders come ashore. One witness claims to have counted 120 infiltrators hitting the beach and running inland somewhere south of Seoul around *Ulchin-Samch'ok*. 120 is about the size of an NK Infantry Company. Speculation was that there were even more, unobserved, landings.

Within the hour, Camp Page was also on full alert. We received orders from Weatherspoon that no one was to leave the Camp. I started stressing about Joyce. Somehow, I needed to get word to her that now was not a good time to be arriving in Korea. Paul came to the rescue. Being Signal Corps, he had his connections, literally, and that night he got me patched through to Joyce in Alabama, via a MARS radio connection. Don't ask me how they do it, but these commo guys can connect radio communications to telephone lines and work miracles.

So there we were, just Paul and I, in a locked signal van down at the end of the runway. Against Army regulations, I'm using military equipment for my own personal means of communication with my wife, half a world away. Some HAM radio operator guy in Topeka, Kansas made the connection for us and got Joyce on the line.

"Joyce, this is Herb, over."

"What ... Herb?"

"Yes Hon, this is Herb; you're talking over radio and you're supposed to say over, over."

"Where are you? ... Over."

"I'm in Korea Hon, but I've got some bad news. You can't come over right now, over."

"But, I've got my plane tickets, I'm packed and I quit my job, over."

"I know Hon; something's happened over here and its unsafe right now, over."

"What's going on? Over."

"Just a bunch of bad stuff; it will probably be in tomorrow's papers, over."

"But we've made all these plans; I have my plane tickets, over."

"I know, I know Hon, but we'll have to wait till this mess blows over, over."

"Well, just as long as it doesn't stop me from coming over, over."

"I'm sure it will pass; just talk to your dad, he'll have ideas about it, over."

"Okay, I miss you so much and I was so looking forward to next Sunday, over."

I could tell by her voice the tears were starting; so, I figured it best to end the call.

"Okay Hon, I love you and I'll talk to you soon, over."

"I love you too. It's just that I'm so disappointed, over."

"I know Hon. I've got to go now. I love you, over."

"What? I can't hear you, over."

"I said ... I love you, over."

"What? Over."

"I said ... I love you, over."

"What? Over."

"Lady, this is Harvey in Topeka, he says he loves you! WOAGM signing off."

The comm-line suddenly went dead. Paul and I just sat there grinning at each other for a moment and then both of us broke out laughing. Paul said it first. "So that's why they call them *over*-seas calls!" Thank heaven for Harvey in Topeka and his unique, but effective way of ending a difficult conversation.

I assumed Joyce and her Dad would have come to the same conclusion without my call. All the news the next day had to do with the Blue House Raid and Korea being on full alert. *Stars & Stripes* newspaper, *AFN Radio* and even the *BBC World Service* were carrying updates. As it turned out, a lot of the overseas flights into Seoul were being cancelled anyway.

It was a good call on my part because things were getting hotter and hotter. There were a couple more DMZ violations the next day and some South Korean fishing boats had been sunk, their crews captured by the enemy and taken up north. But all of this was nothing compared to what happened on the 23rd.

Just two days after the raid on the Blue House, we began getting AFN Radio newscasts and back channel communications about something involving the North Korean Navy and an American oceanographic research vessel on the high seas. As the hours passed, and more and more became known, we began to fully realize just how very serious this incident was. The North Koreans were calling this a "Spy Ship" and we're all thinking, *"Here we go again, with the damned North Koreans trying to make a National Geographic boat, measuring sea current temperatures or something, look sinister."*

By the next morning, there was enough information to half-way piece it together. The ship now had a name; the USS Pueblo, and it was not an oceanographic ship, it was a U.S. Navy ship, a "Spy Ship" to be exact. It was a floating antenna farm designed to intercept all sorts of radio communications emitting from North Korea and China. The U.S. was claiming the Pueblo was outside the fifteen mile limit, in international waters, and therefore, everything was legal according to international maritime law. The North Koreans insisted it was inside their twelve mile territorial waters. Evidently, the Captain of the ship, Peter Bucher, tried to flee when confronted, but his slow moving vessel was easy prey for North Korea's fast gunboats. The Pueblo had .50 caliber defensive armaments but it seemed either the guns didn't work or the crew hadn't a clue how to use them. After a short slow motion chase, the North Koreans took them under fire and Captain Bucher surrendered his ship and crew.

It puzzled us that neither U.S. naval planes nor warships came to the Pueblo's aide. Personally, that leads me to believe this ship really was fifteen or more miles off the coast as claimed. The U.S. Navy probably was not expecting anything on this routine mission and therefore had no back-up plans to assist.

The USS Pueblo ended up being towed into a North Korean harbor. As the next several days unfolded, the Communist propaganda machine was spinning in high gear and having a lot of fun. The captured eighty-five man, crew and their captain were paraded before North Korean news cameras. The bastards beat confessions, true or not, out of some crew members and pieces of communication equipment and documents were shown to the world on North Korean news films.

The U.S. was making demands and threatening the North Koreans with dire reprisals if they did not release and return the crew and vessel. The North was having none of it. They were just having way too good a time with this. Unbeknownst to most everyone, this was exactly what the North wanted. They wanted to make the U.S. mad enough to do something really stupid. All U.S. Army units in Korea were being cautioned to use great restraint and not be goaded into firefights or boarder incidents along the DMZ.

The South Koreans were still extremely upset about the attack on their president just a few days earlier. This, combined with all the other atrocities the North Koreans had committed during their frequent and illegal incursions into the South, had the ROK Army wanting to draw blood in the worst way. During a meeting where there was no press, General Ironbone, the 8th Army Commanding General, said, "When I took over command of 8th Army, I had just one primary mission. That was to stop the North Koreans if they were ever foolish enough to attack south. Now, I have two missions; my original mission and my new one. The new mission is to stop the pissed off South Koreans from attacking north!"

In the south, tempers really were at a fever's pitch. Both countries seemed to have their fingers on hair-triggers.

To make matters even worse, in conjunction with snatching the USS Pueblo, Kim IL Sung began moving large portions of his huge army up just behind the DMZ. The mood at 8th Army Headquarters was grave. The whole situation was seen as being very bad and deteriorating by the minute. Here we had this big international *Spy Ship* incident and then the U.S. threatening North Korea about what will happen if we don't get the crew and ship back. In what appeared to be a reaction to those threats, the North Koreans answered back by assembling 400,000 troops, in perfect attack formation, along the north side of the DMZ. The gun was now loaded and cocked with the safety off. The big question now was, "What's going to happen next?"

All of South Korea went on "Full Alert". The 5th Missile Command was given the word from 8th Army to move the Honest John launchers forward, and up behind FROKA's (First Republic of Korea Army) positions along the DMZ. In an unprecedented action, the KMAG igloos at our MSA were cracked open and the real *"No Shit"* Honest John *"Big Boom"* warheads were loaded onto transporters and moved forward along with their motorized rocket launchers. All firing batteries and support units made their way, under heavy military guard, to pre-designated DMZ firing positions. There, they would wait and wait.

Most of 5th Missile's troops were so sure we were going to war, they did all those desperate and even crazy last minute things GI's do just before going into combat with a good chance of being killed. Many gave away money and belongings to whomever they felt should have them. Final letters were written to Moms, Dads, wives, kids and girlfriends telling them of their love and giving instructions what to do with all their worldly possessions—if they didn't make it back. In just about every 5th Missilemen's mind, this was it! I knew of two GIs who were so angry because all this happened during the last month of their tour of duty. Both were audiophiles and had amassed, what each thought was, the perfect stereo system. They were looking forward to showing off and wowing everyone back home. Rather than have it stolen by North Korean soldiers or Slicky Boys, one beery night, the two took fire axes to their stereos, chopping amps, speakers, turntables and tape decks into bits. That was an extreme expression of just how sure everyone was that we were going to war!

My MPs and I didn't move forward with the rest because we were still designated as the Quick Reaction Force and tasked with base security for Camp Page. Our job was to protect the base and the Hawk batteries while the artillery rocket units were deployed forward. We felt both left out and relieved all at the same time. I remember standing at the gate and watching the launchers and support vehicles roll out towards MSR north. I waved to friends and saluted superior officers as they passed. Most of all, I watched the faces of the soldiers as they paraded by. Some looked excited, and smiled and waived as they passed, while others looked quite serious and worried. Each man was mentally going through, and dealing with, his own reaction to what was happening. It was quite a pass-by. You rarely gain appreciation for the size of a big military unit. That's because you hardly ever get a chance to see the whole thing roll by you, single file, in review. As the last vehicles departed and we closed the gate; a group of us watched until they disappeared from sight up the road. We may not have gone, but our prayers and best wishes went along with them.

Camp Page became a pretty lonely place. Not counting the Hawk Batteries, I guessed, out of the normal 1200 man complement, there were about a 150 of us left. All the communal places on base were pretty much closed and most of the KATUSA's either went forward with the rockets or were sent home because there were no uniforms to wash and starch, no vehicles to work on and not many troops left to feed. The on-base clubs closed, the PX closed and no movies were being sent to our theater. Only one unit mess hall stayed open for the whole camp.

MPs always seem to be a little different from the rest of the troops. If anything, our workload increased. With fewer soldiers around, there was more we had to keep an eye on. All our KATUSA security guards and MPs stayed on with us. We continued to perform just about all our normal duties.

Dictator Kim and his huge army stared across the DMZ at the US 2nd and 7th Divisions in the West and the First Republic of Korea Army in the East. If they sent their whole million man army across the "Z" the US and ROK armies would be overwhelmed by eight or nine to one odds. This is why the Honest Johns were in Korea in the first place. The 2nd and 7th had deployed their rockets behind the 38th Parallel in their sector and the 5th USMC had ours set up in direct support of FROKA.

Sporadic artillery exchanges, back and forth across *No Man's Land,* continued for days. The North was sending infiltrators across to probe our strength along the DMZ and to spy on us. Both North and South were complaining to the world that the other was violating their air-space. We also heard rumors the North and South were talking, but there were no details concerning how it was going.

Unbeknownst to any of us, talks really were going on, only it was between the U.S. and North Korea. I don't think the contents of those discussions have ever been released to the public. I don't know if Kim was threatened, bought off, or some sort of combination of the two. All I know is, after close to two weeks, with everyone holding their breath and *leaning forward in the saddle,* the North Koreans blinked. Their huge Army began to slowly pull back from the "Z". Somehow, clearer heads must have prevailed. Several days of surveillance over-flights confirmed the North was truly pulling back and the Honest John units were finally given the word to stand-down. There was relief everywhere south of the 38th but none greater, anywhere, than in these rocket units. The *"Nuclear Genie"* was once more being stuffed back in the bottle. First and foremost, nukes are designed to be a weapon of deterrence. No American commander or troop ever wants to launch one of these things. These were the *aces up our sleeves*, so to speak, only to be drawn if we were *really* losing.

Back at Page, we got the great news that our troops would soon be coming home. Everyone was smiling and happy, but none were happier than the *Working Girls* downtown in the on-limits clubs. Things got pretty lean for some of them while their American *boyfriends* were up north. More than two weeks, with little or no income, was a hardship for them since they were used to money coming in just about every night.

One bizarre incident did happen while the troops were away; these out of work prostitutes went on strike. I mean they made up signs and walked a picket line in front of the main gate and everything. There they were, mini-skirts, furry short jackets and high heels, all *tarted* up, walking in circles and chanting. "GI go, Army give us dough! GI go, Army give us dough!" Seems the girls had their own twist on this deployment thing.

Their leader, Big Shirley, described it this way.

> "U.S. Army say, 'You work in GI club and only do *Boom-Boom* with GI.' We do what U.S. Army say. We stay clean. We only do with GI. Army take GI away. We no work. We no have no money. We hungry. We need money. We good girls! We no *Boom-Boom* anybody but GI, just like Army say. Army now owe us money. Not our fault North Korea come and GI have to go fight!"

I had to admit, as weird as it might seem, Big Shirley sort of had a point. However, it didn't matter much, because the Stupid Colonel Mixon was left behind to mind the store while Colonel Weatherspoon was up north. He didn't see this as a photo opportunity and a great story for the rest of us to tell when we got back home.

"Royce, I want you to get rid of those whores and get rid of them now. I don't want Camp Page to be the laughing stock of all 8th Army." "*Too late!*" I thought. With those vague orders and an irate Lieutenant Colonel on my hands, I went back to the MP Station to see what could be done. All the MPs were gathered by the windows having a ball and snapping pictures. I had to admit, it *was* a ridiculous sight and a great *Kodak* moment.

I gathered my Korean staff around me and told them about the directions Mixon had given. Cop Chong spoke first, and in his low, sinister voice said, "I fix. You want go, I make go!" I cautioned him, "Okay Cop, I don't mean to tell you you're business, but you know, you can't go out there and just start hitting these women or anything like that. You have to come up with another way." Cop nodded and grunted understanding. "Understand, I no put hand on nobody." He gave me a big grin, turned and left the building.

I don't know exactly what I expected, maybe some negotiating or something of the sort but, about an hour later, what I saw was quite different from anything I imagined. A self-contained fire truck came roaring around the corner with all its lights flashing and sirens blaring. I quickly noticed that Cop was up on top of it, seated behind a water cannon turret. He barked out orders over a bull horn, telling the women to leave. Big Shirley gave Cop the finger and that was all she wrote. A high pressure stream of icy water hit Big Shirley about chest high and knocking her *tail over teacups* into the gathering of working girls. It was like a bowling ball smashing into the pins. Wet whores went flying everywhere! The cannon continued to roll the protestors up the street for about 50 feet. Cop turned the cannon off and over the bull horn, once again, gave directions for the prostitutes to move out. This time, there was no hesitation. The bruised, wet and freezing working girls beat a hasty retreat.

Cop jumped down from the fire truck, came back inside the PMO and with a big gold-toothed smile on his face he proudly pronounced, "They gone and I no put hand on nobody!" Although horrified at the sight of mini-skirted hookers rolling up the road in a blast of ice water; I had to smile at the grinning man's comment. He'd obeyed the letter, if not the spirit of my directions, and in the end, quickly accomplished the mission.

The clubs were now gearing up to welcome the soldiers home. Each was planning a big party of some sort. The working girls were still mad at Cop Chong but were all dried out now and getting ready to show the boys what they'd been missing.

The KATUSAs that stayed behind were happy too because now they also could get back to work. The Mess Halls and Officer/NCO Clubs were gearing up for feasts and celebrations. All our Korean friends were happy because things would now get back to normal in Chunchon. Without the steady influx of GI money, a lot of the regular businesses, not to mention the Black Market, had also suffered.

I was happy, because now I could at least start thinking about getting Joyce over here again. Paul and I worked out another late night MARS call down at the signal trailer and Joyce and now I zeroed in on Saturday, February 10th as her new arrival date. The tenth was perfect because Weatherspoon was going back to Washington to report at a congressional meeting on the DMZ confrontation with the North Koreans.

She talked to me some about the snatching of the Pueblo, but it seems the Blue House Raid and our recent Mexican Stand off with the North Koreans had gone all but unnoticed back in Daleville, Alabama. The reason no one back home seemed concerned about Korea was because just after midnight on the 31st of January, 1968, the North Vietnamese launched their "Tet *(Chinese New Years)* Offensive". Over 70,000 NVA (North Vietnamese Army) troops and VC (Vietcong) poured out of the jungles and into most of the major cities. The U.S. embassy in Saigon came within a whisker of being completely overrun. Thank

God for the 18th MP Brigade! They helped hold the city until the Infantry could get back in there to relieve them. The whole country would be messed up for weeks and U.S. casualties were really bad.

For some fearful and selfish reasons, I elected not to enlighten her about recent events in my neck of the woods, partly because I didn't want to appear like I was trying to push the date back again. In my head, I feared she might think I didn't want her to come over at all. The other reason, I have to admit, was lust mixed with love. I just missed her so damned bad on so many levels. Later, after the call was over, I made the realization she would be arriving just a couple of days before Valentines Day. I would have to set up something special for that too. Then, all of a sudden, it hit me; Joyce would be arriving in Korea exactly one hundred days from the date I kissed her good bye in Providence, Rhode Island.

25

The Round-Eye Has Landed

It was now Sunday the tenth of February … and 0345 in the wee hours of the morning. I checked the luminous dial on my wristwatch. I'd been lying there awake in my bunk for nearly three hours. I went to bed at about ten anticipating I would have trouble sleeping. I was wrong! I must have tossed and turned for maybe forty-five seconds, then, in total emotional exhaustion, I just passed out. I think I must have started dreaming within minutes after hitting the pillow. It was the dreams that were causing problems.

In my dream there were North Korean *Migs* screaming around Joyce's airliner. For some reason, her Boeing 707 was flying like a fighter plane dog-fighting its way through the swarm of enemy warplanes. Now, her 707 was on fire and crash landed on the Camp Page runway. It skidded past me on the tarmac and burst into flames. I was running towards the burning plane but, no matter how far or fast I ran, I could never get to it. Just at that point in the dream, I jerked upright in bed in a clammy, cold sweat. I sat there, disoriented, with my heart racing as if I'd just run a four-minute mile. In a few seconds, the real world slowly oozed back into my brain and I realized it was just a horrible nightmare, but now it was over and, most importantly, nothing bad had actually happened.

It was still very early when I pulled myself together and walked over to my office in the freezing morning air. An eternity later, Kelser and Krippies arrived in a freshly washed Jeep. I instantly noted it had a brand new canvas top. Sergeant Kelser saw me looking at it. "Well, this is a special occasion, Lieutenant; so, I guessed we can risk a new one." I don't remember ever asking the two of them to go with me; they just sort of decided I wasn't going alone.

This was a very cold February 10th and the little box heater between the Jeep's front seats was working overtime trying to keep up. The windshield defoggers were marginal at best. The trip down was uneventful, but we were all glad to be wearing our winter parkas. I brought an extra one for Joyce. Kelser was also thinking ahead and had thrown two Army blankets in the back seat. Our canvas top, even the brand new one, had a lot of air leaks. It was better than no top at all, but not a whole lot better. Military vehicles were never intended to be built to civilian comfort standards. I was concerned how my Alabama bride was going to take the cold but then realized, *"What was I thinking? She's Canadian."*

We got to Kimpo Airport early, drove over to the military side and took advantage of the airbase flight line coffee shop. When Krippies and Kelser unzipped their winter parkas, I immediately noted, in addition to their side-arms, they both had .45 caliber, M-3 "Grease guns" hung around their necks.

"You guys know something I don't?"

"We probably do, Sir! These M-3s are our express line through customs."

"You're kidding?"

"Nope, just wait and see."

Nervous as a cat, I gulped down the last of my coffee and jumped up, "Time to go guys!" It wasn't really and we were just a short drive away from the commercial air terminal but, I was so antsy, I just had to get moving. It was so long since I'd seen Joyce, and now that our reunion was imminent, the wait was becoming psychologically close to unbearable. On top of that, last night's dream kept popping into my head no matter how hard I tried to block it out.

Putting it mildly, at the commercial terminal, the three of us really stood out. All U.S. military flights, including military contract flights with commercial airlines, came in on the other side of the runway at the U.S. military terminal. Korean and other commercial travelers normally didn't get much chance to see too many American soldiers in their civilian terminal; so, we were probably quite a sight. Because of the cold, all three of us were wearing our double-soled *Corcoran* combat boots, which added about two and half inches to our heights. So, that made Kelser and Krippies near monster size while I was just a stubby 6'5". We three giants, in this land of the *Lilliputians,* just strode through the main terminal door with the snow swirling around us. We were wearing these huge, knee-length, OD (Olive Drab), winter parkas with badger fur-lined hoods. Fastened to our shoulder epaulets were our black Military Police brassards with the large white "MP" letters. We're all armed and my two companions now had their parkas wide open displaying their sub-machineguns.

It was like a bad "B" western movie. People stared up at us; some looked afraid, but most just stared in awe at our combined size. *Three U.S. Marshals had just walked into Dodge City.* I had the feeling most of them had never seen three men of this size together in their lives. The bulky parkas, winter head gear and dangling machineguns all added to our menacing size and appearance. We never had to slow our pace or maneuver around anyone. The *little people* just flowed around us like water moving around a boat's prow. We ended up at the *North-west Orient* ticket counter. Even the people in line at the counter stepped aside as we approached. I heard myself saying to the attendant, "Excuse me, Sir, is your flight from the United States due to arrive on time?" I knew there was only one flight, but I asked anyway. The Korean gentleman behind the counter just stared up at us, mouth open and nodded *"Yes"*. *"*What gate?" Still staring up, he pointed to an area over his left shoulder. I thanked him, gave a little bow and we three headed off in that direction. I overheard Kelser say to Krippies, "Ain't this a hoot?"

As it turned out, Kimpo did not really have a very sophisticated way of handling international flights. In 1968, there was no *real* airport security. We three walked into the international area unchallenged. There were also no movable *Jet ways* to transfer passengers from the planes to the terminal. The planes would stop a safe distance away from the terminal and passengers would walk down the roll-up stairways then take a hike from the plane to the terminal. We stood around for awhile looking out the widow, through the now worsening snow; I caught a glimpse of the distinctive *Red Tail* of a *Northwest Orient* plane floating down onto the runway. My heart leapt into my throat and I could feel it pounding a hundred miles an hour. Kelser and Krippies came in on either side of me and Kelser said, "Come on, Lieutenant, let's go find that lady of yours."

A big blast of icy air and whipping snow caused us to quickly flip up our fur-lined hoods and snap a few more snaps closed. No one had stopped us from walking out of the terminal and onto the tarmac, so we just kept walking towards the plane. The anticipation was killing me. We stood there, off to the side, at the bottom of the stairway and watched as each person's face appeared in the plane's doorway. It was a full flight and the wait seemed endless. Finally, at the top of the stairs, there she was. As I had anticipated, my fashion plate bride wasn't quite dressed for the weather. She was wearing a new *London Fog* coat with one of those zip-in winter liners. It was probably okay for the coldest day in Alabama, but another one of those cold fronts had just arrived from Manchuria. I watched as a sudden gust of frigid air made her catch her breath. The wind also flipped up the hem of her coat revealing nylons and a dress hemline that came just above her knees. That same blast instantly destroyed a hairdo, which probably originated in a state-side hair salon about twenty-four hours ago. She seemed such a tiny thing shivering there at the top of those stairs. Looking up at her, she seemed even smaller than her stately, five foot one and three quarter inches and 110 pounds.

I wanted to run up the steps and give her a big hug, but that would be almost impossible what with the steady stream of people hurrying down and towards warmth inside the terminal. As she started to descend, I moved even closer to the bottom of the stairs. Joyce was clutching a large carry-on bag and trying to hold her coat closed at the throat as she braced herself against the freezing wind. She was now shielding her eyes and trying to see where she was going. Her eyes were all squinty and her nose all wrinkled up as she strained to see something familiar. I don't think she even realized the three, large men in the hooded parkas at the bottom of the stairs were not affiliated with airport operations. When she was almost to the bottom step, I reached in and swooped her up into my arms. A look of fear mixed with surprise instantly vanished as I brought her face close enough to peer inside my fur-lined hood. Recognition was immediate, and so was the big hug and kiss. She was squealing with delight and screaming, "I'm here, I'm here, I made it, I made it!" I didn't even mind the fact that she was kicking the hell out of me with the heels of her shoes. We were finally together and, right now, that was all that mattered.

I set her down and quickly wrapped the spare parka around her and flipped up the hood. The parka came down to mid calf and looked absolutely ridiculous on her but its instant protection far out-weighed how thoroughly silly she looked in it. It was then that I noticed a young GI standing behind her carrying several bags. He was just standing there; so, I asked, "Can I help you, soldier?" Joyce quickly turned around, "Oh, I forgot, this is Ned! Ned's just coming back from being on leave and he's been helping me with my bags ever since Atlanta. He's stationed at *Young-Sand* or some place like that." Krippies and Kelser took the bags from Ned. He must have been feeling a little used because as Joyce was thanking him he muttered, "You shoulda' told me he was an MP." Ned faded away into the whiteness and the four of us hurried inside. I introduced my traveling companions to Joyce on the way in.

Now began the old rigmarole of clearing Customs & Immigration in a foreign land. Joyce spotted her bag instantly. I looked at it with disbelief. No wonder she could find it right away. It had to be the hugest suitcase ever put on an airliner. We could have saved a lot of money by just shipping her to Korea inside it. Of course there were no wheels on it and it had to weigh well over the legal airline weight for a single piece of luggage. It was strapped closed with silver *100-mile-an-hour-tape*. I had to ask, "Did you leave anything behind at your folk's house?" She answered with a sheepish smile, "No, I don't think so!"

We breezed through Immigration. The agent just looked at us, and our machineguns, and basically must have thought to himself, "*To hell with it! I'm not pissing these monsters off. If they want to bring the little Round-Eye in, that's okay with me."* I don't think he even looked at her Canadian passport. She opened it; he stamped it and just waived her through.

Customs was another matter. The little bureaucrat behind the customs table looked at the customs declaration form and saw there was nothing declared. Not believing there could be nothing of interest inside such a huge case, he decided he wanted to look inside and see for himself. Joyce panicked and pleaded with me, "Herb, please don't let him. If he opens that bag, there's no way we will ever get it closed again. The reason it's taped shut in the first place is because we broke one of the closer thingies when we sat on it to make it shut. Daddy just wrapped tape around it to keep everything inside. If they cut the tape, it will *sprong* open and all my stuff will fly all over the place It will be one big mess and we'll never get it home without everything being ruined!"

Kelser stepped in. "Sir, please let me handle this!" I stepped back and Kelser turned to the Customs Agent. The agent was motioning for us to open the bag. Kelser leaned in close to him and shook his head and emphatically said, "No! Let us through!" The agent got excited and rattled on in Korean about something and again gestured to open the bag. Kelser walked around the counter and lowered his body until he was eye to eye with the agent. "No! You understand me? No!" The Customs Agent held his ground, and for a third time, only this time he demanded, in English, "You open bag now!" Kelser and Krippies then pulled themselves to their full height and, in unison, un-zipped parkas and grabbed their M-3 "Grease Guns." This, the agent instantly understood. He quickly stamped the form and waved us through, "You go. You go now!"

Joyce's mouth fell open. "You weren't really going to shoot him were you?" Krippies grabbed the oversized bag like it was a toy and we all beat feet out of there. Kelser was explaining to Joyce on the way. "Give these guys a rubber stamp and they'll hold you up for an hour just because they can. This guy knows when an American Army MP says 'No' that's supposed to be the end of it. He's just pushing it. We're getting more and more of that now since our two countries have opened up "Status of Forces Agreement" talks again. It's beginning to piss me off. Flashing the big guns was just our way of making the point a lot faster. We could have argued with him forever and it would have ended the same way it just did with him stamping the customs form. We just did what we did to cut through the crap!"

We got to the Jeep and shortly worked out the only possible solid geometric solution for the four of us and that *Ark* of a suitcase all fitting into the vehicle. Kelser drove and Krippies rode "shotgun." Joyce, the big bag and I all squeezed into the back seat. The bag clearly took up over half the available cubic footage back there. I squeezed my cheeks in between the AN/VRC-12 radio, bolted to the right wheel housing, and that huge bulging bag. The only place left for Joyce was mostly in my lap.

Now, one would think a reunion between a loving husband and his wife in this exotic land would be very romantic. Anyone who's ever had to ride in the back of an M-151 Quarter Ton Truck (Jeep) will attest to the fact that this is not a comfortable place to be, even under the best of circumstances. At first, the idea of being intimately scrunched together with my beautiful bride in my lap seemed like Heaven as Joyce's light frame nestled into my parka-padded lap. The openings in our parka hoods met and we savored a long, private kiss and exchanged *I love yous.*

The problem was; time, bumps and turns. Every bump caused the Jeep's springs and shocks to absorb the bump. As the springs rebounded to their normal size, Joyce's light body assumed, if only for a second or two, the weight dynamics of a 250 pound, "Green Bay" linebacker. Problem was, there were a lot of bumps between Seoul and Chunchon; so, this was a repetitive process. At first, it was relatively entertaining and we laughed at being bounced around. As time passed it became less and less entertaining for me and more and more painful. My kidneys were taking a "heavyweight bout" pounding and during one particular jolt I just knew I'd ruptured my spleen. To further add to my extreme discomfort, every time Kelser would turn left the *Samsonite* monolith would come crashing down from its perch atop the left rear wheel. After being slammed by it a few times, I adjusted my weight so I was practically pushing up against it for the whole trip home. This put my whole back and left shoulder in an awkward and strained position for a protracted period of time.

I know pain's a relative thing, but mine was now the rapid-fire equivalent of giving birth to three sets of triplets, in a row. When we somehow arrived at the outskirts of Chunchon, portions of my body had long since ceased to function. I would have asked Joyce to adjust her position, but the poor, little thing had fallen asleep in total exhaustion about twenty miles ago and her dead weight seemed to have added on even more poundage. As we hit one last big bump approaching the main gate and I just knew my back had cracked in two. The Jeep lurched to a stop outside the floodlit main gate.

Joyce was now wide-awake. She moved and I could not suppress a low painful moan. "Oh, Sweetie, am I too heavy on you?" I grimaced and lied, "No, Hon, I'm fine." Kelser said, "Mrs. Royce, you might want to look at the gate." Joyce and I both looked and there, hanging on the gate, was a large, black on white banner reading, *Welcome to Camp Page Joyce.* Joyce started jumping up and down with me as the trampoline. "Oh look, Herb, isn't that sweet?" All I could do was bite my tongue to hold back the scream.

It was now well after dusk. We rolled through the gate and I was in near panic someone else might have seen the sign. Krippies was reading my mind. "I know we were supposed to be driving you up to your house, Sir, but the guys wanted to meet and welcome your wife. I called ahead on the radio and the banner was only put up moments before we arrived. If you look out the back window, you'll see it's already coming down." Sure enough, the KATUSAs were already wadding up the banner and stuffing it in the gate shack. "Weatherspoon's back in the Sates, Mixon's in Seoul with Huddleston and the Gorilla's shacked up with his *Moose* downtown so, at this moment, the coast is clear."

We pulled up outside the PMO; Kelser and Krippies unfolded out of the Jeep and extracted Joyce from the back seat. I was another matter. Once Joyce climbed out of the Jeep my legs started to hurt like hell as blood finally began to flow to them again. The two giants, unceremoniously, yanked me out and helped me to stand. I had that numb feeling in my thighs like the one you get when you've been sitting on the *John* for about two hours, reading the Sunday paper or something.

Inside the PMO, the whole MP contingent plus my three roommates were present, along with another welcome sign. A big "Hoot" went up as Joyce bounced through the door and I hobbled in behind her, like a little old man. There was pink "bug juice" (punch) and a big sheet cake with white frosting and "Welcome to Korea Joyce" spelled out in red frosting. Everyone came up to Joyce and introduced himself. An MP was posted outside the door, as a lookout, in case of unwelcome visitors.

About an hour later, Kelser drove us up to the house. We got out in front of the place and, in the glow of the streetlights; it looked particularly warm and cozy. From the road, looking up at it, the house seemed huge; Joyce flipped her parka hood back and exclaimed, "Wow, look at the size of this place!" I then explained that we only had the top half. As we ascended the suicide stairs to the front gate, Kelser related that, during the party, *the* bag had been delivered and the Cannon Heater had been lit. He followed us up to the gate then bid us goodnight. Someone had turned on a few of the lights and the place never looked better. I locked the metal sally port gate behind us. Joyce was fascinated and started to explore our small courtyard. She spotted the outhouse and smiled, "I know what that is!" She then walked around front and got her first view from our balcony's scenic overlook of the city. It was still freezing cold and, in the light of the street lamps, I could see the frosty-mist of her breathing. She stood there taking in the sights, sounds and smells of Chunchon. I came up behind, put my arms around her and hugged her tightly. Still looking out over the balcony, in a low voice she said, "I love it, I just love it! This has to be one of the most beautiful sights I've ever seen. I don't know how you did all this, Lieutenant Royce, but it's more than I could have ever wished for in my dreams." She turned, put her arms around my neck, looked deep into my eyes for a moment, then gave me the most wonderful kiss and whispered in my ear, "Thank you!" I then picked her up and carried her, giggling, over the threshold into our very first home.

I kissed her again, then set her down and just let her explore her new home. I followed, delighting in her reactions to what I'd made for her. I pointed her towards the bedroom, as it was the biggest room, and the one with basically all the furnishings. It was not my doing, but there was a new, lavender, silk quilt on the bed and a dozen red roses in a vase on the headboard. The room was romantically lit by a wooden temple lamp. The glow from its small bulb showed off my craft shop-made chest and wardrobe in a very forgiving light. She just stood there in the middle of the room and did a very slow pirouette, taking in all the details, including the red, brocade drapes, the floor cushions, the space heater and the low Korean tables. Her suitcase was standing next to the wardrobe. I had already bought her a pair of red, silk pajamas and laid them out on her pillow.

She came over to me and gave me a surprisingly strong hug. "What's the rest of the place look like?" She laughed at the concrete kitchen with its tiny sink, fridge and stove. "This is going to take some getting used to! I guess we're going to have to eat out a lot. Wow, look at the size of the pantry; it's almost as big as the kitchen! You've even been shopping too; look at all the canned goods." The almost bare living room and guest room rounded out the tour. I was saving the *piece de résistance* for last and could not have planned my surprise any better, if I tried. Joyce looked at me with pleading eyes. "Herb, would you please go outside with me. I need to use 'Buckingham Palace'. I'll get used to it, but tonight, please go out there with me." "Oh, okay, if you insist, but you know you're going to have to learn to be brave and go to the John by yourself; follow me." We covered the few steps to the bathroom and I threw open the door. I'd rigged a small spotlight so it shown right on our wonderful inside toilet. As I revealed my big surprise, I gave out a loud, "Ta-Da!" and showed off the porcelain gem, "Merry Christmas, Hon!" Joyce gave out a little shriek, "You did it; you found one!" Then, she backed inside the small room, and while closing the door, in a low voice said, "I'll be out in a little while; it was a very long flight."

If there's one thing which will crush the hell out of any romantic moment, it's just being plain old bone-weary, out-on-your-feet tired. Joyce freshened up as best she could in the tiny, kitchen sink while I'd already jumped into bed in excited anticipation. While she was out of the room, she slipped on the new, silk PJs I'd bought her. She momentarily emerged, fished a bottle of *White Shoulders* from her handbag and disappeared from view once more. "Be back in a flash." I just knew she was dabbing perfume on all the important places. She came back in the bedroom, but took a moment to briefly warm her bottom near the Cannon heater. "Wow, this funny looking thing sure pumps out the heat!" She then yelled, "Ready, Teddy?" and took a running leap into bed and landed, giggling, right on top of me. One long, deep kiss and she rolled off and dove under the covers. She scrunched down under the quilt and gave a brief shiver. "This bed feels divine." She snuggled backside first into me. She was fluffing her pillow, wiggling in and arranging her nest. I scooched forward so we could be *"Spoons"*. As I inched towards her, I smelled her sweet perfume and felt her soft, silky hair and the smoothness of her skin. She had such soft, flawless, baby skin. I reached up and turned off the lamp on the headboard. In the darkness, as I laid there next to her, I was anticipating a taste of that incredible bliss I'd waited and longed for these past, 100 days. I slipped my left arm around her tiny waist and pulled her in close to me. It was then I heard the passion killer of all passion killers, *"BA-ZAW—WHEEU—BA-ZAW."* My angel was out cold and instantly dead to the world. Over thirty hours of trans-continental and trans-Pacific travel had done her in.

Actually, I didn't seriously mind, as I too was dog tired, but just so damned glad she was finally with me and that the Migs didn't get her. I gazed at her in amazement for a short time. Then drifted off into the best sleep I'd had in weeks.

26

Adaptation

Normally I would stop by the PMO early on Sunday mornings but, this Sunday, I decided to take the day off to celebrate Joyce's first full day in Korea. More correctly, my crew said they'd kick my ass if I showed up. So, after getting completely and thoroughly reacquainted, we ventured out so I could show her around her new hometown. I still wasn't sure how all this was going to work. We talked about it and decided, rather than worry and over-think everything; we would just take it a day at a time until our new Korean lives sort of found their own level of normalcy.

You have to realize that, in this Northeastern part of Korea, there really weren't very many Americans. This wasn't like any of the American Army Division areas or like down in Seoul where there were literally thousands of Americans. Yongsan, for example, was an accompanied tour for many soldiers and they had family quarters, dependent schools and everything you might find on any American Army fort back in the World. In contrast, Camp Page was considered a remote, unaccompanied assignment for American military. Because of this, the Chunchon locals didn't get much chance to see *"Round Eye"* western women and they sure as hell had never seen a *Joyce*. Sure, there were a few females assigned as part of Camp Page's permanent party, but putting it politely, this small group was hardly a representative cross-section of western womanhood.

There was *"Lucy the Librarian"* who was probably nearly seventy, and a very old seventy at that, I might add. I don't mean to be unkind, but Lucy looked every inch a cliché librarian with her thick wire frame glasses, grayish hair pulled back into a bun, not even a rudimentary attempt at makeup, and those long, dull, fashion-less dresses that hung on her thin, devoid-of-curves frame. Lucy was a nice enough lady, soft-spoken, friendly, smart, and a very good librarian; but it must have been a long time, maybe even forever, since Lucy got a rise out of any guy.

Then, there was *"Fat Pat the Craft Shop Girl"*. Pat was a real piece of work. I'm pretty sure Pat kept renewing her contract to stay at Camp Page because here she had no western, female competition and could get all the dates she could handle, something which probably didn't happen much back in high school or college. She was one of those high school types the cute girls always talked about. *"She has such a pretty face; too bad she's so fat. If she lost all that weight she would probably be really cute too."*

Pat was very much into guys. She took keen interest in every newly assigned soldier and officer. She was the absolute opposite of Lucy. Pat always wore bright colored clothing, lots of make up, had dyed red, shoulder length hair to flip around and she always showed lots of cleavage. This was easy for Pat because she had really big boobs. She always seemed to be rubbing them up against some new guys arm when helping them with their craft shop project. Actually, it was probably difficult for her not to bump you with *The Twins* since they were about the same size as her head. She also liked to lean over the counter when waiting on new troops just to let them get a really good peek down her v-neck sweater.

There are a lot of guys in this world who are only concerned with "pussy" and don't care much what the girl looks like. Pat was a magnet for these kinds of guys. She had a working, western pussy and was more than willing to share it with most any guy who took an interest in her. During my time at Camp Page, I can't remember ever seeing Pat "guy-less" … or sober when she was outside the Craft Shop. You see, Pat also had a bit of a drinking problem.

The only other two women at the Camp were the *Nurse Twins* down at our clinic. I knew them through the work we did together trying to keep the on-limits working girls cleaned up. These two women were probably in their mid to late thirties. When I would see them in the Mess or happen upon them downtown, they always seemed to be together. Wherever you found one, the other was always close by.

One wore make-up while the other wore none. One had long hair, the other a "pixie cut". One wore dresses, skirts and high heels, the other, slacks, baggy blouses, sensible shoes and a big watch. Up until now I hadn't been around too many lesbians that I knew of. I just sort of bumped around life in my own ignorance, never picking up on any of the so-called signals.

In 1968, lesbians and homosexuals hadn't really been invented yet. At least, there was no flaunting of it in public and very few would ever dare talk about it to "straight" friends. Those who were, pretty much kept it out of public view for fear of severe repercussions. If the Army found out you were a "Homo" or a

"Lezzy," you might be thrown in the stockade, but most assuredly, you'd be on your way out of the service very quickly on moral turpitude charges.

It was Paul who first made me aware of Sally and Ginger's unique relationship and why no guy had ever been lucky enough to land a date with Ginger ... the okay-looking one. We were downtown looking for something for the house when we saw them coming out of a hotel. We were looking for a place for lunch and I said, "I didn't know they had a restaurant in there." Paul's head snapped around towards me. He had this; *"You can't be this stupid"* expression on his face. "The only lunch they had in there was each other." I must have looked like a deer caught in the headlights. "They're *rug-munchers,* you dope, didn't you know that?" It was then that all the little pieces of the puzzle fell into place for me, "Ooooooh!"

It was a bright sunshiny day as Joyce and I took our first walk together downtown. To Joyce, Chunchon was like a freezing cold "Disneyland"; she was fascinated by everything. The narrow market streets were out of the wind; so, Joyce unbuttoned her long coat revealing her, just above the knee, blue dress with white trim. As we walked along, I became increasingly conscious of the attention she was getting. Men, women and children were all coming out of the little shops to get a good look at this pretty, round-eyed woman. Several people, who weren't satisfied with just one look, began to follow us. I noticed two of them had sketchpads and were busily drawing something on them. At about the halfway point, down the block, we had attracted about twenty or so followers.

A little, old *"Momma-San"* walked up to Joyce and rattled off something in Korean. Joyce smiled down at her and said, "And hello to you too!" The little old lady put her hands over her mouth and laughed, then smiled and began to speak to those gathered around us. I was lost; my two weeks of language school and the little Korean I'd picked up since I'd been here was basically worthless in the market. Here, various Korean dialects, Chinese and even Japanese words are all mixed together. For some reason, all counting of money is done in Chinese. The Japanese had occupied this country from around the end of the Russo-Japanese War until the end of World War II, a period of nearly 40 years. They had forced their language on the Koreans and made them endure many severe and cruel hardships. The average Korean doesn't have much good to say about the Japanese, but they still sprinkle their street-level Korean language with lots of Japanese words.

This little, old woman, who appeared to have some level of stature in this market street, took Joyce's hand and pushed up her coat sleeve with her other hand. This displayed Joyce's smooth, soft, very pale skin. The woman was most impressed and called all the women around her to come take a look. Koreans are a very cast-conscious people. In Korea, lighter skin is viewed as being more beautiful and also a visual cue of a person's *station in life*. Koreans with darker skin are automatically classified as field workers, farmers or laborers. Probably no Korean had skin as white or as soft as Joyce's. The other women gathered around to see and feel her forearm. Amongst themselves they were discussing Joyce's uniqueness in what seemed to be impressive terms. The only words I could really pick up were *arumdaun* (beautiful), *hayan sack* (white), *agi* (baby) and *puduroun* (soft skin). I think I got the gist of it with just those four words. They were saying Joyce was beautiful and her skin was so white and soft, just like a baby's. Joyce was becoming a bit fearful over all this bizarre attention. Then, the darnedest thing happened. This gathering of women abruptly stopped the epidermis examination and gave her many bows, almost as if she were royalty or something. They then formed a loose, moving ring around us as we continued our walk through the market. They chased away the curious and gave us a chance to proceed in peace. Mama San also helped by haggling great prices for our purchases. At the end of the block, we thanked the old woman, bowed goodbye to our protective entourage and jumped into a cab. Inside the cab I turned to Joyce and said, "Sweetie, you're going to have to get a tan!" I then explained some of the things I'd learned about Korean culture.

Our first Valentines Day together was a simple celebration. When you don't have much money and you're in a strange land, you do what you can. A card, a box of candy from the PX and a bottle of "Cold Duck" from the Class VI pretty much took care of the gift part of the ritual. We went out for our first Korean restaurant meal together. I took her to a place that served pretty good *Pulgogi*, a sort of Korean barbecued beef dinner with vegetables and rice. She loved it and all was right with our world.

Over the next few weeks, Joyce's appearances in the market were not nearly as dramatic. It calmed down to the point where she became comfortable with going on her own. "The Pretty Round-Eye" was slowly being accepted by the locals. The old Mama San would still help, but it was way less formal now. It got so Joyce and Mama San even had tea together. Shopping was now her main female, social event. She was even learning how to play a Korean card game with the women in the market. I never understood it, but it consisted of continuous talking, slapping these little, hard, tile-type cards on the table and lots of laughing. To a certain degree, Joyce had begun to make herself at home.

Our lives were making the adjustments we needed to function normally as a western couple in this strange land. It was a huge change for Joyce. Here we were in this interesting and exotic country where many things seemed so strange. But, somehow, we felt safe and shielded from the harshness of what was going on in the world. One evening, while in bed, reading the February 18th edition of the Sunday *Stars & Stripes,* Joyce summed it up. "We're so lucky you're here and not in Vietnam!" I took the paper from her. The U.S. State Department had just announced the highest one-week U.S. casualty toll of the Vietnam War, 543 killed and 2547 wounded. For a moment, I felt guilty being snuggled in bed with my loving wife, hundreds of miles north of the *Big War* yet still on the same side of the globe.

Joyce had started her job at Dr. Han's clinic and was working hard organizing the clinic's system for admitting and treating patients. The other Korean nurses didn't seem to mind this pretty, western nurse with all her new ideas. Even though language was still a problem, Joyce was learning more and more Korean every day. She would give demonstration-type classes to the rest of the nurses on various western medical techniques and this sort of established her as the nurse with the most technical expertise.

Dr. Han was another thing; Joyce could not stand the man. She thought his work was sloppy, he had crummy bedside manner; he was careless with sterilization procedures and, overall, he was just a lousy doctor. When it came to nursing, Joyce was a perfectionist and Dr. Han was driving her nuts. The two of them would lock horns over things Joyce thought Dr. Han should or should not be doing. From reports, it sometimes got quite vocal. Dr. Han was accustomed to nurses who just did what he told them to do and who knew their subservient station in life. The wills of the two clashed frequently, but in the end, Joyce's began to slowly prevail. Dr. Han was paying more attention to proper sterilization protocols and, in return, Joyce started treating him with a little more respect ... at the clinic. At home, she still told me horrible, bloody, nasty Dr. Han stories. "Please, not while we're eating, Hon!"

We had taken full advantage of Weatherspoon's trip back to the States. I had brought Joyce onto post several times, but now that he was back, we had to be more careful. There were actually no military regulations preventing me from bringing a guest on base. It's just that I didn't want the Colonel or his cronies to know Joyce was my wife. So, we moved around the base with a certain level of caution. Most thought she was just this Canadian nurse who worked downtown. We checked books out of the library; Joyce was a voracious reader. We also tried our hands at black & white and *Ektachrome* photo development in the craft shop dark room. We'd lounge around in the evenings with my BOQ roommates listening to LPs on my newest stereo acquisition, a "Dual" 1019 turntable. We'd bring back hamburgers, fries and drinks from the O-Club bar and all just kick back for a relaxing weekend afternoon or just any evening. My roommates and Joyce really hit it off. I think they just liked having conversations with someone whose voice was higher than theirs. I also took her to the on-base movie theater. The first of many movies we saw there was, "Come Spy with Me" with Troy Donahue and Andrea Dromm. It wasn't much of a movie, but appropriate as it fit in with all our sneaking around. However, the most important thing Joyce accomplished during her trips to camp was stealing a hot shower down at the gym. She would bring a gym bag, full of her essentials, down the hill then hit the small female locker room between eight and eight-thirty on weekdays. She had secretly taken up residence in one of the lockers, complete with her own combination lock. Everyone had already finished their PT, showered and was at work well before eight. The gym would be all but deserted when she'd arrive. Joyce, literally, had the whole place to herself and she enjoyed the luxury of long, hot showers. She'd dress, blow dry her hair, put on her makeup then stop by my office for a quick cup of coffee and maybe a donut before she started her day. The route between the gym and my office was not well-traveled and usually she encountered no one.

So, when nothing important was going on at the camp, this became her ritual: A mile walk, shower at the gym, a quick coffee with me or Buck Sergeant God and then another walk back up to the house to change for work. Joyce was never in better shape. Funny thing though, just like our very first walk, she still had women and men with sketchpads popping out of shops as she passed by and making quick sketches of her. I wasn't sure I liked that at all.

It wasn't until about a week later that we found out what all the sketching was about. When we were walking home one afternoon we looked in this dress shop window. Hanging there on a mannequin was the same dress Joyce was wearing. As the weeks went by, we would see duplicates of just about everything that came over in that huge suitcase. We'd even see Korean women wearing the same dresses as Joyce. Without knowing or intending it, "Joyce fashion" had become the hip thing amongst the young, high-fashion set in Chunchon.

Other than this strange sketching, there was only one adverse incident, and this one scared the hell out of Joyce. During those first weeks when Joyce would walk down to the Camp for her morning shower there would be this one man in an alleyway who would call after her. He was speaking in Korean; so, Joyce had no idea what he was saying. As time passed, and she began to understand some of the Korean words, she realized this man was saying horrible things to her. One day she came into my office in tears and told me this man was scaring her. She related some of the things he was saying.

I called Mr. Shin and Cop Chong into the room so they could hear her story and help with translating some of the Korean words Joyce thought the man said. Joyce related what had happened.

"It started a couple of weeks ago. I would pass by this alley where he has this little, outside, knife sharpening shop and he would say something to me as I passed. I had no idea what it was; so, I'd just smile and then he'd call something after me. After that, he started coming out of his alley and looking mean; so, I started walking down to camp on the other side of the street. Then, he started yelling across the street at me. This really started bothering me, but I didn't want to tell you because I still thought it might be nothing and I might just be being silly. Well, this morning, he came out of an alley on the same side of the street where I've been walking. Only this time, he came out and pointed at me and screamed some things at me."

Mr. Shin cut in, "Joyce, you remember anything he say?"

"I think I can remember some of the words he used a lot and one or two I already know are bad words. He said something like, '*derre-unsakkee*' and '*erdee gahser dwejer berryaw*'. Did I say that so you can understand it?"

Cop Chong and Mr. Shin were both nodding. "Oh yes! This not good thing to say; he say, 'Dirty woman, why don't you go die somewhere?'". "He say anything else?"

"Yes, he said, '*ssee-bahl ayawn megook jeejer-boonahn sakee*', was that bad?" The question did not need an answer; all you had to do was look at the winced expressions on Cop's and Mr. Shin's faces. "Oh yes, that very bad!"

"What does it mean?"

"You sure you want to know, Joyce, because I don't want to really say!"

"Yes please, I think I really need to know. I do know '*megook*' means American but that's all."

"Okay, he say, and I really don't want to tell you, but he say, 'Fuck you, American pig!' Now you know why I not want to say."

"Oh! Why would he say such things? I never did anything bad to him!"

"I no know, Joyce, maybe he just crazy man or maybe just ass-hole but Cop Chong and me find out."

The two of them hurried out the Main Gate and headed up the street.

After her shower, I drove Joyce home in the Jeep so she wouldn't be late for work and, also, for her own protection until we found out what this street business was all about.

That didn't take very long. The very next day I walked with Joyce down to the camp; and, we did encounter the knife sharpener. He looked like he'd been severely beaten about the head and shoulders. As we approached, he scurried out to the entrance of his alley, saying nothing; he gave Joyce a very deep and probably painful bow. I also couldn't help but notice that the rest of the shopkeepers along the way also came out and wished us a good morning as we passed. I have no idea what Cop Chong did, but I'm certain this was now the safest street in all of Korea for Joyce to walk down.

27

Dinner with the Pig

Joyce had been working at the clinic in Chunchon for close to a month now and I knew she had this big dinner-meeting downtown. So, on this particular evening, I hurried home after work, because I knew this was going to be a special evening for Joyce and I wanted to be around in case she needed my help in getting a hot tub ready. Tonight, was one of those special occasions where we'd have to press the cramped tub in our tiny bathroom into service. This would entail boiling lots of water and hoping we could get a sufficient amount of it warm enough for a proper bath.

When I got home Joyce had already finished bathing and was standing in front of the mirror busily getting herself ready to go out for dinner with her colleagues. I walked up behind her and watched in the mirror as she expertly applied her eye makeup. I slipped my arms around her waist and nuzzled her neck. She was intent on getting her eyes just right. "Take it easy, big guy, all this fuss tonight isn't for you; well, maybe later tonight, if you play your cards right."

She gave me a little, wicked grin and a wink over her shoulder then continued. "Okay, enough with the hugs already, don't make me put an eye out. Professionally, tonight's very important to me. I've been working very hard to establish myself here. You would not believe some of the primitive ways this clinic still operates when treating certain things. I have so much I can teach these nurses and I'm just glad to be here, both professionally and personally." I got another one of her special little looks as she made eye contact with me in the mirror. "This is really a big honor you know! For all Dr. Han's rudeness and crudeness, he has really taken an interest in the improvements I've got going at the clinic. He's been stopping by several times a day to check on what I'm up to. I think he's really impressed. It's a good thing we have Miss Hong there; she's the only Korean nurse on staff who can really speak English and she's been helping me pass information to the others." Joyce now switched to working on her lips and continued on. "Miss Hong told me my being invited to this dinner with Dr. Han

145

and all the other doctors from the hospital is a big honor. She said none of the other nurses have ever been invited to anything like this. I think she's just a tiny bit jealous but is so nice she's trying to conceal it."

She then stepped away from the mirror, turned towards me and asked, "Well, whatcha' think; will I pass?" She must have, because as she did a slow pirouette for me, I felt that weak in the knees thing again. She was just so damned beautiful. She had on this basic black dress with a single string of pearls perfectly imitating its neckline. Pearl earrings brought the whole thing together. Makeup was immaculate and even her shoes and handbag matched. She added, "I don't know how long this shindig is going to last. It may go late if they have lots of procedural questions. Stay up for me and I might make it worth your while." She gave me that killer grin again.

I called down to the MP station on the field phone to have them send up a cab. We had this one small cab company we all trusted. Cop Chong's brother owned it, so we knew it was safe for us. Joyce was in high heels; so, I steadied her as we descended our suicide stone stairs. We stood there in the dirt street, on this moonlit night, small-talking, while Joyce, trying not to step in anything too nasty, lit a cigarette to calm her nerves. In less than five minutes she was off in the cab for her important dinner date. I gave her the cab company's phone number and told her to have the driver honk when she got back; so I could unlock the gate and help her up those damned stairs.

I toyed with the idea of going back down to Page and pick up some paperwork. Instead, got a Coke out of the fridge and settled down with an Ian Fleming, Bond book I somehow had missed, "On Her Majesty's Secret Service." Every time I was sure I'd read them all, I'd come across another one. Man that guy wrote a lot of Bond books!

Less than two hours later I heard pounding on our iron gate. I stepped outside, un-holstered my 45 and brought it to full cock. "Who is it?" I asked in my best low and authoritative voice. "It's me, ya' twit, let me in the damned gate!" I opened the gate and in stormed Joyce, madder than a wet hen. She went straight into the bedroom, plopped down on the edge of the bed, kicked her shoes off across the room and lit a Benson *& Hedges* menthol.

In her agitated state, I was a little afraid to ask but did so anyway. "Why ya home so early Hon?" First, I got the glare, then a request. "How 'bout a drink?" I went out to the kitchen and got a can of Coke out of our tiny Japanese fridge along with a teeny-tiny ice cube tray full of teeny tiny ice cubes. I walked back in with two rum and cokes. Joyce was now in flannel Pajamas and had already washed off her makeup in the bathroom.

I tried again. "Okay, tell me all about it. Anybody you want me to kill?" This brought a weak smile and she started.

"It's just so unfair! I showed up with my invitation in hand, thinking what I would say. I had this whole little speech put together in my head to introduce myself and get things started. There was this room full of men when I came in. I saw Dr. Han with them. He waved to me and gave me a little bow, but two beautifully, dressed Korean women ushered me into another room full of more Korean women. One of them spoke a little English. I was told this is where the wives were going to eat and that women don't eat with men at these sorts of functions. I told her I was invited by Dr. Han and I was supposed to be in the other room. She said, 'No', I was to stay with the other women until called. So, I thought, what the heck, it's probably just part of a thousand-year-old, Korean custom; so, I should just go along with it.

It actually was kinda' fun associating with all those China-doll type Korean doctor's wives. They were very interested in me. They really checked out what I was wearing, the material and all, and were fascinated with my high heels. They all made fun of my big feet. My feet aren't big; I'm a size six for cripes sake! They also kept holding their arms up to mine and comparing skin color. You're right; I gotta' get a tan. One felt my arm and told me the baby skin thing again. Then they *all* had to feel my skin. That's still a bit creepy to me! They also asked a lot of questions about my makeup. It was sort of like an international pajama party. I ended up dumping my purse out on the table so they could all look at and play with my makeup. Well, I eventually got into it and loosened up a bit. Drinks were served and I figured I'd relax and enjoy myself until I got my chance to talk to the doctors.

Dinner came and that was interesting too. I got a lot of tips on how to use chopsticks, so that part was good. Everything was fine and then the door to where the men were opened and there was Dr. Han. He bowed and smiled. I gathered myself up from sitting on the floor and followed him into the other room. I smiled politely at this room full of distinguished looking Korean doctors, and then Dr. Han introduced me, and it wasn't by name. He just said, in English, 'See, I tell you, all American womans not ugly!' It was as if I were some rare anthropologic discovery being shown off to a gathering of scientists from the National Geographic Society or something. I was speechless!"

She lit another cigarette and continued, "Before I could formulate any kind of reply, or even get red in the face, I was pushed back into the other room with all the Korean women again. I'm standing there with the women and I'm trembling with rage; I just wanted to spit. First of all, I'm not a freakin' American; I'm a Canadian, goddamnit."

Oh-oh, Dr. Han had used the "A" word in reference to this proud Canadian woman. Joyce had once explained to me that Canadians sometimes seem anti-

American but really aren't. It's just that the United States is so honkin' huge that Canadians think it's like sleeping with an elephant. The elephant might not intend you harm, but you're sill afraid it might just roll over in bed and accidentally crush you to death. Because of this, many Canadians are always aware, and sometimes slightly afraid, of their huge sleeping neighbor to the south.

She then continued, "Second of all, who the hell put this toad of a pig in charge of deciding what's pretty and what's ugly? Vomit looks pretty, next to his face!"

Although I was totally innocent in this matter, I somehow knew I was in great danger of being included in with all the dumb-ass males who had ever entered into and agitated Joyce's young life. So, I put any fantasies of a romantic evening out of my mind. Taking on a supportive, consoling role was probably the safest and most prudent path until this entire incident quieted down to a dull roar. I brought her a second rum and Coke, a double this time, and hoped for the best. She curled up in bed with her latest library acquisition, the drink and another *Benson & Hedges*. I decided to be quiet and try to make myself look very small and un-elephant like for the rest of the evening. In the morning, I noted I hadn't been hatcheted to death in my sleep; so, I somehow escaped being lumped-in with all the other rotten male bastards slated for special execution in "Joyce World".

From that evening forward, Joyce would no longer refer to Doctor Han as Doctor. Han; she had now joined Mr. Shin. "Doctor Han, the Pig" was now his official full name in Joyce World; or, for short, she referred to him simply as "The Pig."

28

Stars & Stripes

Life, like water, was beginning to seek its own level again. We were now well into March, and now, other than having Joyce with me, not much else was going on. Colonel Weatherspoon was fully submerged into his disturbing, serious drinking habits again. The North Koreans were continuing their death and destruction campaign while trying to establish a counterinsurgency type war in the South. Problem was, historically, the South Koreans were pretty sick of everyone trying to occupy and control their country. The Chinese, Japanese and North Koreans had all accomplished it in the past. Some even occupied, what is now South Korea, more than once.

In 1968, things were relatively good in the South and slowly getting better for the average Korean. There was also a massive civil defense type effort going on and everyone seemed to be involved in learning how to ferret out infiltrators. But again, the troubles in Korea were overshadowed, in the press, by world events.

The *Stars & Stripes* newspaper, and to a lesser degree, *AFN* (Armed Forces Network radio), were our primary sources of information about what was going on back home. Every solder's day was not complete without reading his daily copy of Stars & Stripes.

On this particular day, according to *Stars & Stripes*, things were not very wonderful in other places around the World either:

- In New Hampshire, Eugene McCarthy was campaigning hard for the presidency. Eugene McCarthy! Where the hell did the Democrats dig him up? He had really bad false teeth and about 2,000 hippy volunteers working for him. They all had cut their hair and changed the way they dressed. Their slogan was: "We're stayin' clean for Gene" and they were going around contacting conservative, Republican voters in New England and trying to sway the vote. Who the hell did they think they were kidding?

- Bobby Kennedy was also throwing his hat in the ring and just about everyone, Democrat or Republican, considered the late President John F.

Kennedy's younger brother and former U.S. Attorney General the legitimate candidate for the Democratic nomination.

- Things were not so hot in Czechoslovakia either. There was a strong independence movement brewing in that country and it was being encouraged by most of the "Free World". Under pressure, their Soviet-backed president had resigned and the Kremlin was not happy about it. The Warsaw Pact leaders were meeting in Dresden, East Germany to discuss what they called "The Czech Crisis".

- In Memphis, Dr. Martin Luther King was leading a peaceful march that suddenly turned violent. Dr. King was lead away from the scene but after he left all hell broke loose. Sixty "Freedom Marchers" were injured and one sixteen year old black boy was killed. Over 150 marchers were arrested by the police.

- For some crazy reason, when the bombing of North Vietnam seemed like it was beginning to really work, President Johnson announced bombing limitations. There would be no more bombing north of the 20th parallel. This was crazy! Why stop something that seemed to be our best chance of ending the damned Vietnam War?

No wonder the rest of the world was oblivious to the strange happenings going on in South Korea. Most of it had no affect on anyone but us anyway; we were hidden away in our own little Korean corner of the world. As Joyce and I lay in each other's arms, peacefully sleeping in our snug little Korean bed, we had no idea that in just a few days, powerful forces, way beyond our control, would radically alter our new life.

29

"Charlie Battery's Been Hit!"

Tomorrow, the 21st of March, was going to be Joyce's Birthday and I wanted to be sure it was going to be one to remember. Just recently, I collected on part of my prize from winning the football pool. On January 14th, my Bart Starr and the Green Bay Packers smeared the Oakland Raiders 33 to 14 in Super Bowl II. I made the point spread and won a hundred bucks and two cases of Champagne. I got the money right away but Dave Ross told me I could pick up my two cases from Class VI any time; so, I decided today was the day. I put the bubbly on ice at the club to ensure it was good and cold for tomorrow's big event.

My simple plan was; get a mess of hotdogs and hamburgers, grill them up on our balcony, invite all the MPs plus my roommates and throw Joyce a proper birthday party at the house. I guess it wasn't much of a plan but at least I had one.

Mr. Shin took me to what he claimed was the best baker in all of Chunchon. He said, "This baker number *han-na* (one). He knows how to make American birthday cake". I was armed with a scrap of paper with the words, **Happy Birthday Joyce**, printed on it, plus several pictures of decorated cakes torn out of old library *Better Homes & Gardens* magazines. With these detailed instructions, Mr. Shin and I trucked on down to visit his baker extraordinaire. "You sure this guy can make a real American birthday cake Mr. Shin?" "Oh yes, very sure, he the best!" I was introduced to the baker and, through Mr. Shin, began to explain what I wanted. The baker studied the magazine pictures, listened to Mr. Shin's instructions and took the paper scrap. His last words were "Okay, I make number one on *krake* for *Joy-cee*." I just had to take it on faith that *"I make number one on cake"* in Korean did not mean the same as it did back home.

I have to admit, I had not seen a birthday cake downtown since I arrived; so, I was apprehensive about what it might look like. My doubts ended up being totally without merit. The baker came through like a champ and brought out what had to be one of the most beautiful birthday cakes I'd ever seen. The pink confectionary script was perfect; all the colors were exactly what I wanted. The little pink roses with green leaves and stems were truly works of art. I was also amazed at how inexpensive this masterpiece was. This big, gorgeous cake—must have weighed fifteen pounds—only cost me about four bucks American.

We, somehow, actually ended up surprising Joyce and everything went well. The MPs were scarffing down the burgers and dogs. My guys had also brought potato salad and baked beans from—I didn't want to ask where. As the evening wore on, and the first case of Champagne was now history, a unique game of skill evolved. We began opening the Champagne bottles on the balcony. We'd shake the bottles vigorously then let chemistry take its natural course. We would take turns aiming the dangerously volatile bottles and try to shoot out a nearby streetlight with the corks as they blasted their way out of the bottles. Our proficiency may have been steadily improving, but our physical ability to accurately aim began to diminish rapidly.

During the course of our marksmanship contest, I discovered I'd been paying for all the streetlights on Ok Chong Dong. There was a power line from our, street light, target which came above the street to our house. Upon closer inspection, I discovered there were actually two power lines connected to the house and this one was taking power *from* our house to the street-lamp post. Later, when I traced the line, it ended up being connected to all ten of our streetlights. Seems some enterprising Korean had found yet one more way of getting money out of Americans. The term, "Steal the radio and leave the music" came to my mind again. Mr. Shin handled this for me and the second cable attached to my house was soon disconnected. Down deep, I just knew this had to be the Dragon Lady's work.

Someone doused the house lights and couple of the guys carried out the huge, beautiful cake with its twenty-two, pink candles all contributing to the festive glow in the room. Everyone ohooo-ed and ahhh-ed as the cake came into view. We all, almost in unison, broke into a passable rendition of "Happy Birthday." Joyce was so happy with her husband's thoughtfulness on her first married birthday; she was actually glowing as brightly as the candles on the cake. Joyce was very impressed with her giant, baked, beauty of a birthday cake and dispatched all the candles with one mighty puff. Buck Sergeant God did the honors and cut the cake. It is Korean custom to wait until everyone is served before starting to eat. I was served the last piece, smiled broadly at my bride and announced, "Happy Birthday Joyce—everybody dig in!" The whole room simultaneously stuffed big chunks of the beautiful cake in their mouths. The first spoken words were those of Buck Sergeant God, *"Wa ta hal?* It tastes just like bread and butter!" And, indeed it did! The cake tasted exactly like *Wonder Bread* and the frosting just like good ole' *Land O Lakes* butter. That's when I realized it takes more than a picture to understand what a birthday cake truly is when you've never tasted one before. I smiled a wide Champagne smile and said, "What the hell!" then improvised and saved the day by passing around a couple big jars of peanut butter and grape jelly. That event was forevermore to be known as the year we celebrated Joyce's twenty-second with a really fancy peanut butter and jelly birthday sandwich.

The party ended early and our guests departed, deciding to walk, as a group, down the hill to the Camp. No Slicky Boy in his right mind was going to take on twenty-something MPs even if a few of them were a bit tipsy. Joyce and I immediately turned in. The Bread & Butter Cake would be something we both would laugh about for years to come.

It was a good thing I didn't really like the way the Champagne tasted because, about four hours into our deep sleep, the field phone on the headboard rang. I fumbled with it for a moment until I wrested it from its snug, spring-loaded cradle. Trying not to sound too sleepy, I answered, "Lieutenant Royce." "Lieutenant, this is Sergeant Oden, Charlie Battery's been hit! North Korean infiltrators are crawling all over the place. I called Sergeant Zack before I called you and he's falling out the QRF *(Quick Reaction Force)*. A Jeep's on the way to pick you up right now."

Immediately, I was wide-awake and jumped out of bed. Every night I'd lay out my gear in exactly the same manner in case something like this happened and I got called out. Dressing in the dark was no problem for me at all. My BOQ roommates and I had developed this process into a fine art. To ensure I had a quick start, I always slept in my underwear. Joyce was now up on one elbow and in her; *I'm not really awake,* sleepy little voice asked, "What's going on?" "Charlie Battery's been hit and my Jeep's on the way up here right now." As she slowly processed this information in her semi-conscious state, I continued to get ready. Through practice, I'd gotten the emergency dressing part down to under two minutes. Joyce was now up and looking very worried. I zipped up the side zippers on my modified combat boots, grabbed my pistol belt with LBE *(Load Bearing Equipment)* and my M-14 rifle. A 20 round magazine was already locked and loaded in the magazine well.

Joyce was now looking very worried and grabbed my free hand in both of hers. It was a scene I'd seen in so many Saturday matinee cowboy movies, *"You jess don't worry your purdy little head missy. Them Injuns is no match for usins."* I wondered if Hop-A-Long Cassidy or Johnny Mack Brown had this same sick butterfly-feeling in the pit of their stomach when facing hostile Indians. I looked down at Joyce, gave her a tiny kiss on the mouth and said, "Don't worry sweetie; it's probably just some sort of drill or something, go back to bed." I kissed her again, gave her hand a squeeze, then pulled away. I could hear the first gear whine of my Jeep's transmission and low growl of its engine coming up our hill. "Lock the door behind me, Hon." *I think I did it; I think I got out of the house without her seeing just how scared shitless I really was.*

I'd had hours and hours of battle drill training, but this was the first time I was actually headed for a real live, no shit, gunfight and, honestly, I was scared as hell. As I stepped through the front gate I balanced myself at the top of those suicide stairs. I could clearly see Charlie Battery atop the mountain, across the valley, about fifteen miles away. A lot of enemy green tracers were lazily arching up the hill; too many to accurately count, but a bunch. Friendly red tracer rounds were raining down from Charley's perimeter fortifications. The red and green streaks of light intertwined in a freakish, spider-like tango. The wind was blowing any sound of gunfire away from me. An 81 millimeter mortar parachute flare popped over Charley adding faint light to the stairs below me, even from that great distance.

A blast of cool night air hit me and helped clear my head. I flew down those treacherous stairs to the street. SP4 Danny Cortez, my resident Hippie from San Diego. He had driven past the house and turned the topless Jeep around. He pulled up just as I hit the bottom step and I jumped in. The windshield had been removed and a few sandbags were strapped down on the hood. The two other MPs in the back of the Jeep were SP4 Hanlon and "The Spaniard." The Spaniard was the M-60 machine gunner and Hanlon, his assistant gunner. They were busily sorting ammo and readying the machinegun.

We met up with Sergeant Cavern, Sergeant Godblood and the other two gun Jeeps at the traffic circle. All twelve of us dismounted and got together by the side of the road in what must have looked like an improvised football huddle. I started, "Look, we don't know exactly what's going on up there, but we do know Charley's getting hit by Bad Guys. I was watching the green tracers and there's a bunch of em'. Since we don't have a good picture of what's going on up there, we're going to have to pretty much make this up as we go. Sergeant Cavern, you're the senior sergeant so I need you to take charge of one Fire Team made up from your Jeep crew plus Godblood and Winslow. Your call sign is *Yankee 2.* I'll take my Jeep crew plus Rickloff and Albinski out of Godblood's Jeep. That gives you two machinegun teams and I get the other one. My call sign is *Yankee 1* and you're *Yankee 2.*

We will un-ass the Jeeps at that big honkin' round boulder next to the road on the last turn before the straight shot up to Charley's main gate. You remember the one we practiced on last month?" Sergeant Cavern nodded. "That rock will also be our rally point, if we need one. I'll assess the situation when we get to the rock and then we'll do whatever we have to do. I'll get on the radio and let Charley Battery know we're on the way. Now listen up! I don't want no John Wayne BS from anybody! Let's just do this like we've practiced. Got it?" Eleven voices gave back a firm "GOT IT!" "Okay, let's mount up!" *Wow, did I really say "Mount up?"*

I got on the AN/VRC-12 radio and made contact with Charley's radio room. They couldn't add much to what we'd already heard. All they knew was they were being fired upon from what seemed like everywhere and their perimeter was being probed. They seemed to be holding their own okay but liked the idea of the *Cavalry* being on the way. The radioman sent a runner to get their commander, Major Lopez.

We were now racing across the valley towards trouble at 65 MPH. The M-60 machineguns were all loaded and ready to go. We had a total of three M-60s and nine M-14s with bipods and full automatic selector switches. So, in affect, we would be entering combat with a dozen full automatic, 7.65 millimeter weapons. That's a hell of a lot of firepower; especially, if we could somehow enter the fray, undetected, from the enemy's rear.

We turned off the main road, killed our headlights, except for the "Cat Eyes" and cautiously drove up the dirt road in "Blackout Drive". Every man was coiled, ready and straining eyes against the darkness. I could feel my throat tightening and was experiencing a really bad case of the "dry mouth".

Now I'm thinking to myself, *"Son of a bitch! I'm about to go into real combat for the very first time in my life and it isn't even fucking Vietnam! This shit's not supposed to happen! This isn't supposed to be a combat tour. I'm not even drawing fucking combat pay. I've got eleven good men with me. I'm supposed to be their leader. Their lives could hang on the decisions and actions I take here tonight. This isn't fucking fair! These guys are depending on me and, right now I feel like a total imposter. How the hell could I be in charge? If I hadn't been such a hotshot and decided to put together a real quick reaction force, we wouldn't even be up here right now."* When I came down on orders for Korea, my Mom said, "Thank God it isn't Vietnam!" Good thing Mom can't see me now!

I could now clearly hear gunfire off in the distance. Another flare popped and silhouetted a big round rock; I now had my bearings. I had all the training; in fact, Infantry OCS guys get more small-unit tactics training in six months than

West Pointers get in four years. The problem, in my mind, was my training had all been oriented towards jungle warfare and this was no fucking jungle. I knew *Fire & Maneuver* and how to do *Suppression Fire* but I don't remember ever getting *Cavalry Coming to the Rescue* training. My hasty plan was just to get close and hopefully get out of the Jeeps without getting our balls shot off in an ambush. Didn't seem like much of a plan right now. If we could just get out of the Jeeps and into some sort of a battle formation I've practiced a mess of times maybe everything would be okay. I knew what to do on the ground with eleven other guys with guns. I'd done infantry squad battle drills literally dozens of times.

To this day, and I don't know how, but somehow we got to that big-ass boulder, undetected, dismounted and broke our twelve-man squad into two fire teams. I could hear the sharp cracking sound of Chi-Com SKS carbines. I'd been trained in the *Crack & Thump* method at Benning and taught how to identify enemy from friendly gunfire and to figure out where it's coming from. Right now it was going away from us, so that was a good sound. I radioed Major Lopez and gave him our position and requested he not shoot in our general direction until we got set up and took cover. I was worried more about his men right now as a few odd red tracer rounds were bouncing down the hill in our general direction. I peaked around the left side of what we had now officially dubbed as *"Big-Ass Rock"*. *Star Cluster* rounds were popping open above Charley's perimeter. In that brilliant, burning, white phosphorous light, camouflage just doesn't work. I could clearly see a mess of attackers all over the rocks at the base of Charley's south perimeter about a hundred yards up the hill from our position. I couldn't count them, but from the ones I could see, I estimated there were twenty to maybe twenty-five of them. One was working hard on getting himself inside the perimeter wire. I froze as he threw something up hill. The *BOOM* was deafening and crap began to rain down on us. Thank God for steel helmets. Small rocks and pebbles were now pelting us from above.

We crouched together in a group. "Sergeant Cavern, you take the left and secure good cover for your men. Set up the machine guns and don't fire until my order, and for God's sake, keep them all quiet. I'm going to be on your right with my right flank up against Big-Ass Rock. Riflemen, I want everybody on full auto for the first three magazines. I want all weapons firing at max capacity when I give the order. We don't know how many bad guys are up there so I want them to think we're a whole fucking Infantry Company. Everybody, helmets on tight and pull your goggles down. Nobody wants a rock chip from a ricochet in the eye." I radioed Major Lopez and told him we were about to go into action and to hold the flares until I asked for them. I reminded everyone to pay attention to their flanks. In the darkness, Cavern and his men slid silently over to the left as my guys and I took up good firing positions to the right. All our LBE gear had been carefully taped down with black "100 MPH Tape" so it didn't rattle. We were very quiet.

Once in position, I radioed Major Lopez to pop three more flares and then keep them coming when he saw we had commenced firing. The flares lit up the night and twelve muzzles opened up full-auto to the rear of the unsuspecting enemy. The North Koreans, who were expertly shielding themselves from Charley's guns, showed momentary confusion before realizing something had gone horribly wrong behind them. They were now caught in a withering crossfire between Charley Battery up above and a large but unidentified unit of undermined size below them. These infiltrators were highly trained and disciplined commando types so they didn't just break and run. They were trying to exfiltrate and methodically fight their way out of this mess in a somewhat orderly manner. Problem was, we had eliminated a great deal of their available cover and concealment. If they tried to seek cover from us, they just exposed themselves to fire from Charley's guns on the high ground. For all intents and purposes they were just "ducks on the pond". Their choices seemed to be: Get shot by us, get shot by Charley or try to get the hell out of there. They chose the latter, returning fire in both directions as they slid over the rocks to our right. I ordered the riflemen to flip their selector switches to semi-automatic fire and search for individual targets. The machineguns continued to do what machineguns do. We must have hit a leader or two because the orderly retreat now became more like a mad scramble of fleeing solders. We just kept firing with all we had. Charley Battery rejoined the party, in earnest, and was raining down some serious lead on the Bad Guys, including 40 Mike-Mike Grenades. A whole world of shit was now being thrown at the retreating infiltrators.

Cavern's team was all charged up, and his men, witnessing the enemy's hasty retreat, started to break cover in pursuit. One or two of my guys started to follow them. I yelled over the radio to re-assemble back at Big-Ass Rock. My team got back to the Jeeps first and started setting up a hasty perimeter. I knew we'd been lucky in our first gunfight even if these kids didn't. I was also so mad I was shaking. It was still dark and I could now see more vehicle headlights coming up the hill. It was still a couple of hours before first light.

Cavern's guys were coming back to Big-Ass Rock talking, laughing and telling each other little vignettes. As everyone gathered around me I shouted, "Shut the fuck up! All of you, just shut the fuck up! Goddamnit!" The men were stunned into silence as I rarely ever yelled at them. "First, is anybody hit; anybody need medical attention?" No one spoke up so I continued, "What the fuck do you think you were doing up there?" The Spaniard chimed in, *"Well Suh Ah …"* "Shut up Jensen, that was rhetorical! Listen up; you don't move out to pursue the enemy except upon my command! You don't expose yourselves to enemy fire unless I tell you to; you got that? You guys were doing great until you decided to go on your own damned little hunting expedition. You started acting like a mob. No, I take that back, even a freaking' mob has a leader. You guys were going to ditch Sergeant Cavern and me and go running off across the rocks. Do you have any idea what's out there?" The Spaniard looked at Godbold and asked under his breath, *"Is thas retorkul too?"* Godbold nodded as I continued, "From my position I saw what I think was about twenty to twenty-five of them. Nobody here knows if that's all there is. They could still be a much superior force. These guys are fucking Commandos, goddamnit … Commandos; you got to respect that! We were extremely lucky tonight. We only drew *some* of their fire because we surprised the shit out of them and they got sandwiched between us and Charley Battery. I only saw two, maybe three of em' fall so right now we don't really know how many went down out there killed or wounded … and we won't know until morning because I ain't stupid enough to try and follow them in the dark. For all we know they may have another squad or more somewhere out there as back-up just waiting in ambush if we pursue. Don't any of you ever, ever break a battle formation on me again, you got that?" "Yes Sir!" "Just remember, your buddy on you left and right are betting their lives that you'll hold your place in formation and do your job. Sorry I blew up, but goddamnit, I don't want to be sending anybody's Mom, wife or girlfriend one of those fucking letters because one of you went and got yourself killed doing something stupid. Do it like we've trained; follow commands and we all stand a better chance of nobody going out of here in a body-bag. Everybody got that?" This time there was a loud and more organized, *"Yes Sir!"* "Okay, everybody check your weapons, make sure they're fully loaded and on safe. We're setting up a formal perimeter around this rock for the night. Everybody find good cover. We're gonna' hunker down here and sit tight until daybreak. Seems like there's a lot of friendly company coming up the hill now anyway. Radioman … let Major Lopez know we're all okay; give him our position and tell him we're buttoning up for the rest of the night. Sergeant Cavern, you and your fire team take the south side of the rock. Me and my guys will take the north side. Oh, and Sergeant Cavern, I want you to put out one LP (Listening Post) to the east of us about fifty yards out. Reload any empty magazines from the ammo in the Jeeps and everybody grab a box of C-rations. One last thing … nobody sleeps! I want all eyes looking for movement in those rocks"

Morning sort of came. We were greeted by one of those gray, misty, foggy, cool, mountain mornings. During the night about ten vehicles had gone past us and through Charley Battery's main gate. Major Lopez called us on the radio and together we decided now would be a good time to comb the area outside Charley's perimeter, sort of an aftermath clean up operation. The Major came down the hill with about ten of his men. I gave a short briefing to the gathered troops about not moving any bodies they found and warned them about booby-traps. The North Koreans were famous for their booby-traps. "No one is to move anything; weapons, equipment or bodies. Call the Major or me." I'm not so sure Major Lopez liked me taking charge but he nodded in agreement anyway. "Okay, let's all stay on line, and call out if you find something. Everybody here has his weapon; now's the time to make sure you've got a round chambered and your weapon's on safe. If we make contact with the enemy, take immediate cover and return fire. The Major or I will give further orders if a serious gunfight breaks out. Everybody be careful out there."

We spaced out the troops about ten feet apart in a long skirmish line and started moving from the road in an easterly direction. The biggest thing I remember was there were pockmarks everywhere from rounds bouncing around the rocks. I thought, *"How the hell could anything have lived through this?"* There were little flare parachutes lying all over the place too. We then found the first enemy body; the left hand was almost severed by direct 7.62 round hit to the wrist. He was lying in a disjointed heap like he'd been hit by a semi-truck, doing a 100 MPH. I suspected he was the first one I saw fall from up above, after being hit. From his crushed, bloody body I figured he was killed more by the sixty foot fall to the rocks below rather than by gunfire. Somebody else found his splintered SKS assault rifle some distance away.

We found another body tangled in the perimeter's concertina wire. This must have been the guy who threw the satchel charge that caused the big blast. His body was riddled. I figured one of our M-60s must have locked on and blew the shit out him. There was another guy who actually made it inside the wire to the base of one of Charley's perimeter bunkers. He had a single bullet hole through the head just below his left ear. He also had an unexploded satchel charge with him and about a dozen hand grenades. I backed everyone off and asked a runner to get to a radio and call Page for EOD (Explosive Ordnance Demolition) support.

After expending, what must have been, over 3,000 rounds from just us, and not counting the ton of stuff Charley must have used up, this was it? Three dead, bad guys, that's all? (*In later years it would always amaze me at how many rounds could be fired and yet nobody gets hit.*)

There was no joy or excitement in the kill. My troops would look in silence at the dead and what they had done. For all of us, except Sergeant Cavern, this was our first firefight. Danny Cortez even up-chucked buttery birthday cake and champagne after seeing his first dead body.

Over time, it slowly sinks in to all soldiers; at the end of the day, this is just two governments sending their kids out to kill each other. Each kid probably thinks his government is in the right, but somehow that doesn't matter much when you're looking at the dead. When you reduce it to its basics, they're all just somebody's dead kids. Soldiers mostly just do what they're told to do. Today, we did it better than they did; tomorrow, it might be different.

We'd only been involved in our search for less than half an hour when a whole shit-load of ROK troops showed up, five *Duce-and-a-half's* (Two and half ton trucks) full. There must have been over a hundred of them from the ROK base near the Dam. The ROK Major in charge spoke some English. He came over to Major Lopez and myself and just took over. "My name, Major Kim. We know what happen. We take *ober* now. We now hunt and kill infiltrator, okay? Bye, bye!" With that, there were now ROKs crawling all over the place just grabbing everything in sight and loading it onto their trucks. Major Lopez and I just looked at each other, shrugged and smiled at each other and both said, in unison, "Bye, bye!" The three dead infiltrators we found were unceremoniously tossed in the back of a ROK *Duce* to be taken somewhere.

Now that it was light, we were becoming more popular by the minute. The Stupid Colonel Mixon and the Gorilla showed up. Mixon immediately started taking credit for our involvement. Officials from the city of Chunchon and Kang Wan Do also showed up along with the KNP and reps from the local newspaper. The Stupid Colonel Mixon latched on to them and I could hear the words, "Good thing I insisted on putting this Quick Reaction Force together. I knew we would be needing them soon." I just kept my mouth shut and walked away. The local Chunchon newspaper people were now hanging on Mixon's every word as he thanked the Chunchon Mayor for his support of the U.S. troops at Camp Page.

Black CIC (Korean Counter Intelligence Corps) Jeeps started arriving and along with them, my "old friend" Prescott Smith and one of his MI flunkies. Smith came up and slapped me on the back and actually said, "Good show old man; jolly good show! I was listening to your radio communications and keeping closely abreast of your adventures throughout the evening. Good show!" He then scurried off after his Korean CIC buddies, with his toady close behind. There was still sporadic gunfire coming from quite a distance away.

Major Lopez walked down to Big-Ass Rock where we were cleaning up and trying to get our act back together. Before I could sort myself out, he saluted me first. I quickly returned it. I knew his saluting a junior officer first was his way of showing respect for what we had done last night. I tried to make light of it but could feel myself blushing with pride at his personal display of recognition. He thanked us all, saluted and walked back up the hill. Who cares what twist the Stupid Colonel Mixon was putting on it? This Major knows what really happened and so did the men of Charley Battery and that's enough. It's just that I was so damned proud of my guys. I'd heard all the stories about how green troops often freeze up in combat situations. After the firefight, I'd checked everyone of my guys out to ensure they all had what they needed and that nobody was injured. However, they all did need something; they all needed ammo, lots of ammo. My guys, to the man, had brought holy hell on those poor bastards last night.

Just then, there was commotion in the rocks some distance away to the east. ROK Army medics and some of the CIC guys were moving towards us as fast as they could negotiate this rough, uneven battlefield. There appeared to be much excitement. A ROK ambulance was now nearing our position on the road. There was a ROK soldier strapped down on a stretcher. They all passed by us, huffing and puffing, and on to the ambulance. I could see that a wounded soldier was swathed in blood and looked all but dead. The Ambulance picked up the wounded man, made a u-turn, and then raced back down the hill.

I turned, and the last ones coming over the rocks were Prescott Smith and his flunky. They were completely out of breath by the time they got to our location. I grabbed Prescott's arm and asked, "Did the ROKs get the son-of-a-bitch who shot that soldier?" Gasping between sentences, Prescott replied, "That's not one of ours; that's a North Korean imposter masquerading as ROK Army. He had a complete ROK uniform right down to the correct shoulder patches. He's barely alive and we're going to see if we can keep him that way." I responded, "I thought you couldn't capture those guys, that they kill themselves before they ever let themselves be captured." Gasping again, "Yes, that's true, but this one was too weak to pull the pin on his grenade. He passed out just as the ROKs were about to dispatch him. I intervened and stopped him from being summarily executed. I've got to go, Lieutenant Royce. This is big; this is really big! I'm responsible for finally capturing one alive! You should be congratulating me on my good fortune." As Prescott scurried away towards his Jeep, I thought to myself, *"Yeah, and I'll bet that's just how it goes into your report: Me, me, me … what a pain in the ass."*

We loaded up and started back down the mountain towards Page. We did it! After all that training, it actually fucking worked! I was silently enjoying myself and feeling a huge amount of pride in the way my guys acquitted themselves. I was damned proud of each and every one of them. We'd engaged a hardened enemy, a superior force, surprised them, took them under fire and successfully met our objective of stopping their attack on C-Battery. It was a good day to be an American soldier. Granted, we actually *got the drop on them* and *bushwhacked* the sneaky bastards from behind; but they did return fire, even if it was during a hasty retreat. Granted, Charley Battery's boys dumped a bunch of lead down on them too, plus kept the place lit up for us with flares so we could see. Crap! Why can't I stop over-analyzing everything? A win's a win! In the end, we won the gunfight. The enemy retired from the field of battle in disarray and we were lucky. We came away with just cuts, scratches, bumps and bruises from banging around in those damned rocks. *The Calvary was now headed back to the fort—que theme music, fade to black and roll movie credits.*

Just before we started the ride home, I was told there were also multiple blood trails leading away from the area. This indicated we had wounded several more of them during the firefight.

I radioed in to the MP Desk, "Yankee Base, this is Yankee-1; we're going to stop by the 'Alternate CP (Command Post—our code name for my house) on the way back to let the 'Boss' know all's okay before we come in. Don't want the Boss to worry … over." The radio crackled and it was Joyce's voice. "Yankee-1, this *is* the Boss. No need; I'm at the MP Station along with about half the base—over! A big grin crossed my face, "Yankee Base this is Yankee-1, Roger that; we're on our way—out."

About two miles from the Main Gate, I ordered an "Administrative Halt". We lined up the Jeeps, locked down the M-60s on their pedestal mounts and squared away all the equipment. If there was going to be any sort of a "Welcome Home Committee" we wanted to look like proper warriors. Helmets at a jaunty angle, chin straps on tight, uniforms squared away, goggles up and all weapons on "Safe".

Ten minutes later we rolled through the Camp's Main Gate with every man *sitting tall in the saddle*. We looked pretty damned good for a bunch that'd been up all night. As we rolled in, there must have been close to 200 people hanging around the gate and MP Station to greet us. The cooks, the library and craft shop ladies, doctors and nurses and just about everybody who could be there was there. We pulled through the gate, made a sharp left hand turn and rolled to a stop by the PMO sign. We were immediately engulfed by a throng of cheering and clapping well-wishers crowding around the three gun Jeeps. It was one of life's unforgettable moments. When the Army gets to do what the Army's trained to do, and it's successful, every soldier wants to celebrate it. That's just the way the Army is!

I heard a voice call out, "Buck Sergeant God, how was it?" Godblood replied, "This ain't no shit man; let me tell you what happened …" I smiled to myself as he started his tale of how he had single-handedly defeated the whole damned North Korean Army. I steadied myself with one hand on the M-60 and stood up on the seat scanning the faces in the crowd for Joyce. I couldn't see her anywhere. All I saw was First Sergeant Zack, head and shoulders above the crowd, moving towards my Jeep. He came up next to me and popped a salute. Over the noise, I yelled, "Hey Top, you seen Joyce?" Zack grinned, "Here she is Sir, and she's been here all night monitoring the radio … and, with all due respect, Sir, she's been a royal pain in the ass." I hadn't noticed it, but in Sergeant Zack's considerable wake, Joyce had been right behind him hanging onto his gun belt. I jumped down and Joyce threw her arms around my neck and kissed me hard. She had tears in her eyes. "I was so worried about you; I came down here where I could hear what was going on." She started to kiss me again and I said, "Not in front of the men, Hon; I'm in uniform and under arms." With First Sergeant Zack plowing the way for us, and with Joyce in front of me, we made our way into the MP Station. Hands kept patting me on the back as we passed through the crowd. I don't remember any of the words being said; I just knew they were all words of praise and well wishes. I was just so damned glad to be with Joyce, hers was the only voice I cared to hear.

Inside the MP Station there were more cheers. Joyce and I made our way past the MP Desk towards my office. As we passed by the desk, Sergeant Oden handed me down an ice-cold bottle of *Coke*. I stopped and silently raised it towards him in a gesture of thanks, than upended it and drained the whole bottle before lowering it. The ice-cold, sweet, familiar taste felt really good going down. It would have made a great *Coke* commercial.

Joyce and I made it to my office where I closed the door and gave her a deep, long kiss and a big hug. It was a few seconds before I realized I was holding her so firmly her feet weren't even touching the floor.

My very-own private nurse then stripped off most of my uniform and started checking me all over to ensure nothing was damaged. Once satisfied that just Band-Aids and mercurochrome would fix everything, she hugged me hard again as tears streamed down her cheeks. She then opened her medical bag and expertly started attending to my various cuts and scrapes.

She told me, after the Jeep picked me up; she got dressed and went out on our balcony and actually watched the light show across the valley. "I could see the red and green tracers and the flares and I remember you telling me 'green' was the bad guys. When the second barrage of red tracers started up from below the green, I knew you and the guys were there. When you opened up, there was so much red I couldn't believe it. Then I saw a lot of the green shift and start coming your way. That's when I got scared, finished getting dressed, and ran down the hill to the MP Station. I spent the rest of the night drinking coffee with Sergeant Oden and listening to the radio at the MP Desk. Did you know he and his wife have a baby boy? She was there too. She's so pretty and so nice! She brought us all lots of hot food but my stomach was too upset to eat." Joyce was now talking a, coffee-induced, mile-a-minute. I had to do something to slow her down, so I kissed her again. This only worked momentarily. The second our lips parted, I heard, "Then right after Mrs. Oden left, it came over the radio that the North Koreans were on the run and you guys were all okay. I went in the ladies room, had a little cry and said a little prayer thanking God you and the guys were all alright." We were sitting next to each other on my desk and I was holding each of her hands in mine. I looked at that beautiful but tired face, smiled and told her, "We're all okay!"

It was a little after eight in the morning and I said, "I'm starved, let's go find some breakfast." We started walking towards my BOQ room so I could change out of my dirty fatigues. Joyce was now a well-known and welcome visitor in the BOQ complex. Ab was on leave visiting his wife and folks in Alabama and the others were out and about already. Joyce flopped down on my bed while I stripped off my filthy uniform for a quick shower down the hall. "Don't fall asleep on me now." With her hands behind her head on my pillow she said, "No chance, if you knew how much coffee I have inside me you'd know that's impossible." I picked up my towel and soap and started out the door. Joyce's voice stopped me and I turned to look at her. "You know, Herb, this is all pretty weird. The phone rings and you get up in the middle of the night and race off to war. I then stand on my balcony and actually watch my husband in combat. Then you come back in the morning and I'm waiting for you. I easily could have said, 'How was the war today Honey?' It was just like any wife back in the world could have asked her husband, 'How was your day at the office?' Now you have to admit, I'll bet there's just about nobody who's having a first year of marriage like ours!" I replied as I closed the door, "No bet."

When I came back, just a few minutes later, I was squeaky clean but poor Joyce finally had her adrenaline crash and was out like a light. I pulled an OD Army blanket over her shoulders and smiled down at that wonderful face I was so in love with. All of a sudden my whole body felt like lead. I crashed in Ab's bunk and passed out from both mental and physical exhaustion.

30

Hooker Poker

We may have been in an exotic setting but some parts of our new life together were just as mundane as any other newlyweds. We both had to get up and perform our morning, get ready for work, rituals. I was almost always first to rise but it was actually easier for me. I got up at 0500, threw on yesterday's uniform and jumped into a waiting jeep at 0515 for a ride down to the PMO. I'd go to my BOQ room and get ready for morning PT (Physical Training) along with the rest of the Camp. After a sweaty hour of exercise including a run around the perimeter I'd take a hot shower, shave, put on the fresh uniform and shined boots Mr. Ahn had laid out for me, then hit the Officers' Mess for breakfast. By 0700 I'd already be at work.

In comparison, poor Joyce had to rough it. She would rise at about seven. The house would be warm when it needed to be because I would attend to the Cannon Heater before leaving for the day. I would also execute the morning flush and refill the toilet tank on the wall before my departure. That's about all I could do to ease her morning. When it wasn't possible for Joyce to grab a shower down at the camp, just like in the old western movies, Joyce would heat water on our little Kimchi stove in the kitchen. She would also collect any hot humidifier water leftover in the can atop the Cannon Heater. With just these meager warm liquid resources she would always emerge for work at the clinic at 0845 looking like she had a suite at the *Plaza Hotel*. Camp showers were preferable but Joyce seemed to cope well when she had to bathe at home using our primitive facilities.

I had asked Mr. Ahn if he would be willing, for a price, to also take care of Joyce's clothes cleaning needs. He said he would be glad to but wanted no extra money. In the end, he lost that battle and was paid an additional eight dollars, plus two dollar tip, for his services. I would carry her laundry back and forth, usually after dark. So, with Mr. Ahn's laundry assistance and her ever increasing visits to the hot showers down at the gym, Joyce, for a "clean freak", was able to stay relatively happy.

The one thing I could not supply for Joyce was female companionship. Lucy Librarian was from a different era, and other than books, the two had very little in common. Fat Pat, the Craft Shop Girl, was too busy servicing half the Camp and really took offense at Joyce's presence anyway. She wanted all the horny GI's to forget that girls like Joyce even existed. To a lot of young solders, after a few months in Korea and a few beers, Pat looked pretty damned good to them; plus, rumors were, she fucked like a mink. None of her dates ever went home disappointed. As for the Nurse Twins, I had no idea what they had going on, but in my ignorance of all things lesbian, I didn't think it was a good idea for the three of them to hang out together in case lesbianism was some sort of a virus or something. There were frequent times when my job required I work late or even stay overnight at the Camp. It sure would be nice if she had a girlfriend to go shopping and do all that other "girlie" stuff with.

I guess, in passing, I must have mentioned some of this to Kuska. He evidently was dating a legal secretary from somewhere downtown who he said spoke English. Although I liked the idea, I guess I wanted to check out the young lady before I agreed. So, we set up a meeting for the next week where I could meet this *Pack, Jin Hee* person. I figured we'd go out for lunch together. Neither of us would push the idea of the two spending time together until I gave Kuska the high sign. That *was* the plan.

My prudish plan short-circuited when I was informed of what Joyce was doing during her off-time while I was working. While shopping, Joyce had met some Korean girls around her age who all spoke at least some English. They started meeting for lunch and they had been teaching Joyce some card game it seemed every Korean woman played. When Joyce wasn't scheduled to work at the hospital, she'd occasionally spend her afternoons drinking a little Korean rice wine, eating Kimchi and playing cards with some of the young ladies she'd met in the market. All this was fine with me but that was before all the details came to my attention.

Kuska and Oden appeared in my office doorway. Looking worried, Sergeant Oden stated, "Sir, during our patrol through the Off-Limits areas today we came upon something we think you should be aware of. Seems the Spaniard and one of the KATUSAs, Corporal Lee, came across your wife drinking and playing cards with … with a bunch of Hookers, Sir." Oden winced when he said the word "Hookers". He was expecting a reaction from me. Other than my stunned expression I displayed none, so he continued. "Madam Kim was also there, talking to her." Once again he winced. I turned to Kuska and asked, "You and this

Jin Hee person free for dinner tonight? I got to find Joyce a girlfriend fast, and it sure as hell ain't gonna' be the Dragon Lady!"

I left the office shortly after this disturbing news and headed straight home. Joyce was already there in the pantry seeing if she could rustle up some dinner-magic from our collection of commissary canned goods and some veggies she picked up in the market. She spoke before I did and I was glad I'd kept my flapping mouth shut for a change.

"Hi, Hon, you're home early; that's good because you can save me tonight by taking us out to dinner." While still talking, she started placing the cans back on the shelf.

"Boy did I have an interesting day! Oh, and by the way, I met your so-called Dragon Lady and another rather interesting woman by the name of Patty. Both introduced themselves to me and said they had met you shortly after your arrival. Patty told me you're a 'very *good* man.' Mind explaining that to me, in detail, Lover Boy?"

"I told you about Patty, the Dragon Lady and the American house."

"Yes you did, but you didn't tell me how lovely these women were."

"One's a hooker and the other's a madam; what more is there to tell?"

"Well, for one thing, you could have told me she owns the house we live in!"

"What?"

"She owns this house! It's our landlord's house; he borrowed the money from 'The. Pig Doctor' and 'MD Piggy' borrowed the money from Madam Kim. So, the Dragon Lady actually holds the deed to our house."

"No shit?"

"No shit Dick Tracy! So, whether you like it or not, we do have, at least, a business relationship with 'The Chunchon Madam'."

"Okay, so what were you doing in the off-limits area?"

"Oh, so you heard about that too. I was having lunch and playing cards with a bunch of Korean girls, just like I've been doing for the last several days when I've been off."

"I'll bet you didn't know those girls were hookers did you?"

"I suspected as much, but after today, I knew it for sure! I'm also guessing Hookers are just about the only Korean women in this town who speak a substantial amount of English! Today was also my first lunch and card game in your evil Off-Limits area, and that's where I met Madam Kim."

Getting all huffy, I replied, "Well I don't think it's proper for the wife of the 5th US Missile Command Provost Marshal to be in the Off-Limits area!"

"Oh, and I suppose renting a house from the 'Chunchon Madam' is?"

"Look, I'm not trying to start an argument or anything; I just think the Off-Limits areas are just too dangerous."

"Of course they are, and that's why Madam Kim had two of her bodyguards watching over us."

"Oh Shit! This is just keeps getting better and better all the time doesn't it?"

"Don't worry mister 'Straight Arrow' it's not going to happen again!"

"It's not?"

"Of course it's not; I was just having fun with a bunch of girls about my age who I could actually talk to. When I met the Dragon Lady and found out who they all really were I knew these get-togethers would have to come to a screeching halt. I'm not going to do anything to compromise you or your job you dummy! So rather than panic and make a big scene, I decided just to enjoy my one day in your forbidden Off-Limits Area. Besides, I'm allowed in there! The signs say 'No *American* Military Personnel'. In case you forgot, I'm neither American nor military!"

"Well, go get ready; we're going out to dinner tonight with another couple, Kuska and his English-speaking, non-hooker type, girlfriend, Jin Hee. I hope you're not too disappointed, but we'll be dining at an *on-limits* establishment this evening, and sorry, but Jin Hee ain't no hooker; she's a legal secretary."

Joyce laughed, "Okay, okay, I broke the code. Anytime I want to go out for dinner, all I have to do is threaten to go back to hanging out with the hookers!"

"Okay, wise-ass, make fun of me all you want, but those places are put off limits for a reason. They're unsafe and crawling with disease." Joyce disappeared to dress and I went out to our teeny-tiny fridge for something that mixes with rum.

Kuska picked a great place for dinner. It was the restaurant on the top floor of the tallest building in Chunchon, all seven stories of it. Even from just seven floors up, it had a commanding view of the city. It was right on the traffic circle and, from our window seats, we could see all the way to the river beyond the Camp. We even walked up onto the rooftop, outside dining area, to see what the view was like. For the 4th of April it was still a little too chilly but would be a great place to come and eat if summer ever arrived.

As it turned out, Jin Hee was just lovely, funny and she spoke nearly perfect English. She was one inch taller than Joyce and made jokes about being the taller of the two. Her nose was more like a small western one and it gave her a different look. It was obvious she was of mixed blood but the combination was the best of both east and west. The really great part of it all was that Jin Hee and Joyce really hit it off. Before the evening was over the two of them had already arranged a shopping trip together to Seoul and a lunch date at a seafood place Jin Hee knew down by the river and described as "fresh and excellent".

Over the next few weeks, Joyce and Jin Hee would bond their friendship. In doing so, and with no particular design in mind, it also brought Kuska and I socially and professionally closer. In 1968, Army Officers were still not supposed to *fraternize* with Enlisted. I'm pretty sure the original intention of this rule was to keep the enlisted men from finding out what *"Assholes"* and idiots many of their officers really were. Lieutenant Prescott Smith immediately comes to mind.

The Friday, 5 April edition of *Stars & Stripes* bore very disturbing news. Dr. Martin Luther King Jr. had been assassinated by some redneck asshole, with a Russian sniper rifle, in front of the Lorraine Motel in Memphis. I felt hugely sad and unsettled because I admired this man's work and believed he held the key to peacefully ending this segregation mess back home. Instead, riots were breaking out in D.C., Newark, Detroit, Kansas City, Baltimore, Chicago and Boston. I feared there would be a lot more racial unrest and maybe even some sort of civil war. That never came to pass but I think we may have come pretty close in some parts of the country.

That night, with rioting going on back in the U.S., Colonel Weatherspoon and the Stupid Lieutenant Colonel Mixon were worried about what might happen with our black soldiers. So, I was ordered to check out what the mood was down at the "Continental." The Continental was the one club out of the six which was almost, exclusively frequented by black soldiers. I don't think it was ever planned that way; because the U.S. Army, even back in '68, didn't put up with any form of racial discrimination. Maybe it was the great Motown music; maybe it was just the number of black soldiers who frequented the place, or maybe it just was what it really was, a place where black soldiers could go and be in the one spot in Chunchon where they were in the majority. For the most part, white soldiers were not made to feel unwelcome and, in fact, a few made the Continental their club of choice and no one ever bothered them. But no matter how you wanted to explain it, the Continental was a black club.

We found the mood inside was like a wake, and maybe that's exactly what it was supposed to be. There were a lot of deep conversations concerning where the equality movement would go from here and several feared it would result in bloodshed instead of Dr. King's non-violent approach. All the MPs went out of their way that night to *cut some slack* for the black soldiers who might have had too much to drink. It seems the Army's system where all races live, eat, sleep, work and play together had a calming effect during this tense time. It wasn't the Army most worried about; they were concerned about what was going on back home. In a strange way, I think all of us, black or white, were glad to be in Korea that night. We were spared direct contact with the terrible political and social events happening back in our homeland.

The news coming out of Vietnam wasn't much better either. On the 11th, Defense Secretary Clark Clifford announced the call-up of an additional 24,500 reservists and increased the troop ceiling in Vietnam to an all time high of 549,500 soldiers. With less than one tenth that number in Korea, it's no wonder my Mom wrote, saying she never hears any news coming out of Korea other than the Pueblo crew is still imprisoned up North and negotiations for their release continued but, even that story was now relegated to about page five or six.

31

The Last Straw

I arrived in Korea in mid-November and it was now Friday the 26th of April and I'd actually been in-country for over five months. To pass the time, about my third week in country, I got involved with the Camp Page Pistol Team. A short time ago, we competed in the 8th Army Pistol Matches and did quite well, and tonight we were to receive our trophies … for the second time.

I walked into the O Club and looked up at the long procession of Brass Plates hanging high on the walls of the bar. As was my ritual, I took a long moment glancing up at those highly polished brass plates with the blue, red and yellow replicas of the 5th USMC shoulder patch and counted them. There mine was, "LT ROYCE", but it now had fifty-one other plates following it around the room. This meant I was closing in on the halfway point of my thirteen-month year in this, so called, Land of the Morning Calm. Despite Colonel Weatherspoon *"throwing chairs on my dance floor"* every time I turned around, I was still here and like old *Friedrich Nietzsche* once said, "What doesn't kill you makes you stronger." I somehow seemed to be surviving and maybe even getting a little tougher and harder every day. The Screaming Eagle was no longer this person to be feared. My relationship with my Colonel was like a fencing match. Almost daily, I had to come up with new ways of fending him off. I didn't exactly hate it here anymore but, then again, I wouldn't mind if Joyce and I were transferred to Hawaii either. Realistically, I knew I had to complete my thirteen-month tour of duty just like everybody else. With my brass plate about half way around the bar, I felt the worse just had to be behind me now.

I brushed those troublesome thoughts from my mind and ordered my usual Cuba Libra. This was going to be a special night for me. Recently, we competed in the annual 8th Army Pistol Championships and I had played a principal part in that feat. Our little Camp Page team had placed second overall in competition with all U.S. Army pistol teams in Korea. I, personally, had come in with the top individual score on our team. There were presentations at the matches but the 8th

Army Commanding General thought it would be appropriate for local commanders to re-present the trophies at appropriate, local ceremonies, in front of our own commands and fellow soldiers. So, the trophies were taken back from us, packed up and sent to our respective commanders. Colonel Weatherspoon had no choice; a four-star general had told him he had to make the presentations; that meant he had to hand me an award and be pleasant in front of God and everybody. He decided to award the trophies at our monthly Hail & Farewell dinner in the Officers' Club. This also meant he was going to have to make two presentations, shake my hand twice, and make two sets of remarks. I couldn't wait. Maybe it was my second drink but I was dying to see how this man, who literally hated my guts, was going to pull this off.

My Dad had been a big time pistol shooter as far back as I could remember. He'd been on several "All Navy" teams throughout his thirty-year career. He was a true expert with the .22, .38 and, in particular, the .45 caliber pistol. On top of that, he'd won dozens of the difficult three-gun, aggregate competitions. I remember him going to the "National Matches" at Camp Perry Ohio just about every year when I was a kid. In addition, he was also a master gunsmith and even hand-loaded his own match and hunting ammunition. At one point in his career, he was ranked as high as the number two, best shooter in the whole U.S. Navy. There was always this guy named *Gunner Seavers* who nobody could ever beat.

I grew up living with and learning my way around guns; as a kid it was just a part of my childhood experience. My Dad had tons of shooting medals and trophies piled up all over the house. There were so many it became an inside family joke. He even built a room in the basement because Mom complained so much about the tacky, trophy clutter.

Dad would even take me to the North Kingstown town dump at night to shoot rats. He said it would sharpen my eye and help me develop reflexive shooting instincts. This meant I was supposed to get better at hitting moving targets. I actually did get quite good at it. I remember one night, while he directed a spotlight, I shot twenty-two scampering rats in a row with my Dad's *High Standard* National Match 22 before I finally missed one. My Dad taught me a lot about both pistol and rifle shooting at an early age. I continued shooting both types of weapons throughout my life. I liked rifle shooting but I loved shooting pistols. I guess it was all those old cowboy matinee movies. I wasn't passionate about it like he was, but I really liked it and I pretty much always knew what to do with a pistol.

My fighter pilot Dad was this strange guy who was hard for me to get close to. He was gone a lot; off to far away places killing foreigners stupid enough to go up against him when he was in the cockpit of a Navy fighter plane. We never had one of those classic Hollywood movie father and son relationships; but he showed affection in other ways. He was continuously worried about the Army giving me some old, worn out piece of crap .45 out of the arms room, then expecting me to go to war with it. When he was still living, and I got posted to a new assignment, he would always ask, "What kind of sidearm they got assigned to you?" I don't know why he asked, we MPs always carried a Model 1911 .45 semi-automatic pistol. A small box wrapped in brown paper and sealed with silver duct tape would always show up in the mail shortly after my arrival at each of my new postings. The box always contained a jewel-like, adjustable trigger, a firing mechanism and a chrome-plated barrel, with matching, hand lapped, barrel bushing. These were precision, replacement parts for my issued weapon. Included would be some special gun grease, a new recoil spring and a recoil-reducing invention of his he called a "Mouse Trap". Intricate, hand-printed instructions were always included. My Dad was never a demonstrative person. But that was okay, because I figured it out a long time ago; those little boxes of bright, finely machined gun parts were his way of telling me he loved me and was trying to protect me from harm. I always knew whoever might engage me in a close range gunfight was always going to have a really shitty weapon in comparison to mine.

When I wrote Dad that I was on the Camp Page pistol team and we were going to compete in the 8th Army pistol matches, he got all excited and sent a whole box full of handmade, precision parts for our .45s plus a course of training instructions for the team. I installed all the gun parts in the team's pistols and after a couple months training and thousands of rounds fired down range, the little Camp Page team was ready to take on the big boys from the mighty 2nd and 7th Infantry Divisions. It was really quite comical because the poor bastards never saw us coming. We ambushed most of the big teams at the matches before anyone caught on that we were for real. We came within a lousy two points of winning the Big 8th Army Team Trophy but Second Place was quite a feat, nonetheless. That's because the Second and the Seventh literally had thousands of soldiers to choose a pistol team from.

The dinner part of the evening was now over and the presentations were about to start. Captain Joe Bartlett was ranking man and team captain for our four-man crew. I was both team trainer and one of the shooters. The Colonel called Joe up front and started in by saying nice things about Joe's leadership and the team's prowess, as a whole. Joe was this rawboned, incredibly strong ole redheaded, Kentucky, country boy who was now about half-lit. He just stepped in and interrupted the "Old Man." "This ain't all about me, Colonel." He motioned to the three of us seated at one of the front tables. "Ya'll come up here with me and the Colonel." To a room full of applauding fellow officers, we all proudly strutted up front and gathered off Joe's left shoulder. I could feel the heat of pride and a little embarrassment turning my cheeks and the back of my neck pink. On Joe's right, the Colonel continued to try and talk about team's effort. Joe, as I said, had had a few drinks and was having none of it. He reached over to his left and put me in a headlock and pulled me in close to him. I was off balance and clumsily complied. Joe grabbed the microphone with his right hand and started in, "Colonel, we all shot real good but we wouldn't of had no damned winning team if it weren't for Herb Royce right here! He trained us; he worked on our guns; he taught us lots of inside competition stuff and he's the best damned pistol-shooter anybody on our team's ever seen! Hell, he's the best damned shooter in Korea as far as I'm concerned and he's getting a trophy right here tonight to prove it." Every officer in the room burst into applause and started hooting. Even the Colonel, obviously irritated, reluctantly put his hands together. The Colonel then handed Joe the 8th Army Second Place Trophy. More applause came as Joe handed the trophy to me and all four of us held it high above our heads to the delight of the room and the camp photographer.

Things started settling down as we four wound our way back to our table. The Colonel then picked up the First Place Individual Trophy and looked at it for a long moment. It was one of those really big and gaudy monstrosities. The room fell silent. Weatherspoon took a long pull on his drink then picked up his cigarette and started in. "Well every event like this has to have someone who comes in first." He paused for a few puffs. "Lieutenant Royce was lucky enough to be that person this year." Again, there was great commotion and standing applause from the room, but instead of being invited up front to accept the trophy and saying a few words, Weatherspoon walked slowly towards our table and set the trophy down in front of me. I, of course, stood up as he approached our table; he briefly shook my hand, gave me a disgusted look and said, "Congratulations Lieutenant". As we shook hands he locked eyeballs with me and I stared unblinkingly right back at him. I could feel his hatred for me and the heat behind those eyes. Everyone applauded again but this time in a more subdued manner as they looked around at each other searching for some sort of explanation at to what was going on. The Colonel got back to the microphone, declared the ceremony over and departed for the bar.

Joe turned to me and said, "Damn Herb! That old SOB really does hate your guts!" With disappointment in my voice I said, "Yeah, I know!" I picked up my trophy, let out an audible sigh and walked back to my room. This one ended early, but most Hail & Farewells usually went late; so, Joyce had invited Jin Hee to a girl's night sleepover up at the house while I was going to bunk in my room on base. Back in the room, I shot the breeze with Paul about the latest Gook DMZ violations in the 2nd ID (Infantry Division) area. We also listened to his new Neil Diamond album for a while, then called it quits, and turned in around midnight. I was exhausted, and still fuming at how the Colonel had pissed all over what should have been a great night for me. I wanted to tell everybody about how hard the team worked and about some of the funny things that happened at the matches, but most of all I wanted to tell them about my Dad. Instead, I just passed out right away in my bunk.

All of a sudden, there was this reddish glow and muffled sounds that made no sense to me at all. For a few seconds I thought I was still asleep. When your eyes are closed and its dark, shouldn't the insides of your eyelids look black to you? When I finally realized I was actually awake, and popped my eyes open, I was staring into the glare of a very bright flashlight aimed right at my face. "Sir, *Sir*, they need you down at the PMO ASAP." Finally, I became aware it was Spec. 4 Cortez shaking my arm and speaking to me. "Okay, okay, I'm coming; just get that damned light out of my face!" It took me a couple of minutes but I threw myself together and followed Cortez and his light beam down the dark corridor.

When we made it out into the night, the perimeter lights somehow seemed brighter than usual. Cortez led me to a section of the fence about a hundred yards down from the Main Gate. There was another MP standing in the middle of the perimeter road with his arms folded looking at something high up on the fence and talking to it. Two KATUSA security guards were nervously standing behind the MP. As I came closer I realized the MP was Specialist Mike Hanlon.

Now this was an interesting soldier. SP4 Mike Hanlon was a schoolteacher from Coventry, Rhode Island; he was twenty-eight years old and had a Master's Degree in education. He was also one of the meanest soldiers I'd ever known. He was pissed-off at being drafted because he had a wife and two baby girls back home. He was pissed-off because he'd been sent so far away from Rhode Island. He figured, if he were stateside, at least he could drive or maybe fly home once in a while. But what he was totally pissed-off about was that he was in Korea and not Vietnam. I once heard him telling someone what he really thought:

"Goddamnit, if they're going to draft somebody, at least they should send them someplace important. When I get home, someone should be interested in hearing about where I've been and what I've done. You know, like: 'Say, Uncle Mike, so you were in Vietnam; what was that like?' But Noooo … I'm stuck here babysitting a goddamned, old, drunken bum of a Colonel. Man that old fart pisses me off every time I see the red-faced bastard. My kids are growing and my wife writes me letters that just make me want to sit down and cry. I worked really hard so I could be tops in my training class and I got promoted out of both Basic Training and AIT. I made Spec Four in six months flat just so I could send more money home. I don't know why, I'm only making about a third of what I made as a teacher. My Mom's watching the kids and Linda had to go back to work just to hold the place together until I get back. Yeah, they'll hold my job for me, but I was supposed to be up for a promotion I really worked hard for. That 4-F bastard Tim Brennen is probably gonna' get it while I'm stuck out here just jerkin' off!"

Yep, Hanlon was really pissed and he pretty much stayed that way twenty-four/seven.

I was now within hearing range of the voices. Holy shit! It was the Colonel up on the fence, drunker than "Cooter's Pig" and calling out. "MPs, MPs, where are you?" In a voice full of disgust and virtually no respect, Hanlon answered.

"Here I am Colonel, what can I do for ya?"

"MPs, MPs, what are your actions?"

"What do you want me to do Colonel … shoot-cha? It's your goddamned fence, Colonel; you can climb on the damned thing any freakin' time you want!"

Hanlon then turned and started walking away. As he was turning, he saw me looking up at the Old Man. "Leave the son-of-a-bitch up there, Lieutenant, maybe if we're lucky this time the drunken old fool will fall and break his freakin' neck."

The Colonel's voice was now much weaker but he was still calling out, "MPs, MPs …" He was also beginning to sag a little and looked like he was going to fall. The fence, including the barbed wire top guard, was about maybe nine feet tall but there was a three-foot deep rain ditch between it and the perimeter road. If he fell it would be over a ten-foot drop. If he got hung up in the barbed wire on the way down it would be even worse. I turned to Hanlon, "Come on, Mike, give me hand." "Jesus Christ, Sir, do I have to?" "Yes, you have to, now come on!" We approached the fence with the two KATUSA security guards close behind. I got a grip on the Colonel first and firmly held on to his left calf. I was trying to steady him against the fence. "Sir, it's me, Lieutenant Royce; let me help you down from way up there. "Oh, Lieutenant Royce, I'm so glad you're here. I'm up on the fence! And you know what? I can't get down! Will you help me get down, Lieutenant Royce?" His speech was slurred and he was a real mess. "Sure will Sir; we gotcha'." Hanlon got into position next to me and locked his two hands together under the Colonel's right boot. Between the two of us we inched him down off the wire. He seemed in an amazingly good mood for being as drunk as he was. Normally, he was just a really mean and nasty drunk when his snoot was full. He was still facing towards fence when we finally got one of his feet on the ground. Problem was, Hanlon's hands were still under the Colonel's foot. "Sir, *Sir*, will you please get your foot off my hand?" Hanlon was wincing in pain and doing all he could not to say what he really wanted to, which probably was, *"Get off my goddamned hand you drunken old bastard or I'll drop kick your boney old ass over the freaking fence!"*

Seeing our predicament and that SP4 Hanlon was in pain, the two Korean guards stepped forward to help. The Colonel still seemed grateful … until he turned around and saw the two immaculately uniformed Korean security guards. Through his blurry eyes, he slowly recognized them and immediately went into the patented "Ugly American" routine we'd all seen so many times before. "You goddamned slope-headed bastards get your fucking hands off me! What the hell is this all about, Royce? You can't control your slanty-eyed bastards … and you can't protect my GD camp either. I climbed on the fucking fence and not a goddamned MP or fucking KATUSA saw me do it!" Hanlon interjected, "That's not true Sir! I saw you hit the warning track and go for the fence. The two KATUSA guards followed you but were afraid to speak because of what you've said to them in the past." The Colonel lurched around in the direction of Hanlon's voice. I had to grab him to stop him from falling on his face. Pointing a finger, he slurred, "You shut the fuck up soldier. You will only speak when I tell you to; you got it?" At this point steam was coming out Hanlon's ears and his face was beet-red. I gave Hanlon a quick nod in the direction of the Main Gate. He and the KATUSAs gratefully took my non-verbal cue and started back up the warning track towards the Main Gate. I was now alone and face-to-face with the Screaming Eagle.

The Colonel was now nose-to-nose with me and yelling. His watery, bloodshot eyes were filled with hate and his alcoholic breath was lethal. "You are supposed to be in charge of my base security and you are fucking up by the numbers, Lieutenant! Your security is so piss-poor that any SOB could get in here any time they fuckin' wanted." I protested, "That's simply not true, Colonel!" His face turned the color of raw beefsteak, "You shut the fuck up when I'm talking to you, Lieutenant, you just shut the fuck up! I tell you what … the next time I or anybody else gets within ten feet of my fucking fence, I'm gonna' court-martial your sorry ass. You got that you smug, MP, son-of-a-bitch, smart-ass? *You got that?*" I can't believe I said "Yes, Sir!" to that old drunk but I did. The Colonel did a groggy about face and somehow managed not to spin in. I watched as his staggering gait drifted off into the shadows of the Quonset hut labyrinth. At that very moment, I was probably even madder than Hanlon.

I got back to the PMO and slammed the door behind me. I was so mad I couldn't see straight. I was muttering to myself and I very sincerely wanted to kill that son-of-a-bitch. I turned on the Desk Sergeant and yelled. "If that son-of-a-bitch, sorry-ass excuse for a Colonel (*I couldn't believe I called the Colonel that in front of the troops*) puts so much as a fucking foot on the edge of the warning track, I want every MP and KATUSA within a mile radius to jump his ass, grab hold of the bastard and call me to handle it. *You all got that?*" There was no "Yes, Sir" coming back. It was then I noticed the Desk Sergeant, the RTO (Radio Telephone Operator), the Desk Clerk, SP4 Hanlon, Big Chong and the two KATUSA security guards. They were all staring at me with saucer eyes. I was trembling and my skin felt hot and itchy all over. I glanced down in the direction of their stare and saw that my .45 was in my right hand. Somewhere along the line, while I was talking, I unconsciously drew my weapon and didn't even realize it. I quickly holstered the pistol and continued to talk as if it had never happened. As I continued talking, the men now looked significantly more relaxed. "I want statements from you Hanlon, and Mr. Chong; I also want you to take signed, translated statements from the two KATUSA security guards. They don't have to worry, their jobs are safe. It's me the Colonel wants, not them. Don't pull any punches; I want it written down just like everyone saw it. Don't hold anything back. Hanlon, if there was anyone else in the area when the Colonel went for the fence or if anyone heard anything he said, I want you to find them and get statements. I want all statement finished, signed and on my desk before anyone leaves. I'll be in my office writing my own statement if anyone's looking for me." As I stepped into the back offices I could feel my itching skin and temperature beginning to return to normal.

I know it was less than an hour because I was still working on my statement. The Desk RTO came running back to my office. "We just stopped the Colonel again on the warning track, Lieutenant. He's really ripped and really, really mad!" I charged out of the offices and into the night. I looked to my right and there he was about a hundred yards down the fence line at just about the same point where he was earlier. He was struggling with two big Korean security guards and shouting at the top of his drunken lungs. I ran towards them as fast as I could. As I arrived, I could hear him abusing the two guards. "Get your fucking hands off me you slope-headed bastards! I'll kill you sons-a-bitches! Let me go, goddamnit! Do you know who you're fucking with?" I told the guards, "Okay, I've got him; you go!" The two Koreans were more than happy to beat-feet out of there. The

Colonel's brief freedom was quickly reversed as I clamped down on his left hand and wrist with both of mine. I bent his hand back in a direction it doesn't normally go, forcing him quickly to his knees. I had him in a punishing, police compliance hold and he was hurting so bad he wasn't even cussing me out. I lifted up his hand and arm with both of mine forcing his head to hit the ground. Standing over him, I released my right hand, grabbed my handcuffs off my belt and secured one around this left wrist. While still forcing his face in the dirt, I reached down, got a grip on his right hand and bent it around behind him and secured the other cuff. I kept my left hand on the handcuff chain and, with the other hand, grabbed him by his fatigue jacket collar and lifted him up. I controlled his pain by applying more pressure when I felt it was needed. His arms were now a fulcrum where I could instantly add pain to his shoulders anytime I wanted to. I now had him bent over at the waist, face looking at the ground and we started walking back towards his quarters. He may have been mad but I was now madder. I'd put up with just about enough of his shit; hell, we all had!

As I walked him down the narrow sidewalk I kept talking to him. "Okay, Colonel, you're drunk and I'm taking you back to your quarters. I want you to go to bed and I don't want to see you out here anymore tonight. I don't want you to ever try and climb the fence again either." I kept his level of pain at a place where he really could not talk. He grunted in pain and made other audible sounds of discomfort which were just short of screams. The beauty of this *come-a-long* hold was, while it was extremely painful, there would be no damage or lasting effects when I released him from it. It just caused pains the human body can't tolerate, so the subject usually does exactly what you tell them to do. Right now, I wasn't interested in hearing anything the Colonel had to say anyway, so when he tried to speak I'd just slowly lift up on the cuffs and he'd go painfully quiet again.

We were now at his door. It was unlocked and I pulled it open. There was no external lock, just a hasp for a padlock. I undid the cuffs but continued to keep pressure on his left wrist. He was still in a head down position when I pushed him into his room. As soon as he was inside, I released my grip and closed the door behind him. I flipped the hasp closed and secured it by slipping an open handcuff through the hasp loop.

I stood outside his door for several minutes. I wanted to be sure he was asleep before I removed my cuffs from his door. I was just about to leave when I heard him try the door from the inside. When he heard the sound of my cuffs rattling in the hasp he went berserk and started yelling. "You unlock my goddamned door right now, you fucking prick. You let me out right now or I'll have your sorry ass court martialed … Do you hear me?" He went on and on for about half an hour, then things went quiet. I put my ear to his door to see if I could detect any movement inside. I didn't; so, I removed the cuffs and cracked his door open a few inches. There he was, in all his glory, passed out on the bed, still in uniform and snoring away. It was now a little past three in the morning. I closed the door quietly and made my way back to my room for a very short, very bad night's sleep.

In the morning I got up with the rest of the guys. It was Saturday, so most of us were just required to work until noon. At Camp Page, Saturdays also started at 0800 instead of the usual 0600. I made it in to the office a few minutes before eight. I walked past the command element's part of the building on the way to the PMO. With the exception of Captain Huddleston quietly attending to a coffee pot, there was no sign of movement in his area. My guys must have seen me coming because Sergeant Godblood had a steaming hot mug of coffee waiting for me as I walked in. "Cream and two sugars, right, Lieutenant?" "Thanks, Sergeant; that is exactly correct." I took a long look at Godblood and noted he was checking me out. I'm sure the off-going Desk Sergeant gave him a complete run down on last night's events, probably including my drawn weapon. The coffee was Godblood's attempt at insuring there were going to be no repeats on his shift. It was strong, hot and sweet and exactly what I needed. I could feel the warmth going all the way down and I instantly started to feel the caffeine rejuvenation process commence deep within my body.

Feeling somewhat better, I sat down to recreate the second of last night's events on paper. I noted there was a small pile of statements neatly stacked on my desk blotter. They included four more from the second incident with the Colonel. Mine would make five. That was a total of eleven statements from last night. I didn't even bother reading them. I had my Army field safe sitting on a 2x4 frame behind my desk. I hunched over, spun the combination, swung the heavy door open and stared for a moment at its contents. Sitting there on the bottom shelf had to be nearly a foot-tall pile of statements concerning Weatherspoon's un-Colonel-like shenanigans over the past six months. I stared at the pile and thought to myself, *"How in the hell can he just keep getting away with this crap? Doesn't anybody give a damn? This guy is a big guy in the Army! He controls Honest John rockets and Hawk missiles. Doesn't anybody realize he's a total alky and not fit for duty let alone command? If war breaks out, he just ain't going to get the job done and, in the process, he's liable to get a lot of good soldiers needlessly killed for no particular reason."* I separated the copies and placed the originals in my ever-growing pile in the bottom of the safe. I relocked it and started to draft my own statement.

How was I going to write this up? I had put my hands all over a superior officer. I cuffed him, I hurt him and I locked him up in his own quarters. Now, how in the hell was I going to justify my actions? Had I not been so pissed-off last night, would I have acted differently? I couldn't even answer my own questions. As I began writing, I wondered what this day would bring. As it turned out, nothing at all happened on Saturday or on Sunday.

Starting that afternoon, I spent the rest of the weekend with Joyce doing what she wanted to do; and I decided not to trouble her with last night's events. During our stroll through the open air market and lunch in a local restaurant, I kept quiet and let her tell me about the fun she'd been having with Jin Hee. That evening, after dinner, I finally told her all about my Friday night awards ceremony and my encounters with the Colonel. I watched the worried expression on her face. I knew she was on my side but, like everyone else that hadn't witnessed the *Mr. Hyde* side of Weatherspoon up close and personal, they had difficulty believing he was the dangerous bastard I painted him out to be. I knew in my heart of hearts the 5th USMC had the very important mission in keeping the peace in Korea. Many a night I had the fantasy of my just marching down to 8th Army Headquarters and turning him in. Problem was, I had this moral dilemma on my hands. On the one hand, he was my commanding officer and I felt duty-bound to support him. On the other hand, and I have to admit it, I was afraid. I had no idea what would happen if a lowly Lieutenant, like me, were to go up against this West Point Colonel who'd fought in both World War Two and the Korean War. What did I know? I was just a lousy know-nothing Lieutenant in comparison to him. I knew, for their survival, the Colonel's entourage would just close ranks around him and there was no telling what kind of book he'd been keeping on me. Even if the stuff was trumped up, I knew his henchmen would back him to the hilt on whatever he said. I've never been a particularly paranoid person but I now felt the walls closing in on me and I knew something had to give pretty soon but, for the life of me, I couldn't think what that would be. On Monday morning I found out.

Monday, just looked like another day in Korea. At least it did until about 1030 hours. The phone rang and it was Captain Huddleston. "Lieutenant Royce, the Colonel would like to see you in his office." "When, Captain?" "Right away, please!" I hung up the phone and stared at it for about thirty seconds ... Something about the oiliness in Captain Huddleston's voice made me feel very uneasy. I checked myself out in the full-length mirror just outside my office door. Boots shined, hair combed and gig-line straight; *lock and load!* I stopped by the Desk and told Sergeant Godblood the Colonel wanted to see me in his office and I didn't know how long I would be. That morning, the hallway between the MP Station and the Command Suite somehow seemed longer. I turned into the Colonel's outer office and Captain Huddleston said, "Go right on in, Lieutenant, he's waiting for you."

I knocked and heard the Colonel say "Enter!" As I opened the door I noted Huddleston was right behind me. Standing to the left of the Colonel was the Stupid Colonel Mixon and the Gorilla was standing on his right. The Colonel was seated at his desk. I strode up to about three feet in front of Colonel Weatherspoon's desk. I could hear my heels click together the instant I assumed a ridged position of attention and saluted. "Sir, Lieutenant Royce reports." Finally, the Colonel returned one of my salutes. "Stand at ease, Lieutenant." I then assumed the position of *Parade Rest* with my feet shoulder-width apart, my right hand over my left and my forearms behind my back. The Colonel shuffled some papers on his desk, picked up a blue folder, opened it, and began to speak:

"Lieutenant Royce, it's been no secret around here that for months I've been less than pleased with your job performance. You've been unable or unwilling to meet my expectations of you. I have tried to be your mentor and to show you the correct way but you've insisted in continuing in you maverick ways. Because there has been no improvement in this camp's security, after I've repeatedly asked for it, I'm afraid you have left me with no recourse. You are here in front of me this morning to receive punishment for failure to do your duties and for placing my command in danger by not properly securing this camp." So, here it finally was. I'm standing alone in the Colonel's office. He has three witnesses and I have none. He's setting me up for a real *"hose job."* I had to force myself to concentrate and listen to his exact words. "Your dereliction of duty is probably worthy of a Court-Martial, Lieutenant, but, since you are relatively new to the Army, I've decided to be lenient and just administer Article 15, Non-Judicial Punishment; so, you should consider yourself lucky." I knew what Article 15 was; At Fort Rucker, I'd given out a few myself. I knew it could cost me a considerable amount of pay, extra duty and restrict me to base for up to three months. I also knew an Article 15 in your permanent personnel file was the kiss of death to an officer's career. The Colonel continued on in his best *Kangaroo Court* manner. I'm guessing he hoped I would explode or show disrespect to him in front of his three goons. If none of that happened, he was counting on my quietly accepting and signing the Article 15 papers.

"Lieutenant Royce, here are the charges:" As the Colonel started to read them I could actually feel myself starting to relax a little. It was somehow a relief to know the other shoe had finally dropped. Deep down, I instantly knew what I was going to do from the second he uttered the words, "*Article 15*".

"Charge 1: Failure to maintain a proper level of base security commensurate with Camp Page's important military mission.

Charge 2: Failure to maintain discipline within the ranks of the 5th USMC Military Police Detachment. This includes the Korean Augmentation to the United States Army Security Guards and Military Policemen, more commonly known as KATUSAs.

Charge 3: Failing a penetration test conducted by the 5th USMC Commander himself after he repeatedly warned you of the consequences if your security was not up to his standards.

You have been read the charges. You now have two choices. You can either accept these charges, as read and be administered Article 15 punishment or you can request a trial by Courts-Marital. What is your choice, Lieutenant?" I looked into the eyes of the three officers in front of me. I looked first to my left at Major Gorilla. Other than being a horny *village rat,* from what others told me, he was a pretty decent guy and a pretty good officer. He clearly was embarrassed to be a part of these proceedings and avoided eye contact with me altogether. I then looked to my right. The stupid Colonel Mixon looked back but he had this almost-grin on his face and was just glad he wasn't the one incurring Colonel Weatherspoon's wrath. Lastly, I looked straight ahead into dark eyes just filled with hate for me. I then asked the one question I knew you're not allowed to ask at Article 15 proceedings. "Colonel, under Article 15, what punishments are you planning to give me?" He gave me a little smirky-smile. "Lieutenant Royce, you of all people should know how it works. You accept the Article 15 first, we sign the papers and then you wait outside. I then sit down, weigh all evidence and decide what level of punishment is fitting. I then call you back in and tell you what it is. I assure you Lieutenant; I'm a fair and impartial man. Everyone in this room knows that!" I watched all the puppets nodding. "So, Lieutenant Royce, have you come to a decision?" "Yes Sir I have … I'll take the Court Martial!"

There was a brief, silent pause as all the air was sort of sucked out of the room. You could have heard that proverbial pin drop. I checked everyone's eyes again. Huddleston's mouth dropped open and his eyes were wincing as if he were waiting for an explosion. The Gorilla's showed fear and Mixon was still trying to figure what the hell was going on. Three, two, one, zero, and the Colonel launched out of his desk chair sending it speeding backwards into the wall with a loud crash. His face instantly turned crimson and he commenced yelling at the top of his lungs. "Goddamn you, Royce, goddamn you!" He was now wagging his finger at me menacingly. "You'll get your goddamned Court Martial and you'll be damned lucky if you don't spend a couple of years in Leavenworth! You son-of-a-bitch, you're just doing this to drag up old, meaningless shit and doing anything you can to stop me from getting my star … you, you bastard!" I had come back to the position of attention as the Colonel came around to my side of the desk. He was inches from my face and I even got some of his spit on my uniform. "You get the hell out of my office this instant before I forget I'm an officer and a gentleman and throw your sorry-ass outa' here! I'm going to get you for this, Royce, just wait, I'm going to make your life so fucking miserable you're gonna' wish you were never born. Now get the hell outa' here." I saluted quickly and I got the hell out of there. As I stepped into the outer office, Kuska and Sergeant Godblood were standing just outside the Colonel's door. Captain Huddleston followed me out and in a surprised tone asked, "How long have you two been standing here?" Kuska looked Captain Huddleston squarely in the eye and with a smile replied, "Quite a long time, Captain. I guess we came in just about the time you all went into the Colonel's office and closed the door." "Did you overhear anything, Sergeant Kuska?" "Well, Sir, it's kinda' hard not to. We came here to pick up our boss for a meeting downtown that we're already late for. I'm sorry but these walls really are paper-thin and, from what I could tell, my boss is gonna' be Court Marshaled and the Colonel is really, really pissed. Does that about cover it, Captain?" Lieutenant Colonel Mixon had overheard our conversation and followed us out into the hall. "Lieutenant Royce, I think when he calms down this will all straighten itself out. Maybe this is all just a big misunderstanding; I'll see what I can do." I knew this was just more mealy-mouthed bullshit but I automatically thanked him anyway and continued down the hall with my two guys.

"What were you two doing down there? I don't have a meeting downtown that I know of." Kuska explained as we quickly walked back down the hall, "No, there's no meeting. Godblood came in right after you left and told me you'd been called on the carpet. We figured it was about last Friday so we ran down the hall just in time to see the Colonel's door closing. We stood by the door and we heard every damned, lying word that came out of the Full Bird's mouth. Buck Sergeant God and I are going to write statements to that fact. Good thing we followed you because that crafty old SOB has three witnesses who will swear to his lies … but now they can't because you've got Godblood and me to back you up. I think that's what's got Mixon and Huddleston all stirred up. We just crapped in their mess kits. Are you really going to go for a Court-Martial?" "Fucking 'A' I am!"

I walked directly into my office and went straight for my safe and opened it. I loaded my foot-high pile of statements into a cardboard box and yelled, "Somebody gas up the Jeep and bring it around front!" It only took a few minutes for my Jeep to arrive. I turned to Sergeant Godblood and said, "Please tell Joyce I've gone to Seoul on important business and not to wait up if I'm late. Oh, and call 8th Army PMO and let them know I'm driving down to see Colonel Condra on very important business." Godblood asked, "Do you want a driver?" I declined, went outside and nestled my box of statements down in the floorboards on the passenger side and started out for Yongsan Compound.

I don't remember much about the drive down to Yongsan. I kept going over in my mind how I was going to do all this. How was I going to present my case? I didn't even know if the 8th Army PM was going to be in. All I knew was I had to get off base. If the Colonel came down to my office and started ranting and raving again there was no telling what I might do. So, it was best I was outa' there and on the road where I could vent my frustrations on drivers I didn't even know. *"Get the hell out of my way, you idiots!"*

I arrived at the 8th Army PMO and strode in carrying my heavy box of papers. Godblood had gotten through and Colonel Condra was waiting for me. "Well, welcome, Lieutenant Royce. I got the call that you were on your way here on important business but there was no elaboration. What's in the box?" We went into his office and closed the door. "Sir, I met you during my first few weeks in country. One of the things you told me at that meeting was that if I ever needed your help to please not hesitate. Sir … I need your help." For about the next two and a half hours I explained what was going on at Camp Page. I kept handing the Colonel statements to back up my charges and I answered his many questions. We had only gone through about half the box when Colonel Condra held up his hand, "Okay, Lieutenant, I think I've got the picture! There's a theme going on here and I think my investigators can go through the rest of this pile and figure it out. I've got another meeting I absolutely have to attend; so, I think we have to end it here." He got up; we saluted, shook hands and he walked me to the door. A small wave of panic wafted over me. *"Was I getting the brush-off? Is this where it all ends? Would this box of statements just be pushed into a corner somewhere?"* I was asking one Colonel to go up against another Colonel and both of them were West Pointers. *"Didn't I hear somewhere there's some unwritten code of the brotherhood that West Pointers protect each other?"* I didn't know; I'd heard jokes about "The West Point Protective Association." That was what I heard it was called. Oh shit, maybe they weren't jokes! I was just a dumb First Lieutenant. So, for some reason, I left the good Colonel with a slightly veiled threat. "Sir, if you need copies of these statements, I have plenty more." His expression changed just a bit as we said our final good byes. I thought about what I'd said all the way back to

Camp Page and wondered if he took my final words as a threat or just an offer. I tried not to dwell on it but it continued to bug me. Now all I could do was just sit tight and hope something was going to be done before I was goaded into doing something dumb.

32

TPI

Monday the 13th of May was a very warm day. At lunchtime I found Joyce hiding out in my BOQ room enjoying the coolness of our antique *window shake*r air conditioner. Everyone in the room owned a share in this lifesaving device. When it was time for a roommate to leave, the other three would buy the departee's share then resell it to the next FNG that moved in. Joyce was talking to Mr. Ahn about the new baby boy he and his wife just had. Boys were still a really big deal in Korea.

Several copies of *Stars & Stripes* were laying on my night table so while the two were talking I thumbed through them. The world was still going mad around us. The North Vietnamese had agreed to meet with the U.S. in Paris before month's end to begin peace talks. None of us thought they were serious, just biding time to lick their wounds. Seems one of the major hang-ups to getting the talks going was the North Vietnam delegation didn't like the shape of the table in the room where the talks were to take place. Now just how stupid was that?

I thought Paris was kind of a strange place anyway. This is because the, then, "Viet Minh (North Vietnamese) had defeated the French at *Den Ben Phu* in 1954 when Vietnam was still listed on maps as *French Indochina,* a French colony. Paris wasn't exactly the most tranquil place for "Peace Talks" at this time either. There was a lot of student unrest at the Sorbonne. This was causing sympathy strikes all over the country. Over nine million Frenchmen went out on strike. President de Gaulle was so worried his government would be toppled he started making frequent radio addresses to the French people. At the same time he directed major French Army movements throughout the country. This show of force eventually would dissipate any revolutionary intentions but the de Gaulle government was permanently damaged by this action.

In the wake of Dr. King's assassination, Ralph Abernathy took over the Southern Christian Leadership Corps and set up an encampment on the Mall in Washington DC. Even after a solid month of rain, there were still over 2500 followers encamped in what they called "Resurrection City", and the government didn't know what to do about it.

Joyce and I had long discussions about all the goings-on. She had the liberal, Canadian view while I had the view of most US Army officers. She once described my political leanings as "A little to the right of Attila the Hun".

Nearly three weeks had passed since I'd visited Colonel Condra and I hadn't heard so much as a peep out of his office concerning my allegations. I guess I'd thought, maybe wished, Weatherspoon would have been called down to 8th Army HQ to answer questions. To the best of my knowledge, none of us who wrote statements had been contacted by any of Colonel Condra's investigators. I talked to Kuska about it and all he said was, "Who knows! These things usually take a long time to investigate, but you know, there's always a chance the 'Good Old Boy Network' or 'The West Point Protection Association' has circled the wagons and nothing's going to be done about it. I've seen it happen before." That was heartening news! I also hadn't heard a word out of Weatherspoon's office about my impending Court-Martial, and that too was weighing heavily on my mind. Not knowing what was going to happen was beginning to drive me a bit crazy.

What I did know, was that Weatherspoon was making good on his threat to make my life miserable. I'd been given some additional duties. I now had to inspect all four Hawk firing batteries every week and deliver written security status reports to him by 0800 every Monday morning. This meant I was spending lots of time on the road. Charlie Battery was the closest. It was only about an hour round trip plus whatever time it took me to do my weekly physical security checks and updates. Alfa Battery was almost two hours away. Including the survey, it took me just about all day to do that one. Bravo and Delta were somewhere in between. Even if I wanted to fudge them I didn't dare because one of his flunkies would occasionally show up to spy on me. Also, I wasn't allowed to farm out these inspections to any of my men, even though several were MP School trained to do them. These additional tasks were deliberately designed to just bog me down with busy work. The rest of the Army gets a facility PS Survey about once every year or maybe two, and here I am doing them weekly on the same units. I could see his plan was to slowly add more and more work to my plate until I either cracked or could not keep up. In either case he would have me cold and be able to give me a well-documented, substandard efficiency report—or worse.

I was also made "Korean Canteen Manager". I had to insure the KATUSA canteen was clean, the food ordered and all monies accounted for. This project was also soaking up several hours of my time each week. While I was messing around with all this busy work, many of my more important duties were suffering. Thankfully, I had a terrific staff and they were working overtime making me look good in my normal duties. Kuska, in particular, would put my name on half his investigations and would brief me on all the details when I had my infrequent free moments back in my office. My guys were taking care of most of the routine stuff. The one thing Weatherspoon had not counted on was the loyalty of my people. Without them I would have been ground into the dirt in very short order.

Joyce wasn't all that happy about this situation either. I was spending far too many nights on base and not enough time with her. It was nothing that was going to affect the soundness of our marriage or anything like that, but she definitely was not thrilled with our current situation. The saving grace was, we both knew come December, we'd be winging our way back to some State Side Army Post. We were hoping it might even be Fort Rucker again, where her Mom and Dad were still stationed.

I still had my duties as commander of the QRF, which meant I continued responding to North Korean infiltrator sightings. It was hardly a daily occurrence, but it certainly seemed to be once or twice a week now. 1968 ended up being the hottest year for enemy incursions into the South with more than 600 documented attacks and incidents.

All my MPs were pretty well trained by now; so, if I was off doing a battery survey they would respond without me and I would try and catch up with them, if I could. The Colonel still expected me to finish my weekly surveys even if I was called away on real, no shit, QRF missions. I confided in Joyce that I didn't know if I could stand a half-year more of this crap and we started talking about what we would do and where we would go if the Army were no longer an option. Outwardly, to Weatherspoon, I never complained and I tried to make it look like I was taking it all in stride. At this point there was absolutely no love lost between us and I was dreaming up stuff just to screw with his head.

It was a Sunday night and I was working late in the office. I think it was about 2030 hours when the Desk Sergeant walked back to my office and told me the tower had called saying there were four choppers inbound with one going to the VIP pad. We immediately responded to secure the pad and I sent a runner over to Weatherspoon's quarters to let him know we had visitors. I was short a man; so, I added myself to the VIP Pad Security Detail. We secured the area and, about ten minutes later, we heard the unmistakable sound of *Huey* rotor-blades beating the air into submission. Colonel Weatherspoon, The Stupid Colonel

Mixon and Captain Huddleston all arrived at just about this time. The Colonel walked over and asked me who was coming in. I told him, "Sir, all the tower told us was there were four choppers inbound with one going to the VIP pad. That's all I know Colonel." Weatherspoon shot me a sideways look of disgust and growled, "Figures *you* wouldn't know what's going on, Lieutenant!"

It was a bright, moonlit night and, by their longer silhouette, I guessed all four choppers were probably the newer Bell UH1-Hs. They were coming in low, up the valley, following the river. They flew over the end of the runway and were coming straight at us, with glaring landing lights reflecting off their whirring rotor blades. As the first Huey pulled up to a hover over the VIP pad, but before setting down, I could see a small, brightly-painted, metal replica of a general officer's flag with four, gleaming white stars on a background of red. *Holy Crap!* There was only one of those guys in all Korea and that was General Charles "Chuck" Ironbone, the 8th Army Commanding General.

I glanced over and Weatherspoon looked visibly shook. The chopper settled to the ground and the whine of its gas-turbine motor deepened indicating the pilot had killed the engine. The blades were now steadily losing RPM. For the next two suspenseful minutes, I could only see silhouettes inside, but no one alighted from the helicopter. The side cargo doors finally slid back and the front right hand door swung wide open and out stepped "The Man" himself. All six and a half feet of U.S. Army General Officer unfolded out of the small Huey door. He stood there for a moment with his back to us as he unhooked his radio connection, took off his flight helmet and shook hands with the pilot. Safety protocols state that military formalities don't commence until the senior officer is safely clear of the rotor blades. When he turned towards us, he looked just like in his command photos. He was every inch the Hollywood version of a four star general. He was very tall, raw-bone lean and ramrod straight with a silvery-white flat-top and a black patch over his right eye. I was told he lost it in fighting on Hill 666 in "The Battle of the Punch Bowl", during the Korean War, in 1951. The man was pushing sixty but looked hard enough to roller skate on. This was one flag officer who instantly commanded respect even before you met him.

He lowered his head and crouched over a little as he walked quickly out from underneath the still spinning rotor blades. As he was walking toward us he shook hands and briefly spoke to two of my MPs. Colonel Weatherspoon started walking towards the General and when he got within six paces he saluted. General Ironblood ignored the salute and grabbed Weatherspoon's hand like they were long-lost buddies. "How the hell you doin', Ralph? It's been a long time, probably too long. Fine looking MPs you got up here! I like 'em tall; they look good just standing there." There was some more small talk between them, then the General and Weatherspoon walked away. The General had his arm around Weatherspoon's shoulder and their two heads were close together; it was obvious Ironbone was bending Weatherspoon's ear about something. They looked like two old friends who hadn't seen each other in a long time, and I'm thinking, *"What the hell? Don't tell me these two went to high school together or something!"*

I didn't have much time to contemplate this because my attention was now drawn to the helo next to Ironbone's. Three Star, Lieutenant General, Vincent T. "Skippy" Mack came out of that one. He walked off to the side of the tarmac apron and lit a short, fat cigar. It was well known that General Mack was Ironbone's "Hatchet Man." Whenever there was dirty work to be done, Skippy would show up so Ironbone wouldn't get his hands messy. No one seemed to know how the General got the nickname "Skippy" but when you're a three-star, there's very few people who will tease you about it.

All four choppers were now offloading troops. There were a handful of officers, a whole lot of warrant officers and a few high-ranking NCOs. There were eighteen of them in all, not counting the two generals. *"What the Sam hell was going on?"* General Mack and a Lieutenant Colonel were walking straight for me. When they came within range I popped a salute, "Good evening, General … Colonel; Lieutenant Royce at your service. Can my men or I assist you in anyway?" Skippy Mack turned to the Lieutenant Colonel and smiled, "So, Joe, we finally get to meet the famous, and prolific, note taker of Camp Page. You sure can write a lot, son!" The Lieutenant Colonel (LTC) smiled and reached out a hand, "Lieutenant, my name's Joe Palladino and my job is to be your worst nightmare for the next week or so." It was then that I noticed the LTC was wearing Military Police branch insignia on his collar. "What's all this about, Sir?" Skippy Mack stepped in with the answer, "This, son, is all your doing; it's what's called a, no-notice, TPI Team Inspection." I must have still looked confused. "Son, because of your allegations, we've got about thirty people coming here to conduct a Technical Proficiency Inspection. We brought all these smart Warrant Officers along with us and, for the next week to ten days, they're gonna' be crawlin' up everybody's butt to see if 5th Missile knows shit from *Shineola* about rockets and missiles! Thanks for offering your help, Lieutenant, but I think we can handle our own gear. We just need to be pointed towards the visiting officers' quarters—if you got em." "Yes, Sir, we do; I'll have one of my men escort you over there."

It took a little doing, but after an hour or so, rooms had been arranged, beds moved around and linens found. I don't know where Ironbone and Weatherspoon disappeared to but I guessed the Four-Star probably had the best accommodations on base.

I don't think anybody on Page got much sleep that night. I called Joyce and told her what was going on and that I would be bunking on base, then tried to cop a few "Zs." After not even two fitful hours of sleep, the base sirens went off. I jumped from my bunk and zipped into my boots. I'd left my uniform on just to catnap anyway. When I came charging out of the room LTC Palladino was standing there, with a stopwatch, *"Click"*. "Morning, Lieutenant Royce! Fine morning for an alert! When you get to your office, you will find an envelope stuck to your door; read it and react." I flew to the office and ripped open the envelope; it read:

TPI—MP Event #01

LT Royce,

<u>The MSA is under attack by infiltrators: Assemble your QRF and arrive at the back gate ready to depart Camp Page for the MSA ASAP. When you are completely ready to depart the Back Gate for combat operations contact the evaluator located at that position.</u>

LTC Palladino, MP, USA

Just as I finished reading the "Event", I could hear the first Jeep arriving in front of the PMO. The second and third Jeeps came within the next minute or so. There was this mad scramble as our Arms Room was opened and M-60s were affixed to the pedestal machine gun mounts and ammo loaded on board the Jeeps. Buck Sergeant God was in the second Jeep and SP4 Danny Cortez had the third. We huddled briefly while I explained the mission. We broke huddle and all twelve of us mounted up. I jumped in right seat of the first Jeep and led the gun Jeeps through a sharp U-turn and headed for the Back Gate. As I turned, there was LTC Palladino with that damned stopwatch again, *"Click"*. As the Lieutenant Colonel grew smaller in my side view mirror, I smiled to myself. *"Those months of QRF drills and our actual missions have pretty much prepared us for this kind of shit."* When we got to the Back Gate, there was a Warrant Officer standing by. I could see him in the glow from a nearby perimeter light. He was enjoying a cigarette and wearing a bright yellow armband with the bold, black letters **TPI** on it. We pulled up next to him in the Jeep and I said, "We're ready to go,

Chief!" He whipped out a stopwatch, *"Click."* "Alright, Lieutenant, you don't mind if I check out your troops do you?" "Absolutely not, Chief!" and he then commenced checking out all our gear, weapons and ammunition. After which, he asked each team member various questions about our Jeeps, weapons and equipment. "How do you clear a jam in an M-60, soldier?" We also had to demonstrate things. "Tear down your 45 weapon and put it back together for me, soldier." Everything seemed to be a stopwatch-timed event. About an hour later we were released to turn in our gear and go back to bed. It was now shortly after 0500 and bed would not make much of a difference; so, we all went to the mess hall for "Early Breakfast." Holy Cow! There were even two TPI Warrants with clipboards checking out the mess hall when we arrived.

About 0800 we were all summoned to the camp movie theater. The place only seated about three hundred but I'll bet there were close to double that in there, this morning. The house lights were turned all the way up as Ironbone walked out onto the stage. There was no tapping on the podium nor anyone saying, *"May I have your attention please?"* There was just the loudest *"TENCH-HUT"* I think I've ever heard and it was followed by instant silence. There he was, hands on hips, dressed in immaculate fatigues, strolling back and forth across the stage. Generals wore these wide black leather belts rather than the web gun belts the rest of us wore. General's belts also had large gold belt buckles. Ironebone's had a raised, gold U.S. Army eagle on it. I also noted he was toting a compact General Officer's pistol in a black holster on his right hip.

I don't know if it was staged or not but, as the General paced back and forth across the stage, the glint off that shiny, gold belt buckle must have hit everyone right in the eyes. We all remained standing at attention while the General formulated exactly what he wanted to say to us. It was a long minute before he said, "This is going to take awhile, so find something to sit on so we can get started." Just about everyone found a place to sit somewhere. The aisles were full of GIs sitting on the floor while the luckier ones had real seats. After about thirty seconds of movement, the room became morgue-quiet and the General started to speak.

> "Men, I've been in the Army for over thirty years now. I've commanded troops in three wars. Some may have their own private opinions about me being an expert on war—and that's okay—but I think just about everyone agrees, after five Purple Hearts and a chest full of medals for doing foolish things in days gone by, I may not be an expert but I'm at least an informed source on the subject. I may be an unlucky SOB, but still an informed source."

The General briefly pointed to his black eye patch and the room laughed. It was a spontaneous outburst at first, but it quickly subsided into isolated nervous laughter before falling quiet again.

"Well, there are a few things I've learned to be true over my years as a soldier and one of them is this: If you sweat more in peace, you bleed less in war! By that I mean, if you expect to survive combat and win battles, you better damned well learn everything you possibly can about fighting your enemy before it actually happens. Being trained and ready to meet the challenges of war is just what TPIs are all about. I'm a firm believer that training wins battles and saves lives. If you men, you NCOs and you Officers pass this thing, you'll have shown me you truly are prepared, as a team, to perform the things you need to be able to do to defeat a determined enemy on the field of battle.

Starting at zero dark thirty this morning, and for the next week or so, you will be tested on pretty much everything you're supposed to know how to do. I'll be surprised if you know it all, because, nobody ever does. This TPI is designed to tell me just what you can and cannot do and where you need further training to get better. So, I'm asking each and every one of you to try your best over the next week to do all the things we're going to be testing you on. This is important! This is not a bank audit. It's not a grocery store annual inventory either. We are the 8th United States Army! There are only 50,000 of us in South Korea … and do you know why we are here?"

A hand flew up about midway back in the crowd. "Put your hand down son, that was a rhetorical question." Hank Jenson turned to Buck Sergeant God and whispered, "Why does theys keep askin' questions if-in theys don't wants no answers?" Godblood just put a single index finger to his lips and glared at Hank.

The General was now saying, "We're here on one of freedom's frontiers. The North half of this peninsula and then westward, for the next five or six thousand miles, and a billion people or more people, is nothing but godless Communism. Red China and the Union of Soviet Socialist Republics stretch all the way from here to a divided Germany where our 7th United States Army stands alongside NATO guarding and protecting Europe's freedom. This is not some game, gentlemen, and we don't get to do '*do-overs*'. The Reds want us all dead and gone. They, like the fucking Nazis before them, want nothing less than total world domination. Once again in our nation's brief history, we are being called upon to be the ones standing in the path of enemy conquest. We are the 'Gate Keepers', gentlemen. If we fail, merciless hordes from the North will come screaming south to swallow up this brave, little country and its fine people. Vietnam is already under attack. If both Korea and Vietnam fall, then Thailand, Taiwan and maybe even all of Asia will follow. We must stop them here!

I was called upon once before to stand at this very same Korean Gate. I was here with the United Nations of the world back in the 1950s. The enemy attacked from the North and overran the South. America responded and I came ashore with General Douglas Macarthur during the legendary *Inchon*

Landing. We drove the bastards nearly out of Korean Peninsula all together. Then, the Red Chinese and the USSR joined in and counter attacked. We were horribly outnumbered by the Red Chinese Army, but somehow, despite heavy casualties, we were able to contain their *Human Wave* attacks and turn them back. After nearly three bloody years of war, both our leaders and theirs decided the 38th Parallel was enough—for now—so they called a ceasefire. That shaky ceasefire has been going on for about fifteen years now. Funny thing is, to this old soldier, it still seems like the ceasefire was signed just last week. Sometimes, gentlemen, I still hear those eerie Chinese bugles in the dead, dark of moonless nights. Those bugles served two purposes. They were the Reds' basic troop signaling device, much like we used during our own civil war. But I'm here to tell you, those damned bugles are one of the creepiest sounds you'll ever hear and they scared the shit out of us. It was scary as hell because it told us what was coming. Hundreds or even thousands of little yellow men carrying stubby, machineguns and big knives were going to be coming at us. When they did come, we'd mow 'em down, by the hundreds, with our machine guns but they'd just keep coming. In between those human waves of the screaming little bastards, we'd have to go forward from our fighting positions just to move the dead bodies out of the way and clear our fields of fire. Sometimes, their follow on waves would come screaming towards us with just ammo. They would take weapons off their dead comrades, load them with their ammo and just keep coming. All of this was done to the sound of those goddamned bugles. We are here in Korea today gentlemen, to make sure those fucking bugles never ever sound south of the DMZ again.

You men of the 5th United States Missile Command play a most important role in all this. We know the Red Chinese and North Korean Armies are just two damned big for us to fight them man-on-man. Because of this, we have to rely on combat multipliers. Your Honest Johns and Hawks are two key multipliers. The Reds know we have them. They also know what your rockets and missiles are designed to do and what they can do. Because of your rockets, they are hesitant to make their massive attacks aimed at overwhelming our defenses along the DMZ. They fear what your Honest Johns will do to them. They're also afraid to make a massive air strike south because they know your Hawk Batteries, all along the border, are ready to knock down hundreds of their Migs before they even encounter our Air Force.

So you see, you missile and rocket men play a key role in this deadly dance … maybe even *the* key role in keeping the Commies at bay. Remember, North Korea's Kim IL Sung, that megalomaniac SOB, has vowed to reunite the two Koreas under Communism before his 60th birthday. Gentlemen, that assholes birthday is just a few years away. We all know what he's been doing this year to try and goad us into attacking him. He wants to turn the Korean Peninsula into a second Vietnam. He can't stand Ho Chi Min getting all the attention. But … he can't do it without the help of the Chinese and Russians. Kim's problem is the Chinese and Russians are all wrapped up supporting another one of their puppet governments against the U.S. and South Vietnamese in

Vietnam. However, the USSR and Red China do have a deal with Kim. They will get involved in Korea if we attack Kim from the south. That's why the Pueblo! That's why the thirty-one man raid on the Blue House in Seoul! That's why the massing of 400,000 North Korean troops just north of the DMZ and that's why all the infiltrations and killings are still going to day. All these provocations are aimed at getting us to attack him first. All his actions show us he's trying to pull any trick he can to make good on his birthday promise. My job is to intercept his deadly incursions into the South. Your job here at Camp Page is to be ready to crash his party if he's ever crazy enough to go it alone and attack south. As long as you men are poised and ready to launch your rockets and missiles on short notice, Kim, as crazy as he may seem, is not about to sacrifice tens of thousands of his troops in doomed attacks. You and your deadly rockets and missiles are blocking his high speed routes to the South. You, gentlemen, are fucking up the old man's birthday party!"

Applause and whistles erupted. Ironbone raised his hands to silence the theater.

"I'm going to be flying back to Seoul later this morning with General Mack. We'll be leaving you in the capable hands of TPI Team Chief, Felix Wendelschafer and his team of technicians. Do your best; and I'll be back towards the end of your TPI to check in and see how well you've done. Before I go, I want to leave you with a couple of thoughts. I often contemplate this when faced with Army-related challenges. There are many professions you could have gone into. In every one of them, there's an expectation you will work hard, learn your job and do the best you can. The big difference between being a soldier in the United States Army, and just about any civilian job, is the level of job importance.

Our primary job in the Army is to 'Protect the United States of America against all enemies foreign and domestic'. When you stop to think about it, that's one hell of a job to be asked to do! If we fail in our jobs gentlemen, there are no *do-overs*. We can't just walk away and find another job. Back on *Civie Street,* maybe the store we work at closes or the company we work for goes bankrupt. Yes it's a personal tragedy, but not really a big deal nationally or globally. In the Army, if we fail in combat the whole country and our way of life are put at risk. If we fail, everything we hold dear may fail! If we fail, we could die, our buddies could die and this dying could extend all the way to our families and loved ones back home, to our nation and maybe even what's left of the free world.

No, gentlemen, this is not just another job! It is your moral and patriotic duty to study and train to be the best soldiers, NCOs and officers you can possibly be. Your nation and the free world are depending on you to block or defeat Communism whenever and wherever it rears its ugly, cancerous head! As I depart back to Seoul, I want you all to know that I have dedicated my life to defending the United States of America. I also want you to know that, professionally, I take everything personally. Lastly, I want you know that I love each and everyone of you as if you were my own sons. Us old soldiers can talk like that ... particularly when we're wearing four stars!"

A ripple of laughter zigzagged across the room.

"Because of my love for you fine soldiers. I feel it's my job to ensure each and every one of you is trained and cared for by your Chain of Command. Those of you who take soldiering seriously have nothing to fear from this inspection; you will do fine. However, and let's be perfectly clear on this one, if any of you ignore training, ignore preparedness or are just hiding out in the Army for a monthly pay check plus three hots, a cot and place to squat, you are going to feel the full wrath of this old one-eyed warhorse."

With his last word, the CG (Commanding General) did a crisp right face and strode off stage. Someone yelled "*Ah-Ten-Shun*" and then the mad, noisy scramble of getting up and into the position of attention commenced. TPI Team Chief, CW4 (Chief Warrant Officer) Felix Wendelshafer then told everyone to be seated and he began telling us about our inspection.

Colonel Weatherspoon tried to make his way out of the theater to see the CG off but it was just impossible to penetrate the crowd; so, he reluctantly reclaimed his seat down front.

The Chief told us to check the bulletin board in the theater lobby at 0600, 1200 and 1700 hundred hours each day for planned inspections of various things. He also cautioned there would be many additional, unannounced inspections required. Thirty minutes later I was in front of the bulletin board discovering I had an arms room inspection at ten, and an in-ranks inspection of my MPs at 1130 hours. It had started!

During the week I saw more of LTC Palladino than I thought possible. I couldn't figure out when the man slept. Paul Gleason told me there were two Warrants checking out all their radio and long-line communications at Page and at all the Hawk sites. I saw Warrants with yellow brassards everywhere, day and night. My QRF got called out three more times that week. One of the times, it wasn't even for a test, it was the real thing. Alfa Battery got a late night visit from Infiltrators. We rolled but it was all over before we even got to the outskirts of Chunchon. The MP Desk radioed us it was a lone sniper and it appeared Alfa's base defense had killed him with an 81 mm, mortar round. LTC Palladino used the event as another test of our being able to roll when we got the call. I was never completely satisfied with our performance; yet, I had the overall feeling things were probably going okay for us. All my guys were working their collective asses off and we had no "half-steppers". Palladino seemed to be loosening up a little. I even caught him sort of smiling once while he was working with Buck Sergeant

God and the Spaniard at the MP Desk. He also seemed genuinely impressed with the KATUSA security guards. What wasn't there to be impressed about? He watched their bayonet drills, *Taekwondo* work outs and witnessed some of their training at the rifle range. They were all very well trained and I had absolutely nothing to do with it. Every one of them had served in the ROK Army. The guard cadre took care of all training. I was so impressed with it I only loosely monitored the guard's training operation. They had another qualification that was equally impressive; for Koreans, they were all very big.

The TPI was just about the sole point of discussion all over the Camp. Joe Bartlett, CO (Commanding Officer) of Headquarters & Headquarters Company, Bill Block, CO of the Engineers, Paul Gleason, XO (Executive Officer) of the Signal unit and I were all sitting in the club one night discussing how the TPI was going. We four, more or less, thought it was going just sort of okay for our operations. We also all agreed those Warrants sure seemed to be writing down a lot of stuff on those clipboards and behaving very secretive about the scores they were giving out.

Additionally, we all had the feeling things were not going so good down in some of the Honest John firing batteries. None of the officers were talking much but their troops were leaking things to our boys at mealtime in the mess halls. Most of the scuttlebutt centered around training screw-ups. Evidently the TPI guys had pulled a no-notice drill and told one of the firing batteries to roll out three launchers and dummy rockets to pre-designated field locations, somewhere in the exercise box, and then conduct a mock launch at some specific hour. They were given enemy coordinates to fire upon but only one launch team, out of the three, was able to successfully do it. The two other units had problems. There seemed to be maintenance issues with one of the rocket launchers. The crew knew how to set up and fire but an electrical launch mechanism on the launcher truck somehow messed-up and failed during the test. The last of the three teams executed a textbook perfect launch. Too bad their math calculations were off. Had the rocket actually been launched in anger, it would have wiped out a friendly ROK Army position nearly 15 clicks off target. That was a really big mistake since Honest John impacts equate to mass casualties.

The week continued on at an agonizingly slow pace with sirens going off at all hours and daily business continually interrupted with those damned no-notice drills and relentless inspections. I think LTC Palladino looked at every scrap of paper he could find in my offices, every piece of evidence in my evidence room and every investigation we had on file. He also scrutinized all our Standard Operating Procedures and questioned my MPs about every damned one of them. As time progressed I was getting less and less confident about how we were doing. The only positive thing Buck Sergeant God could come up with was, "At least we didn't nuke no friendly troops like them other guys did!"

Friday finally arrived and so did the sound of two Hueys. Ironbone and Mack arrived in two, separate helicopters around noon. There was no fanfare this time; they were all business. Both General Officers immediately cloistered themselves in a signal van parked down at the end of the runway. The van was one of the inspection support vehicles that showed up the second day of the TPI. The rest of the day, there was what seemed like an endless stream of Warrant Officers coming and going from the van.

There were TPI teams visiting the mountaintop Hawk Batteries today. The last of the Honest John units were out there, somewhere in the field, defending the Missile Command's honor with three mock-launch exercises. Rumor had it that this was *The Test*. If all went well we might just pass this damned TPI.

Nothing of interest had happened for us all day either. LTC Palladino was among the missing. Today was the first day I woke up at a normal hour, plus there was no one waiting for me in the hall with a stopwatch. I fully expected Palladino to be there with another incident message. He'd handed me a total of nine notes during the week. No member of the visiting inspection team seemed interested in us anymore. So, this warm sunny day we all just sort of hung around the PMO waiting for something to happen, but it never did.

I was standing outside, with my back up against the curved outside of the PMO hut, just enjoying the feeling of the sun-warmed, corrugated metal on my back. I was thinking about nothing in particular and then it dawned on me—I was totally relaxed. I guess it was the combination of mental and physical exhaustion after a very hectic and trying week. It was actually more than that; I suddenly realized this was the first week, since my arrival, where I had not been forced to deal with Weatherspoon in one negative way or another. I guess I didn't understand, until now, just how much he'd been affecting me mentally. I was shaken out of my daydreaming by SP4 Hanlon. "Lieutenant, the TPI teams are convoying in from the field and so are the rocket units.

A small group of us slowly walked over to the vicinity of the Main Gate. Coming down hill from the city center, traffic circle, we could see the trucks and Jeeps all lined up and perfectly spaced like a line of ants on the sidewalk. First, came the TPI Jeeps and ¾ ton trucks. I could tell the inspections and testing were over. The Warrants were kicked back, just "smokin' & jokin'" acting all relaxed like. Kuska was now standing next to me. "Well, Kuska, watcha' think? Did we pass?" Fred gave me a little smile, "Here come the Rocketeers, look at their faces and that will give you the first clue." The first two Jeeps rolled through, then a Duce and then the three, 5-ton launchers, followed by the transporters and cargo support vehicles. The last vehicle was a 5-ton dump truck. Our answer was in the bed of the dump truck. The bent tail fins of an Honest John were sticking up above the high sides of the dump truck's bed.

I know Kuska saw it, but he didn't mention it. All he said was, "I don't see many smiles; how about you?" I was still staring at the back of the dump truck in disbelief as it drove by and headed towards the unit's motor pool. "They dropped a rocket! They must have dropped a rocket! Oh no! Can you fuckin' believe it? Game over, the end, we flunked; we're screwed!" I just stood there slowly shaking my head and watching as the dump truck disappeared into the motor pool complex. "Those poor bastards are dead meat!"

I hadn't had much time to see Joyce since the TPI started and although it wasn't really my fault, I still felt guilty about leaving her alone in the house these past four, or was it five, nights? I did get a chance to talk to her on the field phone a couple of nights, just to be sure all was okay with her up at the house and that she didn't need anything. Most of all, I just wanted her to know she was on my mind. I even popped by the house in the Jeep a couple of times in between alerts and inspections to drop off stuff, give her a quick kiss, tell her I love her and give brief updates on how the inspection was going. She pretty much stayed clear of the camp so as not to raise any unneeded questions about her presence in Korea; that didn't need to be raised.

Towards evening I rang her up, "It's over, Hon. At least, I think it's over. It's probably wise I sleep here one more night in case there's one last alert but, by tomorrow, I think things will start getting back to normal." Joyce had been really supportive and understanding through all of this. These were the times I was glad to be married to such a down-to-earth woman whose father was also a career army officer. She knew the drills. She knew there were times her Daddy, and now her husband, would just not be able to be there with her. Most importantly, she accepted it, for now at least, as our normal way of life. She once told me, "There are easy assignments and there are hard assignments. I have the feeling this one's going to be a difficult, not to mention strange, assignment."

It was late, about 2300, and I was pretty much brain-dead and bone-tired. My mail from the last several days was piled up on the corner of my desk, so I decided to take a break and go through it before I headed back to my bunk. One thing nice about being on an unaccompanied assignment and having your wife with you was there were just about no bills. I mean there was no rent, no water, no gas, no garbage pick-up, no "Gulf" gasoline credit card bill, no car payment and only our small, Korean, electric bill.

I picked out a "Playboy" magazine from my small stack of mail, leaned back in my desk chair, adjusted my desk lamp, put my feet up on my desk, and got comfortable. It may have been May but Miss March looked amazing. I was adjusting the magazine to get my best view of the centerfold when my office door flew open. *Holy Christ!* It was Ironbone! The magazine flew over my shoulder into the corner and crashed into a metal trashcan. My feet lurched up off the desk so fast I came within inches of flipping over backwards. I grasped at the wall and my desk and somehow saved myself from going straight over onto the gray-painted, cement floor. With what was left of my dignity, I snapped to some semblance of attention and saluted.

Ironbone was in no mood for formalities, "Okay Royce, you started this mess! I got the feelin' just about every son-of-a-bitch around here is lyin' about one thing or another. I'm goin' to ask you some straight questions and you better damned-well give me some straight answers; you got that, Son?" I automatically replied with an emphatic, "Yes Sir!" "Okay, I got a Major, a Captain and a Lieutenant Colonel all claiming that accusations of the Commander's drinking and dealings with local nationals are being exaggerated by a small group of non-performing, malcontents who've got it in for the Colonel. They also say any statements I may have seen were probably coerced. All three are stickin' tight to that story. Watcha' got to say about that, Son?"

So, this was how it was going to be? The Command Group had closed ranks around Weatherspoon and it was going to be my word against theirs.

One constant thing about the night shift at Page was that Staff Sergeant Oden was almost always the Desk Sergeant.

"Sir, would you mind if I brought one of those non-performing malcontents back here to talk to you?"

"Not at all, Son, and if ya got it, bring a cup of black coffee when ya come back; this may be a long night."

I walked to the Desk and Staff Sergeant Oden apologized, "Sorry, sir, the General blind-sided me and said if I yelled 'Attention' he was going to shoot me."

"Not so sure he wouldn't have, Sergeant Oden. Please have your Desk Clerk take over? I need you to answer some of the General's questions ... Oh, and do we have any fresh coffee?"

"Sure do, Sir, just made a fresh pot."

While I was filling two cups, Mrs. Oden walked in with the nightly supply of hot, peppery egg sandwiches for the shift. This was too good to be true, so I jumped on it. "Sergeant Oden, would you please bring Mrs. Oden with you and can you also bring a few of those sandwiches? The General might be hungry.

When I walked back in my office, Ironbone was sitting comfortably behind my desk with his feet up and checking out Miss March. He glanced over the top of the magazine and looked me right in the eyes with his one, "No wonder you almost killed yourself, Son, this little girl is down right devastatin'". I found humor in this but didn't dare show it. "General, I've got Sergeant and Mrs. Oden on their way back here to talk to you." I handed him one of the coffees. "Thanks for the warning, Son; I'll just slip your little girlie magazine in your bottom drawer here." I didn't know if he was making fun of me or if it was just the way they talked back in West Texas.

Sergeant Oden and his wife came through the door. Oden was big-eyed, juggling the food and trying to figure if he should salute before or after he put the tray down. Most soldiers never get the chance to talk with a four-star let alone sit down and have coffee with one. Mrs. Oden was trying to make herself very small behind her husband. Ironbone grabbed Oden's hand, "Sergeant, if you got anything to say about the Base Commander's drinking and the way he interacts with the local nationals, now's the time to sound off."

Sergeant Oden started out slowly, feeling his way, afraid he might not say something exactly right or maybe offend the general, in some way. Ironbone encouraged him with a word here and there and Oden started to open up. Mrs. Oden, who had been holding back in the shadows, came over to the edge of the desk and picked up the small plate of sandwiches. Timidly, she approached the General, then bowed and offered him something to eat. Ironbone gave a little bow of his head and said, "Thank you, Mam, *kam-sa-hom-ni-da*, (thank you) this is very kind of you." Mrs. Oden smiled a little smile, bowed and in a tiny voice said, "*Chon-maneyo*" (you're welcome) then scurried back into the shadows behind her husband. Ironbone brought it up to his nose for a brief second. I chimed in, "They're very good, Sir, hot and spicy, we eat them all the time." With that assurance, Ironbone took a sizable bite and nodded approval. Before he took a second, he said, "Please continue, Sergeant and have one of these egg sandwiches; they're great!" Sergeant Oden continued while the General reached for another sandwich.

Conversations continued on for a couple more hours. Big Chong came back and coaxed Mrs. Oden to tell the General how Weatherspoon had cursed at her and called her horrible names. With her head down and eyes averted she quietly spoke, in Korean, of several encounters with our Colonel. Big Chong translated for the General. No notes were taken. It was as if Ironbone just wanted to hear the words first-hand.

Several MPs began to gather around the MP Desk area. They somehow found out Ironbone was in my office talking to the troops. I guess everyone figured this was the one and only shot they would ever have at payback. I informed the General there were several men outside who had written statements in the past and wanted to be available if he wanted to speak with them. Ironbone called several in. The stories were not pretty and there were several of them I didn't even know about because they went back before my arrival. A little after 0200, Ironbone stood up and stretched. "Well son, as Popeye used to say, 'I had all I can stands cuz I can't stands no more!' I'm bushed and confident that damned encyclopedia-thick pile of statements you dropped off with my Provost Marshal are pretty damned factual."

"You actually read it, General?"

"Son, I read every damned word in that thing and you cost me big bucks. You ruined two or three good evenings of poker with some Pentagon people I know I coulda' won a lot of money off of. If I don't see you again, Lieutenant, I just want to say thanks for bringing this whole mess to my attention."

He shook my hand; we saluted and he disappeared into the night. His last words, as he faded into the night, were, "Thank the little lady for those great egg sandwiches and I hope your writing days are now over, Lieutenant!"

I tried to go to sleep that night but my brain just wouldn't shut off. I kept going over and over the fact that for nearly three hours I had been in a one-on-one conversation with one of the great warrior chiefs of our time. I had the opportunity to watch this living-legend up close and talk to him, in between interviews. I watched his every move and listened to his every word. I marveled how he commanded respect, and sometimes fear, yet put soldiers completely at ease with him at the same time. It was apparent every soldier who came into that room genuinely liked and trusted him. It may have been a mini-mentoring session designed so I didn't even realize it at the time. All I know is, I learned a lot that night. I didn't take written notes but the visual impressions he left inscribed on my brain would stick with me for the rest of my life. I will never forget that night or General Ironbone.

33

Don't Pull the Mask off the Old Lone Ranger

A very unusual thing happened the next morning. Ironbone, unceremoniously, climbed into his helicopter, followed by LTC Palladino and a few of the Warrants, and just flew off into the sunrise. Within minutes of the General's lift-off, a convoy of TPI vehicles departed the Main Gate for Seoul with the remainder of his inspection team. Normally there would be a big, hairy, formal exit briefing. The Chief inspector would normally go over what you did well and where you need to improve, then there would be closing comments from Ironbone. None of this happened, not a word! The whole TPI Team was headed south on MSR 17 before hardly anyone in the camp had even gotten out of bed. Nobody, even the old hands, had ever experienced such a thing. Dad Dunkerly said we must have passed because he knew when you flunked one of these things they always relieve the commander, on the spot, and put the XO in charge as an interim solution.

Dad was right; over the next few days, things pretty much went back to our dysfunctional state of normal. Weatherspoon seemed a little shaky for the first few days, but it didn't take long before he was deep in my shit again and getting royally ripped most nights. The only difference I could see now was he wasn't trying to climb fences, screw with the Desk MPs or cuss out Koreans every time he had a few drinks. It may sound strange, but most of us considered these minimal changes as huge improvements over the past and well worth the weeklong TPI rat screw.

The other big change was the emphasis on training. The *Rocket Men* were training just about every day. There wasn't a morning or afternoon that went by without a mock launch exercise happening somewhere on or off base. Weatherspoon was all over the place observing training. He was critiquing solders, encouraging NCOs and admonishing officers. The SOB was behaving like a real, no shit, U.S. Army Colonel who honestly gave a damn about his troops and mission. I figured old Ironbone had fired a shot across the Colonel's bow and was giving him time to clean up his act.

However, there were some things that didn't change. I was still the KATUSA Canteen Manager and still logging hundreds of miles a week in my Jeep visiting the Hawk sites. I still had to hand in my weekly, *busy work*, physical security reports on the anti-aircraft missile batteries. So, although a lot had changed at Camp Page, my life was still pretty shitty; and, I was still the *Old Man's* ace, number one, whipping boy.

It was late morning on the 30th of June. It was one of those beautiful, warm Sundays everyone always hopes for; about seventy-five degrees Fahrenheit, blue sky and just the right kind of summer breeze. Joyce and I decided to enjoy the day to its fullest. We were taking a lovely, long, relaxing walk through Chunchon's surrounding countryside. At Joyce's request, Jin Hee and Kuska joined us. The girls were a few paces ahead, holding hands and giggling, while Kuska and I were in deep discussion over some of the latest crap going on in the world.

As if losing Dr. King to an assassin in March hadn't been enough, on the 5th of June, some asshole Jordanian with two same names, *Sirhan Sirhan,* shot Bobby Kennedy to death after a speech at the Ambassador Hotel in San Francisco. Kennedy had already taken the California and South Dakota Democratic Primaries. He was well on his way to be the Democrats' Presidential Candidate in November and, probably, the next President. Instead he died in a hospital on the 6th of June. I always thought it ironic he died on D-Day, the anniversary of the WW II, Normandy Invasion. No way could anyone ever forget that date! Kuska was convinced it was a Commie plot; some kind of payback for us backing down the Soviets during the Cuban Missile Crisis.

Kuska had told me about the *Prague Spring.* Some guy by the name of Ludvik Vaculic had released his "Two Thousand Words" manifesto criticizing Communist rule in Czechoslovakia and warning foreign powers not to try and control his country. The Czechs seemed to have gotten rid of their Soviet puppet government without a single shot being fired. I told him I thought the Czechs were out of the woods and it was all going to work. Kuska disagreed; he said the Soviet Army was not extending its summer military exercises on the Czechoslovakian border for nothing. I remember his words: "Those poor bastards are going to be crushed by Soviet tanks before the snow flies!" As it would turn out, a short time later, Kuska's words were prophetic.

After that cheery conversation, Kuska and I agreed to drop the political discussion and get back into the moment. The day had turned out to be one of those wonderful summer days that now and then come around, for no particular reason. Nothing had been planned out; we were just taking it as it came and it couldn't have been more perfect. While we were strolling along the river; Kuska noted some sort of a houseboat tied up ahead against the riverbank. When we got a little closer, Kuska and Jin Hee walked up to the boat and talked to a woman on board. From the path where Joyce and I were standing, it looked like Kuska was actually the one doing the most talking. We were far enough away that I could barely hear what was being said, but the conversation was in Korean and all three seemed to understand one another.

As it turned out, the houseboat was actually a floating restaurant and bar. There was some sort of festival starting next week and tomorrow they would be docking closer to town but the woman said if we wanted to come aboard for a drink and snacks we were welcome to. We were all thirsty at this point in our little fieldtrip; so, we gladly took the lady up on her friendly offer. We spent the next hour or so enjoying each other's company and watching the late afternoon sunlight dance on the waters as the river raced by us to join the "Han" on its way south to Seoul. Kuska and I had a couple of *OB* beers and the girls ordered some sort of funny tasting Korean cocktail. All I know was that it was pink, came in a tall glass and tasted a whole lot like ice cold, liquid, *Bazooka* Bubble Gum. It was sicky sweet and disgusting, but must have had a decent kick because the girls were really getting giddy. Jin Hee was pulling on the tip of her nose and trying to stretch it out as far as she could. She was doing Joyce imitations complete with mannerisms and speech patterns. Apparently, by Korean standards, Joyce had quite a honker. We were all killing ourselves laughing. Joyce retaliated by pushing her nose in and did Jin Hee to a tee, ersatz Korean and all. Kuska had tears in his eyes from laughing so much. It got to the point where we were all laughing so hard it hurt. The boat crew finally had to come out just to see what these crazy people were laughing at, and even they started cracking up. The girls' ridiculous floor show was enjoyed by one and all. It had been quite awhile since I'd had such a good, long belly laugh and it hurt really good deep down inside.

The walk back to town was pure slapstick. The girls were goofing on each other and having a great day. I guess I never realized it until now but the two seemed more like sisters than just friends from different halves of the globe. As Chunchon slowly came into view, the effects of the alcohol had pretty much worn off. After our long hike back we were now all starving and thirsty. Jin Hee told us the *Pul-go-gie* at the restaurant in the "Crown Tourist Hotel" was wonderful; so, we decided to have an early dinner there. I'd passed the place many times but had never been inside. It was very nice, dark and woody with sort of an old world, European feeling and charm to it. The dark, carved cherry wood trim and crystal chandeliers made the decor seem a bit out of place here in downtown Korea. I guessed it was designed to attract Western tourists, although I had yet to see any. The prices were high enough so most GIs wouldn't patronize the restaurant or bar except maybe on special occasions. We checked the menu and then our wallets. Between us, we figured we had enough *Won* to cover dinner, a couple drinks and maybe a tip.

We ordered and the girls promptly got up to go to the ladies room. Seems it's the same tradition in the East as well as the West. That left Kuska and I sitting there, staring in silence at each other over two tall glasses of cold beer. I don't know why, but I picked this moment to ask. Something had been bugging me for weeks now and, today, Kuska's impressive display of spoken Korean down by the river brought it back to the front of my mind.

"Kuska, who the hell are you anyway?"

"What? What do you mean?"

"Oh come on! You arrive here in the dead of night, you work wonders with the Investigations Section and you speak absolutely fluent fucking Korean; but you don't tell anybody you can, and you claim you've never been here before. So what the hell really gives?"

Kuska took a deep breath and a long pull on his beer; he quickly checked the room, then looked me straight in the eye for several seconds. We were the only people in the dining room. "Okay, I guess you've earned an explanation, although, I normally never give one." There was a long pause; as Kuska searched for just the right words. "Herb, you're the closest thing I've had to a real friend in and long, long time. I'm going to be leaving soon." I broke in, "What do you mean you're leaving soon? You're not even half way through your tour." Kuska looked me straight in the eye and leaned in closer, "Herb, I'm not *in* the Army. Yes, I work for the government but I'm not really in the Army." I searched his face for hidden clues as to what the hell he was talking about but there were none. "Sometimes I'm Army, sometimes I'm Navy, and other times I'm a U.S. civilian or maybe, sometimes; Polish, Czech, East German or even Russian. I speak all those languages plus Korean. I become whatever I need to be to get my mission done and live to see another day."

I was still having problems digesting what I was hearing. "Well, what the hell are you doing here if you're not in the Army?"

"In three words, I'm hiding out." Kuska could tell from my expression I just wasn't getting it, so he continued. "Before I came here I was working in Prague."

"You mean Prague, as in Prague, fucking Czechoslovakia?"

"Yes! Every morning, first thing, I would get up and go to this open air market before I went to work; I'd buy fresh flowers for my office from this nice little old lady." He looked at me as if what he was saying should make sense. My body language and expression were silently telling him *"Yeah, so what?"* So he continued, "Well, one morning I went to buy my flowers and the little old lady showed me a Teddy Bear; so I bought it." I guess I was looking at Kuska like he had three heads. "Don't you see? That was my signal they were on to me and I had to get the hell out of Czechoslovakia!"

"I found a safe corner in an alleyway and ripped open the bear's back seam; inside were my escape instructions. I was told to go to a particular cabstand with the Teddy Bear and look for a cab, a *Skoda,* bearing a particular number plate. I didn't dare go back to my apartment for fear the police would be there waiting for me. I found the cab, climbed in with my Teddy Bear, and, without asking any questions or even saying a word, the driver took me on several circuitous laps of the city to ensure we were not being followed; we then departed for the country-side. When we got out to some remote farm road the driver briefly stopped the cab by a farmhouse and secured a brown paper, wrapped package from the barn, handed it to me and we drove on. The package contained ski goggles, a lock-back knife, leather work gloves, a small flashlight and a 9 mm *Walther* pistol with two extra clips of ammunition. About fifteen kilometers out of Prague, he dropped me off in a hollow in a heavily wooded area. He went back to the trunk again and emerged with the fully dressed upper torso of a store manikin and propped it up in the back seat. He handed me written directions, a map and a small compass. When he waved goodbye and drove off, it then dawned on me; never once had he uttered even a single word. The cab drove off in the same direction with the dummy riding proudly in back. I stepped into the woods, found a comfortable place to hole up for the day and stayed there until after dark. Using the compass, map and flashlight, I took off overland for about five kilometers to the designated wooded area next to a large meadow. I was to stay there until 2 AM."

I broke in again. "So what do they do, come in, land a plane in the field and pick you up?"

Kuska felt the need to tell me, in detail, how this all worked: "No, that's the way they used to do it, but now-a-days that's way too dangerous. It's a little more dramatic and hair-raising than that. I waited until about five minutes before two, then ran out into the middle of the meadow. At almost exactly 2AM I heard heavily-muffled engine sounds coming straight towards me from the west. When I saw the silhouette of a large aircraft hurtling straight at me, at about two hundred feet off the ground, I turned on my little flashlight and pointed it right at the oncoming plane. A green light in the nose of the aircraft gave me two quick green flashes. A flat, black mass, with the unmistakable silhouette of a C-130 Hercules, flashed overhead. A large canvas bag with luminous streamers crashed to the ground almost on top of me. I knew exactly what it was and went straight to work. When I popped it open, there were five things inside: A five-point safety harness, a black crash helmet, a long length of rubberized rope with D-rings attached to both ends and a deflated midget blimp with a helium cylinder attached to it. I quickly put the harness on, clipped one end of the rope to it and the other to the mini-blimp. I turned the gas cylinder valve on and the balloon began to take shape. I quickly put on my goggles, helmet and work gloves. As I was doing this the now fully inflated blimp had self-separated from the helium tank and was rising into the dark sky, dragging the rubberized rope with it. The little blimp rose about two hundred feet or so in the air with only my body weight acting as a mooring anchor. I adjusted my equipment and attached the helium tank and bag to my harness. I then turned around 180 degrees from the direction the Herc had come from. Per my training, I sat down on the ground and assumed a tight fetal position with my arms folded in and my chin tucked hard into my chest. As soon as I did this I could hear the four powerful turbo props churning through darkness towards me. I snuck a small peek and there was this sinister, black Herc coming in very low and fast straight towards me. The nose on these Special Ops 130s have a large 'V' shaped apparatus affixed to it. The pilot is looking through a 'Starlight', night-vision device; and the mini-blimp has these glow-in-the-dark panels. The pilot lines up the 'V' so it passes just under the blimp. When the rope hanging down from the blimp makes contact with the 'V' device, it automatically locks onto the rope. It also, somehow, cuts the blimp free to float off, to who knows where, on the prevailing winds. Nothing happens on the ground for a second or two as the rubberized rope keeps stretching. Then, all of a sudden, you start coming up off the ground. At first, it's a gentle slow-motion lifting sensation because there's still some give left in the rope. Then, it begins to contract and, I tell you, Herb, you think you've been shot from a crossbow. The acceleration and G-forces are unbelievable. The only thing that stops you from whacking into the Herc is, once the stretching ends and contracting begins to slow, the bad aerodynamics of your body slows you down until you're finally matching the speed of the airplane. So, here you are, trailing out behind this low flying C-130, dangling from an inch-thick, rubber rope at 150 knots."

I thought I knew a lot about airplanes but I'd never heard of this, so I asked, "So how'd they get you inside the plane?"

Kuska continued: "This is where it gets really scary! When the rope passes under the 130, they have this crew of crazy people waiting on the lowered rear cargo ramp and they somehow grab the rope as it trails out behind the plane. They hook it up to this oversized deep-sea fishing rig—for lack of a better term—and they just reel you in like a Tuna. There's this cargo netting attached to the lowered ramp. They reel you into the netting and then you're supposed to grab onto it and help them help you into the aircraft's cargo bay. Remember, you're still doing one-fifty or better and there's a lot of turbulence and buffeting back there. That's why you've got the helmet and gloves. When you finally get close to the ramp they yank you up on it and retract the ramp. The pilot then hits the deck and hauls ass back across the West German border at over 300 knots, hoping to avoid enemy radar, missiles and interceptors."

"Holy Crap, Kuska, how the hell did you know how to do all that?"

"We get one training exercise out in the California desert; so, we know what to expect. The Czech extraction was my third time, if you count the one in training, and I hated every one of them. The other problem is the Air Force has to create diversions along the border and get as much radar jamming equipment in the air as possible to keep the bad guys off your ass."

"So, why Korea?"

"Well, I lied; I've been here several times. Without going into the details, I was even in North Korea once, for a short time, posing as a Russian Army Colonel helping the Gooks with their surface-to-air missile capabilities. I even coordinated with some other Russian officers and got the classified, field manuals for their weapons systems and radars. The Reds are so into security and so freaking scared of their own shadows they don't often ask questions. They just assumed they didn't get the word or were not authorized to have the information.

They've never actively looked for me here so this is where I like to hide out whenever things get hot. The KGB has been hunting for me on both sides of the Iron Curtain but the word now is they've called off their dogs. Our side, somehow, convinced them I'm dead again. There was a mystery body, in a bogus extraction harness, dropped from the C-130 near my pick-up point. Everything was rigged to look like something went wrong during extraction and I plunged to my death. So, now all I have to do is just show up in another place with another identity and start all over again."

"So, I guess your name's not even Kuska?" He smiled and shook his head. Then the personal side of all this hit me. "What about Jin Hee?" "Look Herb, where I go, I can't take anything or anybody with me. My mother and father are both dead and I have no brothers, sisters or even close relatives. Except in some files somewhere in DC, I don't really even exist. I don't even keep photographs of Jin Hee or anybody else for that matter; it's just too dangerous. I take them, but give them all back to her then burn the negatives. I'll miss Jin Hee a lot, she's a wonderful girl and I probably do love her as much as I can love anybody; but I have to leave and I can't even tell her goodbye because I can't answer all her questions. I know I'm going to really hurt her but she's not the first. I can't live like a monk. I love the feel of a woman too much. Sometimes, being with a woman is the only sanity I have in my world. Without that feeling of warmth in my life I think I'd just go off the deep end. So, the decision I always have to make is, either no woman in my life or hurting some lovely girl I've been with for a few months. If I tried to keep a romance going, I'd just be risking both of us getting killed in the process. It's just something I have to do; it's my way of life. What makes me valuable to my country is there is no way the enemy can ever get at me. I have no handles they can grab onto and twist.

I have to have your word you won't tell Jin Hee, or anyone for that matter, about my leaving until after I'm gone. Like the *Lone Ranger*, I'm taking a risk by lifting my mask so you can see who I really am; so, please keep my secret a secret."

I looked back at him with a look of resignation. "You know I will; I guess I can dream up something to try and let her down as gently as possible. Can I write a book in thirty years and tell the world what happened?"

"Go right ahead; I'll probably be long dead by then, and besides, nobody's going to believe you anyway."

"You probably got that right!" We looked at each other for a long moment, then clinked glasses and took long pulls on our beers.

The girls came giggling back to the table and Joyce asked, "Why the serious faces guys, this is supposed to be our fun time after that horrible inspection" We smiled and helped them get seated. "Kuska and I were just talking about the North Korean infiltrators but we promise to stop." Joyce then warned, "Well this is the last time today we're going to leave you two *Gloomy Gusses* alone to talk shop."

I think I did a pretty good job of covering the fact that one of my best sergeants and also a good friend was a fucking spy of some sort and that he was leaving soon for who-the-hell-knows-where?

Jin Hee was right; our Korean steak dinner was delicious. We stuffed ourselves and, in the waning rays of this glorious day, we paid the bill and reluctantly meandered down the hill towards Camp Page. About half way down, Kuska and Jin Hee peeled off, waved goodbye and headed for Jin Hee's place. They had their arms around each other and Jin Hee's bell-like laughter trailed off into the distance. I started to feel heavy inside again. I put my arm around Joyce's shoulder and we continued onto the camp and my BOQ. I had to get my Monday *Hawk Site Security Report* assembled for the Colonel's perusal. I knew it was just busy work, which he never read, but God forbid if they wasn't sitting there on his desk every Monday at 0700.

It was very close to dusk when SP4 Cortez came knocking on my door. "Sir, we just got word there's a chopper in-bound to the VIP pad." I'm thinking to myself, *"What the hell? Don't tell me they're coming back!"* Joyce and Paul were sitting around our card table smoking and reading the back of Paul's new Otis Redding LP album cover. I told them I'd be back and departed down the hall with Otis' words fading in the air, *"2000 miles from home...."*

Cortez's timing was right on. I had just gotten back into uniform and transferred my .45 from the shoulder holster I'd been wearing under my shirt to my Army issue hip holster; so, I was more or less ready to go anyway. We got to the PMO, grabbed a Jeep and got to the runway in record time. The MP Desk had informed the Command Group we had visitors. The Colonel and his driver arrived just a few minutes behind us. Weatherspoon looked a little worse for wear. After all, this was a Sunday and the Army's supposed to take them off and relax when possible. He'd already had a few but was nowhere near his usual shit-faced, lovable self.

Some VIP arrivals are announced and some aren't. It's normally a security precaution or something like the surprise inspection we just had. Anyway, nobody likes having important visitors just drop in unannounced. Weatherspoon neither looked at nor spoke to me in the calm before *whump, whump* sounds filled the air. The Huey touched down perfectly and the turbine whine immediately started dropping. The Crew Chief slid back the cargo door and two figures stepped down onto the tarmac. The first walked out of the darkness towards us. The second walked off the pad away from us, lit a long, thin cigar and gazed out in the direction of the river. As the first passenger walked closer we realized it was General "Skippy" Mack, the 8th Army Deputy CG. Weatherspoon put on his bravest face, smiled, saluted and said, "Welcome, General, good to see you again; to what do we owe this honor?" The turbine had now wound down to just a slight whine and in the still twilight air; from where I was standing, I could hear every word said.

"Ralph, as you know, the TPI didn't go very well." Weatherspoon broke in, "Skippy, we had some bad breaks but, in the past weeks since the inspection, we've come a long way towards making the necessary corrections. If you brought the team back, in a week or two, we could pass the damned thing with flying colors." Skippy looked at Weatherspoon while carefully formulating what he was going to say next. "Ralph, I'm sorry but that's just not going to happen; that boat has already sailed! I'm here because Ironbone knows you and I were West Point classmates together. He thought it best to have a friend tell you; Ralph, you've been relieved of command! My instructions are to pick you up and bring you back to Seoul with me tonight." Weatherspoon looked totally bewildered, "Skippy, I don't know if I can do that. There's so much I have to do. I have to leave instructions for my staff. I have to fill in my XO so there will be a smooth transition. I'll have to pack my stuff." Skippy broke in again, but more firmly this time. "No, Ralph! Listen to me; let's just go back to your quarters, pack an overnight bag and get on the chopper. We'll have your stuff packed out and delivered to you in Seoul in a day or two. You're going with me tonight, Ralph, and we've got less than an hour to get out of here."

Ralph just stood there seemingly not knowing what to do. Finally he said, "But I have to talk to my Executive Officer and my staff to tell them what's happening and give them final instructions." Skippy placed a hand on each of Weatherspoon's shoulders, "Look at me, Ralph, and hear what I'm saying. Ralph, your XO's not taking over either. I've brought your replacement with me and he's going to hand-pick his own staff." Skippy gestured over to where the other passenger was now standing some thirty feet away gazing at the faint pink colors the setting sun had painted on the high clouds in the Western sky.

Skippy said, "Come on, Ralph, let's go!" Weatherspoon balked, "No, I want to meet my replacement first." He then walked with Skippy towards the lone figure whose back was still towards the two. Skippy made the introductions, "Ralph, I'd like to introduce you to Colonel James R. Calvert." The new Colonel was still facing away and puffing on that long, skinny cigar. Ralph seemed to be regaining some semblance of composure and he said to his replacement, "Well, Colonel Calvert, the least I can do, as my last official act, is show you around the Camp a little and introduce you to my staff." Colonel Calvert spun a one-eighty on his heels, removed the cigar from his mouth and locked eyeballs with Weatherspoon. In strong, low tones, said, "The only thing I want you to do, Colonel, is get the fuck off my installation so I can get started cleaning up your goddamned mess!" He spun around again and walked away.

Weatherspoon was speechless and just stood there with a dazed expression and his mouth hanging wide open. Skippy didn't say a word, he just turned to Weatherspoon and said, "Come on, Ralph, let's go get your things." They walked back to the one and only staff car we had on base.

Weatherspoon always made a fuss over that damned car and I couldn't understand why. It was just this crappy, stripped down, black, 65 Ford Galaxy 500 with plastic seats, black-wall tires and tiny hubcaps. The only thing it did was shine. He had a SP4 driver and all that poor kid ever did was drive the Colonel and shine that piece of shit Ford, but I had to admit, he had it looking like it was made outa' black glass. They got in and that's the last time I ever saw Colonel Ralph J. Weatherspoon. I don't know why, but I felt kinda' sorry for him.

I was busy with other things when, about an hour later, I heard the chopper taking off. A bunch of the MPs and the KATUSA Guard Commander went down to the pad to be sure he left. They reported back that Skippy Mack did in fact leave and "The Screaming Eagle" was with him. The news spread like wildfire. Every Korean I saw in camp that night was smiling.

34

Gentleman Jim

In the hour or so between Skippy Mack's arrival and Weatherspoon's departure, I kinda' lost track of our new boss. I just assumed an Army Colonel could find a place to bunk on his own. What I didn't know was it wouldn't be long before I found out where he was.

It was nearly 2130 hours when Joyce and I were in my office gathering our things together so we could head for home. The camp's loudspeakers crackled and a new voice came on the air. "Men of the Fifth U.S. Missile Command, this is Colonel James R. Calvert, your new commander. I need you all to get into your fatigue uniforms and join me in the "Missileman" Theater in exactly thirty minutes, I repeat, everyone in the theater in three-zero minutes. This is not a request; it's an order! That is all."

My office was diagonally across the street from the theater, maybe not even fifty yards away. Since I was already in my fatigues, I got Joyce a *Coke* and today's edition of *Stars & Stripes*, then started walking over to watch everyone arrive and maybe get a good seat. Several of my MPs were already milling around the station; so, we all walked over as a group. I gave orders for Sergeant Oden and Mr. Su to man the Desk and for two KATUSAs to hold down the Gate. The rest of us would make our way over to the theater to hear what our new boss had to say. Colonel Calvert was already on the stage setting up the podium just the way he wanted it. Captain Huddleston and The Stupid Colonel Mixon were fawning all over him. The Gorilla and the Command Sergeant Major were already seated in the first row. Colonel Calvert eyed me as I walked down the aisle towards the stage. I don't know if he recognized me from the flight-line or if it was just that I was surrounded by Army cops wearing MP brassards, but he stopped what he was doing for a moment, straightened up, and gave me a long look. I was sure he was looking straight at me; so I said, "Evening Sir!" He replied with, "Good evening Lieutenant, you must be my Provost Marshal or the most dangerous man in camp; which is it?" I closed both my hands and pointed my thumbs back at my chest, "I'm Lieutenant Royce, your PM, Sir!" He nodded, studied me for a few seconds and then went back to his preparations. My MPs and I took up the third and part of the fourth rows of the theater.

We sat together as a group watching as the evening's entertainment started filing by. Hundreds of soldiers were streaming in. Everyone seemed to be gravitating towards the back rows. It was obvious some had way too much to drink, while others were still half asleep. As more and more arrived, they generally seemed dismayed because they had to move more towards the front, as the back was filling up fast. It was as if no one wanted to be close enough to be recognized by the new commander. Of course, the Command Group took up the front row. I always thought if I were one of the Unit Commanders, I'd want to be in charge of one of the *Hawk* batteries; those guys always seemed to be excused from these last-minute gatherings. The boss usually drove or flew out to their sites for these kinds of messages.

The joint was packed again, for the second time, in just a short while. It was a good thing the "Village Rats" were still somewhere downtown or else the place would have been more uncomfortable than it already was. At what I figured was exactly thirty minutes after the PA announcement, the new boss walked out on the stage. Captain Huddleston yelled a half-hearted "Attention!" and everyone snapped-to in the overcrowded theater. Colonel Calvert, in a soft but authoritative voice, told everyone to be seated. There was the inevitable shuffling and scraping sound of way too many combat boots trying to find a place to sit down in an area much too small to fit everybody. But, in a few seconds, somehow they did.

Our new Colonel began. "Gentlemen, Colonel Weatherspoon has been relieved of this command!" A few seconds of mumbling and shuffling ensued. "He departed this evening for Seoul along with General Mack. My name is James Ross Calvert and I was sent here to be your new commander. Do you know why General Ironbone asked me to come here and be your new commander?" The Spaniard leaned over the back of my seat and cupping both hands to his mouth, in a stage whisper, said, *"Ah ain't askin' no mo questions cuz I'ze knows everthins re-tor-kull rount he-ah."* I silently smiled over my shoulder at Hank and moved my index finger up to my lips. I don't know if Calvert heard him or not, but after a brief pause, the Colonel continued. "I'm here because I'm one of only three colonels in the whole U.S. Army who's been through Honest John TPIs and never even gotten so much as a minor technical finding, and I've been through a bunch of them.

I saw the results of 5th Missile's TPI and, according to that report you sons-a-bitches couldn't hit the ground with an Honest John, if you dropped the damned thing!" He stopped talking for a few seconds then held both arms out with his open palms toward the audience. "Pardon me, excuse me, I stand corrected; you sons-a-bitches *did* prove you could do that!" No one knew whether to laugh or not at that comment, even though there was a note of sarcasm in his voice. A light smattering of laughter could be heard snaking throughout the theater. This drew some craned necks and sinister glares from both Mixon and Huddleston. The Gorilla just sat there looking straight forward and expressionless.

Calvert continued, "I read the whole thing, the whole damned TPI report from cover to cover. According to that report you sons-a-bitches are simply *No damned good!* At first, I thought this report must be some kinda' practical joke old Ironbone was playing on me just to see how I'd react! As I read on, I realized it was the most pathetic readiness evaluation document I have ever laid my eyes on in my twenty-six years of United States Army service. After reading it, I looked our 8th Army Commanding General, in his one good eye, and asked if he was kidding; he wasn't! He gave me the choice of running for dear life back to my comfy NATO desk job or risk my entire Army career, by taking on the near impossible mission of fixing this mess you sons-a-bitches got here. I must be a crazy man! I must be, because I told old Ironbone I'd take the job. I must be crazy because, not forty-eight hours ago, I was sitting at a table in Munich Germany's lovely *"Grosshesselohe"* Beer Garden on the *Isar* River with a really good-looking, big-breasted, blond, German woman—who just happens to be my wife—stuffing myself with great German food and drinking the best damned beer in the world. Now, barely two days later, I'm here in this Godforsaken, hole in the ground, where there are no Oom-Pa bands, no big breasted, blond, German woman, no wiener schnitzel and beer that tastes like panther piss. I got jet lag you wouldn't believe and an aspirin-proof headache to match.

Okay, so now that you've all seen what I look like, I'll tell you what I'm gonna' do. I'm gonna' leave here tonight, take half a bottle of aspirin, find a bed somewhere and get about twelve hours sleep. I'd advise all of you to get some sleep too because tomorrow you're gonna' be joining me in building the new and greatly improved 5th U.S. Missile Command." His voice now steadily and slowly began to rise. "I guarantee you, it will be a rocket unit unlike any you have ever seen or heard of. It will become a legend in the annals of military lore and it will be greatly feared throughout the godless, Communist world. Those of you who survive—and a lot of you won't—will be proud members of the soon-to-be best damned Honest John ballistic rocket unit in the whole damned United States

Army. We will work, we will study, we will drill and we will learn together like never before in your lives. We will do this because, in 90 days those freakin', nit-pickin', TPI Warrant Officer Pricks will be back. But, most of all, we will work our collective asses off to get this mess squared away because this, gentlemen, is a nuke rocket outfit and you don't screw around with nukes.

I enjoy being a Colonel; I'm quite proud of it. But, as much as I enjoy being a U.S. Army Colonel, ever since I was just a little boy, I've always wanted to be a U.S. Army General. In order to become a U.S. Army General, I have to turn this sorry-ass excuse for a missile outfit into the best and most feared Honest John unit in the world. And, before I do that, we have to ace another TPI, which we will be getting, probably, in less than 90 days. In less than three months, I have to undo years of neglected maintenance and training. So get your sleep tonight, gentlemen, because you'll be getting damned precious little of it for quite awhile. I repeat, I've never flunked a TPI and I ain't about to change my ways now!" With clenched fists he shouted at the top of his lungs, *"Do you sons-a-bitches understand me?"* The theater instantly exploded with a resounding, *"Yes Sir!"* in response. His voice was lower now, just above a whisper and he looked physically drained. "Good, good, just so we understand each other. I'm going to bed now, see you sons-a-bitches bright and early tomorrow."

No one called it but the room leaped to their feet and stood silently at attention as our new Colonel came off the stage walked up the center aisle and out the front door. The aisles were packed with soldiers but, somehow, everyone squished together and made a clear path for Colonel Calvert's exit. The room remained dead quiet and nobody moved. From somewhere in the theater I heard Buck Sergeant God's booming voice. "Alright all you sons-a-bitches let's go get us some shut-eye!" The whole place instantly cracked up laughing and everyone started to slowly file out into the night. I figured it was safe to go home. I collected Joyce, who'd spent most of this time enjoying a nice, hot shower and shampoo down at the camp gym. The MP town patrol dropped us off at the house. Wow, this had been a long day!

Time passed quickly and Colonel Calvert had told the truth. He set up an intense training program and we were all working and training twelve hour days, six days a week. He was cramming two weeks of work into every week. It was important to him that every aspect of 5th Missile be perfect, right down to the smallest detail. We all worked really hard but nobody worked harder than our new Colonel.

As the weeks passed, people began disappearing. The smug Captain Huddleston and The Stupid Colonel Mixon didn't even make it through the first week. I never really noticed their going; they were just, sort of, conspicuous by their absence. New faces started appearing and all of them seemed to really know what they were doing. It got to be a game, with soldiers and officers betting on who would go and who would stay. The camp's barracks odds makers would readjust the odds after every day's work. The screw-ups and the stellar performances would affect the betting.

After a few weeks, even the lowest ranking GIs were getting swept up in the program and boasting about how good their firing battery was getting. Everyone was bone-tired but there was something else happening here. This sneaky new Colonel was somehow instilling pride and esprit de corps in soldiers who hadn't had any for a long time.

In spite of all the work, I still found time to be with Joyce most nights and our Sundays—my only day off—became very precious to both of us. We would lie in bed during the week and plan what we were going to do with each up coming Sunday. It was Joyce's job to play tour director and make all the arrangements so none of the day would be wasted.

Life for Joyce was taking on new dimension too. I thought it wise to let Colonel Calvert know I had a wife living in Chunchon and that she was this headstrong Canadian nurse who just came over to be with me. He was going to find out sooner or later anyway; so, I figured it best for me to be up-front about it with my new boss. His reaction to this was quite a surprise. Up 'til now, I sort of had to semi-sneak Joyce around the camp and, to the best of my knowledge, Weatherspoon never realized she even existed. I pretty much know he didn't because, if he had, I would have been restricted to the camp every night. My MPs would just let her on base even though her Army dependant ID card was not supposed to be recognized on Camp Page. She would sneak those hot showers down at the gym whenever no one was around or hang out with Mr. Ahn, in our BOQ room until I got off work. We'd order burgers or something to the room and Joyce would just step into the closet when the food arrived. My three roommates enjoyed the feminine company and she would help them find nice, Korean gifts for their wives in the local markets. She would also buy things for Mrs. Ahn and their new baby. Joyce's knowledge of the kind of Korean spoken in the market by the common people was getting quite good.

Reading was always her passion; so naturally, she established a friendly relationship with Lucy Librarian. When she wasn't working she'd spend hours in the library, reading quietly in a secluded corner or drinking tea, and talking books with Lucy. Joyce was the only one who called her Lucy. To the rest of us she was Miss Thompson or just "The Library Lady".

Calvert evaluated everything in his world in relation to how it could improve his command. Now that he knew about Nurse Joyce Royce, it was easy for him to figure out how she could help. He asked if she would be interested in helping out at the camp's medical clinic. It had to be on a volunteer basis, of course, but, in exchange, he would figure out some way to get her command sponsored. This meant she'd get her own ration card and a Department of the Army Civilian ID card, which would officially allow her on military bases throughout Korea. No more need for her to sneak down to the gym for those quick, hot showers. She could now go to the PX, Commissary, Snack Bar, Movie Theater, Craft Shop, Gym and Library on her own. As a command sponsored officer's wife, she was also allowed to dine in the Officers' Club; this meant no more hiding in closets for hamburgers. She was even allowed in the big Yongsan PX and Commissary and I knew this was going to cost me big bucks. To maintain her Korean work visa status, she couldn't just quit her job so she told The Pig doctor she was experiencing migraines and couldn't come to work for a while. Headaches were a really big deal in Korea, so she got the time off. Anyway, I think Doctor Pig was ready for a rest from Joyce. The very next day after her talk with the Colonel, Joyce started as a volunteer nurse at the Camp Page Clinic.

TPI preparations were lighter for the MPs and some of the other support units. Evidently we had done okay on the first go-round and the Colonel wasn't on our case as much as he was on some of the other units. It was the firing, maintaince, logistics and motor pool units that were catching hell from the Old Man. Heads were still rolling and new faces showing up on almost a daily basis. A lot of them had worked for Colonel Calvert in other assignments and all seemed to love the guy. My brass plate, on the bar wall, lurched forward about ten or eleven places in just a couple weeks. The base was looking really good, too. There was nothing broken and everything seemed to have a fresh coat of paint on it, including the rocks that lined almost every sidewalk. I never understood exactly why it is the Army tries to paint every rock white on every Army post I've ever been on.

The continuous stream of activity reminded me of a coastal, Florida community preparing for a hurricane. Everyone was involved and working hard towards a deadline. I may not have had specific directions, but we continued working on everything we could think of to make sure we were ready for anything the TPI Team could throw at us. Besides, everybody else was working their tails off and we wanted to be associated with that. If the inspectors were going to find anything wrong in the MP shop, it wasn't going to be because we hadn't checked it.

One other thing happened during those weeks that made several of us sad. I lost a good friend. I went into the office late one evening and noticed an envelope on my desk. I zipped it open and instantly got this sinking feeling.

Herb,

I want to thank you and Joyce for your friendship while I was here. It means more to me than you guys will ever know.

I had a visitor last night and … well, I got to go. Evidently everything's cool again and I can get back to my real job.

Please take care of Jin Hee. That little girl really got under my skin more than I would have liked. I didn't tell her I was leaving, too chicken; so, if you and Joyce could cover my six on that one, I sure would appreciate it.

I left her quite a bit of money and a note. Tell her it's in our <u>secret place;</u> She knows where that is. It's enough to take care of her for a long time and she can go back to her government secretary job. I made sure it's still open for her.

Well, got to go! Hope to see you again some day … I'll call you!

Warm Regards,

K

I just sat there for about half an hour thinking and re-reading the note to see if there was something I missed, some hidden meaning. Here's a guy I only knew for less than half a year, and yet, I felt closer to him than some friends I'd known since high school. I knew he was this real world, *James Bond*-type guy. No question, he had to go off someplace and save the world for democracy by foiling another diabolical Commie scheme; but that didn't help the empty feeling in the pit of my stomach.

I went home and told Joyce the news. She just started crying. Her tears weren't for Kuska, although she would miss him too; they were for Jin Hee. Evidently, I'd forgotten we were going to a birthday dinner for Kuska at Jin Hee's apartment this Saturday night. I also wasn't privy to all the girl talk that had passed between the two of them. Evidently, for Jin Hee, this was *the* guy, as far as she was concerned. Joyce was now going to have to take on the mission of being with Jin Hee, when I told her about Kuska. Tomorrow was going to be a tough day!

Telling Jin Hee was more horrible than I imagined. She just seemed to come apart at the seams and collapsed in quaking spasms of never-ending tears and incoherent blubbering. I stayed there for about as long as I could stand it, then Joyce mercifully gave me the high sign I could leave. As I was departing, Joyce gave me a quick kiss and whispered she would be staying the night with Jin Hee. I beat a hasty and cowardly retreat back to my BOQ room just thankful to be out of that oppressive atmosphere.

It was no secret to any of us that my roommate, Paul Gleason, was quite infatuated with Jin Hee. Secretly, Paul thought she was the most beautiful, enchanting woman he'd ever seen. What none of us fully realized was that Paul was totally *Full Goose Bozo* in love with her and had been for some time. He'd been suffering in silence for months knowing Kuska was her guy and there was absolutely nothing he could do about it. He would die a little inside every day when he'd see Jin Hee and Kuska together.

When I went back to the BOQ, I told the guys what a miserable day I'd had and how totally crushed Jin Hee was over Kuska's disappearing act. The boys were concerned because they all knew and liked Jin Hee too. Over the months, she had become one of our gang. I didn't know it then, but Paul had just hatched a plan to win Jin Hee over. "Herb, I know you and Joyce are going to try and be with Jin Hee as much as possible to ease her through this but please call on me so I can help, too. I know Jin Hee pretty well and I can help you guys out. You know; maybe take her to a movie or out for a bite to eat." Abercrombie and Dave Ross chimed in too; so now there were five of us on this, sort of, "Cheer up Jin Hee Team".

I don't know where the hell June went; we were all working so hard it just sort of morphed into July without really being noticed. The only thing memorable about July was the 4th and that's only because Colonel Calvert gave us the whole day off. Jin Hee was still a total *Sad Sack* but Paul's tag team idea of having the five of us keep Jin Hee company seemed to actually be working. At least, the screaming had stopped. Oh sure, there were still tears but, now at least, there were a few brief smiles mixed in. Had I really been paying attention, I would have realized Paul was actually doing the lion's share of Jin Hee's babysitting.

35

Sid & Earl

It was about noon on the 4th of July and the whole Korean Peninsula was locked in one of the hottest summers any of the local nationals could ever recall. In remembrance of our nation's birthday, this was a non-work day at Camp Page. The potato salad was chilling in the mess hall reefers and the hotdogs and hamburger patties were beginning to sizzle on every charcoal grill on base. Little columns of greasy smoke could be seen billowing skyward between several of the pale green Quonset huts. All this cooking only made the day seem hotter and it was only approaching noon. The real heat of the day was yet to come. Piles of softball equipment had already been dumped at the ball field along side tug-o-war ropes and horseshoes. A small group of us were huddled in my BOQ room dreading the unraveling of this sweaty, uncomfortable, national birthday.

Chief Warrant Officer (CWO-2) Sid Luckman and Warrant Officer (WO-1) Earl Elwin were two pilots on loan to 5th Missile. They and their semi-new, *Delta* model *Huey* helicopter had recently arrived to help us with rapid transportation missions between Camp Page and our four Hawk sites during this period of increased enemy activity. The arrival of this UH-1D Huey team now gave us true "Air-Mobile" capability, as this bird could haul up to twelve troops at a time. Up 'til now, our aircraft had nothing above aerial observation, light MEDEVAC (Medical Evacuation) and very light transportation capabilities. Captain McCabe's helicopter was a vintage Bell OH-13. So many parts had been switched around on the old bird that no one knew for sure just how old his helicopter really was. Parts of it probably were Korean War vintage. We also had an only slightly newer Hiller, H-23G *Raven* flown by Lieutenant Rudy Rydel. Neither of these little bubble-type choppers could really haul much. The pilot plus one passenger, or maybe a litter patient, was about it on a hot day. There was also Captain Song's trusty U-6 *Beaver* and a-soon-to-be piloted old L-19 *Cessna Bird Dog* which, I don't think, had been in the air since my arrival. Rumor had it we were getting an Air Force FAC (Forward Air Control) pilot assigned to help coordinate air and ground enemy infiltrator search operations. So, Sid & Earl's bird was the only thing we had that could actually haul a fully armed squad of troops and set them down almost anywhere.

Sid & Earl looked like an old vaudeville comedy team. Sid was this tall, lean Oklahoman with a Southwestern, cowboy drawl. Sid's droopy moustache and longish sandy hair hardly met Army regulation. Earl was Sid's exact opposite. He sported a high and tight buzz cut and his mustache met regulations perfectly. He was this short, sort of chubby, little guy from Clarksdale, Mississippi. Earl came equipped with a Southern accent even thicker and slower than Abercrombie's. When I say short, I mean his size small flight suit hung on him and bunched up around his ankles. I'm not sure how he even got in the Army; he certainly didn't meet the minimum height requirements. Earl Elwin's name was totally unpronounceable to the Korean tongue. *Wer Wer-wen* was about as close as it ever got.

Sid & Earl came from way down south, somewhere around *Pusan,* before being temporarily assigned to us. Since coming north, the two were becoming increasingly paranoid. They convinced themselves they were going to be shot down and captured by North Koreans. This fear caused both of them to buy lever action, *Winchester* 30-30 carbines at the *Yongsan Rod & Gun Club.* They carried these unauthorized weapons, plus a shit load of ammo, with them on all their flights. The Army issued .38 caliber, *Smith & Wesson* Model 10 revolvers to pilots but the boys thought they needed a little more firepower. The *Winchesters* were just about the biggest guns they could buy at the gun club. Carrying these cowboy saddle guns was definitely against Army regulations so the boys sort of snuck them on board every time they flew.

Despite their paranoia, these two quirky flyboys fit right in with our BOQ room #103 group and we all became fast friends. Because of rotating assignments, most Army guys make friends quickly. In Korea, you only had a year or less to get to know somebody, so you had to make friends fast and some even became fast friends.

On this particular holiday afternoon, we were literally frying in our BOQ room. It was the hottest day so far and our ancient, communal air conditioner decided to just freeze up and pack it in. It was still making a sick, sort of humming noise; but no cool air was coming through, and the room was getting hotter by the minute. Upon closer inspection, I noticed this geriatric device had simply become a solid block of ice and that's why no air was making it through. To just survive, I shut it off and we abandoned the hot and humid tin can of a room for some fresh air. Outside, it was only marginally better but it too was steadily getting hotter. There was no breeze and the sun was blazing down. Joyce, the two pilots and I ended up in my office because it had a big floor fan and a bit of cross-flow ventilation. It wasn't much but, at least, it was something. My three room-mates abandoned us in search of something cold to drink.

Joyce reached into her oversized purse for her cigarettes. To get to them, she pulled out a blue and white striped, two-piece bathing suit she'd stuffed in there. We thought about going to the base swimming pool but, when we walked over there, it was already wall-to-wall, beer-soaked GIs immersed in standing-room-only, tepid water; probably not a fun place for guys let alone a female round-eye. Sid's moustache twitched and then he stood bolt upright and with his crooked smile announced his solution. "Earl and I are going to get our bathing suits. Meet us down in the hangar in ten minutes! We're going swimming in the Sea of Japan!" Joyce and I looked at each other, smiled and silently agreed, *"Why not?"*

Down at the hangar, Joyce changed into her bathing suit and put on one of Earl's tiny flight suits. It looked huge but still fit her better than it did Earl. We put a flight helmet on her and pulled down the smoke-tinted visor. The combat boots didn't fit either but she clunked her way across the tarmac out to the Huey with the rest of us and no one seemed the wiser. Sid had filed a quick flight plan with the SP4 at airfield operations and the four of us were now inside the Huey with the blades spinning. As soon as we lifted off and headed out over the river, I slid the cargo doors open. A cool, life saving wind came whipping through the cargo bay. As we gained altitude, the air temperature cooled and life got a lot better. Sid set a heading for due east. He said he knew of a stretch of deserted beach he thought would be perfect for our little holiday swim. The flight was probably a little less than an hour. Now, joyriding in military aircraft is not something I normally do. I mean it's just not me! I don't misappropriate government equipment; I investigate people who do things like that. It's just that today was so damned hot, I said, *"To hell with it all!"*

We set down on sort of a sandy pinnacle about thirty yards above a beach. Sid said, "I think we should do this in shifts, me and you and then Earl and Joyce. That way, we will always have a pilot with the bird in case we have to get out of here fast." I didn't like the sound of that. Now that I'd cooled down, our little adventure seemed to be getting dumber by the minute. Sid reached over behind the pilot's seats and pulled out the two *Winchesters*. "Herb and I will go for a swim first and then you two can go. Earl, show Joyce how to work my gun." Joyce's eyes got really big as she was handed the cowboy carbine.

Sid and I stripped down to our bathing suits, raced down the dune and across the hard packed sand towards the cobalt blue waters. We ran straight in splashing the life saving liquid all over us. At waist deep, I plunged in and it was wonderful!

I hadn't been in an ocean since our honeymoon about seven long months ago. I surfaced and swam parallel with the beach for a few minutes. We probably hadn't been in the water for more than ten minutes when Sid said we ought to switch with Joyce and Earl. I think Sid was finally realizing just how much trouble he could be in for commandeering a U.S. Army helicopter for a private joyride. We jogged back towards the helicopter. As we approached, Joyce and Earl were already stripped down to their suits and poised to run down the dune. Joyce sure looked great in that two-piece and I couldn't but notice that Earl's eyes were bugging out a bit more than usual. As we got to them, Joyce asked, "How's the water?" She and Earl were already half-way across the beach as I yelled after them, "Wonderful!"

Sid and I dried off a bit, put our flight suits back on, then manned the guns and watched the two frolic in the water as we enjoyed the cool ocean air. Shortly thereafter, we noticed bushes moving. We hadn't seen them before because they were so well camouflaged but there must have been a ROK Army Infantry Company deployed along this section of beach, probably on infiltrator watch or something. Some ROKs were now walking out onto the beach in the general direction of Joyce and Earl and I was beginning to get a bit nervous. At that point, an English speaking ROK Army Captain popped up beside our helicopter. He was wearing a helmet with grass interlaced in his net-type helmet cover. "What are you Americans doing here and do you know where you are?" Sid took the lead, "Yes, of course we do Captain. My name's Raphael Sabatini and I'm escorting a famous American singer on a USO tour of American and ROK Army Camps here in Korea. That little lady over there is Patsy Cline the famous American Country and Western singer. She wanted to take a swim in your beautiful ocean on the way to our next show." Not wanting to seem uninformed, the Captain lied, "Oh yes, I've heard of her. My men thought she was Bunny from *Prayboy Crub*." I guessed most Korean soldiers didn't get much chance to see a shapely, round-eye woman in a two-piece bathing suit very often, if ever.

The Captain then got very serious; Mr. Sabatini I regret to inform you but you *dangerousry crose* to DMZ." He pointed to a pile of rocks near the shoreline a couple hundred yards up the beach. "That is DMZ! In fact, your *he-ree-copter* has interested North Koreans. One of my outposts say North Korean scouts coming this way. We would *rike* very much to ambush them, so *preeze* to be so kind to get Miss *Crine* out of here fast so we can shoot North Koreans. It would make me very happy."

I quickly thanked the Captain as Sid started cranking the turbine up. "*Oh Shit!*" Joyce and Earl had been swimming up the beach toward the pile of rocks, and North Korea. The second the low RPM warning light went out, Sid nosed the Huey over and slid down the dune, skids inches above the sand, and straight towards the two swimmers. Earl heard the Huey and grabbed Joyce's hand and the two were now running south along the surf line towards us. Sid flipped the Huey around so the bathers were now on the south side of chopper. The helicopter became engulfed in swirls of stinging ocean spray and sand. By the looks in their eyes, no one had to tell Joyce and Earl something was seriously wrong. They both dove in on the floor. As soon as Sid could see they were mostly inside, he poured the coal to it. I could now clearly hear sporadic gunfire as I pulled Joyce in close to me on the floor and hugged her tight. Sid had the Huey nosed over so far and gaining speed so fast he was actually using the cabin's bulkhead windows as a windshield because the Huey's nose was close to pointing straight down at the sand. He then set the collective and cyclic for maximum climb. The three of us were G-forced flat to the floor. Within seconds we were above small arms range and still rapidly gaining altitude. Sid yelled over his shoulder, "Whose fucking idea was it to go swimming anyway?" We all gave a nervous smile at Sid's attempt at humor.

Not wanting to risk having our phony little mission being discovered upon landing, Sid set the Huey down for five seconds in the school yard across from our house, then hauled ass out of there. After a careful post-flight inspection, Sid and Earl discovered we had a souvenir from our little adventure. One small bullet hole in the left horizontal tail stabilizer was the only evidence of our dumb stunt. Thankfully, it just punched harmlessly through the aluminum skin. A little sheet aluminum, a few pop rivets and a tiny daub of OD touch-up paint and the Huey would be fine. Most importantly, no one else would ever know about our being involved in a shooting clash between North and South Korea along the DMZ or our rescue of *"Patsy Crine the famous Prayboy Bunny."*

36

Red Goose, Buster Brown & Paul Parrot

There were several orphanages in and around the city of Chunchon. At this time in South Korea's economic progression, children were not a luxury; they were still a necessity. The future of the country would depend upon their children. So many Korean men had been killed during years of Japanese occupation and then the Koran War that the country was still trying to recover from it.

Like China, in Korea, male children are the preferred offspring. With no real social system for taking care of the elderly, it fell upon the children to provide for their parents when they were no longer able to care for themselves. In most cases, sons were expected to provide for and take care of their aging parents. A Korean couple with three or four sons was considered to be extremely fortunate, while a couple with no sons pretty much feared growing old.

Because of this custom, sons were generally more prized than daughters. It was not unusual for some daughters to find themselves in orphanages at a very early age. Many would simply be left on orphanage doorsteps in hopes someone wanting a daughter would adopt them. Seems cruel by our present day standards but then we aren't dirt-poor Koreans, trying to scrape out an existence there, in 1968.

Of course, there were boys in the orphanages too but the ratio of girls to boys was about six to one. Boys only seemed to end up in orphanages if both parents were killed and there were no other adult, family members who could or would take them in. In other instances, if a boy child was infirm or had some sort of birth defect, he too might end up in an orphanage. I saw a lot of little boys, and a few little girls, with cleft palates, or what we used to call "hair lips". Every time we would come across such a child, we'd report them to our clinic. From time to time, our chief doctor, Jimmy Wunder, would operate on these poor kids and correct these deformities. He gave dozens of little kids a great smile, a chance at adoption and he definitely changed their lives. We can sit here in the West making judgments about dumping little, unwanted kids in orphanages but it's simply the way it was back then, in that part of the world.

U.S. Army troops, the world over, have one universal commonality; they love kids and puppies. Because of this, just about every unit on Camp Page was involved in some way or another with one of the orphanages downtown and the MPs were no exception. Since Joyce was working at the clinic and the MPs were one of the smaller units, it only made perfect sense for us to join forces with the medics and work together.

We worked with a "little kid" orphanage where the children ranged in age from about two to five years old, or after they were helpless babies but before they started school. It was probably the most rewarding and emotionally draining work most of us had ever done. There were about 250 of them in this small facility and, no matter how much you could give; it simply wasn't going to be enough.

We were always looking to see what we could do for the kids; and what these kids desperately needed was shoes and socks. It was still summer but winter would be coming on soon and only a few of them had real shoes; and most of these were practically falling off their feet. The kids were either barefoot or had these cheap plastic or rubber-like shell shoes; GIs just called them *E-de-wah* Shoes (come here). Winter coats were going to be another needed thing.

Warm winter clothing wasn't the only thing these kids needed; they also needed a lot of love and attention. Our visits were looked upon by the kids as special events, something on the magnitude of a Christmas. I say Christmas, because we strange-looking, giant men came and played with them and always brought candy, cookies, sweet milk and, maybe, some toys. To these kids, our visits may have been some of the very few bright spots in their otherwise basic, little, routine lives. The medical staff would try to come once a month and check the kids out and we MPs would fill in at other times. We built them a little playground in their dirt courtyard complete with swings, slide and sandbox. You would have thought we had brought "Disneyland" to Korea.

The clinic staff took care of their basic medical needs and gave the kids all the same shots American kids get. On one particular visit, all the kids got their Polio protection, not from shots but from the vaccine dropped in small cups of sweet liquid. I remember Joyce doing the "Kimchi Squat" for what seemed like hours as these, little, dirty-faced darlings paraded past her in well-behaved order. She spoke a little Korean to each child and the kids just seemed to be fascinated with her. She'd give each one their vaccine-laced drink, along with a very warm Joyce smile, a big hug and a *Tootsie Pop*. She would then switch all her attention, for the next few minutes, to the next wee human in line. I heard several of the little ones talking together after their vaccine and I asked Mr. Shin what they were talking about. "They call Joyce '*yeppun sungnyo*'; it means 'Pretty Lady'. They've named her 'The Pretty Lady'."

The shoe thing bothered me so much I wrote my Mom about it and asked if she could ask her church if there was anything they could do to help some of these kids. I asked some of my guys if they would write letters home too. Now, if you knew my mother, you would understand all you needed to do was mention a worthwhile charity project and she would get it organized and rolling. What I did not expect was the magnitude of her efforts.

In just a few weeks, some very big boxes began piling up in my office. The boxes were sent from three, different shoe companies that made children's shoes: *Red Goose, Buster Brown* and *Paul Parrot*. There was a note from each hoping the contents of these large boxes would help us in our work with the children's orphanages. When we opened these crates, there were hundreds of boxes of children's shoes of all sizes plus huge bales of thick, warm, white socks. There were enough shoes for all our kids and probably some others. We were all so excited about handing out the shoes, we just couldn't wait 'til Saturday afternoon and our next visit with the kids. It was our main topic of conversation for the remainder of the week. We told the head of the orphanage we had a special treat for the children and we wanted to meet them all inside with their feet freshly washed.

Our truck, filled to capacity with wee foot-covers, pulled up outside the orphanage and dropped the tailgate. All the little ones were inside with their freshly washed faces pressed up against the windows, as we wheeled in the great boxes with hand trucks. They were all excitedly bouncing up and down and bursting to know what was inside.

Joyce, with Mr. Shin's assistance, had all the children sit in circle rows around the edge of the room with the big boxes and GI's in the middle. Armed with tape measures and foot-size charts, we all started to measure the children for the shoes. This was also the perfect opportunity to tickle little bare feet and hand out Tootsie Pops, the children's favorite candy.

When the first big box was opened and a tiny pair of red leather lace up shoes came out, the room came to almost a complete silence. The little ones stared in fascination; I don't think any of them had ever seen such shoes. For the better part of two hours we sat on the floor with the children fitting them for shoes. Each child got a new pair plus five pairs of warm, white socks. Even the orphanage staff was overwhelmed by all this.

I sat there in the middle of the room just trying to take this all in. It truly seemed just like Christmas and we had just given these little guys the best presents they'd ever gotten. I got the biggest kick out of one little girl wearing a shiny new pair of black shoes. She just stood there staring down at her feet and smiling. She then started walking in a very wobbly fashion. Suddenly it dawned on me; this was probably the first time this little girl had ever walked with real shoes on her feet. All the children were fascinated and delighted with their new shoes. Of all the little children, in my mind, one has stood out above all the rest. This little cherub-faced girl, probably about three, wore her shoes for about ten minutes, then, sat down, unlaced them and took them off. For the longest time, she clutched them to her tiny breast and cheek and just rocked back and forth with her eyes closed; she had this unbelievably, beautiful smile on her little face. She just stood there rocking back and forth while humming some little tune. After this little five-minute ritual, her eyes popped back open and she plopped back down on the floor and solicited the nearest GI's help in putting her new, blue leather shoes back on. We spent the remainder of that Saturday afternoon sharing milk and cookies and trying to teach the little ones how to tie shoelaces. I look back on this day as one of the most emotionally rewarding days of my life.

When it was announced we would be leaving, we were mobbed and hugged around the knees by these miniature people. I don't think any of us wanted this day to end but it was time. I noted several of my guys trying to hide the tears in their eyes. These big, tough soldiers were touched by the day and they too would probably remember it for a very long time. The frustrating thing was there were so many of them and, by comparison, so few of us; they needed so much emotionally as well as materially. We all wanted to do something more but we knew, no matter how much, it just wouldn't be enough. It was never enough, so we had to settle for just doing what we could.

That night I wrote Mom a long letter of thanks telling her all about the day, how wonderful it was and the kids' reactions to it all. I took dozens of pictures and promised to send them along as soon as they were developed so she could share them with her church. I asked her to thank everyone involved and to especially thank those three, great guys: *Red Goose, Buster Brown* and *Paul Parrot.*

There was always sort of an "afterglow" from our visits to the orphanage. During the week, the guys would talk about it. After this amazing experience, several of them decided we should go back for another milk and cookies playtime with the children. You have to think about this for a minute. Here's a bunch of eighteen to maybe twenty-five year old males who could be drinking, throwing a football around or be downtown with the girls; yet, they would rather go see the kids.

That's just how far these wee creatures had wheedled their way under our skins. So, at two the next Saturday afternoon, we loaded ice cold milk and cookies into the truck and about ten of us ventured off for a surprise visit to play with the kids.

This was not to be a good day! We arrived and, through the fence, saw some of the children playing on the little playground we made for them. We also noticed none of them were wearing their new shoes. None of us said anything because we were all probably collectively thinking, *"Oh, right, new shoes, don't want to scuff them up on the playground!"*

We knocked on the door and, rather than greeted with the normal warm smiles, we were confronted by a shocked, almost terrified, woman. She rattled off something in Korean. My ever-faithful Sidekick, Mr. Shin, had joined, us even though, technically, he had the day off too. Mr. Shin rarely left my side if he thought his services might be officially or even semi-officially needed. "What's she saying, Mr. Shin?" "She don't want us to come in, Lieutenant; she say this not a good day for visit. I find out why." Mr. Shin started an animated discussion with the woman in Korean and his voice began to get shrill like it always did when he became agitated or angry. Mr. Shin was always content to stay in the background, keeping me apprised of everything; including the meanings and subtle nuances of what was going on as well as just the basic translations. I was shocked when this thin, quiet, little man gave the woman a great shove, knocking her out of the way. "Follow me, Lieutenant; something here very wrong!" As we filed in, we encountered a few more members of the staff who, rather than greeting us with the usual big smiles, cast their eyes down to the floor. We got to the rooms where the children were and noticed none of them were wearing their new shoes. Like a mad man, Mr. Shin started going through the barracks-like rooms where all the children slept. Each child had a thin, rolled-up floor mattress and a small, open cupboard containing all their meager possessions. The shoes and socks were nowhere to be found. Mr. Shin pushed a female staff member up against the wall and screamed at her. All the woman did was put her arms up to protect her head while screaming, *"Tas-reejee mah"* (Don't hit me!) then cowered, staring at the floor. He reared back to strike her but I grabbed his hand. "What the hell is going on, Mr. Shin? This isn't like you!" "There no shoes, Lieutenant! Shoes all gone, but she don't tell me who took!" Now the magnitude of the situation began to sink in. "You mean to tell me 250 pairs of shoes are missing?" "That's right, but nobody here will tell me who took; I go call Cop Chong!"

Mr. Shin went outside and I tried to assess the situation. There were only women here. Mr. Cha, the guy who seemed to be the head *Honcho* was not in the building. I was looking around when I felt a tug from below, on my fatigue pants. I looked down and, holding onto my leg, at about my knee level, was the same little girl who had clutched her new, blue shoes to her chest. When she saw she had my attention, she lifted up one of her tiny bare feet, pointed at it and said in her little voice. *'Koh-yand-ee naui koodoo?"* She wanted to know where her shoes were. Now, I can take a lot but I couldn't take this. I could feel my neck getting hotter. I ordered my guys to search the place. There were only two pairs to be found and both were in Mr. Cha's little office. We were without a translator until Mr. Shin returned with Cop Chong; and during this time, I found the lack of being able to communicate most frustrating as I had my questions.

The door opened and I expected to see Mr. Shin but it was the orphanage honcho, Mr. Cha. He was shaken by our presence. Our truck was out back and apparently he had not seen it. I knew Mr. Cha spoke basic English so I went over to him, probably with fire in my eyes. Mr. Cha made a quick check to his rear but SP4 Cortez was now standing in front of the door. "Where are the shoes, Mr. Cha?" Rather than answer, Mr. Cha assumed the posture and facial expression of someone who completely didn't know what was going on. This only pissed me off further; so I repeated myself, only this time, I was much louder. "Where are the fucking shoes we gave to the kids last Saturday, you bastard?" Mr. Cha was now looking very frightened as I walked with deliberate steps towards him. He then uttered the absolute wrong thing, "Shoes, what shoes?" I grabbed him by his coat lapels, lifted him completely off the floor and slammed him up against the wall. At that moment, thankfully, Mr. Shin and Cop Chong arrived. Mr. Shin apparently had already filled Cop in about what was going on. Cop walked over to where I was with Mr. Cha. "This Korean *bidness* now, *Rootenant*, I take!" With those words, Cop grabbed Mr. Cha by the upper arm and literally threw him into his office and slammed the door.

Cop was an interesting person, both well-known and feared all over Chunchon and Chang Won Province. Without a doubt, he was one of the *"Top Deputy Sheriffs"* in the Chunchon KNP. He was respected, but, more importantly, he was universally feared throughout the provincial area. In Korea, power equates to fierceness, in addition to political and physical strength. His power and ability to educe fear was that of an "Al Capone," who's legally sanctioned to operate by both the State Police and the Governor. Cop Chong would stay within the law when he could but he would willingly go outside it when it suited his purpose and all the crooks knew it. Cop was a no-nonsense, results oriented kind of guy. He was sort of a shorter, more physically fit and politically powerful "Dirty Harry".

The women moved all the children to another part of the orphanage when Mr. Cha's screams of pain got so loud it began to scare even me. The guy sounded like he was being slowly killed. In less than thirty minutes, Cop Chong emerged from the office with his big, gold-toothed smile. "He tell me where shoes are. We go pick up shoes at warehouse tonight. Piece of shit tell me decision made by big orphanage honchos to sell shoes and make lots more money for orphanage. He say it better than just letting children wear shoes out. I tell him shoes not his to give; they gift from American Army GI. He say he sell, get cheaper shoes for children, then use rest of money for food, coats and warmth for children. He say shoes too good for orphans and money help them more. I tell him bullshit!" He then lie some more. I get tired of lies, knock him around a bit, then stick gun in mouth tell him I blow fucking head off if he not tell me truth. He then decide it best to tell me truth. Money not go back to kids. Money go in bosses' pockets. I go now to warehouse. Mr. Cha, he come with me so he don't warn warehouse. See you here tomorrow—with shoes!"

Once again, Cop had cut through to the quick in his fast, brutal and efficient manner. As promised, the shoes and socks were just about all returned; and the extras we had back at the camp made sure all the children were once again outfitted with warm, quality footwear. I sorted through the shoes 'til I found what I thought were the correct blue ones. I sought out my special little girl and personally placed the blue shoes and socks back on her feet. Mr. Shin conveyed my message to her that these were her shoes and, if anybody ever tried to take them away again, to let me know. I sat there on the floor and, as I handed her the rest of her socks, she threw her little arms around my neck and gave me a kiss on the cheek and a huge smile. I had to get up and leave the room because I didn't want anyone seeing the big, brave Army Lieutenant's tears.

Somehow, Mr. Cha never returned to the orphanage and I never heard too much about him after this event. I didn't ask either for fear of what Cop Chong might tell me. The orphanage ended up being adopted by the local, Roman Catholic Church missionaries and things got considerably better. The nuns started filtering many of the children into the Seoul orphanage system where they had much better chances for adoption. This Seoul system was also the only Korean orphanage where foreign adoptions were allowed. I knew this would give the beautiful little girl with the blue shoes a great chance at being adopted, now that prospective parents worldwide would have the chance to see that little angel face.

From that day on, we made it a routine that, at least some of us, would go to the orphanage every weekend just to let all concerned know we were still greatly interested in the wellbeing of all *our* kids.

We now turned our full attention back to the job of passing our TPI re-inspection. We all knew it was looming and it would be happening soon.

37

Let's Play Lawn Darts

Colonel Calvert was not the kind of guy to screw around. When he's ready, he knows he's ready. So, instead of waiting for the TPI folks to announce their re-inspection date, he just goes out and gives them an invitation to come back now and get it over with! I suspect old Ironbone got a big chuckle out of this, probably because nobody has ever invited a TPI Team back before. So, about a week later, the TPI Team was back at Page just to see how good this brazen Kentucky Colonel really was.

Not only had our Colonel invited the TPI Team back, he also invited *Stars & Stripes,* promising them multiple chances to get spectacular shots of Honest John launches for their newspaper. You see, during *The Weatherspoon Reign of Terror*—as it was now known—not much got done by way of training. Calvert found a stockpile of Weatherspoon's leftover rockets and practice warheads. Ralph was supposed to have used them up in training, but there they were, seven of them, still stuffed away in the back of a hanger.

This time, the TPI lasted only three days. It didn't take long for the inspectors to realize *"Calvert's shit was all in one bag."* Our new boss had it *"All right and nailed down tight."* So, the third and last day was pretty much a picnic and an old fashioned game of really big *Lawn Darts.* Unbeknownst to everybody but us Camp Page troops, Calvert had mixed a little P. T. Barnum into the event. It was going to be more show than missile exercise. The Army's training standard was to get an Honest John launcher into position, assemble and load the rocket, launch it, and get the warhead successfully down range and on target in less than five hours from being placed on launch alert. Worthington's intentions were to launch all seven in two hours or less, if he could do it. This was going to be a pretty cute trick, because we only had six launchers. That meant one of the launchers would have to reload before it could launch its second HJ rocket.

What only a handful of people knew was that there was a long forgotten, seventh launcher rat-packed away on Page. It was an experimental, air transportable, mobile launcher stashed in a crate in the back of a warehouse. There were only two known to be in existence in the entire Army inventory and it seemed we had one of them. The other one was supposed to be somewhere in West Germany. Ours had never been uncrated and no one really knew if it would even work. Calvert personally checked it out and proclaimed he saw no reason why it shouldn't.

Another thing our new boss did was survey all our pre-positioned launch sites. During these surveys, he also plotted all likely target areas within range of our Honest Johns. He targeted mountain passes and any other piece of turf large enough for division-sized or larger enemy units to form up. Just about every other choke point or target of interest he could think of was also plotted. Rather than troubling his firing units with working out the targeting math when they deployed to the field, he did most of the calculations for them, then kept the information in classified launch books. This info would be issued to his commanders, if ever the "balloon went up". The cleverest thing he did was pound two-foot long, iron rebar stakes all the way into the ground where the front, left and right tires of the launcher trucks were supposed to be. Then, he plotted the location of all these stakes on maps. This way, the firing teams could go to the exact location on the map, find the hidden iron stakes with metal detectors and quickly get the launchers into their approximate firing positions. This greatly reduced the time needed to calculate the traverse, elevation, range and azimuth to target information. This was because most of it was already in those classified books. He then drilled this tactic until every launch team could set up to fire in an amazingly short period of time, even in the dark.

After the final period of training, Calvert lit another of his long, thin, trademark cigars. I watched him standing there in the shade of one of the rocket launchers, while smoke swirled about his head. His aviator sunglasses shielded his eyes but not the smile on his lips. The smile told it all. He announced to his commanders, "I like it! And, if I like it, it's gonna' tickle the hell out of anybody else. If that Son-of-a-Bitch Kim is ever damned dumb enough to send his army south, I'm gonna' kill 'em all." He took another puff on his cigar, folded his arms across his chest, and stood there for the longest time looking north towards the DMZ. The rocket's shadow was pointing in the same direction and shielded the Colonel's eyes against the late afternoon sun.

The stage was now set for the *Gentleman Jim Calvert Show*. At the morning briefing on the third day, the TPI Team Leader gave his minimal instructions. "At ten-hundred hours, the *Alert Horn* is going to sound. At that time you will be given a fire order for two targets in the impact area. You are cleared today to do live fire launches." Gentleman Jim interrupted, "Excuse me Chief, I'm actually gonna' need seven targets. I have seven old, leftover training rockets to fire, and I need this opportunity to get rid of them. They're sort of cluttering up the place." CW4 Felix Wendelshafer, the lead inspector, grinned, "Seven … you're going to launch seven rockets in less than five hours with just six launch vehicles?" "No, Chief; we're going to give you something you've never seen before. I'm going to launch seven rockets in under two hours! You're going to have to figure out how to grade the seventh launch!" The Chief Inspector looked a little confused but said, "Okay, Colonel. At ten-hundred hours I'm gonna' give you seven targets, but understand this; you will be graded on all seven launches. You shoot seven … we grade seven." Gentleman Jim smiled at the Team Leader, "I wouldn't have it any other way, Chief." Calvert took a very long pull off his cigar and blew seven perfect smoke rings towards the Chief, then strode out of the briefing room.

The horns went off right on time, and Gentleman Jim was given the mission order. Six mobile launchers and their associated vehicles, men and equipment rolled out the gate towards the river about ten miles away. The launch location ended up being in a remote area, nestled within a mountain pass, along a large section of almost-dry riverbed. All our firing teams had been there many times during the past few weeks and they knew every inch of the place. It took about thirty minutes for the launchers to begin arriving at the river. It was obvious the TPI Team had secretly selected this place a couple of days ago, because it was all set up. There were tents, portable observation bleachers and even latrines already in place. The Brass from 8th Army had already arrived. Ironbone wasn't in attendance, but Skippy Mack was there along with a large entourage, including several ROK Army Colonels and Generals. Several Hueys were sitting near the riverbank about a hundred yards downstream.

There are four vehicles in an Honest John firing team: The actual M-386 Launcher, an M-55 Rocket Transporter (Honest Johns came in three sections: warhead, motor and tail fin assembly), an M-54 Cargo Truck for all the miscellaneous stuff, and an M-62 Medium Wrecker. The wrecker hoists the components onto the 5 ton truck launcher rail. A six man team puts it all together and it becomes a complete M-50 Honest John artillery rocket, ready to launch. Because this test called for a mock nuclear launch, everyone who was going to be anywhere near the warheads had to be in full, protective gear including masks, hoods and full CBR (Chemical, Biological, Radiological) suits. I watched our teams practice this procedure a dozen times or so. It was amazing how fast they'd become at putting one of these monsters together.

It was quite a sight from the bleacher seats. Everyone from Camp Page who could get away was at the launch site. Joyce was even there with Lucy Librarian.

We all wanted to see our new Colonel's "Seven Ring Circus". The launch teams were finding their "Marks" with metal detectors and began positioning launchers. The Rocket Transporters, Wreckers and their assigned security units were making a mock stop at the MSA. If this had been real, they would have picked up the "Real McCoy" warheads. Instead, the transporters were bringing practice warheads. These warheads had just enough smoky explosives in them so evaluators could easily spot where they hit in the impact area, and hopefully, they would.

The transporters and wreckers began arriving and the transfer and assembly operation was now well underway. As each launcher unit came on line and ready to fire, they waited. They waited until all six launchers were fully "up and ready." Then, at Colonel Calvert's signal, from left to right, the units began a staggered launch countdown. The first Honest John leapt off its launcher rail with a deafening roar. Billows of white smoke from the solid fuel motor engulfed the entire launcher truck in a dense, white cloud. The instant the tail fins cleared the rail, the spin rockets erupted with their quick two second burn and the rocket accelerated away at an amazing rate of speed. Within five seconds, the rocket was clean out of sight, with only a rapidly dissipating trail of white smoke as fading evidence it had even passed by.

Within seconds of the smoke clearing from around the first launcher truck, the second rocket blasted off and, it too, was almost instantly out of sight, just like the first. This second one seemed so loud, it was truly frightening. Everyone in the bleachers now had hands cupped over ears because there were four more launchers all set and ready to go, and the noise was truly deafening.

And go they did! Exactly like the first two, the following four went off just like the same movie scene being played over and over again. There were a lot of people around trying to take perfect pictures of these picture-perfect launches. The *Stars & Stripes* photographer was having a field day, as were the official Army photographers, film crews and anyone else who'd brought a camera. The incredible sound of the first launch caused poor Lucy Librarian to drop her camera and hug Joyce tightly.

Six launches at ten second intervals! No one had ever seen six Honest Johns launched within a minute. We were witnessing military history. We were seeing what it probably would be like if these tactical nukes were ever launched in anger. That's why Colonel Calvert had asked for an official Army film crew for his rocket shoot. He knew it was going to be significant.

A five-minute sound movie of this event would be played over and over at the U.S. Army Artillery School at Fort Sill, Oklahoma and throughout the Army as an example of how these launches could and should be done. There would probably be no way that a copy of this film would *not* be deliberately leaked, through intelligence channels, to the Soviets and Red Chinese. I suspect this short fire-power demonstration film would give our enemies second thoughts about crashing across the DMZ. It demonstrated how quickly *Honest John* would vaporize their hoards of screaming troops, bent on overwhelming our defensive positions. I wouldn't doubt it if the Soviets showed it to *Krazy Kim,* himself, just to calm him down.

I was standing close to Colonel Calvert when his Jeep radio started crackling. Someone, from twenty-five to thirty miles down range, near the impact area, was calling in the results. All six rockets had hit within the target-area. Remember, these were free-flight, nuclear rockets. Of the six, three were precisely on target. These three were graded as one hundred percent target destruction. Two more were credited with seventy-five percent target destroyed and the last rocket with over fifty percent target destroyed. These percentages were just from the blast and fireball. Fallout and other residual radiation would eventually achieve one hundred percent target destruction for all six rockets. Had this been for real, it would have destroyed six division-sized, North Korean Army units and up to 100,000 enemy troops. The results announcement was made and the bleachers erupted in cheers.

While we were all celebrating these almost unbelievable results, Chief Wendelshafer chimed in. "Very impressive, Colonel, very impressive indeed, but, by my count, you're still one rocket short." Calvert gave the Chief a sneaky little side-glance, out of the corner of his eye. He then nodded to his radioman and told him, "Tell Fire Team Seven they are a 'Go' for launch." He then lit another long, thin cigar and smiled at the Chief. "It'll be here in a few minutes Felix." The radioman adjusted frequencies, "Ground Fire Seven, and this is Hellfire. The fuse is lit. I repeat … the fuse is lit!" From out of the radio speaker came, "Roger Hellfire, Ground Fire Seven on the way approximately five mikes out." Another quick radio frequency adjustment and then, "Sky Fire Seven, this is Hellfire. The fuse is lit." Someone answered back with an odd whining sound in the background, "Roger that Hellfire, Sky Fire Seven on the way … Out!"

Within minutes, a lone wrecker arrived and parked a little further up the river-bed. As soon as they arrived, you could see that one of the occupants was talking on the radio to someone. Just then, the other occupant dropped a yellow, beer can, smoke grenade. A dense, bright yellow cloud billowed and slowly rose into the air. Next, a solid, whirring sound grew increasingly louder and a giant, twin-engined H-37 *Sikorsky,* Mojave helicopter came flying low, up the river bed, with a strange device sling-loaded beneath its fat belly. It headed straight for the smoke. This was one strange looking helo. As it approached, retractable landing gear lowered from under the twin outboard engine nacelles. The pilot followed directions from the soldiers on the ground and set the load down exactly where they were told. As soon as it set its sling-load down and released the cables, it moved slowly sideways and set down on the river rocks. Giant, clamshell doors, under the cockpit, opened and soldiers in full CBR gear came running out. They immediately rolled out tail fins, a solid rocket motor and a warhead. Using the wrecker, the team rapidly assembled the rocket on this strange device.

The TPI Chief came up to Calvert. "Where, in the bowels of Hades did you ever find that thing, Colonel? I've read about air transportable HJ launchers in Field Manuals but I've never seen one." "That's because there's only two of them in the whole damned world as far as I know, Chief; this one, and one other someplace in West Germany. Other than being test fired at White Sands, New Mexico to be sure they actually worked, this may be the first time anybody in the Army has ever actually used one. Sure hope the damned thing don't fall apart!" "Me too, Colonel; this, I gotta' see!"

What the Colonel was not telling the Chief was that he had been fooling around with this contraption for weeks, had pretty much figured it out, and was pretty certain, at least in theory; that it was actually going to do what it was designed to do. There was also a lot of pre-planning involved.

The rocket was flawlessly assembled, loaded on the portable rig, aimed and fired without a hitch. We then knew why there were only two of these things left in the Army inventory. After firing our rocket, there was now only one operational, air-transportable, Honest John launcher, and it was still somewhere in West Germany. Seems these things were pretty much an emergency, fire and forget device. After the launch, there just wasn't much left of it that wasn't all burned, bent up or melted by the intense heat. The important thing was, it worked like a charm, and this seventh rocket flew straight and true to its mark. We ended up seven-for-seven, and 5th Missile Command was now in the Army record books. Somewhere, I knew old Ironbone had just put down a phone and was smiling to himself.

38

Bus High Dive

With the weight of the TPI off our collective shoulders, life at 5th Missile took on a whole new and purposeful dimension. Everyone walked a little taller and spoke of his job and unit with newfound pride.

The infiltrators continued to make everyone a little jumpy. We had more alerts, but not much came from them. There were a few shots fired and a few shadows evaporating into the night, but that was about all. My MPs were still keeping pretty busy with our everyday security duties and Quick Reaction Force mission training.

I had to make an early morning run to Yongsan to attend an hour-long intelligence briefing but, this time, the trip was going to be different in more ways than one. For nearly half my tour, Bob Kelser had sort of taken care of me and shared many of my adventures … but that just wasn't going to happen anymore.

One of the sad things about the Army is saying goodbye to friends, and this time it was really going to hurt. Sergeant Kelser, SP4 Jensen (AKA the Spaniard), Sergeant Godblood, SP4 Crippies and Sergeant Boon were all going back to the world. They came from different states, but all of them went through "Boot Camp" and AIT (Advanced Individual Training) together. All had arrived in Korea on the same plane and all had taken three month extension tours. And now, they all would be mustering out of the Army together and going back to civilian life. The big difference was, this time, they would all be going their separate ways. That's just how it was during the "Draft" years. All these fine, young men were called up as *American Citizen-Soldiers* and, after they did their duty, they were now going to return to civilian life. No longer were they the same boys who left home to serve their country. Men would be coming home, and they would be forever-bonded together by their shared experiences in the Army.

These four young men had something else in common. Sergeant Kelser told me about it and it confirms my sometimes-feelings that there must be Angels here on Earth, and they certainly come in strange packages.

These four GI's, fresh out of Military Police AIT at Fort Gordon, Georgia, all came down on orders to go to Camp Page, Korea. They all climbed on the same plane in Atlanta and headed for Oakland, California. The five of them checked in at Oakland Army Depot. Their orders had them all leaving out of Oakland for Korea the next day. They all checked in, at exactly the same time, with an NCO who just happened to be relieving another Sergeant for lunch. He took one look at their orders and said, "Shit! Come with me." The five followed, and the Sergeant drove them to the end of big warehouse looking building at the Oakland Air Terminal. In a far corner of this musty old building, a few cots were tucked away behind some piled-up wooden cargo pallets. There was also one tiny room close by with just a single toilet and sink. The Sergeant instructed the group to drop their duffel bags by the bunks and said,

> "Listen up you guys! There are no flights leaving out of Oakland for Korea. All Army contract flights out of here are currently going to Vietnam. Some idiot assignments clerk back at the MP School messed up your orders. You're supposed to be at Fort Lewis, Washington. Military contract flights out of Seattle are the ones going to Korea. I've worked here for awhile and I know we're having problems filling the planes with 'fresh meat' for Nam. If you Bozos had shown up, even a few minutes earlier, your orders would have been changed and tonight you'd be on your way to the 90th Replacement Depot in Saigon. I've seen it happen dozens of times when there've been screw-ups like this and I'm sick of it. So, if you *don't* want to end up being cannon fodder in some Vietnam rice paddy, you'd better do exactly as I say. Stay here, keep it quiet and keep the lights off. I'll be back later with something for you to eat. Tomorrow morning, get up at five, get dressed in your khakis and wait here for me. I'll have new orders for you and get you on a plane headed for Seattle.
>
> If anybody comes by, just tell them you're the new nighttime security detail for the warehouse. By the time they check it out, if they do, you'll be long gone outa' here"

That night the boys did as the Sergeant said. The Sergeant returned later with pizza and Cokes, and in the morning, just as promised, he picked them up, drove them to the airport and handed each of them a set of amended assignment orders for the 5th Missile Command, Camp Page, South Korea, via Seattle-Tacoma Airport.

Had they gone to Vietnam, they would have been there for the "Tet Offensive" and the peak year for American soldiers being killed and wounded in that war. As I said, Angels come in strange packages and this one was disguised as an Army Sergeant.

I got out of the Infiltrator intelligence briefing at about ten and, of course, we made a quick, obligatory stop at the big PX. When I came out, I was the proud owner of a new *Minolta* 35 mm, SLR camera and a 50 mm lens. This was my first trip with SP4 Danny Cortez as my driver. I knew this trip to Seoul was more of a PX run for Danny, but I didn't mind. Having someone to talk to on the slow drive south was always better than going it alone. We got back on the road and headed towards Chunchon at about 1100 in the morning. I wasn't totally at ease with Danny's driving yet and I missed Kelser's perspective in our conversations. Cortez and I were talking photography when he made a radical change in speed and exclaimed, "Oh shit! That little kimchi bus ain't gonna' make it! We'd better get the hell off the road!" He maneuvered our Jeep to the left and stopped behind the protection of a rock overhang. He jumped out and I followed.

Korean buses came in two basic sizes, the big, or regular bus-size buses, and smaller ones, which are about a third the size of the big ones. For some unknown GI reason, the smaller ones were called *Kimchi* Buses. This particular kimchi bus was still a ways off but racing downhill and careening from side to side as it came. Each successive swing was getting wider and more out of control. Cortez and I were standing in front of our Jeep, mesmerized by the drama. The bus driver had either died or totally lost control of the little bus. Every time the bus would recover from just about going off the road, the two of us would grimace and cringe. We'd be emitting sounds. "Ahhhh! Ohooooh! Jeezee! Oh my God!" My guess was the brakes had failed and there was no usable emergency brake. It was either that or the driver could not or did not know how to downshift into a lower gear. So here it came, caroming down the hill. Miraculously, the driver got the bus down the hill and onto a flat, straight stretch of road. We both breathed a big sigh of relief. The bus, somehow, made it out of danger. It was still rolling fast, but at least it was now on a flat, straight road and back under the driver's control. It was even beginning to slow down. It was then that it happened. The hapless little bus lurched violently to the left, like the steering just broke or something. Its two left-side wheels came up off the ground and the bus made a slow motion quarter roll onto its right side then slid off the road. In semi-slow motion it started to slide on down a 200, or so, foot gravel embankment. The bus' body was making horrible, metal-scraping sounds against the softball-sized rocks that made up the embankment. Sparks were flying out from everywhere. I could see there was still a bunch of people inside, bouncing all around. The bus flipped again, this time, ending up on its roof. A few screaming passengers tumbled out from where the door had been ripped off. Two more passengers were ejected just before it hit the water with a huge splash. The bus then instantly disappeared beneath the dark waters.

I don't remember us saying anything to each other but, even before the bus hit the water, both Danny and I were already scurrying down the loose, rocky embankment as fast as we could. We had no plan; we were just going. Some Koreans had stopped their vehicles and were coming down behind us. We passed by some of the passengers who'd been thrown out. Two were pretty bloody and banged up and a third appeared dead as we scrambled past them and down the embankment.

We were at that part of the Soyang River, which is about a quarter-mile above the dam. The Soyang Dam and hydroelectric facility had only been in operation for maybe a year. The water here had to be two or three hundred feet deep.

Still, with no plan, I automatically started ripping clothes off as I slid down the rocks.

For two summers, as a teen, I'd been a lifeguard at our town beach. When I got to the water's edge, right where red bus paint scrapings were all over the rocks, I sat down hard and unzipped out of my combat boots and jettisoned my fatigue pants and jacket. I dove into the cold water, opened my eyes and saw that the bank fell away fast. The sun was bright, almost right overhead and the water was unexpectedly crystal clear. I expected the bus to be gone but, maybe, there would be someone I could pull up. To my amazement, there the bus was, resting on its roof, in about fifteen, maybe twenty feet of water. I could see bubbles rising from it getting ever bigger as they neared the surface. Instead of going straight to the bottom it somehow got hung up on an underwater outcropping just about the same width as the bus. I surfaced quickly and yelled to Cortez, "It's right here below me; I'm going down!" Cortez was already undressed, in the water and had gotten a rope from somewhere.

I always looked forward to Friday nights during those miserable, Rhode Island winter months when I was in high school. Just about every Friday evening, my Dad would take me and, sometimes, two of my cousins to the enormous, indoor pool at Quonset Point Naval Air Station. The Navy used this pool for various types of water training. We used it to practice our underwater swimming in preparation for summer snorkeling and spear-fishing. I remember it was this huge, Olympic-sized pool and 20 feet deep at the deep end. With just swim fins and a mask, plus weeks of training, I got so I could underwater swim the entire length of the pool and back before surfacing. I would slowly swim along the bottom of the pool, starting and finishing at the deep end. Even though I was conserving my air as best I could, it would always feel like my lungs were going to explode as I surfaced from the deep end. Slowly, I got so I could hold my breath for a little over three minutes.

I breathed in as deeply as I could and made a well practiced surface-dive. Three or four strokes and a few scissor kicks and my hand touched the front, right tire. Sound magnifies underwater and I could hear screaming and thrashing about inside the bus. I quickly pulled myself down so I could see inside. It was amazing! No one seemed to be trying to get out. They were all frantically fighting to get their faces into a small air pocket on the floor of the upside-down bus. I stuck a hand inside and tried to grab a young girl. She grabbled back, and with amazing strength, almost pulled me inside. I managed to get both my feet on the outside of the bus. Using them as a lever, I just stood up. My leg muscles were way more powerful than her arms. She popped out the door and I quickly flipped her into a cross-chest carry and made for the surface with my lungs bursting. I blew out what little air I had left just before surfacing and somehow came up right where Cortez was standing. He tossed the rope over and pulled us in. This young girl, probably in her early teens, was coughing her lungs up. Koreans swarmed into the water and grabbed her.

I looked Cortez in the eye, "Jesus Christ, Danny, there's a lot of people alive down there! Give me one end of that rope!" I quickly tied it around my waist. "They grab hold of anything down there. Give me a two-minute count, then pull me up if I'm not back before then."

I surface dived again and there was still a lot of noise. I, again, braced myself on the outside. A teenage boy was near the door. I just snatched him outside in one quick pull and put his hand on the rope. All of a sudden, he knew just what to do and was flying hand-over-hand up the rope. I grabbed another hand, this time an older woman. Again, I swam to the surface with her. She went limp a couple of feet from the surface. I came up yelling for help and saw the teenage boy being attended to on the rocks. Koreans were all over me and took the woman.

I told Danny I was going to make one more dive, but after that, he would have to take over because the water down there was so cold I was running out of steam fast. Halfway back down, I got the bright idea to take the rope off me and lash it to the bus and just pull as many as I could out and onto it. There was still noise and movement but not nearly as much. I reached in until I felt something alive and pulled it out. It was a man and I gave him the taut rope to grab. Next, I pulled out a young woman and, then, an older woman. The younger two went up the rope and I swam up with the older woman. There was now pandemonium on the rocks. There must have been a hundred local nationals all over the water's rocky edge. The road above was jammed with dozens of parked vehicles. Cortez was now waist deep in the water and he handed me the rope. He could now just quickly pull himself down hand-over-hand and save precious seconds of air. Three or four others popped to the surface on their own and everyone was trying to help them ashore.

In some lives, and mine must be one of them, you have to accept that there's a power in the universe watching over you. You have to just blindly accept it because, sometimes, you end up alive when you know you should be dead, and coincidence just isn't an acceptable enough explanation. Cortez had no sooner given me the rope than I got a mighty tug on it. I figured another of the passengers, a heavy one, was pulling himself up the rope; so, I braced myself and pulled back. The tug was so strong it pulled my arms and face under water. There was no one coming up the rope but I hung on anyway. To my horror, I saw the bus slowly sliding off the shelf. Through the darkening waters I helplessly hung onto the rope for a few seconds as the bus continued scraping its way down the long, underwater slope. My last visual image from the bus was the face of a young woman with the palms of both her hands pressed flat against a heavy, metal-screened bus window. She had this sad look on her face like someone departing a home she loved. The piercing pressure in my ears became intolerable and I must have involuntarily let go of the rope. For a few seconds, I watched the tiny bus slowly dissolve in the liquid gloom. My natural buoyancy started to drift me back up towards the surface. I had no concept how deep I had been, but with lungs screaming and head pounding, I started swimming as hard as I could toward the mirrored surface. I exploded out of the water gasping for air.

After a dozen or so deep and painful gasps and a coughing spasm, I numbly turned and looked at Cortez. He was talking to me. "Give me the rope, Sir, I'm ready, I'm ready!" A lump instantly formed in both my stomach and throat at the same time. Even though I was now beginning to realize I was chilled to the bone, I could feel warm tears welling up in my eyes. I slowly shook my head at him, "It's gone, Danny—it's gone!" I hauled myself out on the rocks with help of two, young, Korean soldiers and sat there staring into the dark waters and, mentally, started playing the "*Coulda'—Woulda'—Shoulda'*" game. I shoulda' figured it out from the beginning. It coulda' ended differently if I woulda' just taken the rope and tied it to the bus during my first dive. Maybe, if I hadn't been so damned stupid, I coulda' got more of them out. My adrenaline rush was fading fast and along with it came both the emotional and physical letdown. I sat there shaking violently on the warm; dry, rocks and, then, I began sobbing uncontrollably. Part of this emotional release was for the poor people down there that I was just too damned incompetent to help, but, another part, was the now frightening realization that I could have just as well gotten myself tangled up and slid to the bottom with the rest of those poor people. I couldn't get that young woman's face and sad expression out of my mind.

You simply never know what life is going to throw at you. I read a quote by some guy where he said there was no such thing as *luck*. He said, "Luck is the word we use to explain what happens when opportunity meets preparedness." In other words, if you don't have the training, strength, speed or knowledge to do something when a fleeting opportunity presents itself, you won't be able to take advantage of it. I guess that's sort of what happened this day. If I hadn't been trained as a lifeguard, plus spent all those dreary winter evenings seeing how long I could hold my breath and how far I could swim underwater, I would have just stood on the bank, like everybody else, and stared at the surface of the river.

The Koreans have another, equally complex belief. They are believers in fate! They translate what we call "Luck" into something much more. They believed I was sent to Korea by the almighty somebody—Not sure; they never said which one—for the specific purpose of being at that particular place along the river, at that exact time, to save just those five people. Three more popped up on their own; but one didn't make it. It didn't matter, because the Koreans gave me credit for all seven. Because of this belief, they went way out of their way to make a really big deal out of this event. What's a "Big Deal?" A Korean big deal is a celebration. Try this on for size! They held a huge presentation ceremony at the City Hall. The Governor of Kang Won Province presented me with a high provincial award for saving those people. He gave Cortez a smaller, framed award. A ROK Army band was on hand and played "The US Army Song" and "God Bless America." It looked like the whole Korean National Police force was there standing at attention. There were several Korean officials, including the Mayor of Chunchon, and they all made speeches followed by much applause. My Colonel was there along with most of my MPs and, of course, Joyce. I was self-conscious about the fuss but it was only the beginning. The Mayor made me "Honorary Public Safety Director for the city of Chunchon." I then had to sit behind a desk in city hall, with my name and title on it, while pictures were taken.

The last thing that happened was truly a surprise. The five-star General in charge of the entire Korean National Police, personally, awarded me the rank of Second Lieutenant in the KNP. The General pinned on the appropriate collar rank insignia while another KNP Colonel removed my Army Eagle and affixed a KNP hat badge on my uniform saucer cap. The General then took an ice pick and punched a hole in my khaki uniform pocket and screwed on a solid silver

KNP badge, saluted and bowed. He shook my hand with both of his. Mr. Shin stayed at my side throughout the piercing and kept up a running commentary on what was being said and what it all meant. At first I didn't believe it when he said,

"Don't worry, he not stick you; just making hole in uniform for your badge. This not honorary thing, you now real deal Second *Rootenant* in KNP."
"You're kidding?"
"Not kidding! When you get out of Army you come back Chunchon and be KNP *Rootenant.*"
"What's it pay?"
"Fifty bucks a month and all you can steal!"
I smiled widely and looked over at him. Mr. Shin was smiling back and his pride in me showed. "It no shit; you now real KNP Rootenant … Rootenant!"

The official part of the ceremony was coming to an end. There was a standing ovation, which really embarrassed me. As I looked over the crowd I kept seeing people I knew. Most gave a little wave or a "thumbs up" as our eyes made contact. Behind the dignitaries, was my biggest fan, Joyce, and she had Jin Hee and Paul with her. They all waved and called out.

Then, there was the formal lunch with lots of talking, handshaking, bowing, saluting and picture-taking by the Korean papers and official U.S. Army photographers. At the end of the meal, the families of the survivors came forward and presented me with a Korean temple rubbing of Buddha ascending into Heaven. Mr. Shin told me this was part of the "Fate" thing they all believed in. This was the moment I would most remember. It wasn't the temple rubbing; it was the look in the eyes and the words of all those family members. Each of the seven survivors who came up from the bus walked up and personally thanked me, shook my hand and bowed. Mr. Shin relayed every word and feeling to me. I have never felt so humbled. In the swirl of emotions that afternoon, I somehow felt an unexplainable link to each of these families.

There were other awards given out to several people who helped on the riverbank that day. Danny Cortez was among them. We sort of got separated during lunch festivities when I was directed to sit at the head table with all the "Lord High Muckety-Mucks", but I saw him at another table, across from me, sitting between two lovely young Korean women who were paying him a lot of attention. At one point, we made eye contact; he smiled, and gave me the high sign. All was "A-Okay" at his end.

Because of Korean custom, Joyce was not allowed at the head table with me and all the brass. She was towards the back of the room seated with Paul and Jin

Hee. When we finally made it home, another little celebration was waiting for us. My guys brought wine up to the house and we spent the rest of the afternoon drinking it and talking about how strange life really can be.

39

R&R

I had this big emotional letdown after all the fuss over the bus incident and I wanted to see if Joyce and I could just get away by ourselves for a few days. Lo and behold, the opportunity to go on R&R (Rest & Recuperation) in Japan presented itself. R&R is actually an old GI combat term from World War II. During the Vietnam War, the GIs bastardized it a bit and said R&R stood for "Rape & Run". Those with nothing strong drawing them home, would, for a short time (two weeks), go to Hawaii, Bangkok or even Australia, where I understand the women were quite accommodating and had the advantage of looking pretty much like the girls back home ... even if they did talk a bit funny. Most GIs just wanted to get drunk, chase women for a week or two and try to forget about war. It's simply a chance to mentally get away, even for a short while and *"get out of the line of fire"*, so to speak. All I know is, a lot of Army guys I've met over the years have these lovely Australian wives they first met while on R&R from Nam or Korea.

We really didn't have the money to go on this little five-day vacation but we said "Screw it!" and decided to do it anyway. We were young, and after what we'd recently been through, it would take a lot to deter us from at least trying. Joyce and I had a couple hundred bucks between us and Paul insisted he loan us a couple hundred more. I was going to get paid the day before we left, so the money end should be barely enough for some real fun, if we didn't get too carried away. However, the execution of this mission would be like a challenging military operation.

The *Stars & Stripes Flight* was an interesting way for GIs to travel from Korea to Japan. The *S&S*, Korean Edition, was printed in Japan. At zero-dark-thirty, in the wee hours, each and every morning, they would fly the papers from Japan into Kimpo. Various transportation methods would then get the daily edition to all the Stars & Stripes Book Stores; usually these were co-located with the PXs. This left an almost empty Air Force C-130 to return to Tachikawa Air Force

Base, in Japan. So, they allowed military personnel to hitch *space available* rides from Korea to Japan.

This would take care of my half of our transportation requirements, but what about Joyce's? Well, there was no way out of it; I had to book her a roundtrip ticket on KAL (Korean Air Lines) into *Haneda* Airport near Tokyo. We also had to arrange her flight behind mine so I could land at Tachikawa Air Force Base, grab ground transportation to Haneda and get there in time to meet her plane. After painstaking research and listening to those who'd already done it, we came up with a mathematical formula to accomplish the mission.

The return flight was going to be equally difficult. I'd have to put Joyce on her commercial flight, then, catch an Air Force bus back to Tachikawa. From there, I'd have to put my name on a waiting list for a "Space-A" flight back to Kimpo on the next S&S flight, an Air Force parts flight, or maybe even on a C-9 "Nightingale" medical evacuation flight, if there was one, and if it had space available.

So, with just a small amount of money at hand, I had to be creative and patient while traveling. I, myself, could basically fly anywhere for free on military planes, but with a wife who really wasn't supposed to be there, traveling anywhere was a real adventure. Amazingly, somehow, it all seemed to be coming together.

I made it to the KAL gate at Haneda almost just as her plane was rolling up to the gate. My bubbly bride got off the flight gushing about how nice everyone had been and how fast her flight was. The night before, we had both stayed in the transient billeting facilities right on Kimpo Airbase. I had to get up about five hours before she did to catch my flight. Now, here she was fresh as a daisy while I'm already sweaty, exhausted and dragging tail. I rode into Japan in a sling hammock-like seat on the *S&S* C-130 along with several other guys and a strapped-down helicopter going back for major depot-level repairs. From Tachikawa I took a bus, a train and a subway to get to Haneda.

We were now faced with getting ourselves and two suitcases from the airport to the *Sanyo Hotel* in downtown Tokyo. This hotel was a contracted U.S. military billeting facility set up for troops who wanted to visit Tokyo on R&R but couldn't afford the very high hotel prices. Even in '68, Tokyo had the reputation of being god-awful expensive.

I had written instructions on how to get to the hotel; so, I picked up both our bags and off we went. Japanese subways are unique by western standards. For one thing, they have professional "pushers" on their payroll. The pusher's job is to literally shove people into the cars at each stop along the way. This allows each car to be packed with its maximum number of passenger. So, there we were, jammed in like canned sardines. I had no idea where our suitcases were because I couldn't see anything below passenger shoulder-height. Joyce and I ended up facing each other, but crammed in between us was this very short—shorter than Joyce—Japanese gentleman. He was old, really dirty and smelled of beer, sweat and fish. Thanks to the *Pusher*, he was pressed in tightly between us. Joyce and I were both hanging on tightly to the bulkhead hand-straps. This wee Japanese guy's looking at me intently, studying every inch of my formerly immaculate dress green uniform. I only had about four ribbons on my chest at this point in my career, but this short, smelly guy stood in front of me studying them. The little man then, somehow, turned a 180 and commenced studying Joyce's pretty face and breasts. He did another about face and again stared at me. He repeated this process several times. Then, all of a sudden, with incredible fish breath, he began pointing at us and loudly announcing, in very Basic English—first pointing at me, "*Hey rook! Mare-can War Hero!*" He then turned towards Joyce and loudly announced, "*Hey, rook! Moo-bee Star!*" Next, he did a ninety degree turn wedging himself, sideways, between the two of us and repeatedly pointed back and forth at us while saying, "*War hero—Moo-bee Star, War hero—Moo-bee Star!*" This continued for the rest of what was, thankfully, a short train ride to our downtown exit. I towered over everyone in the car and felt both amusement and alarm as literally everyone in the car was straining and craning their necks to see the war hero and movie star. At our stop, the sea of short humanity, including the fishy little man, passed by us taking one last look at what I'm sure they told family and friends was their chance encounter with Audy Murphy and Natalie Wood. Finally, I could now see the floor and, miracle of miracles; our suitcases were right where I last saw them.

Our five days in Japan went by in a whirl. After living in the Korean countryside for about nine months, Japan seemed like *Disneyland* to us. We went up the Tokyo Tower, had Kamikaze taxi rides, and took the incredible, 200 MPH *Bullet Train* on day trips to both Kyoto and Nikko. On our last day, we had two *must* things left to do; souvenir shopping at the big, downtown *Mitsukoshi* Department Store and catch the *Ginza* area at night in all its glory. The Ginza is like a combination of Times Square and the Vegas Strip all rolled into one. Coming from dimly lit Chunchon, this was a real treat for the eyes.

On our last night, the hotel gave us complimentary tickets to the *Nichiguchi* Theater to see their Las Vegas/Follies Bergere-type floor show. We didn't understand a word of it but both agreed it was great. In particular, I liked the topless, Eurasian show girls festooned in brightly colored ostrich feathers.

The return trip was uneventful. A bus from the hotel took us back to *Haneda*, where I put Joyce on her return flight, then caught an Air Force bus to Tachikawa. Paul was waiting for Joyce at Kimpo, with Jin Hee, and they all took the train back to Chunchon. I was lucky and got a ride back right away on a Nightingale Med flight and arrived home only three hours behind them.

We sat there on the floor cushions in our bedroom playing cards and hoping all the treasures we bought in Japan would arrive okay. There was a small "Army Post Office" in our hotel; so, we mailed most of our souvenirs to my APO address at Camp Page.

We both agreed it was good to be back home in Chunchon. I guess, without knowing it, we'd somehow become Korean country folk. The bright lights and incredible pace of Japan was interesting, and a welcome holiday, but, when it came right down to it, we were now pretty comfortable in our little home in the Land of the Morning Calm.

40

The FAC Family

The morning after Joyce and I returned from Japan, I was told the long promised Air Force FAC (Forward Air Control) Pilot had finally arrived at Camp Page. I, for one, had been dreaming up ideas about how he and his little L-19 Bird Dog could help us in our QRF missions. The Bird Dog could spot for us the same way they did for Air Force fighters and bombers. They carried these little smoke rockets under their wings and it would sure help if he could mark any enemy positions sighted. We could have one of our MPs fly with him and act as his spotter. Sid & Earl could then rush the QRF to the area and set us down where the bad guys were, without getting us in too close of course. This was going to be a lot faster and more efficient than what we'd been doing.

I walked down to air operations and there on the flight line was this tall, slim, dark haired, Air Force Captain kicking the Bird Dog's tires. I mean it; he was literally kicking the tires! I walked up behind him and initiated conversation. "Take it easy there, Captain; you're liable to knock the wheels right off that poor little puddle jumper." The Air Force FNG turned and gave me a big, friendly grin as we exchanged salutes. "Yup, I recon I might just could do that. Ah hain't flew anything this small since my Daddy's old Piper J3. Hey, Lieutenant, my name's Harry Sanders." He stuck out his hand. Harry was a, no shit, Arizona cowboy with a really firm handshake and an infectious grin. I introduced myself and asked, "You been a FAC pilot for very long, Harry?" I was expecting to hear a few Vietnam stories. "Nah, other than a check ride in one of these little guys, this is only the second time I've even been near one. Up until now I've been in SAC (Strategic Air Command) flyin' KC-135 tankers. Not really sure how I got here. There's dust inside the cockpit; you got any idea how long has this thing been just sitting here?" I told Harry I saw it the night I arrived back in November of last year. "I've never seen it in the air, Harry. I've been down here when the mechanics started it up a couple of times but that's about all I can tell you." Harry let out a big sigh, "Well, I guess I'm gonna' hafta' see if the damn thing flies! You wanna' go up with me Lieutenant?" To this day, I still don't know why I said, "Sure!" The only thing I can think of to say in my own defense is, *"Hey, I just love airplanes and flying!"*

There were no crash helmets involved, just ball caps and earphones. The little tandem L-19 could be flown from the front or back seat; Harry picked the front and I wedged myself in back. He fired it up, and let the engine warm up for a few minutes as he checked all the gauges and then, over my earphones, I heard him get permission from the tower to do a local "Check Ride". The takeoff was uneventful; it was just like Harry really knew what he was doing. It was then I noticed he was looking around for something. I pressed the *push to talk* button on my mike, "Wacha' lookin' for, Harry?" Harry's voice came back over my earphones, "What a dummy! Here I am lookin' for the controls to retract the landing gear but, as we both know, there ain't none! I've just been flying the big stuff way too long."

Harry piloted the little Bird across the river and started gaining altitude He then flew into a pass between two good-sized mountains. "Hey, Harry, flown in mountains much?" I asked because I'd been flying in them for months now with Captain Song, Captain McCabe and Sid & Earl. I knew up and down drafts plus the tricky winds made it a good idea not to get too close to the hard stuff. "No, Herb, most of my flyings' been at twenty to thirty-thousand feet; them 135s are nothin' but flying gas stations. All's I had to do was keep it straight and level and let the guy with the 'flying boom' do all the refueling work. Why ya' askin'?" "Well, Harry, you're the one wearing the pilot's wings, but I know something about the air currents around these mountains and they can be a little tricky. You might want to move a little more away from those rock cliffs." No sooner had the word *cliffs* left my lips than we instantly dropped 50 to 60 feet. Before I could catch my stomach, we popped back up again but more to the right. My knuckles were pure white as I panic gripped the instrument panel in front of me. Harry nonchalantly craned his neck around to look at me, "See whatcha' mean! I think I'm gonna' just slide this puppy over a bit away from them cliffs." The air smoothed out some and I began to breathe again. "Hey Herb, ya'll got any more tips that might make me look a little more like I know what I'm doin'?" "No Harry, just, in the mountains, stay away from the sides and keep some sky under you!" "Herb, what say we take her home now and call it a day? I think I might need to find another flight suit; besides, all I really wanted to do was make sure this here toy airplane really flies … and it does." Well, at least he had a sense of humor. Truth was, he caught it quickly and did just the right things to get us back under control.

We touched down smoothly enough and taxied towards flight operations at a brisk pace. As we came towards the hangar, Harry made a sharper-than-he-should-have right turn and all hell broke loose. He must have been thinking he was in a heavy multi-engined jet tanker with a nose-wheel. When he jammed the little tail-dragger into the tight turn it went up on its left wheel and banged the left wing tip hard against the tarmac. The wing rebounded quickly off the ground and knocked the little Bird Dog up on its right wheel and banged the right wing tip almost as hard. After rocking back and forth a few times Harry killed the engine and we both just sat there in silence as we rolled slowly towards the hangar.

The damage looked minimal but, needless to say, there were a whole bunch of people who were not very pleased. Harry filled out an accident report and we both walked slowly towards my office. Even though the damage wasn't all that bad, I knew Harry was feeling really dumb about his silly lapse in judgment. "I hope I didn't blow my last chance." I looked at Harry with a questioning expression. "Well, let's just say I didn't exactly leave SAC tankers in the best of graces. Forward Air Control is about the end of the line for Air Force pilots. I was never good enough for fighters; I flunked out of bombers, transferred into cargo planes for awhile, then transitioned to tankers and now I've been given a job flying little planes that cost less than the nose-wheel on a KC-135. So now what do I do? I go and bang even that up on my very first flight. I'm probably up *Shit's Creek* and this is gonna' be the end of the line for me."

Harry was looking pretty dejected; so, I tried to lighten things up a bit. "It's after five Harry; how-bout I buy you a drink at the club."

"Thanks but I have to meet my wife and find a place to stay tonight." I was dumbfounded.

"Your wife is here?"

"Well, actually my wife and sixteen month old son."

"How the hell did they get here? This is an unaccompanied tour you know!"

"Yeah, I know! I was, or thought I was, going to be stationed at Kimpo down in Seoul and I was authorized to bring Nancy and Rusty. I guess my reputation preceded me, because; when I got to the Yongsan Replacement Depot I was handed orders to come here. I guess I was supposed to make arrangements to send them back but Nancy said 'No way, Jose, we're here and we're stayin' and here we are. You don't know how headstrong a woman can get!"

"I wouldn't bet on it, Harry!"

"She and Rusty are over at the Chaplain's office seeing if he has any ideas about a place for us to stay. Wanna' walk over there with me and meet em'?"

"Sure, why not!"

When we got to the Chaplain's office there was this thin woman with short brown hair and a baby sleeping in her lap. She looked frail and so very tired. Harry leaned over and kissed her on the forehead.

"How ya' doin', Babe?"

"Well, I finally got Rusty to sleep and there may be some good news. The Chaplain has an idea."

"Yeah, what's that?"

"Well seems there's this Lieutenant who has his wife over here; she's a nurse who's working part time at the base clinic. They actually have a real house in town and the Chaplain thinks maybe he can talk them into putting us up for the night. His name is Royce and the Chaplain's out trying to find him right now. So, at least we have a chance at a place to stay tonight."

"Well ain't this interesting! You know Hon; I met this Lieutenant Royce today."

"You did! Was he nice?"

"Well, yes, yes he was, real nice in fact; I tried to kill him twice today and he still offered to buy me a drink. Honey, this here's Lieutenant Royce."

Nancy's head snapped around. First she looked at my face then read the name on my uniform.

"Oh my, I'm so sorry to be talking about you like you weren't even here. I'm so embarrassed!"

"No need to be, Mrs. Sanders, I actually got a kick out of it. The Chaplain's right, we do have a tiny, sort of, guest room and I'm sure Joyce won't mind you guys using it for a night or two, until you can find something."

"Oh, thank you, thank you so very much, that's such a weight off and please call me Nancy!"

Nancy then started to cry a little and Harry put his arm around her and said to me. "Good thing I didn't get you killed; your wife definitely would be too pissed to let us bunk with her tonight." You gotta' like a guy with Harry's sense of humor.

It always amazes me how things sometimes just work themselves out. Joyce and Nancy really hit it off. Now she had two girl friends, Nancy and Jin Hee. The three of them had a ball paling around together. Baby Rusty was a new and welcome diversion in their lives. This had to be the cutest male, Caucasian baby ever. He had long, strawberry-blond, ringlets, the biggest and brightest blue eyes, a permanent ear-to-ear grin and an infectious little, baby giggle. Jin Hee had never seen a western baby and was totally fascinated with Rusty. She was always first to run to him when he'd cry and she loved carrying him for what seemed like hours. He became the center of attention for all three women.

I know I failed to mention it, but, as you've probably already guessed, the Sanders ended up staying more than one night. After the first night, the weekend and then the next week, the three Sanders' sort of blended into our life. Without any conversation, somewhere along the way, everyone just sort of stopped looking for a place for them to live. We all started doing a lot of things together. Not to be the "Odd Man Out", Jin Hee increasingly started asking Paul Gleason to come along with us on our various little adventures. Paul was delighted, of course, and I suspected, through the process of osmosis, the two of them were slowly becoming more than just friends. Taking in boarders ended up being the best thing that could have happened. I semi-learned how to play bridge; then Harry and I started spending more time away from home searching for infiltrators.

41

Run Over by My Own Jeep

We got a call from Bravo Battery that one of their vehicles had been fired upon while returning to their mountain top location. The ¾ truck luckily made it backup the hill, but not without about a dozen bullet holes in it and not without the driver being wounded by flying windshield glass. When his windshield exploded in flying shards, the driver floored the truck and raced through the "Kill Zone" just like we were all taught to do back in basic training. This probably saved his life.

It was a rainy, nasty day and the low-hanging clouds canceled out just about any chance of our being able to get there by helicopter. Sid & Earl, of course, were more than willing to fly us but flight operations put the squash on that idea due to crappy weather conditions and poor visibility. I didn't like the idea much either. Hueys' are noisy things and flying very low would make it a pretty high-risk operation if Bad Guys were around. We also were missing our first chance to use Harry and his Bird Dog to spot for us.

We knew it would take about an hour by road; so, we *saddled up* two gun Jeeps and took off towards Bravo Battery, hoping nothing serious happened while we were trying to get there. Our response time would not be great but it was the best we could do under the circumstances.

We were nearing the mountain road turn off to Bravo but were still on the main road. It would be about five miles uphill to the Hawk unit. Danny Cortez was sitting in back, on the spare tire, and hanging onto the pedestal-mounted M-60. I was driving and SP4 Hanlon was riding shotgun. An FNG named Skip Avritt was seated low in the back of the Jeep opening up another can of 7.65 MM, linked machinegun ammo.

Skip was a former Marine who'd already been to Vietnam. He got out of the Marines but was having problems with adjusting to civilian life again; so, he joined the Army. Skip may have been a little strange, and he drank too much when off-duty, but he was one hell of a good worker. The only other thing worth noting about Skip was he had a lot of American Indian blood in him and he looked it.

As I started into the left-hand turn off the MSR, Cortez screamed, "There they are!" The instant those three words came out of his mouth, our Jeep started taking fire. I yelled, "Jump!" and everyone did. Everybody, that is, except Skip Avritt. He was wedged in behind my seat, on the floor. Danny Cortez did a back-flip off the spare tire and actually landed on his feet; a stuntman couldn't have duplicated that maneuver. With bullets bouncing all around, he somehow still had the presence of mind to take the M-60 and a couple of yards of linked ammo with him. Hanlon, with a mighty leap, ended up in a ditch on the right side of the road. The Jeep bumped into the same ditch, did a slow motion rollover and then came to rest upside down. It was hissing steam and all tires were still turning. The hood was on one side of the ditch and the back end on the other. Skip was unceremoniously dumped out under the Jeep along with a whole pile of heavy, ammo cans falling on top of him. Danny Cortez was already in the ditch when the other two arrived. Danny could really move when he needed to! He immediately started returning fire. I don't think Danny knew where the Bad Guys were because he was spraying every high rock he could see.

I, on the other hand, ended up on the opposite side of the road with my left leg hurting like hell. There was no blood showing through my fatigue pants but the pain was just killing me. My M-14 rifle was left behind in the Jeep but I still had my .45 pistol and lots of clips. The three on the other side of the road had gotten their collective act together. Skip and Hanlon had spotted some enemy muzzle flashes and were returning firing up into the rocks with their M-14s. Danny Cortez was chewing up the hillside rocks with the M-60. I was in the opposite ditch, clutching my .45 while my left leg swelled up like a balloon. I yelled across the road. "Is everybody okay?" I heard Hanlon's voice, "Yeah, except Danny's been shot in the face but I think he's okay." *Shot in the face? That could never be okay!* "Anybody got a radio?" Skip yelled back, "Nope, it got smashed in the crash."

Our trail Jeep saw us get hit and Sergeant Cavern immediately slammed his 151 Jeep into reverse and backed down the hill and around a corner. I assumed they had gotten out of the kill zone and were working on something. No sooner had I thought it than I heard a voice behind me in my ditch, "Sir, it's me, Specialist Kreick." George Kreick was one of our FNGs who'd only been with us for a couple of weeks. He came low-crawling up beside me. "PFC Winslow, Sergeant Moppet and Sergeant Cavern are working their way up through the rocks behind us." We then heard a quick, five-round rip of automatic weapons fire and a uniformed body, along with a bunch of loose rocks, came crashing down on the dirt road, about six feet in front of us. It was a very dead Korean in a ROK Army uniform. I yelled out, "Somebody please tell me we didn't just kill a fucking ROK?" SP4 Kreick rolled him over and assured me, "No, Sir, definitely Gook, and definitely dead! Look—he's wearing last week's shoulder patch and that ain't one of *our* guns!"

Because the infiltrators were masquerading as ROK Army soldiers, the real ROKs had to come up with several identification plans. One of the things they did was keep changing shoulder patches. The bad guys may be able to copy or steal uniforms but they couldn't keep up with frequent insignia, shoulder patch and headgear changes. I privately wondered what happened to the ten percent of the ROK troops who didn't get word of a change. A ROK Captain gave me a simple reply, "They too stupid to know, they die!" Well, no beating around the bush there.

Sergeant Moppet came trotting up the road with his rifle at the ready. "I just got off the radio with Bravo Battery. There's nothing gong on up there Lieutenant. They think it was probably just a little sniper-fire and the infiltrators moved on. A bunch of ROKs are already there and crawling all over the place. I guess this one here was a lookout, watching their backdoor."

Sergeant Cavern was still hunkered down up in the rocks keeping over-watch. We checked the dead infiltrator's pockets for maps and any written material. The infiltrator got hit with a clean head shot. The lack of bleeding indicated he must have been killed instantly. My concern now switched to my own men. "Somebody said Cortez was shot! Is he okay? Danny, where the hell are you?" Cortez came out of the far ditch carrying the M-60. "*I'm ober here, Sur.*" Danny looked okay to me but he was talking funny. As he came closer I noted a little pink ball sticking out the side of his face. I took a closer look. "*Ith my thung, Thur.*" "It's your tongue?" A little more agitated this time, he repeated, "*Yeth, Thur, ith my friggin' thung.*" Danny then opened his mouth for me and stuck his tongue out. At that moment I saw daylight shining through a hole in his cheek. Apparently, Danny had been shot in the face when his mouth was wide open, probably while he was warning us that the saw the enemy. It looked like the bullet had punctured the thin wall of his cheek and passed out through his open mouth. Danny pulled a pen out of his pocket and stuck it in his mouth and out the hole in his cheek. "*Thee!*" For once in his life, Danny's constant chattering worked in his favor and probably saved his life. If his mouth had been closed, that Chi-Com round would have surly hit his teeth. His teeth would have shattered like so many grenade fragments, severely wounding or killing him. The bleeding started up again, so Danny poked the tip of his tongue back into the little, almost perfectly round, hole in his cheek and it stopped.

I asked Sergeant Cavern to take Danny and two of the others back to Page in his Jeep. We used his radio and called for a wrecker and transportation for the four of us who were going to be left behind. We then took up positions in the rocks and waited.

My leg was really killing me now, so I took the time to examine it closer. I pulled my fatigue pants out of my boots and looked at my leg; it was nasty! Both sides of my leg were badly bruised from the knee all the way down to the top of my boot. It hurt to even touch it. As I pulled the fatigue pants material down carefully over my swollen leg, I stretched them taut for a moment. I looked down at my pants and immediately knew what happened, but I didn't know how. There, on the leg of my fatigue pants, was the dusty, ground-in, print of a tire track. The only thing I could come up with was, when the shooting started, I un-assed the Jeep so fast my leg somehow ended up under my Jeep's back tire. I must have actually run over myself!

The wrecker eventually came and we all helped flip the Jeep back right side up then watched the wrecker, with my Jeep, head on off down the road. There was only room for one more in the wrecker cab; so I told Skip to go along in case the driver needed help on the way back. It also gave the driver somebody to literally ride *shotgun*. That left just the three of us, and we still had a dead infiltrator to hand-off to the intelligence guys.

About an hour later, our transportation arrived along with Military Intelligence and some ROK Counter Intelligence folks in their black Jeep. We turned the dead guy's body over to MI, answered a dozen or so questions, then we're on our way back to Page. The ride home was painful; my poor leg was throbbing like hell and I felt every bump on the hour-long ride back to Camp.

When we pulled up in front of the PMO, Joyce was there along with Captain Gavin Green, our Newbie, preppy doc from Newport, Rhode Island. Joyce came running up to me, looking very worried. "Are you alright?" In my best John Wayne imitation, I replied, "O course I'm all right, little lady!" I grimaced and let out a brief groan when I got out of the truck and put full weight on my bad leg. I immediately lifted it a little off the ground and hopped a few tiny steps on the good one. Dr. Green and Joyce jumped in to help me keep the weight off my bad leg. It was a bit comical because both he and Joyce were about a foot shorter then me. It looked like two tiny tugs helping the "Queen Mary" into port. Once inside the PMO the doc had me sit down on a desk to take a look at my leg. He whipped out a pair of scissors and slit my pants up to over my knee; it was totally deep purple now with some orangey-yellow, nasty-looking stuff around the edges. Dr. Green made a painful face then looked over the top of his black-framed glasses, "You, my friend, have a broken leg." Joyce had this pained, sympathetic look on her face and was nodding in agreement. I instantly shot back, "I don't have a broken leg damn it! I've been walking and even running on it!" The doc chimed in again, "Don't be silly, Lieutenant! Look at your leg! I've never seen such hematoma in a living person. What the hell did you do, get run over by a truck?" This diminutive, pseudo-aristocratic doc with his thick, Cliff Walk, Newport accent was now beginning to really piss me off. Like a wounded dog, my pain was now making me very disagreeable. I leaned forward and looked him dead in the eye.

"Matter of fact Doc, I did get run over by a truck, a quarter-ton truck to be exact!"

"You got run over by a Jeep? What idiot ran you over?"

"I'm the idiot that ran me over!"

"That's impossible! How in the hell could that happen?"

"What the fuck difference does it make; how bout something for my pain Doc?"

"You have a broken leg. I'm sending for the ambulance, we'll x-ray you, and then see about casting and medication."

"I don't have a broken leg, Doc; I'm just in a whole lot of pain right now."

"Don't be obtuse; your leg's clearly broken."

"You wanna' bet a hundred bucks on it?"

"Stop this, Lieutenant, it's broken and that's final!"

"I'll bet you a hundred bucks in front of all these people that I, knowing my own leg, and am smarter about this than you and your whole damned Harvard, or wherever, med school education."

That was just too much for the pompous, little New Englander to take. "How dare you damn *Havad*? I'll take your damned bet, Lieutenant! Now let's go x-ray your damned *broken* leg!"

The x-rays proved me right—no broken bones. The X-Ray technician looked at the lighted wall covered with a half dozen smoky-looking, gray pictures of my innards and exclaimed, "Hey, Doc, come over here and look at this; he's got leg bones as thick as a freakin' kangaroo. He's right; his leg ain't broken!"

Joyce was a little upset with me for the way I'd spoken to Gavin. Being relatively new to the-nursing profession, she was still brainwashed into thinking of all doctors as god-like beings who should be revered above most mortals engaged in lesser professions. *My Mom was a nurse too and she'd told me lots of dumb doctor stories; so, I wasn't automatically impressed by them. They had to earn my respect, just like everybody else.* I normally didn't cuss in front of Joyce so I was a little apologetic about that part. It was also a good thing I was hurting and her nurse-like, caretaker instincts outweighed any other feelings she may have had at the moment. Even so, she still chewed me out.

> "You scared the hell out of me today, Mister! First, the desk calls and tells me you've been involved in a firefight up the road but you're all right. Then, poor Danny comes back with three of your guys and has a hole in his face where he's been shot. I spend the next hour or so helping Doctor Green patch him up. Then, four more of your guys show up in a Jeep and keep assuring me you're okay. Then, your Jeep comes back full of bullet holes and all smashed up. Then, that new, Skip-guy, comes back with the wrecker and he keeps telling me, 'Don't worry, the Lieutenant's all right.' But, I also notice you're still not here. So, with so many people telling me, 'Don't worry!' I really began to stress out. Then you finally show up and you almost can't stand. Then … then, you're rude and combative with poor Doctor Green and you expect me not to be upset! If we had a real couch you'd be sleeping on it tonight, Mister!"

She then gave me a big bear hug. "Don't you ever scare me like this again, and tell your boys, if you are ever hurt again, just tell me what it is right away so I don't have to foolishly steel myself to the possibility of being a widow before nightfall. They, unconvincingly, kept telling me, 'Everything's okay, Mrs. Royce; everything's all right Joyce." Those bums are such bad actors they couldn't even understudy for a bit part in a junior high play."

Trying to break the tension and lighten things up I said, "Well, now that we all know it's just a big old bruise, let's all stop worrying and go get a drink." "You don't get it do you?" Joyce's eyes flashed and her lips got tight. "This kind of severe bruising could cause blood clots. A clot could break loose, go straight to your heart or your brain and you'd be doornail-dead before sunrise. We're getting that leg up in the clinic tonight and pumping you full of blood thinners and pain killers until that poor doctor you yelled at thinks it's safe to take you off them. How's that Mister 'You can't break my legs'? You'd probably been better off if you'd just broken your leg like any other normal person, you … you, big dummy!"

So, I ended up spending a couple of days and nights in the clinic with my own private nurse. I also figured it was in my best interests to apologize to Dr. Gavin Green, who, in return, gave me some really good drugs to thin my blood and make it so I didn't remember a damned thing about my two-day stay in the clinic.

42

Search & Destroy

I had to put up with a nasty-looking purple, blue and yellow leg for the next few weeks; it still hurt, but at least it wasn't killing me to move anymore. Joyce did a great job nursing me and my poor leg back into shape. Physiotherapy, lotions, and leg massages along with painkillers, blood thinners and lots of TLC got me up and about in no time at all. I wasn't exactly at one hundred percent, but at least I was now officially fit for duty. My quick recovery was fortunate as I was soon to need two good legs. If the Koreans thought fate brought me here for the bus accident, then fate must have been involved in what was about to happen.

Shortly after my medical release, I was asked to join Colonel Calvert in his conference room. When I walked in and reported, I noted there was quite a gathering; it seemed like half the brass in the Korean Army were in attendance, including General Suh, commander of FROKA (the First Republic of Korea Army). After some brief introductions, my Colonel directed me to take a seat to his left. There were about a dozen maps and briefing charts already pinned up on the wall. "I wanted you to see and hear all this, Lieutenant Royce!"

The ROK briefer began, in near perfect English. He gave his presentation using some aerial photographs and maps on an overhead projector. *Where did the ROK's get so many officers who speak English so well? All the Americans I knew could barely be understood ordering a beer in Korean.* The briefing focused on recent North Korean infiltrator activity. The overhead transparencies and information on the walls depicted the recent succession of enemy infiltrations into the South. According to this ROK Intelligence Captain, there were sixty-four infiltrator incidents during the past month. These figures were quite alarming, as were the horrid photos of dead Korean civilians. The briefer talked on about large enemy troop insertions along the south coast as well as some less publicized insertions within a hundred kilometer zone along the east coast just south of the DMZ. The little hairs on the back of my neck went up when I realized two of the insertions being shown were near where Joyce and I went swimming with Sid & Earl.

"What the hell were we thinking?" These coastal events seemed of particular interest to General Suh. There was one insertion in particular which the General found extremely vexing. According to eye witnesses, over a hundred enemy troops were put ashore by NK patrol boats in this one area and then they simply vanished. Two days later, a small mountain village of thirty-seven was massacred. Every man, woman, child, goat, pig and chicken was killed. If it drew breath, they killed it! Naturally, all the other villages in that whole region were now in total panic. A truck load of ROKs was dispatched to find the Bad Guys but ended up being ambushed instead. The ROK's were so heavily mauled they never took up pursuit. The enemy raiding party then disappeared again into thin air. One of General Suh's problems was he didn't have enough free troops to launch a full blown "Search & Destroy" mission to try and end this terror.

As I listened, stories I'd read about "Quantrill's Raiders" came to mind. I remember a matinee movie about this band of cutthroats terrorizing the southwest by killing everything in sight. Quantrill's biggest atrocity was the murder of 150 men, women and children and the burning of 180 homes in Lawrence, Kansas in the 1870s. These North Korean bastards sounded like they were doing the same sort of thing.

I found the briefing all very interesting and understood why Colonel Calvert wanted me at the presentation; after all, I did command his only Quick Reaction Force. Then General Suh took the floor. "I *hab* to find way to kill all North Korean infiltrator before *day* kill more farmer and *famrees*. I worry about infiltrator here." The general used a pointer and tapped on the lighted screen in an area just below the DMZ. "Dis area *hab* many small farm and *viv-ridges*; infiltrator get in *dis* area *dey* kill *may-knee* South Korean. It be *rear* bad *dey* get in *dis* area."

Colonel Calvert twisted around in his chair and looked at me. "Lieutenant Royce, I told the General I was going to loan you and a reinforced squad of your MPs to assist him in hunting infiltrators in the 1st Republic of Korea Army area of operations. You're the closest thing I have to Infantry troops and General Suh needs more Infantry. He's going around to all the U.S. camps and recruiting. General Ironbone has instructed me to support General Suh in any way we can." Here I was thinking I was just getting some *Gee Whiz* information when it was really General Suh giving a recruiting pitch for additional help. Son-of-a-bitch I'd been drafted again, but this time into the Korean Army. I must have looked stunned because Calvert followed up by saying, "Don't worry; you've got a couple of days to get your team ready. Sid & Earl will be at your disposal and you can have anything in any of the arms rooms you think you might need. I also want you to join the General and me, at the club tonight for dinner so you two can get better acquainted. The General will explain how you and your troops are going to fit into his *Search & Destroy* plan." I thanked the Colonel and was on my way over and pay my respects to General Suh but he was pre-occupied with his intelligence officer so I figured I'd meet him at dinner.

Dinner was interesting to say the least. General Suh and his entourage seemed to really like American bourbon. When we were finished with dinner, the General turned his attention towards me.

"So, *Rootenant Roy-cee*, I hear you and your men already kill Communist infiltrator"

"Yes Sir, we've been in two firefights with them so far. We ambushed them once and they ambushed us once."

"I hear one of your men was wounded by infiltrator; he okay now?"

"Yes Sir, Specialist Cortez was lucky his wounds were only minor."

"You *rike* killing Communist infiltrator *Rootenant Roy-cee*?"

"Honestly General, I'd rather be playing baseball!"

"Well, I *rike baseball too* but I *rike* killing infiltrator better! I want to kill all infiltrator. You *wait*, you see what they do to farmer, womans and *rittle childrens, den* you maybe *rike* it too."

I wasn't ready for that question, and I would think about it often; *"Did I <u>like</u> killing North Korean, Communist infiltrators?"*

The General continued his conversation with me.

"*Rootenant Roy-cee*, you pretty tall guy but you not tall as me! How tall you?"

"I'm about six foot three, General."

"I'm *sich* foot *sich, berry* tall for Korean. Almost no Korean as tall as me. You know how *day* pick general in Korean Army?"

"No General, I don't."

"Well it work *rike dis.*"

The General was now standing and he held the edge of a flattened, horizontal hand, palm down, up against his chest. "Private solider about *dis* tall." He then raised his hand to about shoulder height and announced, "Sergeant about *dis* tall." He then continued to move his hand upward stopping at his chin, lips, nose and eyes while saying, "*Rootenant*, Captain, Major, *Cor-ner.*" He then placed his hand flat on top of his head and said, "You get to be tall as me, you get to be *da* big General!" Everyone around the table laughed, including me. This huge Korean then put an arm around my shoulder and with a hard squeeze said, "I *rike* you *Rootenant Roy-cee*! You and me kill many Communists *togeter*!" After much drinking and talking, the evening slowly began to peter-out and I was able to sneak off home and tell Joyce what had happened and what was going to be happening very soon.

For the next week I was extremely busy selecting which eleven MPs were going with me. Mr. Shin was a civilian; so, even though he volunteered, I would not be taking him. He protested, but I stood firm, telling him I would be taking two of the KATUSA MPs with me to serve as both translators and riflemen. This was an argument Mr. Shin could understand and still not have his feelings hurt. I needed shooters who could also translate! Selection of which KATUSAs was a no-brainer. Corporals Lee and Park both spoke great English and both wore "Expert" rifleman badges. When I broke the men down into two fire teams, one KATUSA would be assigned to each.

I would be in overall command and lead one Fire-Team but I needed an NCO to lead the second team. This was another time I wished Bob Kelser was still around. Sergeant Cavern was my next best guy for the job. Now all I had to do was pick ten more men, five for Sergeant Cavern's Fire-Team and five for mine. Twelve was the magic number because that's all that fits in a Delta Model Huey—if you don't carry a Crew Chief. From what I was being told, we would be spending a lot of time wedged tightly in Sid & Earl's Huey. A couple of those big, weird looking, Mojave helicopters would move our three gun jeeps around, if or when we needed them.

Monday, the seventh of October arrived soon enough. I greeted the day with anticipation and reservation. It was 0400 and I was wide awake lying on my back with my hands behind my head. Joyce had a fitful night too. The two of us just lay there talking. We decided it would be best to say goodbye at the house because I would be really busy down at the airfield checking out my men and all the equipment.

In a little voice Joyce asked, "Do you know what you're going to be doing?"

"Pretty much, we're going to be inserted by helicopter on the high ground along likely avenues of enemy approach—probably mountain trails—and General Suh will have a bunch of his ROKs, trying to drive the bad guys into the traps we're setting up. We're going to be just one of many Ambush Teams he's setting up all along the mountain trails. Sid & Earl will drop us off just before daybreak and we'll get into position. If nothing happens, our helicopter will pick us up around dusk and fly us back to Page for the night and we'll start all over in the morning. This is going to be like a giant chess game with General Suh acting as chess master. He's going to keep moving us around his chessboard until the infiltrators bump in to us. Hopefully, I'll be here with you most nights but if he really thinks we're getting close to making contact, then we may be staying up in the mountains overnight."

"What happens if you find them or they bump into you?"

"Well, if any of the other teams make contact with the bad guys, the choppers will drop down and pick up as many of the teams as possible and move them into supporting positions around the point of contact where we can either block the infiltrators advance or cut off their retreat. As I said, it's gonna' be like a big chess game; they move and then we move to block them and try to knock them out."

"Sounds dangerous!"

"We'll be okay Hon; we've got the high ground, lots of support, big guns and if things get tough, we've always got Sid & Earl to yank us out. Heck, even Bill will be up there spotting for us in his "Bird Dog.""

This brought a little smile to her lips.

"You just be careful Buster; don't take any more chances than you have to! We've got a long life ahead of us and I don't want you screwing it up with any of your stupid cowboy movie BS! I want kids some day you know!"

Now I smiled, grabbed her and gave her a big kiss on the lips and in my best John Wayne imitation said, "Now don't you go worrying your *purdy* little head missy, I want to stick around long enough to see just how cute you're going to be when you're a little old lady."

Joyce punched me hard in the chest. "Just go and get this over with, wise guy!"

I jumped from the bed and assumed the position of attention. Giving her a big, exaggerated salute, I yelled, "Yes Sir!" I did an about face and started to get my gear together.

By the time I got to the airfield, the place was crawling with troops and more helicopters were landing. My guys were all crowded around our Huey and being entertained by Sid & Earl. "This ain't no shit guys; them tracers was swarming around us so thick I thought we was flyin' through 4th of July fireworks at Disneyland!" Sid was telling war stories about his Vietnam tour of duty with the 1st Air Cav. Sid already had both the Silver and Bronze star plus a bunch of Air Medals and a Purple Heart; so, most of what he was telling probably was the truth.

General Suh's ground troops had been moving into position over the past few days and I'd been given the coordinates where he wanted us to set up our first ambush site. I got us all together around a big map and, with my flashlight, showed Sid again where we wanted to be dumped off. According to my briefings, we were one of about ten ambush teams which were being inserted this morning along a line in the mountains. The concept was familiar to me because it was very much like those old, black & white, "Great White Hunter" jungle movies where hundreds of native "Beaters" make lots of noise and drive whatever games' being hunted towards the heavily-armed hunters.

We lifted off a few minutes after 0500 for a forty-five minute flight into the gloom. Our helicopter was operating without running lights. Sid & Earl were on instruments the whole way and the only light was the faint red glow coming from the cockpit. A year of combat flying in Vietnam taught Sid things most helicopter pilots would never learn. He set the chopper down in total darkness on a ridge line above a dry riverbed. The ridge was so narrow he never really set it fully down. As much as I could tell he had just one skid resting on the ridge. The chopper would float up and down a few inches as we were getting out. Sid was expertly adjusting power and pitch for aircraft weight changes as each of us jumped out onto the ridge. I was thinking back to our adventure on the DMZ beach and it reminded me again what an amazing pilot Sid really was. When Sid lifted off, he went straight up for several hundred feet into the darkness, then did a one-eighty and moved off in the same direction we came from. The distinctive *"Whump-whump"* Huey sound trailed off into the early morning gloom. We were now on our own, in the dark, on a rocky ridgeline somewhere in the *Sobaek* Mountains. The small town of *Yongpo*, I think, was supposed to be a few miles behind our position. The rest of General Suh's ambush teams were strung-out both to the north and south of us.

We positioned ourselves out along the ridge, just below the crest and took up positions about fifteen feet apart. I've always been amazed how well one can actually see at night, even in pitch dark. Just the stars reflecting off the rivers and lakes provided this tiny bit of faint light, but tonight it was enough to get my bearings from the salient terrain features below. Using my red filtered flashlight and map I was able to confirm we were on the highest terrain feature in the area, right where we were supposed to be. Everyone nestled in, quietly prepared their fighting positions and waited for first light.

The second person in, at both ends of our fighting formation, was turned around and facing in the opposite direction. This was to protect the other ten from a surprise attack from the rear. It would be really difficult for anyone to come up behind us. They would be physically exhausted if they tried, but "Ranger Rules" applied here, and this particular rule is, "Expect the unexpected". So we picked the least likely avenue of attack into our location and fortified it. You do this because you have to think like your enemy. They often attack from what they think will be your least protected direction. In our case, it was a near vertical rock formation plunging off to our rear.

The first rays of sunshine were most welcome because of warmth as well as light. It had gotten pretty chilly just sitting there and I was fascinated by the steam rising off the left sleeve of my fatigue jacket as those first rays of sun vaporized the light coating of frost which had settled on my field jacket during the night. I don't know who selected this position, but from our high perch I felt like an eagle with a perfect three hundred and sixty degree circle view of my killing ground below.

We had binoculars, four scoped M-14 sniper rifles, two 40 millimeter M-79 grenade launchers, two M-60 machine guns and one, tripod mounted, M-2, Heavy Barrel, .50 caliber machine gun. In other words we were geared to take on anything from up close and personal to maybe something five hundred or more yards away. The term *"Loaded for bear"* comes to mind.

We may have been loaded for bear but as the day wore on, the novelty and excitement of our high perched mission evaporated into uncomfortable boredom. Even in October, the rocks were still reflecting the sun's midday heat. We hunkered down, staying as still and quiet as we could, just waiting for something to happen … It never did. Just after dusk, Sid & Earl swooped in and pulled us out and back to Page.

General Suh made the decision to move us a few clicks further south and we set up there the next morning. We spent another cold day in ambush formation but, again, nothing happened. This routine continued for the next four days with absolutely no success.

Our fifth day was different. We had nestled in again atop another ridge in a "Horseshoe" formation. The .50 Cal was set up in the middle with the two M-60 machine guns anchoring the flanks. The four snipers and two M-79 Grenade Launchers were spread out in between. At just about daybreak we picked up on some activity below. There was movement coming up a narrow, dirt road. Through my artillery binoculars it appeared like ROK soldiers were moving at double time pace up the road. I radioed our command and control element.

> "Fox Hunter, this is Fox Team Six. Do you have soldiers in the vicinity of our location? I count maybe eight to ten below our position."
> "Fox Team Six, are they wearing helmets or soft caps?"
> "Roger, Soft caps!"
> "Team Six, you have enemy, I repeat, you have enemy! All of our men are wearing helmets today. Take them under fire; back up is on the way."

We had our pre-set plan. The .50 Cal would open up first and we would just see what happened before we revealed our other firing positions. 50s speak with authority and there's just about no soldier, in any army, that doesn't fear this weapon. .50 caliber tracer rounds were now ripping up the ground in front of the lead infiltrators. The ricocheting tracers were putting on a crazy light show while bouncing in, around and all over the rocks. The infiltrators halted their forward progress and were now scurrying for any cover they could find. As soon as they tried to shield themselves from the .50 Cal., the M-60 Team to the left had them dead in their sights and commenced firing. As two more enemy fell wounded or killed, the rest started to panic. Some enemy were still in positions where they could not be seen. The two Grenadiers started lobbing 40 Mike-Mike grenade rounds behind the rocks. Five or six bad guys made a break from cover and headed for the opposite side of the road. The M-60 Team on the right started ripping away. While all this was happening, the four snipers were scanning the rocks through their scopes for anything trying to escape the "Kill Zone". There was almost no return fire reaching our position. The bad guys were in such a panic all they could do was try and hide, although, even this was not working for them.

From our high above perch I could see why they were scurrying up the road. Two Deuces full of ROK troops were coming up the road behind them. I gave the order for the machineguns to cease firing. The Snipers and Grenadiers would take on any targets of opportunity but we would now let the ROKs come in and earn their pay. We put up just enough noise to let the ROKs know where we were. ROK soldiers tended to shoot first and ask questions later. We also established radio contact with the "Friendlies" below, gave them our position and told them what we knew. We now just watched as the ROKs went in and kicked ass with what was left of the infiltrators. It was all over in a matter of minutes.

Intelligence sources stated there were a lot more than the eleven killed here this morning. Based on this information, the FROKA commander made the decision we would all now sweep the entire area in a massive *"Search & Destroy"* mission. We would all come down from our lofty positions and join the troops on the ground. My team, because we had the gun Jeeps, was designated as the Quick Reaction back up team to reinforce other elements as needed. We radioed for our Jeeps. About midmorning two of those weird looking Mohave helicopters arrived with our three Jeeps and a quarter-ton trailer. Sid & Earl also arrived with a crap load of ammo, some C-Rations and water. We got rid of the heavy .50 Cal and picked up the other M-60 we requested. We now had three gun Jeeps armed with M-60s. We loaded four men to a Jeep and were, once again, one hundred percent "Mobile, Agile and Hostile". My Jeep pulled the trailer with all our food, gear and extra ammo. We were now ready to be self-sustaining for the next week or so, if we had to.

Sid handed me a note from Joyce and I tucked it in my fatigue jacket pocket. As Sid and the two Mohaves lifted off, I couldn't but marvel at the differences in design of these helicopters. The bulbous Mohaves had two big piston engines sitting outboard on awkward looking stalks while Sid's smaller Huey had a lone gas turbine engine nestled inside the fuselage. It was like I was looking at the past and future of Army aviation at the same time. Seems most of the newer stuff was going to Vietnam and we just got what was left over. We had to soldier on with the old Mohaves because all the new CH-47 *Chinooks* were going to Vietnam. They even had the new M-16 rifles over there while we carried the older and much heavier M-14s. I'd fired the M-16 at Benning and it was really small and light in comparison to the 14. All the M-16 gunstock parts were plastic. It seemed so toy-like we dubbed it the *"Mattel Machinegun"*.

I picked up my heavy, but extremely reliable M-14, climbed into the driver's seat of my gun Jeep and led the other two down the road to a pre-planned location. We nestled into a protected area, threw camouflage netting over the Jeeps, set up security and tried to get a little rest. It was now mid-afternoon and we knew it was always best to rest if you could.

Another of the Ranger Rules that really made sense to me was: *"Don't stand if you can sit and don't sit if you can lie down."*

43

The Discovery

We moved further north twice during the day but, both times ended up being false alarms. The ROK Intelligence guys seemed to have it in their minds that the North Korean infiltrators were making their way north and east towards the DMZ, or maybe some coastal pick up point. General Suh's axis of advance did appear to be northerly, but now, more and more, we were shifting to the east. Because of this, the ROKs were adjusting their positioning of troops in the "Destroy" part of this Search & Destroy operation.

It was now late afternoon and we, pretty much, knew we were going to be out overnight again. I pawed through the C-Rations and found a box of *"Turkey Loaf"*. Now, I don't know if I really liked Turkey Loaf or if it was just that it wasn't quite as bad as the others. I opened the C-ration can with my P-38 can opener. I always kept one on my dog tag chain. I found a smooth, flat rock to sit on; and in silence, I savored this antique meal. I read the date on the can, "August 1953". *"Huh! Only fifteen years old. What luck, I got one of the fresh ones this time."* I remembered Joyce's note in my breast pocket, pulled it out, and began to read.

Herb my Love,

I've got no earthly idea about what you're doing up there in those mountains. All I know is it scares the hell out of me. I see Sid & Earl on base quite a bit and they tell me you're just on this harmless little camping trip or something but, I can tell by their eyes you're in some kind of real danger. I just hate every moment you're away. It was okay at first, when you were still coming home every night, but these overnighters are beginning to get to me now and I'll be glad when this is all over. I'm tired of being afraid every time you go out on one of these missions. I've enjoyed Korea and all the neat and fun things we've experienced together, but now I can't wait to get out of this crazy dreamland and back home to the real world, the one we know.

I just have this funny feeling this mission you're on right now is different, in someway, than all the others. I just want you to promise me you will be careful. Keep your eyes peeled, stay particularly alert this time and don't let anything escape you. As I said, I just have this premonition that this time it's different than all the others.

I know I'm probably being silly but, this feeling is so strong, please be careful. I love you so very much; I can't bear to think what life would be without you.

Love, Joyce XO

I sat there thinking about her words; I just didn't understand what she was talking about. I'd been on a lot more dangerous missions than this one. I thought back to my first gunfight up at Charlie Battery. On that one, we were green and pretty much on our own. Now, up here in the mountains, we have just about the whole freaking 1st ROK Army backing us up. We're better trained and experienced now and we even have helicopter and spotter plane support. I felt so much better about the way things were these days. *"Keep my eyes peeled and stay particularly alert."* I found myself thinking aloud, "Wonder why she's saying that? Normally, she just tells me to be careful … Oh well!"

There was a lot of action in the mountains that night. The ROKs were spreading out all over and combing every valley and crevasse they could get into. We heard some ROK Air Force, ground attack, jets come in low and we could see bright flashes from whatever it was they were dropping. We figured it must be napalm. It had to be napalm because there were no big explosions to go along with all the light. Later, it looked like the mountains, off to our north, were on fire. We were now certain it was napalm because; there just wasn't much of anything around here that could burn like that.

At first light, we got the word to move out and head up the road as quickly as possible. A village in a valley ahead of us had been hit by infiltrators sometime late yesterday and the ROKs were hot on the trail of some Bad Guys. We were given the mission of checking out the village to see if any of the infiltrators were still there, report back if they were and engage any left hanging around. With all my guys alert and at the ready, we drove as quickly as we could towards a little, no name village, about ten miles to our north. We passed hundreds of ROK soldiers along the way. All of them seemed in good spirits and waved as we hauled ass by in a cloud of dust.

At one location, along the route, I saw that the ROKs had set up a small PW (prisoner of war) cage and had a dozen or so prisoners. Dead bodies were piled near the road and two of those black CIC jeeps were parked close by. I surmised the ROK spooks were going through the equipment of the dead ones and interrogating any live ones. All-in-all, it looked like there had been some major activity during the night and it appeared the Gooks had gotten the worst of it.

Over the Jeep's radio, we heard that a major firefight had just concluded up ahead and the ROKs were now in the mopping-up phase. This firefight was supposed to have been with the same Bad Guys who attacked the village we were headed for. I asked if they needed our assistance and was told to just continue on to the village and see what's there. I put my hand mike back in its cradle and looked up. In the distance, I could see black smoke rising from the village.

Through binoculars, I could tell the village had, pretty much, been razed to the ground. All the little thatched roof farm houses were now just smoldering, roofless shells with only the mud, or whatever, walls left standing. Most of the stacked crops had been torched and there seemed to be no movement at all coming from the village. About a quarter mile out I halted my three gun Jeeps and gave everyone their instructions.

"Drivers and machine gunners, you stay with the Jeeps. Cortez, you take over driving my Jeep. Everyone else comes with me. I want the six of us with M-14s and M-79s to form a skirmish line, right here, in front of the Jeeps. We're going to move out slowly and search through this village. Take the scopes off your rifles and flip your selector switches to full auto. I want max firepower if we need it. I want you gun Jeeps behind us to the right, left and center of our formation and stay about thirty yards in back of us. We're depending on you guys to be our cover fire and back up if we need it. If any of us draws fire, we will all hit the dirt and return fire. If this happens, I want you gun Jeep guys to halt and shoot the shit out of anybody firing at us. Got it?"

They did; so, I took up my position in the formation, with two men to my right side and three on the other. We spread out, with about thirty feet between each of us, and slowly started walking forward, with the 151s creeping slowly behind and matching our pace. We watched our flanks, while the machine gunners scanned ahead for movement.

A creepy feeling began to sweep over me as we approached the first of the burned out hooches. It was just that it was all so damned quiet. The air was even still; there were no ducks quacking, no chickens flapping their wings and making clucking sounds, no goat, pig or cow sounds either. You *always* heard those kinds of sounds, plus small children laughing and playing around in these remote mountain villages. I figured the villagers were probably still in hiding, yet, the stillness gave me this incredible heavy feeling inside. My "fight or flight" adrenalin dump had boosted all my senses to a razor's edge. It was then that we saw the first body. We all stayed on line as to not be out of position if shooting started. I told everyone to halt, as I bent down to check this old man for signs of life. I knew, even before I checked his pulse, he was dead. A large part in the side of his skull was caved in. The severe dent in his head was oblong in shape, or about the same dimension as a horizontal butt stroke from a Chi-Com assault rifle. I'd seen this kind of wound before; so, I knew right away what probably caused it. The body was unarmed. I gave the signal, and we slowly moved further forward in between more still smoldering ruins. Off to my left I heard, "Got another one, Lieutenant!" We all halted and went into crouched positions while this body was checked out. Each of us scanned the area for danger. "This one's dead too, Sir. I count three bullet holes in the chest." Six or seven more bodies were encountered as we slowly, progressed through this eerie, smoky place. One of the guys called out, "Jesus Christ, Sir! They even shot the fucking pigs and goats!" Every animal we came across was dead, even the chickens. Something went really horribly wrong here and I couldn't really figure it out until I came across a Gook with a pitchfork through his throat. There were two dead villagers lying on top of him. Whatever went on in this little village, there was one thing for sure; these people were resisting and fighting back as hard as they could.

We continued forward and were almost through the tiny village when we encountered the complete horror of the event. Inside the walls of a burned out storage room—as best I could tell—were sixteen badly burned bodies of women, old men, children and two infants, all dead and all charred black. There was a large quantity of shell casings lying all around the outside of the small storehouse. In my mind's eye, I reconstructed what probably happened. The Gooks had rounded up the villagers who were home and put them in this building as sort of a make shift jail. The men who were working in the fields came home and some-how tried to protect their loved ones and attempted to fight off the intruders. Farm tools and knives are never a match for assault rifles. During the skirmish, one determined farmer killed an infiltrator with his pitchfork. After which, the rest of the Gooks must have freaked, went on a killing spree, burned the village in retaliation and then moved on. With all the younger adult male villagers dead, they torched the storage room with the old men, women and children inside then machine gunned down anyone trying to escape the burning building. *What kind of fucking animals were these God damned Commie bastards?"*

My heart was now so full of rage. I wanted to find live Gooks just so I could kill em', spill they're blood, then burn their bodies. In less than a year I had grown to admire, respect and maybe even love the hard working people of this strange land. It had gotten to the point where I felt about them pretty much the same way I felt about Americans back home. I felt it was my duty, as a soldier, to protect them too. Today, I had failed them miserably and I was in total rage because of it.

ROK army units were now coming up the road behind us. We saddled up and got our three gun Jeeps rolling towards the road leading north out of the village. At this very moment, I was totally enraged. I had so much adrenalin pumping through my veins I felt like the "Hulk" when his eyes go all funny and things start turning green. I was so pissed; all I wanted to do was kill. It was probably this chemical condition that was to change my life forever. All my senses were on that razor edge as we started north.

Have you ever had something happen in your life, yet you can't explain how or why it happened? I've thought about this moment a thousand times since that day. It could have been luck. It could have been the adrenalin dump sharpening my senses or it could even have actually been divine intervention. Anyway, shortly after we got underway, up ahead, I glimpsed small movements in the tall grass about fifteen yards in from the side of the road. At first I was willing to ignore it and drive on, but something told me not to. I signaled Danny to stop the Jeep; then I jumped out with pistol drawn. I whispered, "Cover me!" Three M-60s silently swung in my direction. I hunched over as far as I could yet still be able to walk. Carefully, with pistol at the ready, I moved towards the area where I'd seen tall grass moving. I was down as low as I could get and still have my feet under me. The tall grass concealed my movement from the target area as I closed in on it. With my left hand and right gun-hand, I carefully parted the tall grass in front of me before taking each step. This gave just a few more feet of visibility to my front before taking the next step. I knew after my next step or two, I would be on top of whatever or whoever was out there. Without thinking about it, every muscle in my body tensed like a cat preparing to spring. I licked my dry lips and visually checked my pistol once more to ensure the safety was off—it was. The tall grass was still shielding me from the target area. I parted the grass in front of me once more and a lightening bolt passed through my body.

There on the ground, in what I can only describe as a hastily prepared nest of grass, was a tiny, still infant. Its eyes were closed, and it was only protected by a thin, threadbare blanket. One of its tiny legs gave a little kick, *"My God, it's still alive!"* I whipped off my field jacket and ripped out the liner. As I gingerly lifted the infant; it emitted a full body shudder. The tattered blue blanket fell away revealing that the baby's umbilical cord was still attached. *"It's a girl and she's just been born!"* As I picked the baby up, I realized she weighed nothing! She was so very tiny and boney. I wrapped her tightly in my field jacket liner and held her close to me. I yelled back to Cortez, "Danny call in a chopper now, now, *now!*" I quickly covered the ground back to the Jeep.

Sid & Earl were already in the air, on the way to one of the staging areas in the event we needed them. I took the hand-mike from Danny and talked directly to Sid. "Sid, get word to the clinic to have my wife meet us at the helipad with an ambulance. I need her there and I need you at LZ (Landing Zone) Whisky ASAP, over." I turned to Cortez. "Whisky is about two clicks up this road Danny, get us there pronto."

As the Jeep lurched forward, I held tightly to the little critter. I ungloved one hand and placed my little finger in the ice cold palm of the infant's tiny hand. I got the faintest squeeze as her miniscule fingers tried to close around my warm pinky. I quickly ensured everything but her little face was covered and held her close to me, inside my field jacket, where she could feel my body warmth. As we approached the LZ, the now familiar *whump-whump* sound was getting closer. I turned command of the mission over to Sergeant Cavern. "I'll be back quick as I can Sarge. Go back to the village and wait there." I turned and ran towards the chopper as it was just setting down.

Sid lifted off the second I was on board. I picked up a head set and mike so he could hear me over the turbine whine and rotor blades popping.

"Sid, did you get hold of Joyce?"

"Yep, she's in an ambulance and on the way to the pad right now. Are you okay?"

"Yeah, I'm fine, but this baby needs medical attention fast."

"Baby! Is that what you got in the bag?"

"Yeah, I think this baby may be the sole survivor from a village back there. The Gooks attacked it sometime last night. Don't mean to tell you your business, Sid; but this baby needs you to make this thing get to Page as fast as it can fly. Hey, where's Earl?"

"He was taking a leak or something more serious back there when I got your emergency call; so, his ass got left."

Page was in a valley by a river and we were up in the mountains. As we cleared the last mountain top, Sid put the Huey in a shallow dive and literally dove it towards the Camp. I don't know how fast a Huey is safely capable of flying but, by the way the thing was vibrating and whistling, Sid probably exceeded the speed any *Bell* test pilot had ever achieved. We arrived over Camp Page in what seemed like less than half the time it normally takes. Sid wasted no time in setting it down by the tower. Joyce was already there, standing next to an ambulance. I jumped out and ran towards her.

Joyce came towards me. "Are you okay? You look and run okay!" I told her I was fine. She started to scold me about scaring her into thinking I was horribly wounded and wanted to see her one last time before I died. I opened my field jacket liner and the little face peered out at her through tightly squinting eyes. Joyce immediately understood. "Oh my God! How did this happen?" "I'll tell you later Hon, but right now you got to get to work on this little girl!" Joyce gave me one last look, touched my face and then instantly changed back into *Super Nurse*. She yelled at the ambulance driver to get moving, then the two of them jumped into the Dodge Power Wagon and sped off towards the clinic.

I turned towards Sid, who was now standing next to me. "Well, did we break it, or will it make it back to my troops?" Sid smiled, and his mustache curled up on one side. "I think she's got maybe another flight or two left in her."

On the slower flight back, we talked.

"I don't know Sid; I just can't figure it out. Everybody in that village died except the weakest most helpless person. How does that happen?"

"Can't tell ya' Herb. Could just be the good Lord movin' in those strange and mysterious ways again. Maybe it's that meek inheritin' the Earth thing. Ain't nothin' meeker than a newborn baby.

"I've been trying to figure out how the baby got there in the tall grass in the first place. I don't know how big Korean babies are supposed to be when they're first born but I know they aren't that tiny. I'm thinking the baby is probably premature; it can't weigh more than two and a half or three pounds. When I opened the baby's blanket and saw the cord was still attached, I couldn't help but think she looked about the size of skinny frying chicken. I don't know if it was a regular type premature birth or if the attack on the village caused the mother to violently abort. I'm thinking maybe the mother tried to hide the baby from the Gooks. Then, maybe she acted like one of those funny birds that lead predators away from their ground nests by pretending they're easy prey themselves."

"You mean 'Killdeer?'"

"No, not deer, birds!"

"Killdeer is the name of them birds! We used to get a kick out of watching them when I was a kid, stationed with my dad way up north in Michigan. Those little critters would fake broken wings and flop around on the ground. Then they would hobble off and lead any predators away from where their nests were."

"The umbilical cord still being attached is what makes me believe it was an all of a sudden thing, that, and that scruffy, thin blanket. The mother probably just grabbed whatever she could and ran to hide the baby. I don't know how the baby made it through the night. It was below freezing last night, Sid, and that baby was ice cold when I picked her up. Sure hope she makes it."

"She will!"

"She will? What makes you so sure?"

"Well, gettin' back to that Lord thing. Why would you be sent to find her if God was gonna' let her die? Another question: Why was it you and nobody else?"

"You really believe I was sent there to find her? You're beginning to sound like the Koreans."

"Yeah, it's just like you were supposed to be there when the bus went in the drink. Whether you like it or not ole' buddy, you're being used. Heck, even bein' run over by your own Jeep didn't stop you from bein' ready to go on this mission. Anybody normal would have had a broken leg and been laid up for a couple of months. The only reason it didn't break was because you were supposed to find that baby. Think about it for a minute! You're also the only son-of-a-bitch over here with a wife—a wife who's a nurse, I might add. You got to get hit over the head before any of this dawns on you?"

I sat there in befuddled silence as we descended to pick up Earl.

When we landed near the village, I bumped in to a ROK MP Lieutenant who knew where the *Me-Gook Hum-Beyongs* (American MPs) were. He gave me a lift to where my guys were. They were eating chow with a ROK infantry company, less than a click south of the village. Another ROK unit was cleaning up the slaughter in the village. In the short time I'd been away, General Suh had called an administrative halt to the operation while he and his staff assessed the situation. Apparently, there were several more successful ambushes last night, as well as during the day. The ROKs were assessing the need to continue an operation of this size. Intel reported some infiltrators had made it back across the DMZ and lived to fight another day. More tunnels were detected and there was even evidence some of the Bad Guys had escaped the General's net by boat. Approximately, twenty infiltrators were still unaccounted for out of the, estimated, hundred or so who originally landed. They may or may not have made it to the tunnels with the rest.

According to Korean intelligence gained during recent interrogations ... we call it torture. Of the few infiltrators captured, one of them revealed what their orders were. If they could no longer fight as a unit, they were to breakup into two man cells and scatter. They were to blend in, live off the land, move only at night and create as much havoc and destruction as they could while still trying to exfiltrate north. To General Suh and his staff, it looked like this tactical switch had already happened sometime last night. The Search & Destroy missions would now morph in to road blocks, more random searches and a massive public information effort. ROK Army Information teams would travel all over, instructing and asking the people to report anything suspicious or any strangers appearing in or around their villages and towns. Later in the day, we were radioed, thanked and told that General Suh had contacted our commander and told him our services were no longer required. At dusk, the weird Mohave helicopters, along with Sid & Earl's Huey, lifted all of us and our equipment back to Camp Page. I guess we were now officially discharged from our unofficial stint in the First Republic of Korea Army. I would miss the great summer kimchee in the ROK C-Rations but, that was about all.

44

Everything Changes

Hours later, when we landed back at Page, I went directly over to the clinic. I was told Joyce and the baby had been driven back to the house; so, I hooked a ride up the hill. When I arrived home, Joyce was sitting close to the Cannon Heater on one of the old couch cushions. Nancy and little Rusty were in the room keeping her company. Rusty was fussing and Nancy said it was his feeding time. The two of them went back to their room as soon as I arrived.

Joyce was wearing my ancient green, terrycloth bathrobe and I quickly noticed something else. She was holding the baby under the robe, against her bare skin and using her own body as something akin to a natural incubator. As I moved in closer, I saw that Joyce's eyes were red and dewy like she'd been crying earlier. She gave me a weak smile and said, "I don't know, Herb; this baby is so tiny, so premature and so weak I just don't know. I've done all I know how to do but I don't think it's near enough. The baby has colic and I'm pretty sure she's allergic to regular baby formula—she keeps spitting it up every time I try to feed her. When I got her to the clinic, I suctioned her airway, clipped and tied off the umbilical cord, put drops in her eyes and washed off all the dried afterbirth. That was the easy part. It's just that she's so tiny; she only weighs two pounds nine ounces, Herb! I feel so helpless." Her eyes began to well up again. "There's also another problem. How long did you say she was outside?"

"I didn't say because I don't really know … maybe anywhere from twelve to twenty-four hours."

Joyce took one of the baby's teensy arms and said, "Watch this!" She pinched the baby's arm between her thumb and forefinger. When she released pressure, the baby's skin did not snap back like it's supposed to. It was as if there was no elasticity left in her skin. It just stayed peaked as if Joyce was still pinching it together. Joyce could tell this demonstration was not resonating with me, so she continued. "The baby's really dehydrated; I have to figure out how to get fluids into her and get it to stay in her. She's not taking normal baby formula; so, I think I need some infant soymilk formula or something like that. If I can just get enough distilled water in her, it may help with hydration but it has no nourishment. So, even if I can get her to take some fluids, she'll still be getting weaker. The other problem is the baby is just so premature—look at this!" Joyce showed me that the baby's fingernails and eyelashes had not even fully formed. "Herb, I'm thinking this baby may be only about six months, or maybe not even that old. She hasn't even developed a sucking reflex yet. I've been trying to feed her warm, distilled water through an eyedropper. This baby needs to be in a big hospital with a proper incubator. We have nothing here for newborn infants at the clinic and the Chunchon hospital is straight out of the Stone Age. I'm doing all I know how to do and this brave little thing is fighting to live as hard as its weak little body can."

I sat down next to Joyce; she opened the bathrobe a little and I peered inside at this miniscule creature nestled up against her bare breasts. All of a sudden Joyce blurted out, "Honey!" And, of course, I said, "What?" "No, not you Honey; I mean honey, Honey!" I was still not comprehending, so she continued, "There's a jar of honey in the pantry, bee honey. It's supposed to be nature's perfect food and it has plenty of energy. Go boil some water, then get the measuring cup and mix one part honey with three parts boiled water. Mix it up and bring it to me."

That night, Joyce arranged the floor cushions, along with some bed pillows, into a makeshift bed and slept, with the baby on her chest, next to the heater. *Slept* is not really the right word. It was the continual process of eye-dropping as much of the honey-water mixture as possible down the baby's tiny throat while trying to catch a wink or two in between feedings. Joyce got the baby to take four, sometimes six eyedroppers full of honey-water at a time.

In the wee hours of the morning, I got up and made coffee. The baby was still alive but showed no real signs of improvement. It was now Monday and I'd been playing soldier all weekend; so, I was going to call in and see if I could stay home for the day. Joyce reminded me; Nancy and Rusty were going to be there and we always had the field phone in case she needed me. I kissed Joyce on the forehead and took a long pensive look at the baby who lay almost motionless, clutched against her bosom. I noticed some faint finger motions and I could actually see the little thing's heart beating fast beneath her boney, little chest. I tried not to think about it. This was like the time I brought home an injured baby bird. I knew in my heart the poor thing wasn't going to make it, but I still went all-out trying to save it. At the same time, I tried to distance myself emotionally so it wouldn't hurt so much when the inevitable happened.

This, of course, was different, even if I tried to pretend otherwise; this was a human baby. I could tell Joyce had been up most of the night because, unlike me, she's the type who really needs all her sleep. She had these big, dark circles under her eyes and just looked out on her feet. I touched Joyce's face and said, "I'm going to try everything I can to find some of that soy milk stuff. I'll put my whole crew on it. There has to be some somewhere, even if I've got to drive to Seoul and hunt for it."

She smiled and in a very tired voice said, "Good, good, you do that. The baby seems to be taking a little more honey-water from the eyedropper the last few hours; I think she likes the sweet taste. I've been trying to force feed her several droppers full every half hour or so; but she doesn't seem to be getting any better. Her little skin still has no elasticity to it and that's got me really worried. She also hasn't peed since we got her … and that's been what … more than twenty-four hours now? I'm so afraid her tiny kidneys may have already shut down. If that's happened, then there's no hope at all of her making it. Oh, while you're out hunting for soymilk, can you see if you can find one of those soft plastic baby doll baby bottles at a toy store or someplace? Maybe I can squeeze more fluid into her with something like that. Her little mouth is too small for a regular baby bottle. Since she hasn't learned to suck yet, I need something better than an eyedropper to squeeze more fluid into her. I was thinking about trying to take her to the clinic and see about starting an IV but she's so tiny and dried out I'm sure I couldn't even find a vein. I'm just going to continue working on her and put the rest in God's hands."

Her words reminded me of what Sid had said so, I passed it on, hoping it would bring Joyce some sort of comfort. "Sid said the baby was going to be fine. He said God wouldn't have sent the only guy with a nurse for a wife out here to find this baby if he didn't intend on saving her." Joyce gave me a tired smile, "That's a nice thought; let's hope and pray Sid's right."

Nancy came back into the room carrying Rusty. "Anything I can do for you guys?" I smiled at her, "Thanks, Nancy! I gotta' go in; I made some fresh coffee for everybody. If you could just help Joyce out today, that would be tremendous." "Don't worry; I'll take care of Joyce while she's taking care of the baby." With that, I called the MP Desk, blew a kiss to Joyce and went outside to meet the Jeep.

I burned up the phone lines trying to find soymilk and the toy baby bottles. I had my whole crew out hunting everywhere. Paul stopped by the PMO with a brown paper bag. He pulled out a brightly colored box with a baby doll in clear view through the cellophane wrapper. Along with the doll was extra clothing, a baby blanket and two, soft plastic, toy baby bottles. "This was supposed to be a present for my niece, but she's only four and I'm sure she won't miss the bottles." I gave Paul a big hug and another one when he offered to take them up to the house for me. Apparently, he saw the baby yesterday when she was still with Joyce at the clinic. I later found out that most of the camp had heard about the little, miracle baby ... the sole survivor from the massacred village.

Colonel Calvert walked into my office and I back-briefed him on the results of our mission with the ROKs. He already knew about the baby and asked how things were going. I told him about the infant soy formula problem. "Well, don't just hang around here; go get Sid and fly your ass down to the big commissary in Yongsan, they probably got it." It was just then that Sid walked through the door. "Way ahead of you, Colonel, already called and they got the stuff. I had a kid that had to have that nasty soy crap too; so, I know what I'm looking for. Colonel, you need to cut this boy loose so he can be with his wife and the baby. You been workin' him way too hard the last few weeks and he needs some R&R!" Colonel Calvert smiled; Sid always made him smile. "You're absolutely right, Sidney. Herb, you go home and take a few days off! Sidney, go get that formula stuff back here pronto!"

When I got home, Paul was still there. Joyce was feeding the baby honey-water through one of the tiny baby bottles Paul brought. "This seems to be working a little better. The problem with the eyedropper was the amount it held. I'd squeeze in the liquid and then I'd have to re-dip it, fill it up again and then try to get it back in the baby's mouth. That's not as easy as it sounds. With this toy bottle, I can leave it in her little mouth and just keep squeezing the honey-water in when I think she can take it. I've been brushing her cheek with my finger when the bottle is in her mouth and I think she's starting to get the idea of how to suck. Tiny bits of progress, but at least its progress."

I spent the rest of the day close to Joyce, helping out wherever I could ... which was practically nothing compared to what she was doing. I was even trusted with holding the baby when Joyce had to go to the bathroom. She would remove the baby from under her robe, wrap her tightly in one of Rusty's soft blankets and hand her to me. I'd gingerly take the blanket containing this precious, fragile cargo and I'd sneak a peek at the little critter. To me she still looked dehydrated and had a sort of gray, rather than a normal pink, baby color. *Wait! What the heck did I know about normal color for a Korean baby?* She also had wrinkles; babies don't have wrinkles, they have creases in between fatty parts. Problem was, this baby had no fatty parts; she was pretty much just skin and bones. I couldn't get the comparison of the baby to a small frying chicken in a supermarket cold case out of my head. They were about the same size, weight and her little chest bones couldn't have been any bigger than a frying chicken's.

Sid arrived around noon with two cases of soymilk formula. The crazy guy landed his chopper in the schoolyard across the street and came running across the road to the house with it. We heard the racket as the chopper came in for a landing and I went outside to greet him. Sid took the suicide stairs three steps at a time and I just held my breath hoping he didn't slip and break his ass. "Make way; milk man coming through!" His momentum carried him past me and through the metal gate. "I got a connection on this stuff and can get you all you need." I tried to pay him but he wouldn't accept it. I tried again but gave up when he said, "You wanna' pay … okay, let's see … around a hundred gallons of JP fuel, a couple hour's use of a U.S. Army helicopter, then there's Earl's and my time, maintenance and then the milk of course. I'd say your lieutenant's pay for a month should about cover it!" I just threw up my hands and gave him a big hug.

Sid stopped in to see Joyce. He set the prize cases of formula down in front of her, gave one of his infectious moustache trimmed smiles and said, "Damn, woman, you look like shit!" Joyce smiled weakly back at him; Sid could always make Joyce smile. "Thank you, Sidney and I see you are your normal charming self today!"

"I sure hope you look this way just because you're just super tired. Lem-me' take a look at the little critter that's been gettin' the best of you lately." Joyce turned her back toward Sid and discretely removed the baby from inside her robe, wrapped her in the blanket and handed her to Sid. He looked inside the blanket and said, "Damn, woman! It looks like you got a fifty year old midget in here, all wrinkly and such!"

"She actually looks a little bit better today, Sid. I hope and pray she's slowly getting better."

After paying his respects—as only Sid could do—he excused himself and flew away. I always wondered what the school thought when Sid would land on their playground. He did it six or seven times that year and we never got any complaints.

This second night was pretty much like the first. One of the scariest parts about all this was this baby still didn't or maybe couldn't cry. Babies are supposed to cry when they are unhappy and this baby certainly couldn't be content. Sometimes, she'd screw up her little face and look like she was going to cry. She'd open her mouth but no sounds came out. There were still no diapers to change either. Nancy had given Joyce some of Rusty's diapers. She had to cut them in half, and even then, they looked comically huge on the baby.

I catnapped while Joyce continued the every thirty-minute feedings all night long. She tried the soymilk with some success. After two days of sweet honey-water it was taking the baby a little time getting used to this funny tasting white stuff. I must have dozed off for a couple of hours. When I awoke, it was almost dawn. I rolled over to look at Joyce; she was sitting near the heater, slowly rocking back and forth, crying. I knew what that meant and I moved over beside her and put an arm around her shoulder. "Oh Honey, I'm so sorry; you did all you could; it just wasn't meant to be." Joyce slowly looked up at me with red, tear-filled eyes, smiled and said, "The baby just peed all over me!" I didn't understand; so, she continued. "The baby just peed all over me! It means her little kidneys finally started working. It means she now has, at least, a fighting chance of making it. I was so scared her little kidneys had shut down, but they haven't. I'm crying and thanking God that your bathrobe and me, are soaked in baby-pee. There sure was a lot of pee in her little bladder; and look at this!" Joyce pinched the baby's arm the same way she did three days ago but this time it slowly relaxed and went back to normal. As the first rays of dawn streamed in through the dusty windows in our little Korean home, we sat there together on the floor hugging each other and crying.

With Joyce's motherly love and her skills as a nurse, the baby started slowly to recover from her very rough start in life. The first time the baby cried, it was comical; it was the most ridiculous tiny little squeaking noise I'd ever heard. We missed those cute, bird-like squeaks, when in just about a week they morphed into window rattling, ear-splitting screeching. We had to keep reminding ourselves this was good; it was a sign she was getting stronger.

When Joyce was relatively sure the baby was going to make it, we sat down one night and decided to finally give her a name. It had dawned on us that ever since she came into our lives we'd been referring to her as either "it" or just "the baby." Joyce wanted her to have a western name, but something that had sort of a Korean ring to it. She narrowed it down to Cindy, Mindy, Wendy or Sandy but decided "Mindy" sounded more Korean than the others. Mindy even rhymed with Jin Hee.

I don't think either of us gave much thought as to what was actually going on; we were just too busy with the mechanics of it all. I had snatched an almost dead infant off a battlefield. Joyce had the skills, stubbornness, stamina and loving compassion to work medical miracles and literally bring a dieing infant back to life. We both—but mostly Joyce—were so intent on turning this tiny critter into a normal, healthy baby, we sort of lost sight of everything else. I don't remember the word "adoption" ever entering our conversations. I think, in the beginning, it was just sort of understood we needed to get the baby healthy and then to get her to some family or agency for further care. Somewhere along the way, things changed, even though we hadn't really talked about it. I think it happened somewhere around the time we named our little, injured, baby bird "Mindy".

It's funny how things sometimes unfold. One day, I went to work as usual, while Joyce was at home taking care of Mindy. I came back around dusk and we sat there on the floor having dinner. We sat cross-legged on the floor cushions with our dinner plates in our laps and our teacups on the floor next to us. We were both unconsciously eating and staring at the glow coming from the small glass window in the Cannon Heater. Little Mindy was all wrapped up in a blanket and sleeping on a pillow next to Joyce. The baby stirred and made a little noise. Joyce set down her plate and picked Mindy up to ensure all was normal. She looked at the sleeping baby for a long moment. I was watching Joyce and realizing I was seeing something in her eyes these days I hadn't seen before. I knew what it was and I knew it was going to change our lives forever. I too was feeling different but not quite ready to talk to Joyce about it.

Satisfied all was okay, Joyce put the baby down and turned to me with a sad smile. "You know, Herb, I don't know what to do; I really don't think I can ever give this baby up. I feel as if she's my natural child; like I actually gave birth to her. I don't think I can give her away to strangers or put her in one of those dreary orphanages. Without saying a word, I got up and went over to the canvas shoulder bag I brought home, then came back and sat down next to Joyce. I could tell she had no idea what I was up to. I reached into the bag and withdrew a blue folder and handed it to her while slipping my arm around her shoulder. "I know; I feel the same way too. That's why I took the Jeep down to Seoul today. If you look in the folder you'll find all the information and papers we need to get an adoption process started". Instant hugs and kisses ensued from my lovely wife. We huddled together there on the floor with our sweet little baby Mindy in between us, sort of in both our laps.

I sat there silently pondering the bigger problem, the one that was growing bigger every day. It was now getting close to the second week in November and, by my rough calculations, I had about seven weeks left in-country. I had absolutely no idea how much time all this adoption business was going to take and I was totally ignorant about anything that might cause a problem for us. All I knew was I'd better get cracking if I was going to make this all happen in seven weeks.

Let's review:

(A.) Adopt by Korean law

(B.) Adopt by American law and

(C.) Immigrate to the United States

Freaking piece of cake!

I sat down the next day with Captain Troy Cleveland the Camp's one and only SJA (Staff Judge Advocate) Officer or, in other words, the Camp's Army lawyer. "There's a big 'Catch 22' in accomplishing all this, Herb. There is only one orphanage in all of Korea authorized by their government to grant foreign adoptions and it's the big one in Seoul.

This little baby you have here has never been classified as an orphan and she's never been registered in any orphanage let alone *the* only orphanage working with foreign adoptions. According to Korean records, she doesn't even exist. No birth records are on file anywhere because of the annihilation of everyone in that farm village within minutes of her birth."

As soon as Captain Cleveland told me of one problem it seemed to be, some-how, connected to another 'Gotcha'. "You do have one more really big problem and, given your seven week timetable, this one could be a real 'War Stopper' for you. By Korean law, when an orphan is found and placed in the Seoul Orphan-age, the child's name and particulars have to be advertised in the main Seoul newspapers for six months before anyone, other than a family member, can adopt them. This actually is a good law because, under normal circumstances, it allows any of the woodpile relatives, or anyone else knowing anything about the child, time to come forward and possibly take the child back into the family and give them a stable home life. Korea's had a lot of wars on its turf and a lot of family displacement. They are very careful in these kinds of matters. Your problem, as you've told me, is you're pretty damned sure all the child's relatives or anyone else who might possibly know she was even born are now very, very dead, right down to her pet duck … if she had one. So, this part of their adoption laws is going to be working against you"

I came out of Captain Cleveland's office more confused than when I went in. I wondered what would be the best way to tell Joyce there were a lot of chairs being thrown on our dance floor.

45

Gunfight at Oak Chong Dong

When I got home that night Harry, Nancy and Joyce all had glasses of wine in hand and dinner was all set out on our short-legged table. We all gathered around, sat on the floor cushions and had a great meal. Harry had flown down to Yongsan, and while there, stopped by the Commissary, returning with a precious cargo of steaks, Idaho Russet potatoes and most importantly, more soymilk formula. Any meal with fresh red meat from the "World" was a special occasion. Harry had charcoal-grilled the steaks to perfection and was just bringing them in from the balcony as I walked through the door. With this impromptu feast before us, I decided not to spoil the evening with all the roadblocks I'd discovered; tomorrow was another day.

After the great dinner, it became time for the ever increasingly popular bridge game. Popular, that is, with everyone except me. I stayed semi-lost most of time and needed a lot of coaching from Joyce. Harry and Nancy were long time players and seemed really good at it. Joyce had a knack for cards while I continued to be hopeless at just about all card games. I just don't have a head for cards. Bridge, as I've been told, is almost a science. It's sort of "The Chess" of card games; so, I was doubly lost.

Everyone arranged their seating cushions on the bedroom floor; while I cracked open a bottle of *Cold Duck*. We were settling in for an evening of Bridge. I hung Army blankets over the bedroom window drapes. It was my normal night-time ritual. This totally blocked light from emanating from inside the room and also acted as a bit more insulation on these cold nights. Little Rusty and baby Mindy were snuggled together, in our big bed and blissfully out for the count.

It was nearly 2300 hours when we heard the first shots. These were quickly followed by a cacophony of gunfire. Everyone in the room went dead silent. I craned my neck and cocked my head as if this was going to help my hearing. Some of the sounds were the unmistakable firing rhythm and bark of a Soviet Block AK-47.

I always stayed in uniform until bedtime to avoid having to get dressed if I got called out by the MP Desk. I also always brought my .45 pistol and M-14 rifle home. Harry was already in his normal off-duty jeans and USAF sweatshirt. Following my lead, he started bringing his newly issued M-16 home too.

I snatched the bundled babies off the bed and handed them to their mothers and started barking orders. "Take the babies to the pantry, close the door and get down on the floor." I was unconsciously stuffing quilts and blankets in their arms and herding them towards the small windowless concrete room. As I got them all inside, I fully cocked my .45 pistol, put the safety on and handed it, along with a flashlight, to Joyce. "It's cocked and on safe Hon, just like we practiced. Harry, you secure the house and douse the lights. You and I are going outside to check this out". We had past discussions concerning what to do should danger ever come to our door, but this was the first time we'd activated our little "Emergency Plan". I'd even taken Joyce to the Camp Page firing range and let her shoot my .45. She never got particularly good with it, but she learned the basics and attained a basic level of proficiency, even though she personally had no use for guns. Just before going out into the dark, I told Joyce, "Lock the pantry door and get on the floor in the corner over there, spread out the bedding and try to get as comfortable as you can. We'll be back when it's safe." I had put a stout locking bolt on the inside of the pantry door just in case a situation such as this ever happened. "Harry and I are going to lock the doors on our way out. Don't open this door for anyone unless you hear one of our voices." I lied and said, "It's probably nothing but we can't take chances."

I closed the pantry door and heard the sound of the locking bolt behind me. Harry had turned out all the lights and was making sure the two other doors were locked. We grabbed our weapons and let ourselves out the kitchen door. I locked it and slipped the skeleton key into my pocket.

We were now in our small courtyard and the gunfire was distinctively louder. Whatever it was, it definitely was coming our way! The moon was up and its faint bluish light lit our way as we crossed the compact, walled courtyard and slipped out through the small, *sally port* door in the spiked Iron Gate … I padlocked the gate from the outside and we gingerly negotiated our way down those stupid, suicide stairs.

At the bottom, I quickly whispered to Harry what I thought our actions should be. "Okay Harry, we got good guys and bad guys shooting at each other and it sounds like it's all headed up our road. Our job is to protect this house. Whoever is out there, they have to come by us if they're coming up this road. If they get past us, they can get behind the house where the wall is low; so, right here is where we need to set up and stop them. You take the rain ditch at the foot of our stairs and I'll take this ditch across the road from you. I can see down the road better from there. You protect the house and shoot anybody who even comes near those damned stares. I'm going to fire at anything coming up the road before it gets to you. Do not—I repeat—Do not shoot in my direction, and do not shoot until you hear me open up. If we can surprise whoever this is, we stand a good chance of winning this gunfight.

We broke huddle and jumped into our respective ditches. I head Harry exclaim, "Damn … this stinks like shit!" Harry was right, and that's probably just what it was. Thankfully, my nose had been broken so many times my sense of smell was only marginal because my ditch was just as disgusting as his.

Gunfire was sill echoing off the buildings and I could tell it was still getting closer. I always kept a round chambered and a full twenty round magazine inserted in the magazine well of my M-14. I clicked the safety off, flipped the selector to "Full Auto" and checked to be sure I had my four additional magazines. I knew I did, but I nervously checked again anyway.

I finally glimpsed movement way down the road, maybe a hundred yards away. I could clearly see green tracers streaming down the hill towards whoever the pursuers were. I yelled over to Harry, "I think there's only one Bad Guy". My other concern was the a few odd red tracer rounds which were now beginning to ricochet and bounce up the road towards us. We were going to have to duck friendly fire until our enemy got close enough to safely take em' out without hitting any of the pursuing South Koreans.

I took up a semi-prone position in my stinking, gooey ditch. My thinking was: *"If I can get myself in this ditch at some kind of angle where I can see the Infiltrator when he gets within fifty feet, yet, avoid exposing myself to friendly fire, then that's what I need to do."* So, I flattened myself out into the ooze and took up the best defensive, firing position I could.

The gunfight was coming straight at us and the gunfire was much louder now. Red tracers were whizzing and ricocheting over me. I could tell we would soon be right in the middle of it. From my angled position I figured I would be able to see the Bad Guy's head first, then his shoulders, his waist and so on. His proximity to me would be different, depending upon which side of the road he was on. I also figured he'd be hugging the inside of the curve close to the hill to get as much cover as he could. If he came up the hill that way, it was going to put him on Harry's side of the road. I didn't know how Harry was going to react; so, I pretty much decided I was going to have to handle this as if I were alone.

The gunfire now sounded right on top of me but I still couldn't see anything; so, I lifted my head just a little and there he was, not fifteen feet away and backing up towards me. The salient features of his evil-looking AK-47 assault rifle were unmistakable. Most GIs can instantly recognize an AK as they've been a distinctive symbol of world Communism for decades, and more recently, that of world terrorism.

All my calculations had been total crap! My adrenalin afterburner kicked in full throttle and I reacted. The rest of the engagement, again, seemed like everything flipped into slow motion. I came up fast outa' that filthy rain gutter and rose to my full height, while still standing in the ditch. Lots of red tracers were now bouncing all around. The North Korean soldier had paused momentarily to reload and had just completed the process of recharging his weapon. He was bringing the AK up to his shoulder when he picked up my movement out of the corner of his eye. My rifle was already up in firing position and I had my gun barrel leveled at his center of mass. As he wildly and desperately spun, swinging his AK towards me, I emptied all twenty-one 7.62 mm rounds into his jerking, body. I pumped the last seven or eight rounds into him while he was still convulsing on the ground. I just could not come off the trigger until my weapon was empty! In retrospect, I figure I must have needed some kind of psychological release or closure for my frustrations at not being able to kill the Infiltrators in the mountains before they murdered everyone in that village. Maybe he was even one of them. Subconsciously, I must have been saying to myself, *"Take that all you murdering bastards!"*

A few more sporadic shots rang out, but things quieted down quickly after my intense burst of gunfire had literally blown the infiltrator apart. I think those in hot pursuit saw my blast of red tracers and the NK Agent go down. Shortly, the road in front of the house was swarming with ROK troops and KNP. I recognized a Police Captain and he came up to me, smiled and excitedly said *"Jos a me da, Jos a me da!"* I stood there for a minute looking down at the mangled, snuffed out life at my feet. I never realized people had that much blood in them. This wasn't the first enemy soldier I'd killed, but with this one, it was up close and personal. With the street light's faint help, I saw his fear the second he realized I was so close. I saw his determination, as he tried with all he had, to get me before I got him. I saw the incredible pain in his face as my rounds ripped into his body; but what I remembered most of all was what his eyes looked like the instant life left his body. The lights really do go out! I remembered the night at the roadblock when Captain Song told me, "If you want to live through a war, never give the enemy a chance. Kill them instantly, without thinking, or they will kill you and your men!"

I then noticed just about everyone was giving me a wide birth and it suddenly dawned on me; I literally had shitty mud caked all over me. Harry came up and put an arm around my shoulder, "Holy Crap do we ever stink! The girls ain't even gonna' let you and me back in the house tonight. By the way; you got any ammo left? You sure wanted that son-of-a-bitch dead!" I smiled wryly, as we made our way up those damned stairs.

I unlocked the kitchen door and yelled out, "Joyce ... Nancy ... it's all over; it's safe to come out now." I could hear the pantry door unbolting and then saw Joyce's worried face. "Make sure the .45's on safe and hand it to me Hon." She started to come and give me a hug then recoiled. "Yeah, I know, I know! Just hand me the gun and get on the field phone and tell the MP Desk to send up a Jeep to pick us up for a shower ... and tell them, for their own good, to find one that's topless.

Harry and I went back down the stairs to wait for the Jeep. Our street was still an anthill of activity so we decided to walk down the hill a bit to catch our ride. Once more, my life seemed like a "B-Western". Good guys protecting the women folk from the bad guys in a wide open western town. It was like it was *Chunchon, Kansas* in the 1850s.

46

The Ordeal

The next morning, Harry and I decided to walk the mile down hill to Page. When we reached the traffic circle there was a large group of people gathered around a ROK Army spokesperson. Behind the speaker, strung up by his armpits to a lamp post, was the messed up body of last night's North Korean infiltrator. It was one of the public awareness talks we heard were going on all over Korea. In the light of day, I didn't really want to look at him, so I picked up our pace, averted my eyes and cleared the traffic circle before resuming my normal gate. I knew what I did was the safe and right thing to do, at the time, but now it was the next day and I wanted to put last night's events out of my mind as quickly as possible. It was sort of my own mental health program for dealing with the bad things in life. I knew deep down I'd never forget last night, but if I didn't think about it, maybe those sorts of memories would get shoved further and further to the back of my *Mental Bus* as new, and hopefully, more happy memories came on board. Besides, today I had a lot of other things to mentally work on. How was I ever going to be able to cut through all this Korean "Red Tape" and get little Mindy back to the States? It was either going to be that or fly back to Chunchon from time to time to visit my wife and baby, because, I knew Joyce wasn't leaving without her.

At Page, I was sequentially greeted by a string of MPs, starting at the gate and ending up inside the PMO. They would salute with their right hand while holding their noses with their left. My reply was, "Very fucking funny guys".

I briefed the Colonel on what went on up at my house, then took the opportunity to speak to him about our plans to adopt, and what I'd already found out. Most of my problems were about things he had no control or influence over, but he did say he'd give me all the time I needed to try and get it done. "You have my full support on this Herb. If you need me, for anything, just give me a call. Put one of your Sergeants in charge of the MPs and spend the time you need to get this done."

He then asked if I had come down on orders back to the States yet. I told him I hadn't and that I was getting a bit concerned as I had less than two months to go. "I have friends in Washington that might be able to help; where do you want to go Herb?" That question caught me flat footed. I thought of Joyce first and that her dad still had over a year left on his liaison officer assignment at Fort Rucker. We had talked about how nice it would be if we could go back to Rucker; so, I just blurted it out. "Probably back to Fort Rucker, Alabama, Sir. That's where Joyce's Mom and Dad are, and with the new baby, it would be nice if we could be around them for awhile."

"Okay then, I'll see what I can do."

After my talk with the Colonel, I walked back to my office and gathered my Korean staff around for a "Brainstorming" session. I told them what Troy Cleveland had said about the Seoul Orphanage and Newspaper advertisements. I watched as they quickly talked amongst them selves, in Korean. What they told me made it sound easier than I thought, but it was also going to be an expensive. Mr. Shin acted as the spokesmen for the group:

"In Korea, money get a lot done and open many locked doors. Cop Chong and me, we go to Seoul and talk to orphanage and newspaper guys. We find out how much. Sad to say, but in Korea money always talks, and American Dollars talk loudest. I think we can do this, but it takes time and money."

"You mean I have to bribe somebody, Mr. Shin?"

"Not 'Bribe' Lieutenant, 'Gift'! In Korea those lousy money hungry *dolttaegaril* (dick heads) want gift for every little thing they do. They make it sound like it your idea and not something they asking for! They say something like, 'Oh, what you ask for is very difficult to do, but if you really want, then maybe a small gift when you visit will convince my boss you are an honorable and sincere man.' They pull that sort of crap, over and over, for each little thing you want. To get baby on Seoul Orphanage rolls, get official Korean adoption papers and get newspaper to sign off they've advertised Mindy for six months going to cost you big American bucks."

"What's 'Big Bucks'? What's a normal bribe, excuse me, I mean gift?"

"Sorry to say, but normally, one hundred Dollars American from a GI works."

"You said I'd have to pay for each service. What does that mean?"

"It mean, if there three or four documents needed you will get only one at each visit and it cost you one hundred Dollars each time you go."

"Can you and Cop go down there with the three or four hundred dollars and come back with all the documents?"

"Does not work that way, Lieutenant. This is business deal, as these *horo saekki* (Bastards) see it. Remember, it not 'Bribe' … it business! They put on big front, this is accepted way of doing business with foreigners in Korea. It not official, accepted way, but it is normal way. Most things can get done without gifts, but it takes a long, long time. But, in your case, you asking bureaucrats to do something which is actually not normally done; so, this is going to cost you big time!"

"How much, Mr. Shin?"

"Let Cop and me go talk to them again. We find out, then you come with us, bring money and we pick up documents. I wish this were Chunchon and not Seoul, because here, Cop Chong just walk in and everybody give you all the papers you need same day for no money!"

Afterwards, I sat there at my desk and reviewed the family finances. It was a short and depressing review. I may have been a First Lieutenant in the United States Army but before taxes and expenses, I figured out I made just about $474 a month or a lousy $119 a week. Calculated on a normal forty hour week, that would make my earnings about three dollars an hour. But, the Army isn't exactly a normal job. You often end up working much longer hours, plus, you're on call twenty-four hours a day. On a twenty-four hour, seven-day-a-week basis, that's only seventy-one cents an hour. If these damned Korean bureaucrats wanted a lot of gifts, I was going to be in big trouble. My brass plate on the club wall now had only about ten others in front of it and my remaining time left, in weeks, was down to single digits!

I'd already paid Paul back for what he'd loaned us to go on R&R in Japan and last payday I finished paying off the last piece of stereo equipment I had on "Lay-A-Way" at the PX. We hadn't really anticipated any major expenses; so, we hadn't been seriously saving for anything. We were pretty much like just about every other newly-wed couple. This meant, we were living from paycheck to paycheck, having fun and not so much worried about the future because it seemed like such a long way off. I was counting on the "Key Money" from the house to pretty much buy Joyce's airplane ticket and finance our way back home. Uncle Sam wasn't going to give me any family dislocation allowance, because; I wasn't even supposed to have a wife, let alone a family, over here with me. I'd talked to Harry and Nancy about taking over the house at 14 Oak Chong Dong and they were all for it. All I had to do was get them to give me the $1500 now instead of the week we left. Then, I would at least have some *Gift* money ready for whatever was to come.

Other than when I payed him back, Paul and I hadn't seen too much of each other since the baby came into our lives. I knew he was about to leave; because his plate was number two or three in line the last time I looked. I figured his plate would soon come down for the next Hail & Farewell. I also knew he and Jin Hee were spending a lot of time in Seoul, visiting her family, and that Jin Hee was now as crazy about Paul as he was about her. It was really nice to see that these two wonderful people had finally gotten together. That's why I was really glad for the break when Paul walked into my office.

"Paul, how the hell are you? Where the heck you been?"

"Oh, down to Seoul a lot. I took two weeks leave. You know I'm leaving next Wednesday back to the World don't you?"

"No, not really; I knew it was soon but we've been so engrossed in this baby thing, we haven't had much time for anything else. You know were going to try and adopt?"

"Yeah, I heard, and that's part of the reason I came to see you. The other reason is to show you this and ask a favor."

With that, Paul shoved his left hand toward me which was now bedecked with a shiny, new, gold wedding band.

"Paul ... Are you and Jin Hee married?"

"Yep, we got married by Korean law, in Seoul, to keep her parents happy. Then we got married again, by an Army Chaplain in Yongsan. So now, we're married by both Korean and American law. Colonel Calvert helped us."

"Why didn't you tell us?"

"Well, Jin Hee was worried about letting her folks know first, and then, it just sort of got away from us. We had to work fast; because I'm rotating back to the states next week. I have about sixty days left in the Army. It's too short a time for them to send me to Nam, or anyplace else; so, they're letting me out a little early. My home town is Harristown, Pennsylvania; so, they're assigning me nearby, at Carlyle Barracks for a few weeks and them I'll out process. Again, Colonel Calvert pulled a few strings."

"That's just great Paul." I pulled him towards me and gave him a 'big guy hug'.

"So you're bringing Jin Hee with you ... and what's she think about going to the States?"

"Well, that's the favor part. We may be twice married, but now we have to immigrate. I went down to our wonderful U.S. Consulate office in Seoul and handed in all the paperwork to this guy and he says it's going to take a little time for the approval papers to come through. Herb, this immigration guy is a real son-of-a-bitch. Seems he has a thing about Koreans; he's like Weatherspoon was. He looks down on em' like none of em' should be allowed to immigrate to the U.S. In other words, he's a first class prick! I just wanted to warn you about him, so you can try and deal with anybody but him when you file your request for the baby. His name is John D. Bruin and he's the asshole bureaucrat of all asshole bureaucrats. Anyway, I wanted to ask if you and Joyce will look after Jin Hee until asshole Bruin processes the paperwork. I just know he's going to drag his feet as long as he can possibly get away with it. Bruin's the kind of dickhead official that can make you hate the American government! I gave him all the necessary paperwork including the completed background investigation. All he needed to do was rubber stamp it and we could fly back together, but 'Nooo, he's going to toss it in a hold box, leave it there for awhile and screw with us, just because he can."

"Sure Paul, you know us, we'll take care of Jin Hee and thanks for the heads up. I'll be sure to avoid the immigration asshole guy."

We talked a little longer about Paul going back to the same company where he worked while in college and before the Army. Seems he was going to have no problem getting his old job back and maybe even a promotion. Lucky bastard worked for a commercial construction company which was owned by his dad. I, on the other hand, wondered how my live would have been if I had this sort of safety net.

By nightfall, Mr. Shin and Cop Chong had yet to return from Seoul; so, I went home and talked with Harry about getting the key money back early. He said, "No problem!" He would wire home for the cash in the morning and the money would arrive in a few days. That would give us close to $1500 to work with. As I understood it, there were going to be transportation costs for the baby, as well as Joyce, on an international, overseas flight to Seattle. I had yet to find out what the connecting flights from Seattle to Dothan Airport, Alabama, via Atlanta, was going to cost. One of my tasks, during the next few days, was to stop at the Yongsan JMTO (Joint Military Travel Office) and see about airplane tickets; roughly, I figured, I was looking at maybe $600 in just air fairs alone.

Mr. Shin, Cop and I met the next morning.

"So, Mr. Shin, what did you and cop find out?"

"We find out you can do this from Korean side, but it gonna' cost you big bucks. Bastards at orphanage been doing this sort of thing for years. Head Honcho's spokesmen say, 'Well we have to find baby a name; then we have to make sure name no longer needed.' What they mean is, they got to find name of orphanage baby who die around time your baby born. Then they sell that name to you for your baby."

"And this is all going to be legal under Korean law?"

"It seems crooked as hell, but officially, it legal. It the Korean way bureaucrats do business. When they get done, there no difference. Officially, by Korean law, your baby been registered in Seoul Orphanage. Korean government agency swear to it and issue you official papers with all the correct stamps and signatures. It an ironclad legal Korean document!"

"What are all these stamps and signatures going to cost me?"

"Well, that another whole deal. Let's see … one gift for just asking it be done and another two gift for baby's new name and research into name. They also going to need to check with police to be sure police have no information on this name. That gonna' take two more gifts. Then, we got to get signatures and stamps. I think there maybe four more signatures we need to do that. So, I figure you can adopt baby for about $900 U.S."

"Holy crap, Mr. Shin, and your sure this is the only way?"

"Legally, Lieutenant, I'm embarrassed to say, it the only way. $900 and Korean baby become Royce baby."

"What about the newspaper and the six months advertising thing?"

"Well, this part of the deal that orphanage say is so hard to coordinate. They say, name they give your baby has to match dead baby who was advertised in newspaper. It just way to get more gifts. Newspaper much cheaper, they only want gift for first meeting, gift for research, gift for giving orphanage name and gift for document with signature and stamp. So you get out of there for just four-hundred more bucks."

"So, Mr. Shin, you're telling me it's going to cost me around a thousand dollars just to adopt Mindy by Korean law."

"I'm afraid that's the best deal Cop and I could make. Seoul's just not our territory and Cop has no influence with KNP down there in big city. We pick up newspaper documents and papers from Seoul KNP then go over to orphanage and get adoption papers. There one other thing I suggest."

"What's that?"

"Just in case some other bastard has hand stuck out, suggest you bring more gifts along with you, when we go to pick up adoption papers. It not unusual for this to happen at last minute."

For a few minutes, I sat there stunned. The scenario Mr. Shin painted for me meant my plans to have the *Key Money* finance the adoption and airfare home had just blown up in my face. I would be lucky if it paid for just the Korean adoption. There was no question I had to do it. Joyce wasn't leaving Korea without Mindy, and for that matter, neither was I. If all else failed, maybe we could write Joyce's or my folks for help, but I really didn't want to do that. I wasn't going to admit to the Major that I couldn't, financially, take care of his daughter and brand new granddaughter; besides, he still had a wife and three other daughters to support. I also had to move fast on this because the adoption had to be legal by Korean law before I could approach the U.S. Consulate to adopt by American law. To raise my blood pressure further, my *"Time Left in Country Clock"* was ticking faster and faster.

In a few days, arrangements were made for me to accompany Mr. Shin to Seoul. I'd gotten my Key Money cash back from Harry, and per Mr. Shin's instructions, I placed fifteen one hundred Dollar bills in individual, plain white envelopes and sealed them.

Just to be cautious I quickly reviewed my personal finances and estimated I had about $257 in both Won and MPC combined. I went down to the Camp Page Finance Office and spoke to Lieutenant, Morris Fishbine, our finance officer. Everyone knew we weren't supposed to carry U.S. Dollars but Mo did me a little favor anyway and exchanged my MPC and Won for two more crisp hundred Dollar bills. I think Mo made the transaction without question because he felt he owed me for not writing him up for his serious lack in judgment one dark night.

One dark night, awhile ago, it was my turn at being the Camp Page SDO (Staff Duty Officer) and I was just out walking around checking on things. I was rattling door knobs ensuring everything was secured for the night when I came to the Finance Office. I turned the door knob and to my shock, the door creaked open. Instantly, the hairs went up on the back of my neck and I felt that itchy skin feeling I always get when I feel I'm in physical danger. I drew my .45, brought it to full cock, and quietly stepped inside the building. Hand-held radios weren't available yet, so I had to go in alone.

The offices were dark as I inched my way along the corridor wall towards the back offices. When I got closer to the back, I noticed light coming from under the door where the safes and money cage were kept. With pistol at the ready, I slowly and quietly opened the door. There were four men inside the brightly lit money cage and both of the big safes were standing wide open. Won, MPC and Dollars were stacked high on a field table in the middle of the cage. Each of the four had a huge pile of money piled up next to them. Mo then said, "I'll raise you fifty thousand!" The crazy bastards were playing Poker!

I recognized all four of the players; and then it then totally dawned on me what was going on. These stupid, highly intoxicated bums were playing poker with U.S. Army, payroll money. Unnoticed, I stepped in to the room. After observing them for about two minutes I holstered my weapon and announced my presence. "What the hell do you four assholes think you're doing?" In unison they all jerked their heads around and looked at me with their silly, dumbfounded faces. The giant Lieutenant, Bill Block, rose to his feet and smiled at me. In a boozy slurred voice he said, "Hey, Top Cop, ya'll wanna' play some poker?" "No thanks, Alabama! You guys did know you left the outside door open didn't you?" Lieutenant, Mo Fishbine chimed in, "Crap Bill you were last one in and I asked you to lock the damned door!" Bill looked as guilty and sheepish as any giant could. CW4 Dad Dunkerly was there too, so I had to ask, "What the heck are you doin' here Dad?" He lit another unfiltered Camel. "Well somebody has to keep an eye on these young whippersnappers and besides, I ain't leavin' while I'm up by about three-hundred grand." The last person at the table was a very drunk Ab Abercrombie. "Well I do declare; ah think our fearless sheriff has come to incarcerate us for our transgressions." I then went into my speech. "If you idiots are going to do something this stupid, the least you could do is lock the damned door! Look at you! If I had been a bad guy, I coulda' locked all your asses in the cage and beat feet out of here with—how much you got in there Mo?" "Oh, I recon about two million. We just wanted to see what it must feel like to be in a really high stakes poker game." I had to throw cold water on the evening's activities. "Okay, party's over. You three out of the cage and leave all the money on the table. Mo, you get all this cash back in the safe. I'm walking these guys home and locking you in here. I'll be back for you later!"

I made up two more envelopes, just in case I needed them. All seventeen envelopes were placed in a large manila folder which would double as my document protector for the precious official paperwork I hoped to pick up. This was a huge sum of money for me at the time. These seventeen envelopes represented close to half a year's take home pay. Mr. Shin told me he thought everything was worked out, but in these kinds of matters, one is never entirely certain. Cop Chong had commandeered a KNP *Shingin* police car for the day. He said this show of authority might not help but it certainly wouldn't hurt.

We arrived at the central Seoul police chief's office first. I can honestly say, I have never been so diplomatically and formally screwed in all my life. There were little cups of coffee and sweets. There was polite conversation with the various uniformed officials and much smoking of American cigarettes. It was followed by my profusely thanking them for all their assistance and hard work. This was followed by my offering them my not-so-little gifts of thanks for all their help, hard work and friendship. The little white envelopes were picked up and opened. The various officials showed great surprise at my generosity and thanked me profusely. They summoned some underlings to go fetch my treasured documents. The paperwork was handed to me with much explanation concerning how difficult it was to obtain. The meeting concluded with the requisite amount of bowing, hand shaking, saluting and smiling. We were now off to our next stop, minus four envelopes and four-hundred bucks.

The same basic BS went on at the newspaper but, seeing the police were in on part of that, it only involved two gifts, one to the editor and chief of the paper and one to his "Fact Finder". It made no matter to me; because, I now had in my hand, proof that proper notification of my baby girl being orphaned had been made to the public and advertised for the amount of time required by law.

Armed with the police documents and the newspaper notification, we headed for the orphanage. Other than the sitting around with more tiny cups of coffee and making small talk, this visit was basically the same as the other two. However, this was going to be the most expensive stop. The documents, signatures and stamps ended up costing five of my dwindling supply of envelopes. I was now down $1100 and I had one stop to go.

The big government building was massive and looked very much like something out of Europe. I mentioned this to Mr. Shin. "Good eye, Lieutenant. Koreans like European architecture. Even our main Seoul Train Station is copy of train station in Amsterdam, *Horrand.*" There were still certain words Mr. Shin just could not get to come out right no matter how hard he practiced.

Finally, at our last stop, no less than five officials poured over my paperwork, then asked meaningless questions. "You went to police station today? Is baby going to go to United States? Is new father in the U.S. Army? Are you going to be the new father?" All of this was just to make the sham seem more official. They brought out the paperwork and, with great flourishes, signed and stamped the documents. A few minutes and five envelopes later and we were standing out on the front steps of the building. Mr. Shin smiled, shook my hand and said, "Well Lieutenant; how it feel to be Korean Daddy?" I answered, "Poorer, Mr. Shin, poorer!"

It had cost me $1600. There was just one envelop left in my folder, but officially, by Korean law, and forever more, little Mindy was now our baby. The next big step was to adopt by American law, and after what Paul told me about his trials and tribulations with Jin Hee's paperwork, I was not looking forward to it.

47

The Ugly American

There really was no time to celebrate the Korean adoption because, we now had to focus on adopting Mindy by American law and immigrating back to the States. It made no matter to the American government what the Korean government thought or did; the U.S. just wanted to see all the Korean adoption documents to verify them as being genuine. Then, if they felt like it, they would recognize the Korean adoption procedure and grant reciprocal adoption by U.S. law. The only good part about all this, other than nominal documentation fees, was it wasn't going to cost us another small fortune. I had all the needed Korean documents with all the correct signatures and seals; so, why was I worried?

The day after I got back from Seoul, Colonel Calvert called me into his office and presented me with my new assignment orders; somehow his contact in DC was able to pull the right strings and I now had orders to go back to Fort Rucker, Alabama. I was being assigned as Commander, Detachment H, 3rd MP Group CI. That was a CID (Criminal Investigation Division) assignment. These guys are like the Army's FBI and deal only with felony type investigations involving Army personnel. I was going to be responsible for Army investigations for all of Alabama plus the Florida Panhandle. The job was also going to require a lot of additional training at Fort Gordon, Georgia. Although I was excited about the new challenge—only a small percentage of MP Officers get CID assignments—I was even more excited about giving Joyce the good news. There was also bad news; I was supposed to report for duty just after Christmas, which was now just a few weeks away. As expected, Joyce was really happy about the prospects of she and the baby being co-located with her Mom and Dad for the next year or so, but she shared my concern about the timing of all this.

The next day I burned up the phone lines trying to get an appointment with an Immigration Official at the embassy. We wanted to get the paperwork rolling. I wasn't going to be able to get an appointment until next Monday, but everyone assured me not to sweat it, because it should be almost automatic. This was a

308

common procedure and other Army families had adopted Korean children. I was told I would be out of Immigration in less than an hour with U.S. adoption approval and the immigration papers in hand. That was just how routine it was.

With appointment confirmed, I turned my attention, and worry, to other matters. I went down to our Personnel Office seeking Dad Dunkerly's council. I liked Dad, and trusted him as my best source of information about the Army; he'd certainly been in it long enough. I explained to him, given the time available, there simply wasn't going to be enough money to get the two women in my life back to Fort Rucker. I needed to purchase overseas commercial plane tickets from Seoul to the west coast; then, get connecting flights as close to Fort Rucker as I could and that would probably be Dothan, Alabama. Then, I needed a car and a place for us to stay. I had $157 to my name, not counting December's end-of-month pay. Like a lot of newlyweds, money had not been the big issue with us; we were just living on love because we had no real responsibilities. Now Mindy comes along and changes all that. The $1500 *Key Money* nest egg had evaporated in bribes (Excuse me … gifts) and now we were basically broke.

Dad sat there behind his desk listening to my tale of woe while chain-smoking his cigarettes. After laying it all out for him, he took his feet down from the desk and rolled his swivel chair close to me and said:

"Borrow against your pay."

"What do you mean … borrow against my pay?"

"There's an Army finance provision where you can borrow up to three months pay."

"You mean I can borrow something like $1200?"

"Yep, with no interest, and you have a year to pay it back. It's set up specifically for covering the expenses of moving from one Army post to the next. In your case, you won't be getting much by way of a relocation allowance because Joyce was never officially here. So, this is about your best option."

"I don't know, Dad; we have enough problems just making ends meet on what I make now. How the heck are we gonna' make it back in the States if the Army's taking an extra hundred bucks a month out of my pay for the next year?"

"What happens on January 11th, 1969?"

"Sorry Dad, I've got no idea what you're talking about."

"On January 11th, you're going to be promoted to Captain.—Lieutenant! There's this thing called Vietnam, and accelerated promotions are what're going on right now. Your military records tell me you have an automatic promotion to Captain coming up exactly two years from the date of your commissioning and one year from the date of your promotion to First Lieutenant. Last time I checked the Army pay scales, promotion to 'Captain' will be about $150 a month pay bump for you. So, you'll be able to pay back the hundred a month and still be money ahead come next year."

"I knew there was a reason I came to you, Dad. You know it all!"

"Slow down, Lieutenant; there's also a downside to all this. You're coming up on enough time in service to resign your officer's commission and get out of the Army. I don't know if you're thinking in that direction, but with Vietnam still going on, a lot of junior officers are. For instance, your buddy, Paul Gleason, is getting out within a couple of weeks. You could be doing the same, if you wanted. You're coming up on a total of four years in service, if you combine your enlisted and commissioned time. If you borrow against your pay now, it will lock you in for another year. You're going to have to sign an agreement that will lock you in for that time."

"Dad, right now all that's important to me is getting my two girls home safe and sound. I'll take a gamble on the Vietnam thing."

"Okay, let's fill out some paperwork. Then, you and I can walk over to Finance and seal this deal."

With Dad's help, about 45 minutes later, we walked out of Finance with $1200 and I had signed my life away to the Army for another year. Joyce and I had talked about getting out of the Army and starting a new life as civilians, but since we were both military brats, it was pretty much just talk. As strange as our lives were at this moment, we figured things would more or less settle down when we got back to the States. In actuality, since we decided to go through with this adoption and immigration thing, we really didn't have much of a choice.

I wasn't too concerned about Vietnam; the national election results were in and Eisenhower's old VP, Richard Nixon, had won in a three-way race for the presidency with only 43.4% of the popular vote. Alabama's Governor, George Wallace, scooped up 13.5% of the votes with his impressive third party bid (9,906,000 votes) and that probably cost the poor Hubert Humphrey, the Democrat candidate, the election. Humphrey ended up a close second with 42.7% of the vote. I didn't particularly like Nixon, but he did promise to get us out of Vietnam; so, just about every military guy I knew voted for him.

Stars & Stripes also reported that the South Vietnamese government had finally agreed to meet with the North Vietnamese and join in the Paris peace talks. So, it was looking like the war would be over soon anyway. *(It would actually take almost seven more years before it ended.)* This was good, because back home, on college campuses across the country, November 14th was being designated as, "National Turn in Your Draft Card Day". Campus unrest was getting progressively nastier.

For me, things were now falling in to place faster than I had hoped. I was making all the arrangements I could think of to move my little family back to the States. I'd gone over to the JMTO and gotten all the information for Joyce and Mindy's flights back home. It would be Seoul to Seattle, Seattle to Atlanta, then Atlanta to Dothan, Alabama. The plan was for me to send the two of them off a day or two before my military contract flight back home. I now had my orders in hand and I was flying out on the 22nd of December. All I had left to do was get the adoption and immigration papers for the baby and we'd be on our way. After all we'd been through; this should be a piece of cake.

Joyce and I, along with baby Mindy, traveled to Seoul on the train and were now seated in the waiting room of the U.S. Immigration office. We had all the paperwork and I just knew this was going to be a "rubber stamp" operation. The door to the inner offices opened and a voice said "Lieutenant and Mrs. Royce!" We walked into the office and were asked to, "Please take a seat." I looked down at the name plate on the desk and got chills. "Excuse me, Sir; I think we were here to see a Miss Wynell Bradley-Craig." "I'm sorry Lieutenant, Miss Craig is on home leave for a month and I've taken over her workload. The cold fish I was talking to was none other than John D. Bruin, the same SOB Paul Gleason had warned me to avoid. He was the same guy who was supposed to be working on Jin Hee's application. I hadn't told Joyce about this because I didn't want to give her anything more to worry about.

There seemed to be no one else around; so, I swallowed hard, and gave him all the required documents. He took little Mindy's very expensive pile of paperwork, stood up and said we would be hearing from him. We were being dismissed after no more than two minutes in his office. I asked how long this would all take and explained that I was going to be leaving in less than a month. He then repeated emphatically, with a slightly raised voice, "You should have planned better, Lieutenant. You will be hearing from me when the paperwork is ready!" I pushed it. "When will that be Mr. Bruin?" "It will be ready when it's ready, Lieutenant!" He paused, for a moment, looked at Mindy, then said something which pretty much confirmed everything Paul had told me about him. "It's a cute baby … except for the eyes." As he stood there looking down on our little Mindy, I just wanted to come across the desk and rip his face off, but I gritted my teeth and kept my mouth shut. At this point, I saw no reason in antagonizing him; after all, he was a representative of the U.S. Government and the one with all the power at this particular moment in time.

48

Cleaning up the Bits & Pieces

Life becomes confused when one is forced to compress months of important work into just a few weeks. Mostly, it involves trying to suppress panic while attempting to prioritize a myriad of tasks needing accomplishment. It's especially trying when the successful accomplishment of each task depends on correct time phasing, the difficulty of the task, its level of importance, its do-ability and sometimes all of these factors at once. Our paramount problem was getting the damned U.S. adoption and immigration papers in hand. All the other facets of moving back home were a bother but amounted basically to nothing if we didn't have the needed entry papers for our baby. Our massive frustration was that the "Keystone" to getting all these tasks done was totally out of our hands. Our fate rested with some petty, racist, bureaucratic son-of-a-bitch in Seoul.

My replacement hadn't arrived as yet, so even with maximum delegation of my workload, I still felt I had to show up for work just about every day to keep the Provost Marshal's Office functioning. I was no longer detailed to work in the mountains with the ROKs so at least that load was off my back. There also were some interesting things happening which periodically took my mind off our plight, even if only for short periods.

The Wounded Infiltrator: For instance, after all those months, I got word that the wounded North Korean Infiltrator from our first firefight up at Charlie Battery had somehow survived his wounds. Like most all of these highly trained Commie fanatics from the North, he was programmed to kill himself rather than be captured and to take as many South Korean or American soldiers with him as he could. This particular enemy Second Lieutenant ended up being too weak from loss of blood to pull the pin on his suicide grenade—they all had them. ROK medics stopped his bleeding and got enough plasma in him to keep him alive until they could get him back to a U.S. Army MASH unit for an interim patch-up job. From there, he ended up in the big U.S. Army Hospital in Yongsan. He was held there for months as a reluctant celebrity in a special ward where he was watched very closely. He had to be restrained in his bed every night and he lived in leg and hand irons during the day. Even with these precautions, he'd tried to "Off" himself by eating a whole bottle of pills; another time, he tried to jump out a five-story window. His stomach got pumped after the first incident and in the second, five-hundred pounds worth of MPs caught hold of his legs as he was going out the window.

After he began to realize the Americans weren't going to eat him for dinner or do any of those other things he'd been told we'd do, he sort of calmed down a little. It was still very difficult for him to reconcile maybe twenty years of political brain washing. He was forced in to having long sessions with both ROK and American MI (Military Intelligence) interrogators. Now that his physical wounds were almost healed, the MI types decided on an interesting experiment. MI was going to give this guy a new set of civilian clothes, a pocket full of South Korean Won and then turn him loose in the streets of downtown Seoul—well not really turned loose.

It was a daring plan because MI desperately wanted this guy to spill the beans about what he knew concerning their infiltrator training and their missions. No one really knew if this Bad Guy was going to use some of the money to buy a knife and kill himself or just find some tall building to jump off of. You have to remember, all these guys had been programmed to kill themselves rather than be captured. Because of this uncertainty, the ROK intelligence guys had assembled a small army of agents to shadow his every move. There were three or four plainclothes ROK MI or KNP guys covering every city block in the drop-off area. It would be almost impossible for the infiltrator to know for sure he was being tailed. No matter what direction he moved, the MI guys would keep ahead of him, flooding the area with new faces.

They stopped the car in Seoul's city center and gave him a phone number to call when he wanted to be picked up. The MI guys then drove off, leaving this Northerner in the middle of his enemy's capital amongst several million South Koreans.

What followed was pretty amazing. The infiltrator stood on the street corner, where he was let off, for about an hour. He just stood there watching the people and downtown traffic swarm by. He then started walking the streets in ever-widening circles. He went into a bookstore and browsed for another hour then took up his walking again. Next on the agenda was lunch in one of the nicer restaurants and another hour was killed. In the main train station he watched thousands of people getting on and off the trains; then he bought a map of the city.

When he came back out on the streets, he took a cab ride to the "East Gate" Market where he strolled along, buying some more food and eating it as he walked. While passing a schoolyard, he stopped awhile and watched the boys playing soccer. After another hour or so, he got on a streetcar and rode it right back to the hospital where this long day started. He walked up to the ward where he was kept and asked the Sergeant if he could talk to the CIC agent who had questioned him. The Korean Intelligence Captain came out and the infiltrator quietly asked, "What do want to know?"

The interview was more than amazing. The infiltrator sat down and started to cry and said:

> "My whole life, for as long as I can remember, has been nothing but a lie! My comrades and I have been told all of South Korea is nothing more than hundreds of concentration and labor camps overseen by the capitalist American oppressors. We are told all of South Korea is enslaved and the people are so very unhappy. Our mission—all of the training and hardships we've been through—was to free the South Korean slaves, destroy the American monsters and to overthrow their puppet South Korean government. It was our sworn duty to free our brothers in the South, lift the yoke of American oppression and reunite the two Koreas once more under our glorious leader. But today, for the first time, I see now that my whole life, all twenty-two years of it, has been nothing but a cruel lie.
>
> I am disoriented because I see no prisons here. I see thousands of Koreans and very few Americans. I have never seen such a sight as this city; to me it is overwhelming. There is so much food, such big buildings and I hear laughter everywhere. In my mind, I said to myself, 'It must be a trick.' So, I explored as far as I could. I then realized, this city is just too big to be a trick. You have spoken to me about freedom; today is the first day in my life I have ever experienced it.
>
> Since up to now my life has had no meaning, I have made the decision to change all that. You and even the American doctors and nurses have been good to me. You have treated me with respect, even though my mission was to come south to kill as many of you as I could. I want the rest of my life to have some meaning. The only way I can do this is to help you stop the infiltrations and stop the lies. So I have decided to tell you everything I know and all the things I was told."

This ended up being a tremendous intelligence coup for the South. This North Korean, Second Lieutenant was way above average intelligence and he had a wealth of knowledge about infiltrator operations. He explained how their missions worked. He took the CIC guys to places where, during nighttime boat landings, they had hidden extra supplies of food and ammunition. He even showed them where three of the tunnels under the DMZ were. He participated in PSY-OPS (Psychological Operations) where he spoke over ROK Army PA systems in the mountainous areas where infiltrators were suspected to be hiding. Because he knew things only a real North Korean infiltrator would know; it helped persuade a few of his comrades to surrender. For the first time, the South was beginning to accumulate real intelligence information about this shadow organization of mysterious intruders.

The Spooky Lieutenant: One of my tasks as Provost Marshal was to review our files for derogatory information anytime the 5th Missile Command was about to promote someone. This was done as a precaution to insure the Command wasn't accidentally promoting someone who had a Military Police record and therefore not worthy of promotion. It also meant I knew about every promotion even before it happened.

I would get these "Record Review Requests" about sixty days prior to the promotion dates; so, I would usually wait until I got a small pile, then sit down and check all the names against our files. Well, low and behold, I looked in my inbox and there's a request to see if we had anything on Prescott Smith. And I'm thinking, *"How in the hell is that jerk making Lieutenant Colonel?"* I didn't know his age but he can't be that much older than me. It was then that I read *"For promotion from Second Lieutenant to First Lieutenant."* That lying son-of-a-bitch told me he was a Major! All this time I thought Smith was some sort of MI *Whiz Kid* and was on the promotion fast track, when in fact, I had outranked him for most of my tour and was even going to be senior in grade when he made First Lieutenant.

I met this goof ball during my first week in country. He seemed like an odd duck, but then he was in Military Intelligence, and I never considered any of those guys normal. The Spaniard had warned me way back at the beginning of my tour that this guy was a gold-plated phony. Once again, as he always seemed to be, the Spaniard was dead on correct.

Unfortunately, we had no adverse information on Prescott Smith. Telling lies was part of the MI business but, after so many times of bending the rules for his guys, I was feeling a little used. After all, hadn't I honored Smith's request to always let them off post after curfew, without question, and never challenge them even when we bumped into them in the Off-Limits areas? There was even the time we rescued one of his guys and probably saved his life. We arrived in the nick of time and pulled this guy's naked butt out of a Working Girl's hooch. One of those damned charcoal block heaters leaked carbon monoxide fumes in through a crack in the floor and came within a whisker of killing both the agent and girl he was with. Smith asked me not to write a report on it because his man was on an information-gathering mission of great importance. For some reason I went along with Smith, even though I never really believed a word out of his lying mouth.

Call it Karma, or whatever, but it's funny how things sometimes seem to even out. The very night I signed off on his promotion papers, I saw Prescott Smith sitting at the bar with a gaggle of newly assigned Second Lieutenants intently listening to him. Smith was at the center of the group regaling them with his version of his many exploits. While asking him questions everyone in the group was addressing him as 'Major'. I'd had enough of this crap; so, as I was walking by, I grabbed his hand and said, "Congratulations on your up-coming promotion to First Lieutenant, Smith!" I then kept walking. Was it a mean thing to do? Some people might say it was; and I don't normally go out of my way to be mean to anyone, but I'd had enough of this phony. The Spaniard was dead-on right.

I guess, when I exposed Prescott Smith, his ego took such a hit he felt he had to retaliate; so, he singled out my operation for special attention. This attention came in the form of "Penetration Tests". He would try to get into areas guarded by MPs or my KATUSA Security Guard force. They tried to get in to high security areas three times within a short period but we discovered them in the act every time. I began to realize he wasn't going to stop; so, I had to come up with a plan. If he was successful, just one time, it meant I would automatically be relieved and maybe it would even end my career as an Army Officer. Sooner or later, this jerk was going to get lucky; so, I had to put a stop to it now.

When we intercepted the next intruder, we were exceptionally rough with him. He was all camouflaged and crawling up a rain ditch. A KATUSA guard saw him first. He was in the process of cutting through some barbed wire when a group of us jumped him. He saw us coming and was getting up to run when we slammed him hard to the ground.

"Okay, okay, you got me! My name's Staff Sergeant David Evans, U.S. Army Military Intelligence, this has been a penetration test and congratulations, you passed it. You can let me up now." I consulted Danny Cortez. "What do you think Specialist Cortez; does this man look like an MI Agent or does he look like a North Korean spy?" Danny sounded very concerned. "I don't know, Skipper; he doesn't look like no North Korean I ever saw."

"You're right, so how 'bout a Russian? I hear there's some Russians up north helping them learn how to use the weapons systems they're giving them." Danny kept playing along with me. "I'll check his pockets and see if there's anything to help ID him."

At his point MI Agent Evans was getting pretty uncomfortable. We'd cuffed him in back, tied his boots together and then ran another rope from the footropes to the handcuffs and cinched it up tight so his heels were now touching his fingertips. Agent Evans yelled, "What the hell do you think you two are doing? I identified myself and told you this was an MI penetration test. I can prove who I am; my credentials are in my right breast pocket." Danny unbuttoned Evans' right pocket and handed his *creds* to me; I carefully inspected them. "I don't know Danny; this picture doesn't look very much like him."

"I agree, Sir."

"Tell you what I think Danny. I think he's a spy because an MI friend of mine told me all MI Agents carry their creds in their left breast pocket next to their hearts; it's one of the little secret procedural things they learn to do in Spy School. We don't have a proper D-Cell to lock him up in, but the KNP have a jail downtown. I'm sure Cop Chong can get him put up for the night until we can check this guy out and verify who he really is." At this point Agent Evans started screaming at us and demanding we call the SAC (Special Agent in Charge), Prescott Smith. I told him I knew Prescott Smith and he was way too important a man to be bothered at this time of night with a North Korean stooge trying to break into a maximum-security area. He was just going to have to cool his heels in a Korean jail until morning.

In the morning and on purpose, I forgot to call Smith. What the hell, it was Saturday and I had things to do with Joyce. I figured, on his own, Smith would discover his guy was missing and call the MP Desk. At the time, we figured Smith must have gone to Seoul or someplace for the weekend because we didn't hear from him until midmorning Monday. After spending three nights in a Korean jail, Sergeant Evans was not a happy camper.

Smith burst into my office.

"I demand to know where Staff Sergeant Evans is!"

"Who's Staff Sergeant Evans?"

"Now listen here, Lieutenant Royce; you know perfectly well who he is! Now where he is?"

"Well there was this guy who was trying to sneak into a controlled area late Friday night but … he didn't make it."

"Yes, that was Staff Sergeant Evans! He was conducting a penetration test; now where is he?"

"I've never seen this guy before. He said he was this Sergeant Evans you're talking about but I know all your guys and he's not one of them."

"I know; I borrowed him from the Yongsan MI Detachment for a penetration test of the MSA because he's a face you and your men don't know."

"Yeah, about all this testing of security; I wanted to talk to you about that. By regulation, we're supposed to get one of your tests just once a year. If we were to have flunked, then we would be re-tested. We've had three tests in the last few weeks and we've passed them all. You're not singling me out just because I got tired of hearing all your Bull Shit, are you *Lieutenant*?"

Certainly not ... I just think the mission here is so important that all components of the Honest John weapons system must be properly protected!"

"Smith, you're so full of shit your eyes are brown!"

"Well, no matter what you think, I demand you release Staff Sergeant Evans!"

"We don't have him."

"What do you mean you don't have him? I demand to know what you have done with him!"

"Well he's in a Korean jail being held as a possible Russian spy."

I thought Smith was going to faint.

"I want you to get him out right now; I demand he be released instantly!"

"I'll release him when I have proof he's who he says he is. You know we wouldn't want to make the mistake and release a Russian spy."

"Russian spy? This is getting ridiculous! He has MI credentials; didn't he show them to you?"

"About those creds ... they looked a little phony to me; so, we sent them off to be verified."

"Sent them off to my office?"

"Not exactly, we sent them to your higher headquarters."

"In Yongsan?"

"No, a bit higher than that, we sent them registered mail to Military Intelligence Personnel Branch in Washington DC. We figured that would be the best place to send them. I also figure I'm going to continue doing that from now on until you run out of agents."

"What? You bastard! It will be weeks until those credentials come back; MI Agents can't work without them!"

"Yes, we heard that; tragic ain't it?"

"Yongsan's really going to be pissed at you Royce! He was loaned to me for just the night and he was supposed to be back down there for duty on Sunday. They've already called me wanting to know his whereabouts!"

"Well, Prescott, you can tell them he's in a Korean jail and now we'll see who they're pissed at. You can also tell them you singled out my operation for personal reasons and that you've given us three penetration tests this month and we've passed them all. You can also tell them you took off for the weekend and didn't monitor Sergeant Evans' penetration test and that you were unavailable, for three days, to vouch for who he was. So, that left the Camp Page Provost Marshall with no recourse but to send his credentials off to DC for confirmation. Had you been around, you could have confirmed them yourself or directed me to Yongsan; but you weren't here, were you, *Lieutenant* Smith? Who do you think they're going to be pissed at now?"

"Don't be so smug, Lieutenant Royce; I was off on an important assignment."

"That so! Well it also seems one of my patrols saw your Jeep parked out of sight behind an American-looking house at the base of Useless Mountain. You know it; it's the place owned by the Dragon Lady ... the Chunchon Madam."

"You have no proof of that! It could have been anyone of my men and I'm sure they were there on official intelligence business!"

Lieutenant Smith was now looking a bit worried.

"Proof—you want proof—so how about this for proof: A. It was your Jeep behind her gold-plated whorehouse. B. It was parked at the Dragon Lady's place from Friday night until early this morning ... I have photos. C. All three of your agents are accounted for and have been seen on post this weekend. We talked to all of them and all were asked your whereabouts; they all said you were away on assignment. And then there's D. Proof D. is my personal favorite. I've got a little dirt on our dear Dragon Lady; so, she's more than willing to give you up in exchange for my not going to the KNP about it."

I threw some pictures down in front of him and started talking. He took one look and turned white as a sheet. "These are blackmail photos of you from Madam Kim's personal collection. You can deal with Yongsan and Sergeant Evans anyway you want but penetration tests or any other fucking around with my unit stops right now or these pictures get sent to your headquarters and DC. Do you understand me, *Lieutenant* Smith?"

Smith, with his eyes bugging-out and an open mouth, slowly nodded in agreement as he uttered the words, "Yes, Sir."

It all ended up being moot because two weeks later another one of Smith's renegade troops flipped his Jeep on rain-slicked roads and killed his lone passenger. She just happened to be a working girl. Death of a local national is one thing even MI can't mess around with. The KNP investigated the Jeep accident and death and determined the MI Agent was so drunk he couldn't even stand up. Prescott Smith was called down to Seoul by his higher headquarters and none of us ever saw or heard from him again.

49

Hail & Farewell

I had promised Paul Gleason we would look after Jin Hee until he got her immigration business all straightened out … and we did. Jin Hee was included in just about every dinner or little excursion we took. Our job was to keep her happy until Paul could wade through all the immigration red tape and get her home. Paul had been gone for quite awhile and Joyce and I knew the only reason Jin Hee was still here was because of that same bastard immigration guy who was holding up our paperwork. That's why we were both surprised and delighted when Jin Hee came bubbling into our, now almost nightly game of Bridge, and announced; "I got a phone call from Paul and my immigration papers are at the American Consulate. I can pick them up in Seoul tomorrow. Paul is arranging for airplane tickets right now and I will be leaving to be with him in just six days."

There were hugs all around and both Nancy and Joyce were bouncing around with her. The excitement for Joyce was at two levels. Firstly, we were so very happy for Jin Hee and, secondly, Joyce was secretly hoping this meant our paperwork wouldn't be far behind. I had just nine days left in Korea before my military, "Red Tail" contract flight home left out of Kimpo. That was the "elephant in the corner" we were both trying not to think about. When we did, Joyce would just start crying; so, we didn't talk about it much. By Army regulation, my wife and Korean daughter were not the Army's problem. The Army hadn't authorized either of them to be with me; so, by regulation, it was as if they didn't even exist. Only locally, had Colonel Calvert bent some rules and pulled some strings to make her presence on base even semi-official.

My "Hail & Farewell" dinner send off was set for tomorrow night and I would finally get that brass plate with my name engraved on it. I'd watched that plate slowly advance around the Officers' Club bar wall for the past fifty-five weeks. Yesterday, at lunch I stood there staring at it high up on the bar wall; it was now at the head of the line with more than a hundred other shiny brass plates following. I remember just a year ago when it was at the very other end of the line near the club entrance and I thought it would take forever to make it around the room. Now, here I was, in what seemed like an eye blink later, wishing I could push that damned plate back a dozen or so spaces. How the hell did my thirteen month year zip past so quickly?

The Army has two kinds of formal dinners—Dining Ins and Dining Outs. The difference between the two is, the *'Ins'* are just for the unit's officers, while the *'Outs'* include wives, dates and other guests. Our Hail & Farewells were of the *'Ins'* variety. At times, these events could get a tad raunchy, as stories were often told in graphic detail, liberally sprinkled with words our Moms used to wash from our mouths with *Lifebuoy* soap.

My Hail & Farewell ended up being very mild. The steak dinner was excellent and I had the chance to shake hands or hug the guys and pay my respects to all the ladies of the club staff who had taken care of me for the past year. Miss Woo of course was my favorite because of her wonderful personality. She caught my eye from across the room and said, "You come here, you big MP guy!" Miss Woo gave me an amazingly strong hug for such a little woman. "You know you come here without your pretty wife and I be your girlfriend. You be taking me home instead of her!" Miss Woo pulled my head down and gave me a warm kiss on the cheek. "You take care yourself, *Rootenant!*" She then turned, with a little wink and a smile, and briskly walked away. I may have been imagining it but I thought I saw a tiny tear in the corner of her eye. This wonderful lady spent a big part of her life making GIs smile when they had troubles and felt down or lonely. She had this uncanny ability to make just about anyone smile or even laugh out loud. I often wondered if she really did miss each and every one of us when we left Camp Page. She always referred to us all as "My boys".

After dinner came the welcomes and goodbyes. Two new lieutenants and a captain were hailed and then it came time for the farewells. Ab Abercrombie, my roommate for my entire tour, and I were the only ones departing in this December's Hail & Farewell. Ab was at his Southern best as he accepted his brass plate from the Colonel and was asked to say a few words. "Ah have enjoyed bein' heah in this exotic land and ah feel a kinship with these people. Bein' *South* Koreans with aggressors to the Naugth reminds me of the plight of the Confederacy durin' the unfortunate war of Northern Aggression." Linen napkins and various other soft objects accompanied by 'Boos' began raining down on the head table while Ab feigned great indignation. "Well, ah nevah'! Y'all must be ill mannered damned Yankee-boys." Ab then placed his right hand over his heart and started singing "Dixie" at the top of his lungs. About half the room joined in while the other half retaliated with a less organized and less enthusiastic rendition of "Battle Hymn of the Republic".

Colonel Calvert rose to his feet and the room became conscious their commander was requesting their silence. "Settle down, gentlemen, settle down. We have one more of our team to say goodbye to tonight." The room regained their chairs and sat down. Colonel Calvert said a lot of nice things about me and I could feel the heat of embarrassment rising on the back of my neck. He recounted the major event of my tour and even covered parts that happened before his arrival. Adding a few embellishments, he recounted the exploits during the firefight at Charlie Battery, The Big PX Caper, The Bus High Dive and my assignment chasing infiltrators with the ROKs. Then, breaking with tradition, he said, "There's one other thing this officer managed to do that no other officer in this command has ever accomplished. He figured out how to bring his wife along with him on what's supposed to be an unaccompanied tour of duty in Korea." With that, the curtain behind the head table rustled a bit and out walked a smiling Joyce carrying baby Mindy. The whole room rose cheering and clapping. Because of Joyce's work, there probably wasn't anyone at Camp Page who hadn't encountered her smiling face down at the clinic. She walked up beside me, and I instinctively put my arm around her.

The room quieted down again as the Colonel continued. "I've got a couple of little trinkets to give Lieutenant Royce. I kinda' feel upstaged here tonight because he and Joyce already figured out what they really wanted to bring home from Korea. What I've got to give him really can't compare. He then asked Joyce to open the baby's blanket and show the room Mindy's sweet little face. Most of the officers had heard the story but not many had actually seen the baby. It was an interesting moment as this room full of guys strained and rubber-necked to get a look at baby Mindy.

That night, the Colonel presented me with an 'Army Commendation Medal' for my accomplishments over the past thirteen months. As he was pinning it on my chest, in words I could only hear, he told me I deserved something else but, even with all the infiltrators and all the shooting going on, Korea was still not officially listed as a "Combat Zone" by the Department of Defense. Therefore, this meant no combat pay or wartime, combat medals.

I think the real reason it was not declared a combat zone was because Washington didn't want to trouble the American people with the fact that there were actually two shooting wars going on at the same time. There was the big, newsworthy, one in Vietnam and then there was this little "Backwater" war going on in Korea. From '61 to '69, North Korea waged a bloody military campaign against the South which some historians now refer to as the "Second Korean War". All I know is there sure seemed to be a lot of bullets flying around during the thirteen months I was there in 1968.

The Colonel handed me my brass plate and then it was my turn to say a few words. I looked around the room, and for the very first time, I knew what it felt like to be a seasoned soldier. I was standing there, saying goodbye to 'Family'. These were 5th Missile Men; the same people I'd worked and played with for more than a year, and now, I was the one leaving all of them behind. So far, during my tour of duty, individual friends had left and that was emotional enough, because I never knew if I'd ever see them again. This time it was different; this time, I was the one leaving and it meant saying goodbye to all my Army and Korean friends at once. I tried not to get emotional, but the moment was overwhelming. All I could do as tears welled up in my eyes and the lump in my throat got bigger was say, "Thanks! I love you guys and I'll miss all of you." From the standing ovation, you'd think I just gave an award winning theatrical performance. I guess it was just that everyone in the room knew my few words were from the heart.

The Colonel quieted everyone down once more and said, "We have one more thing to hand out. I've got a plate here that never made it up on the club wall with the rest, but this person was a member of this command just like everyone else in this room." He then opened a box and brought out a shiny brass 5th USMC plate with the words 'Mrs. Royce' engraved on it and he held it up high for all to see. The room sprang to their feet and a thunderous applause of approval rang out. Joyce had touched so many in the less than ten months she'd been in Korea. The room quieted and Joyce began speaking. "We both want to thank you for your friendship. I, in particular, want to thank Colonel Calvert for welcoming me into this command and making me a part of it. Working with you all at the clinic has been great." Applause broke out again but died away as Joyce continued. "Everyone wants to bring something home to remember Korea by. She then uncovered sleeping Mindy's little head one more time and held her up high for all to see. "Well, look what we're bringing home!" The room exploded once again. Joyce smiled up at me and with tears in my eyes I looked back at her and the still sleeping infant and wondered how this tiny child could possibly sleep through all this commotion.

The rest of the evening involved just about everyone we knew coming up to us to say goodbye. The MPs drove us back our little home at the base of Useless Mountain. We lay there in bed talking about life and the future for what seemed like hours and then fell asleep in each other's arms to the sound of Mindy's little baby snores.

The next four days went by quickly and we all went and saw Jin Hee off at the Chunchon train station. There were hugs and kisses all around, exchanges of mailing addresses and vows to keep in touch forever. Jin Hee had family in Seoul and they were picking her up at the other end of the tacks. They would also be taking care of getting her on the plane, which would ultimately land somewhere around Harrisburg, Pennsylvania. After a year in Korea, "Harrisburg, Pennsylvania" sounded like such a foreign name. Paul was going to meet her overseas flight at the Seattle Tacoma Airport and fly with her the rest of the way to their new home. Waving goodbye to Jin Hee was one of those "Happy-Sad" moments. We were sad to see a good friend leaving but, at the same time, we were happy her new life was finally getting started with another good friend. As we waved goodbye to the tearful but smiling face in the railroad car window, we silently wished her happiness in her new life with Paul.

50

The, The, That's All Folks!

Funny thing about time, when you want it to pass, it goes by at a snail's pace, but when you do want it to go slowly, the clock hands spin like an airplane propeller.

Just the day before, I had said my goodbyes to everyone I knew on Camp Page. It was hard saying goodbye to my Korean staff—especially Mr. Shin. He, however, put it all in context for me. "We miss you Lieutenant. You one of the best bosses we ever have, but now we get new boss to take care of for another year. We do this same thing every year. Sometimes it's hard, sometimes it's not so hard, but it is the way we know. You are the fifteenth boss I have in last sixteen years. So we have to think of life one year at a time. You go back to States, have a good life and take care of your family. We be still here doing what we do, one year at a time."

Mr. Ahn was also very difficult to say goodbye to. I had not forgotten Christmas and I handed him a package from "Sears". It was another wool, Pendleton shirt. I stuffed a twenty dollar bill in the pocket. He would find it after I left.

Afterwards, I made the rounds saying goodbyes to those I knew who were still around. I paused at the main gate one last time and surveyed this strange place that had dominated such a big part of my life for the past year. It now looked so much more impressive than it did on the day I arrived.

On this particular December morning, I found myself standing at the top of our hated suicide stairs at 14 Ok Chong Dong. With moist eyes, I was visually surveying every inch of our wonderful little first home and trying to burn its image into my mind forever. Joyce had her arms wrapped around my middle and was hugging me tightly. Her face was buried in my chest and she was sobbing so hard I could feel her body quaking right through my thick Army overcoat. I had my right arm around her shoulders and my left hand cupping the back of her head and holding her in close to me. Our whole life together was still in front of us, but somehow, on this cold and snowy morning, we both were thinking it was more like the very end of it. What was most pressing on our minds was that I was leaving my wonderful wife and baby behind in this strange and dangerous land; and neither of us knew when we would see each other again. This was because I had no idea how long it would take to get little Mindy all legal for the trip back to the world.

Danny Cortez was standing by the Jeep at the bottom of the stairs. He had already come up and grabbed my two bags and stuffed them in the back seat. I noticed it had one of the older canvas tops just in case. Bob Kelser had taught Danny well. Danny bounded up the stairs and said, "Lieutenant, we have to get moving if we're going to make your flight." Joyce and I exchanged last words, kissed hard and then, I tripped my way down those damned, stupid stairs for the very last time. As we drove down the hill, I craned my neck and watched Joyce until she was no longer in sight.

Colonel Calvert, because he was a great leader and a good friend, officially took over sponsorship of my little family. He was moving Joyce into the female BOQs on Camp Page. I'd given Joyce $1,000 of the money I borrowed from my future pay and stuck the remaining $200 in my pants pocket. Having her on post was going to be a real comfort for me; just knowing she was safe on a secured Army base was a big relief.

With hardly any time to even think about it, we got to Kimpo. I hugged Danny and told him to take care of himself, then I was on a roaring "Red Tail" 707 headed for Seattle, and then on to Rhode Island. Because of Christmas, my reporting date at Fort Rucker was 27 December. It was now the 22nd. The only thing I remember about the flight home was the pilot coming on the intercom and announcing that the first manned Saturn V Moon Rocket was streaking towards the Moon with Frank Borman, James Lovell and William Anders aboard. Somehow, being up in the sky at the same time made me feel a little closer to them and I paused to say a little prayer.

I'd gotten word that Mom had not been feeling too well again; so, I wanted to stop by home, *in route* to Alabama, just to check on her. In 1968, the word *Cancer* was even scarier than it is today. Even though no one had said—and I didn't ask—I suspected that she had it again. I guess I felt it wouldn't be Cancer if I didn't say the word out loud or ask questions.

My first day home, I called Paul and Jin Hee, in Harrisburg. Jin Hee's trip went well. She was gushing over the phone and talking a mile a minute about Paul, Harrisburg and her new family. All of a sudden, in the middle of all her news, she paused. "Joyce and Mindy … when do they come?" I told Jin Hee I didn't know and that we tried not to but ended up with the same guy she had working on her paperwork and that was a big worry for us. I'd heard rumors some of his cases had taken up to a year to be processed, and this had caused many GIs just to give up. In a hesitant low voice, Jin Hee said, "No promise, but maybe there is something that can be done. I tried something different and it worked."

"Jin Hee, I don't care what it is; I'm willing to try anything." The phone call ended, and I still had no idea what she could possibly be talking about. What could this young Korean woman do to make this all right? Hadn't Paul had a bunch of problems too?

I spent Christmas Eve morning drinking tea and talking to Mom about the baby and how Joyce had pulled off the miracle of keeping the baby alive. Late morning, Mom told me she was tired and wanted to take a nap. So, I wandered down to the basement where Dad was in his work clothes and had the old *Maytag* all pulled apart. He asked me if there was anything I needed to do while I was in town. I told him I sort of needed a car and he got all excited. Now, if there was anything that interested Dad more than guns, it was cars. His eyes lit up. "Watcha' interested in?"

"Well, they had these neat little four door sedans over there called *'Shingins';* they seemed to be pretty tough and they sorta' interest me. I think they're something new and I read where they're imported over here now but they're called Toyotas. I'd like to go and at least see what one looks like, if there are any around." My Dad scowled at me. "Don't know why you want to go lookin' at Jap-crap when there's perfectly good American-made Chevys around." Dad was a dyed-in-the-wool Chevy-man through and through. He then said, "Funny thing you mention that, while you were gone, Gunner Seavers, an old flyin' buddy of mine, you remember him? He opened one of those Jap car dealerships right here in North Kingstown. Son-of-a-bitch is part owner and seems to be doing okay. Grab your coat and let's go." I got ready and when I walked into the kitchen, Dad was having one of his daily dozen or so cups of coffee. He was still in his greasy old work clothes. "Aren't you going to change Dad?"

"Nah, I know Gunner and I still have to fix the damned washer when we get home."

We walked into the *Toyota* dealers; it was small but sort of fancy inside. The two salesmen were in suits and two, little, four-door Toyotas were sitting inside on the showroom floor. Dad pointed to the baby blue one. "Is that little thing you're talking about?"

"Yep, it looks just like a Shinjin but it has a different grill and trim. Dad walked over to it and popped the hood. The two salesmen kept their distance. He must have surveyed every square inch of the engine compartment. He was making all sorts of positive comments about how well engineered and screwed together it seemed to be. Dad started out in life as an auto mechanic in my grandfather's Pompton Lakes, New Jersey garage and then became a Master Aviation Machinist Mate before becoming a Naval Aviator. You had to believe he knew what he was talking about when it came to machinery. Without saying a word, Dad dropped down on the floor and slid under the car. "Wow, there is some real interesting stuff under here. The suspension seems pretty stout."

One of the salesroom suits had enough of this greasy old man under one of his shiny new showroom cars. "Excuse me, Sir, may I help you?" Dad slid out far enough so he could see the salesman's face. "My kid here is interested in getting one of these little rice burners; how much are they?" It was evident the salesman was more interested in getting this crazy old man and his kid out of the place. After all, he was professionally trained to spot real buyers, and he also must have had his own opinion about who could afford to buy. I guess Dad and I fell into his, "Don't waste your time and energy category." "Well we would like to help you but we're about to close now. Maybe you could come back at a later time." Dad hauled himself out from under the little, blue car and we walked out to his 1948 Chevy Sedan Panel Delivery truck. Dad liked old Chevys almost as much as he liked working on them. Mom always got the new cars and Dad would drive whatever his hobby project was at the time. The two salesmen watched as we drove off the lot.

Instead of going home, he drove straight to "Gordon Chevrolet" and we walked into their expansive show room and Dad asked, "See anything you like? I also know Paul Gordon." As luck would have it, there was a brand new 1969, bright red, *Corvair Monza* convertible sitting on the floor, and it was calling to me. I'd owned a red 1964 Corvair coupe before I was drafted, and I loved it. Paul Gordon came up to Dad and greeted him like a long lost brother. Because I was an Army Officer, I walked out of the place about forty-five minutes later with a "no money down" brand new Chevy convertible and a full tank of gas. It was a good choice all around. Dad had maintained the family Chevy tradition and I was happy with my splashy, new, red convertible. In the end, I was glad I didn't get the *Rice Burner*.

When we got home, Dad went right into the bathroom, took a shower and got all spiffed up. He put on dress slacks and a nice shirt then told me to get in uniform because there was someone he wanted me to meet. He asked if he could drive my new car so I threw him the keys and we drove straight to the Toyota dealer. We walked in and Dad spotted Gunner Seavers over behind a desk. Gunner immediately stood up when he recognized Dad. He greeted Dad with a handshake and a big hug. "Herbie, you old dog, how you been'? You finally ready to get rid of those shit-box Chevys you've been driving all these years and buy a good car?" Dad smiled, "Gunner, this is my son, he's an Army Lieutenant and just back from Korea."

"The pleasure's all mine, Lieutenant; welcome home. Your Dad's told me a lot bout you. Second place team in the 8th Army pistol matches, that's really good shooting! Okay, Herbie, what's the deal? I know I couldn't pry you out of a Chevy with a crowbar, so what can I do for you?" Dad started in, "Funny thing, we thought you were closed."

"Where'd you ever get a silly idea like that? It's Christmas Eve and we're open until six hoping somebody wants to buy a big, last-minute Christmas present. You interested in a new car, Lieutenant?" That was just the opening Dad was waiting for. "Well Gunner, matter of fact, he was. See that shiny red Chevy convertible out front? That's his second choice. We were in here earlier looking at that little blue one over there. My kid really liked it."

"Well what happened; why didn't you buy it?" My Dad spun around and pointed at a very sheepish looking salesman in the corner and said, "Because that condescending son-of-a-bitch over their treated us like dirt, then lied, and told us we had to go because you were closing." Well, that's just the way my Dad was and has been for as long as I've been around. Don't know if the salesman got fired or not, but at least I'll bet he got a severe ass-chewing for losing a sale, not to mention pissing my Dad off.

The next day was Christmas and I awoke to the smell of turkey coming from the kitchen. Dad had gotten up early and was wrestling the turkey while Mom was still resting. I lay there in bed feeling guilty as all hell. I was here with my Mom, Dad and sisters while my wife was now the one overseas. Officially, we'd now spent our first two married Christmases apart. Here I was worrying about having enough money and there's a brand new, red, no money down convertible parked in the driveway.

Christmas with the family was nice but I just could not fully enjoy it because my mind was about ten-thousand miles away, so I decided to start driving south that Christmas afternoon. That would give me two and half days instead of just two to get to Fort Rucker and sign in by midnight the 27th.

Mom seemed to be doing much better. She did have Cancer but she would beat it again and be with us for another ten years. So, it was with a tearful farewell that I threw my two duffel bags in the back seat of my new convertible, then hugged and kissed everybody goodbye. Dad slipped me a hundred bucks and said it was his Christmas present and it would help with the trip and getting things set up for Joyce and the baby.

The trip went by uneventfully because I spent most of the time replaying mental movies of Joyce and Mindy over and over in my head. I also prayed a lot that God would keep them both safe from harm. I pretty much drove straight through to Alabama with maybe just two hours sleep in a truck stop parking lot. I didn't worry too much about my safety because my other Christmas present from Dad was a brand new acurized .45 automatic, which was loaded and ready.

I signed in at my new posting at about 0600 on the 27th. I would now have to face the in-laws, including, my recently promoted, Lieutenant Colonel Father-in-law. I would have to explain why I was there without their daughter and new granddaughter. Lucky thing Dad gave me the .45.

51

The Long Wait

Facing the in-laws was not near as deadly a prospect as I thought it might be. Evidently, Joyce had been keeping them informed of every step in our process and had painted me as a gallant, bureaucracy fighter. She also said staying behind was her idea, not mine, and she was doing it in spite of my protests. This alone probably saved my cookies.

Ma Shackelton had me over to dinner just about every night during the long wait whether I wanted to or not. We would exchange our latest news, even when it was just a re-hash of what we'd just gone over the night before. I also told the whole family about all the trials and tribulations Joyce and I had to go through to get to where we were.

The new job was pretty interesting and I would soon be going away for ten weeks to learn the things I needed to know as a CID commander, but my mind and heart weren't in it. They were with Joyce and Mindy half a world away. My first two weeks at Rucker literally dragged by and, then, I was summoned to drive up to 3rd MP Group (CI) in Atlanta to meet with my new District Commander. I drove up on Thursday, January 9th and spent the night in the Fort McPherson transient BOQs. The next morning, I reported in to my new boss, Colonel Tom Kusant. I'd forgotten what the 11th of January was and Colonel Kusant ambushed me with a little surprise promotion ceremony. A shiny pair of silver railroad tracks (Captain's Bars) were pinned on my shoulders by the Colonel, assisted by his pretty, southern belle secretary. "I know it's a day early, Captain, but I decided to pin them on you today because I was sure you didn't want to drive up here on your well-deserved weekend off." There was cake and coffee plus a little face-time with my new boss. It was all very nice and it took my mind away from my troubles for a little while.

An hour or so later and I was back in my convertible, with front end pointed south, towards LA (That's Lower Alabama). I thought about Ab Abercrombie, my strange little Southern, Camp Page roommate, and wondered if I was driving anywhere close to where he might be living these days. Ab was supposed to be mustering out of the Army soon and going to law school at Auburn University, then into the family business. I was the only one of our little room 103 group staying on in the Army. I was also thinking that, come tomorrow, it would be exactly two years, to the day, from my Infantry OCS graduation back at Fort Benning, Georgia. Now, here I am, a U.S. Army, Military Police Captain, one of those guys who's supposed to know everything. How the hell did all this happen so fast?

When I opened the door to my BOQ room that evening, there was an envelope on the floor. Someone must have shoved it under my door. I picked it up and my heart jumped; it was actually a telegram. To my way of thinking, telegrams usually mean bad news; so, I played that mental game so many of us do. For a few moments, I went over all the bad things I thought it might be. Coming to my senses, I quickly opened and read it:

Herb

Tell Joyce to be at U.S. Embassy Seoul at exactly noon next Monday (Stop)
Your U.S. adoption & Immigration papers will be there (Stop)
You will have no problems with Bruin (Stop)
Good Luck & God Speed!

K

"K"! Who the hell is K? Son-of-a-bitch; it has to be Kuska! He's the only one who could unclog this log jam so fast. How in the Sam hell did he know? I then remembered Jin Hee's words when I called her from my folks' house and told her about our problems at the embassy. *"No promise, but maybe there's something that can be done."* The "K" had to be Kuska. That crazy son-of-a-bitch lied to me again. He said I'd never hear from him. Jin Hee must have, somehow, gotten word to him about our predicament with the baby? All that talk about leaving and never hearing from him ever again. It's like he's sitting up high someplace just watching what's going on below. Jin Hee must have asked him to expedite her paperwork and now she's asked him to take care of ours. I'm guessing he left her some way to communicate with him in an emergency.

No telling how he got the immigration process going again, but in my mind, there are two possible scenarios. In the logical one, where Kuska just knows some people in high places, makes a few calls and, maybe, pulls in a few favors. That's the more logical of the two. However, in the other one, the one I prefer to believe, it involves the sinister, *Super Spy* Kuska who I know and love. In this version, he does those things I know he's capable of doing.

I've seen Kuska, with one hand, grab hold of a big man by the wrist and just squeeze. The big guy went down to his knees with his mouth open like a fish on a riverbank. Kuska's vice-like grip was so great and painful, the guy couldn't even cry out. I often wondered exactly what he was doing when he got all those confessions, but deep down I didn't really want to know.

When I play this second scenario over in my mind, it's Hollywood Kuska; in the dead of night, he's coming in through the 7th floor window of the bureaucrat's apartment. If anyone happened to be watching, all they would have seen was just the hint of a shadow fluttering across the bedroom wall. Kuska, all in black, kneels down next to Bruin's pillow framed head. He moves in close until his mouth is within inches of the sleeping man's ear. A young Korean woman sleeps soundly next to him. Kuska quickly puts his left hand down hard over the now startled man's mouth. Bruin tries to lurch upward but the powerful intruder has him firmly pinned to the bed. Bruin freezes in terror as he sees that the nocturnal intruder has already reached around him with his right shoulder and arm. The bureaucrat's head is now encircled on the pillow. The shadowy man is holding a shiny, evil looking, serrated knife blade at a perfect focal distance in front of Bruin's eyes. He lets Bruin get a good look at this razor-sharp, eight-inch weapon with its deep blood grooves. With instant comprehension, Bruin ceases to struggle.

With lips almost touching the side of his victims face, my favorite spy hisses in his ear. "I ought to slit you from asshole to appetite right now, you piece of shit … and I will if you so much as breathe too hard. If you wake your *Yobo* (Korean girlfriend) you're a dead man. You don't seem to learn very fast, you racist bastard, so listen to me again, and this time, listen well. You got some adoption and immigration papers for the Royce family, that's R-O-Y-C-E. If you want to live to see next Tuesday you will see Mrs. Royce at twelve sharp this coming Monday; Again, that's twelve sharp. You will see her right away and not keep her waiting. You will be extremely nice and polite to her. You will have all the necessary papers she needs one hundred percent ready to go at that time. You will hand them to her and wish her a nice day. You will do nothing to interfere with her afterward. If you do not do exactly as I say, I will hunt you down in the night and stick this very same knife straight in the side of your neck then rip it straight out the front of your throat severing your arteries and windpipe all at once. Your heart will stop beating thirty seconds after your brain's already dead. You can't stop me from killing you if you don't do exactly as I say. Nod your head, if you understand. That's good; I can tell by the way you pissed your Pajamas you believe what I'm telling you. Now, after I leave tonight, don't go getting brave on me, because I assure you, I know Brian, your favorite son, is at Amherst, and I can kill you or yours anywhere in the world, anytime it suits my purpose. And, yes, I am the same mad man who visited you a few weeks ago about the Korean girl's immigration papers. Oh, and one last thing, wouldn't your lovely wife, Deloris, vacationing back in DC, just love to know about your Korean girlfriend? I do have some interesting pictures of the two of you, you know."

Kuska then kisses Bruin on the forehead and disappears silently in the darkness without a trace of his ever having been there.

To this day, I still have no proof of how the fire got lit under this embassy stooge, but I do know Kuska—as well as anyone can know Kuska—and I know how intimidating and frightening he can be. Deep down, I truly believe something like scenario two must have happened because I can't come up with any other explanation for what was about to transpire.

I spent the rest of the evening down at the Signal Company where a very bright buck sergeant got me through on an overseas line to the Camp Page Military Police Desk. None other than *Buck Sergeant* Danny Cortez picked up the phone. For a few minutes it was like "Old Home Week", Danny said the new MP Lieutenant was a good guy but the place wasn't the same since the old gang transferred out. That's normal, because it's the way it is in the Army; you're always under constant personnel changes. That was enough small talk; I congratulated Danny on his recent promotion and quickly got down to business. I had him copy down the information that was in my "K" telegram and give a firm promise to get it to Joyce as soon as he put the phone down. I thanked Danny in advance and told him to have her telegraph her flight number and arrival date information to her Mom and Dad's house as soon as she knew it. I also told him to tell Joyce I loved her. I signed off saying, "Take care Danny, keep your head down and your mouth open."

I tried to calculate what the time was in Korea and roughly figured it must be somewhere around eleven in the morning. That meant Joyce had two full days plus the rest of today to get ready to go to the embassy.

I spent the weekend and Monday, in agony, wondering what was going to happen. By the time Monday rolled around I was a total mess and jumping every time the phone rang. I ended up being invited, by the family, to spend the night vigil waiting for word from Joyce. We all gave up about midnight because the

Colonel had to fly in the morning and I had to work, too. I was turning the key in my room's door when I heard the phone inside ringing. I was so nervous; I ran to it and almost ripped the cord loose from the phone. It was Mom, and she was so excited I had difficulty understanding her. She settled down a bit and said, "Joyce just called and she has all the paperwork. She's in Seoul right now but she's going back to Camp Page to make flight arrangements at the Travel Office. She will let us all know flight numbers and arrival times as soon as she gets them. She said she doesn't know how you did it or who you called at the embassy but that bureaucrat guy couldn't have been nicer. She said he was almost bowing and scraping like she was royalty or something. Now isn't that a welcome change in fortune?" I'm thinking to myself. *"Scenario Two, it has to be Kuska in Scenario Two!"* But, I said to Mom, "It sure is, Mom, its great; I'll call you tomorrow after I find us a place to live."

"No rush, Herb, Joyce and the baby can stay with us and you have the BOQ room for the time being." I could hear her Dad in the background, "Are you out of your rabbit-ass mind, woman? The two of them are going to find a way to be together, alone, even if they have to pitch a tent in the woods. For crying out loud, what are you thinking?" I had to suppress a laugh. That night, I got my first full night's sleep in weeks.

The next day, I went about a mile outside the Fort Rucker Main Gate to the "Daleville Inn" and rented a "no-money-down for officers", furnished, one-bedroom apartment. Mom came over to check the place out; and after seeing it, she said she had some things to brighten it up a bit and make it more comfortable and homey. I didn't protest because the Colonel said, "Just let the hen nest or she's going to drive you nuts, but more importantly, she'll drive me nuts if you don't." So, I gave Mom a key and turned her loose. It gave her something to do, while we waited; but more importantly, it made the Colonel happy.

The weekend somehow passed and Mom, with Joyce's sisters' help, moved half the contents of their on-base quarters over to the apartment. She and the girls cleaned everything to Mom's specifications and they even went grocery shopping to fill up the fridge, freezer and tiny pantry cabinet.

Tuesday morning, four February, the Colonel called me at work saying, "Joyce and the baby are arriving at Dothan Airport, out of Atlanta, on Saturday the 8th at 1641 hours, aboard "Southern Airways" Flight 224. She'll be flying out of Seoul aboard "Northwest." Their Port of Entry will be Seattle-Tacoma Airport and then they catch a "TWA" flight into Atlanta. Herb, you're going to have two tired little girls on your hands come Saturday evening on the eighth. Congratulations, you two pulled it off."

I was thinking; why was it taking her four or five days to get a flight out and then I remembered stateside flights don't depart out of Kimpo every day. They only flew on something like Tuesdays and Fridays. Hers was on the Friday, *Northwest Orient* Red Tail.

Up to now, if I had troubles sleeping, the rest of the week was even worse. Just like when she first flew to Korea, every night I had those same damned nightmares with those same damned North Korean, Migs chasing her airliner. My dreams may have been bad, but nothing compared with what Joyce was going through.

52

Showdown in Seattle

Joyce had made arrangements and gotten things together. She had two, big suitcases and the baby. You have to remember, this was in the days before wheeled luggage and she was coming out of what was then still classified as a third world country. But, all of that was okay because Joyce is a very competent person. In short order she had pretty much gotten everything organized, plus, we both still had a lot of friends at Page. So, friends helped her box up what would not fit in her suitcases and took it to the APO to be mailed home. Danny Cortez and Mr. Shin were going to drive Joyce and Mindy down to Seoul, the afternoon before their flight. Mr. Shin had an elderly, married cousin who lived on a main city road only five or six miles from the airport. Joyce would stay with them that night, and then get up at zero-dark-thirty for her 0730 flight back to the States. Her plans were to go to the street corner—not a hundred feet away from the door—and hail a cab to Kimpo Airport. Mr. Shin said cabs ran by there all the time and it was no problem getting one. I liked the plan; it was a nice, simple and there wasn't much that could go wrong.

In Seoul, Danny and Mr. Shin hugged and kissed Joyce goodbye then left the two of them with his non-English-speaking cousin. They all ate dinner together and then went to bed early. Joyce set two alarm clocks, just to be sure, then, settled down with little Mindy for a fitful night's sleep.

The alarms went off at 0400; Joyce got ready and closed the two large suitcases for the last time. The cousin's wife graciously got up and made Joyce some hot tea. Joyce packed up the still sleeping Mindy, wrapped her up in a blanket and fastened it to her back, Korean style. She hefted her two bags and the cousin opened the front door for her. A blast of cold air raced in along with a heavy swirl of snow. Joyce set the bags down inside the door and stepped outside. She was in the midst of a howling blizzard; there was already nearly a foot of drifting snow on the ground. A freak winter storm had blown in from Manchuria during the night. Without AFN Radio, Joyce had no warning.

Joyce looked up and down the road; there were no taxies, in fact, nothing was moving on the snow-clogged roadway. She stepped back inside, closed the door and said aloud, "There is no freaking way I am going to miss our plane!" She plopped down on the floor, snapped open the two big bags and started unloading. In one bag she consolidated just the essential items needed for the trip. Most of it was baby stuff. She also packed just her most precious personal belongings. Ten minutes later, with a quick goodbye to the elderly couple, she was out the door with only one half-filled suitcase and a baby warmly strapped to her chest with blankets. She was wearing a pair of winter fashion boots which were hardly designed for a trek through deep snow.

Still, nothing was moving on the road. Joyce looked at a street sign at the corner depicting an arrow and the salient features of an airplane. Under it, in both Korean and English, it read "Kimpo Airport". Joyce squinted at her watch; it was 4:44 AM and still dark. She figured she had, just under, two and a half hours to walk the five miles to the airport. With determination in her heart and tears of frustration in her eyes, Joyce commenced her trudge through the mid-calf deep snow towards Kimpo.

About forty minutes had passed since she set out and reality began to set in. There was no way she was going to make it in time. The icy, flying snow was stinging her face. The suitcase wasn't all that bad because it was lightly loaded it was sliding like a sled on top of the snow behind her. The problem now was her fashion sense; it was getting the best of her. Her hands, feet and face were freezing. Feeling helpless and resigned to the reality of the situation, Joyce slowly turned around and wondered if she could find the warmth of the cousin's house again.

Just then, her miracle happened. A lone pair of headlights came out of the gloom straight towards her. Snow was wildly swirling in front of its headlights. It was then she realized that somewhere along the way she must have wandered off the sidewalk and into the road. It was still dark out, and there was such drifting snow she was having trouble getting to what she thought must be the curb. When she got somewhere close to the side of the road, she set her suitcase down and flailed her arms wildly at the vehicle. As it approached, she was frightened by its sheer size, but stepped into the road anyway. The massive vehicle crunched to a stop just a few feet from her freezing toes. Until it stopped, the dazzling headlights had masked the fact that this was a gigantic snow plow. The assistant driver stepped out of the cab and dropped to the ground. He was Korean and Joyce soon discovered he didn't speak a word of English. She asked him if he could take her to the airport but he did not understand. She started making hand gestures of a plane taking off and then she remembered the Korean word for airplane. *"Be-hang-gee, Kimpo Be-hang-gee."* The lights went on inside the snow remover's mind. Now he knew what she wanted. At first he seemed reluctant to help and that's when Joyce uncovered the baby's sleeping face and said *"Egg-gee"*. The worker then uttered the only English word he probably knew, "Baby!" That must have been the magic button because he grabbed her suitcase and helped both of them up into the wonderfully warm truck cab. The driver looked confused but his partner barked some orders at him in Korean and off they went in a swirl of flying snow.

Joyce remembers the truck smelled of kimchi and winter sweat but it didn't matter because it was warm and they were now moving down the road in the right direction. She unwrapped Mindy and both men looked at her and smiled. This was one of those times in life where one had to take a chance and put their trust in God. These two strangers could have just as easily raped Joyce and maybe killed her or thrown the two of them out into the snowy cold to die; but instead, they were angels sent from heaven to help. We'll never know what route they were supposed to plow but they plowed right up to the airport turn off, then made a right turn at that exit and plowed her right up to the front door of the terminal. Joyce thanked and kissed them both, then tried to get them to take the last of her Won, but they refused.

You would think the airport would have shut down, due to the heavy snows but the main runway is shared with the United States Air Force and, as such, it had to be ready at a moments' notice to launch jet fighters. A squadron of snowplows and blowers had been working throughout the night and the runway was constantly kept in near perfect condition. The Northwest Orient 707 had arrived the night before so it was already on the ground and waiting for her. A small army of airline workers were continuously sweeping snow off the wings. After just a thirty-minute delay, her plane lifted off at about eight in the morning with its precious cargo and banked east towards the Pacific Ocean. The plane was only about a third full so the flight was as comfortable as it could be for a stressed-out mother and upset infant.

Hours later, when the airliner set down in Seattle, Joyce breathed a big sigh of relief. She was home, or more exactly, she was close to home. Her husband, parents and sisters were in Alabama but here she was just a relatively short car ride to Canada and she felt comfort in that. It was now time to go through the normal rigmarole that one has to do when entering a foreign country and, to Joyce, the U.S. was still a foreign country.

She picked up her one light bag and headed for Immigration and Customs. At immigration, she proudly handed the agent her Canadian passport and the envelope full of all the baby's official looking documents. The agent meticulously went through the envelope, occasionally pausing to apply a stamp or signature to the volume of forms. He then opened her Canadian passport and paused.

"I'm sorry, Mrs. Royce … your child's paperwork is all in order but I'm afraid your's is not."

"Why … what's wrong with it? Everything was okay when I left for Korea last year from this very airport."

"That's right, Mrs. Royce, according to your passport you did, but you also left here with a Korean visa. You're a Canadian citizen entering the United States from a third country, and to do that, you now need an entry visa."

"Well I'm here now; what do I do?"

"Well you could fly to Vancouver then drive or fly back across the U.S. border and it would be a legal entry because you wouldn't be entering from a third country then."

"Look … I'm sorry I forgot to get a visa; it would have been easy for me since I was at the U.S. Embassy in Seoul just a few days ago. My husband is a U.S. Army Officer and we are just coming back from Korea; but he had to come in ahead of us. He's waiting for us in Alabama right now! Isn't there anything you can do, like maybe give me a temporary visa or something? It's not like I'm Bulgarian or anything like that … I'm a Canadian for crying out loud and we don't bother anybody! Look, I even have a U.S. Army Dependant ID Card!"

"All that may be, Mrs. Royce, but I cannot authorize you to enter."

"Well, I'm not sure my baby is going to be allowed into Canada either. What happens if I fly there and they won't let my baby in?"

"I'm sorry, Mrs. Royce, but that's not something I'm responsible for."

Joyce stiffened, "Look Mister, I've been waiting to come home for two months now. We had problems with a racial bigot at the embassy in Seoul. I had to practically walk five miles to the Seoul airport in a blinding blizzard. We've been up for more than twenty-four hours; my baby is colicky and has cried continuously the entire width of the Pacific Ocean and, on top of that, it's my time of the month. So, if you want to mess with me that's okay, but here's how we're going to fix all this so as to not upset your precious Uncle Sam's rules." With that Joyce thrust the baby plus all the accompanying bottles, diapers and other baby paraphernalia into the startled Immigration Agent's arms. She spun on her heels and addressed him over her shoulder as she strode away.

"Okay, per your advice and your damned rules, I'm going to Canada. You take care of the baby until I get back, or you can have someone take the baby to my husband in Alabama—I don't care—I'm going to Canada, see you in a few days with a U.S. visa!"

She broke him down. The Agent panicked and he called after her, "Mrs. Royce, Mrs. Royce, *please*, I think there may be something we can do!" Joyce slowed her rapid pace and then stopped. She paused for dramatic affect, facing away from the agent and stood there in silence for a five count; she then slowly turned and inquired from that distance, "Do I get to come in or not?"

"How about a five day emergency visa Mrs. Royce? That would give you and your husband the chance to straighten this all out." Joyce walked slowly back toward the immigration portal and picked, a now screaming Mindy, out of the agent's arms. She couldn't help but notice the unmistakable color of pee on his otherwise immaculate white uniform shirt. He stamped a document and handed it to Joyce. "Welcome to the United States. Mrs. Royce." Finally, she and Mindy had officially and legally entered the United States of America.

Joyce and the baby were the last passengers aboard the TWA flight for Atlanta. Zombie-like from lack of sleep and deaf from the continuous screaming of the tiny infant, Joyce walked the length of the jet to her seat in the very last row. She never spoke of the flight or the plane change in Atlanta; so, I can only assume they must have passed in some semblance of normalcy or it was something she'd rather forget all together.

The Colonel had put his foot down and told Mom I would meet her at the airport by myself and then bring them by the house later; after Joyce had time to freshen up and take care of the baby. But Mom was persistent,

"Why can't we all go to the airport to meet them?"

"I'll tell you why … it's because of the Russian Army."

"The Russian Army … that doesn't even make sense!"

"Sure it does! What's the second thing a Russian soldier does when he comes home from the war?"

"How should I know!"

"He takes off his boots!"

"What on the good Earth has that got to do with anything?"

"Remember when I came home from the Koran War in 1953?"

"When you came home from the war? Oh, oh my yes!"

"That's right, woman, and that's why Herb will be going alone to pick them up and bring them back to their new apartment before anyone else sees Joyce and the baby."

"Yes, yes, you are perfectly correct. We might even want to wait until tomorrow to see them."

So, I went to the Dothan Airport; a welcoming committee of one. I'd stopped by a florist and bought a dozen roses. I had no idea what to do; so, I just bought flowers. You can't go wrong with flowers and roses say, "I love you", right?

The Southern Airways DC-9 out of Atlanta was right on time; it rolled up to the control tower with its precious cargo. At least I'd hoped they were on board; I hadn't really heard from her since she telegraphed her flight information from Korea. I was a little miffed; just how hard could it have been to give us a call when she landed in Seattle?

Dothan really didn't have much by way of a terminal; so, I was standing outside where the planes pull up. I decided to wear my dress greens with my new Captain's Bars to surprise Joyce. It worked in my favor too, because nobody even questioned my walking out of the terminal and on to the tarmac, even before the jet shut down its engines. Seems everybody thinks an Army Captain knows what he's doing. The little twin engine DC-9 is an under-slung airplane and stows its own set of stairs in a compartment just below its passenger door. These early models were designed to fly into small regional airports with short runways and limited facilities.

I don't know why, but Joyce always seems to be just about the last person off every plane she's ever been on and this was no exception. I stood at the foot of stairs and waited for what seemed like forever. Finally, a very weary and drawn-looking Joyce appeared in the doorway holding a pile of baby blankets and a screaming infant. It was not one of those picture book reunions between man and loving wife. Joyce had run her race and the physical and emotional strain of the last thirty, or so, sleepless hours had taken its toll. I decided it would be best to just take the baby from her and schlep all the baby gear to the car. I plucked Mindy from Joyce's arms, took the diaper bag and threw it over my shoulder then pulled my wife in for a one armed hug and short, soft kiss. I said, "Come on Hon, let's get you and Mindy home as fast as we can so you can get some sleep." It was then that Joyce stopped short and got instantly angry with me. "She's not crying!" She peeked inside the baby's blanket and little Mindy was sound asleep against my chest. "Well that little devil! She has cried and screamed for over twenty-four hours straight and the minute you pick her up she's out for the count! This is just not fair!" I knew better than to comment. I put the baby in the back seat in her brand new *Sears and Roebuck* car seat and strapped her in. I quickly retrieved Joyce's one suitcase and off we went.

When we arrived at the "Daleville Inn", I thought of doing something cute like carrying her over the threshold of our new apartment but it was too much trouble. Joyce hadn't said anything about the flowers, my Captain's Bars or the new car. She was on a solitary mission of getting into bed as fast as she could. "I'm so tired, Herb, I feel sick. Please forgive me but I have to get some sleep." She showered quickly then slipped into a pair of PJs. She put Mindy in a fresh nightee, too. She hadn't even noticed that her Mom had moved all her clothes into the apartment's closets and drawers. When she went to her bedroom dresser; her PJs were right in the top drawer where she always kept them. The two of them curled up in the bed like two peas in a pod and Joyce passed out cold as soon as her head hit the pillow. Mindy was still asleep from the time I first picked her up.

I stood there in the bedroom doorway for a long while looking down at the two exhausted women in my life. Watching them sleep, I found it difficult to believe all that had transpired during my thirteen month Korean odyssey. Now, here we all were, finally back together, safe and sound in our little, Alabama apartment. Life seemed somewhat normal again and everything was so very familiar. We left from Alabama and here we were back at the same place. It was as if those thirteen months in Korea never happened ... but they did. All I had to do was look at little Mindy to verify that.

I stood there in the doorway thinking back upon those thirteen whirlwind months and all the things that went on. So much had happened in such a shot time. I knew other things were going to happen in my life. I didn't know what, but knew nothing was going to match my elongated year in The Land of the Morning Calm in 1968.

I called Mom and told her all was fine and we would be over tomorrow after the girls caught up on there sleep. I wasn't the least bit tired; so, I looked in the fridge and found a half a box of "General Jackson's" fried chicken and a six pack of Cokes ... a feast fit for a king. The printing on the chicken box read, "The General's Chicken is better than the Colonel's." This was a pretty lofty accolade for fried chicken sold out the back of a *Gulf* gas station in Daleville, Alabama.

I set the chicken box and bottle of Coke down on the coffee table and turned the TV on with the volume way down low. I couldn't believe it; I'd just tuned into an old Randolph Scott western movie. My girls were back with me, safe and sound asleep in the bedroom. I had a box of really good old southern fried chicken and an ice cold coke; and an old cowboy movie I hadn't seen was just starting. Life doesn't get any better than this.

Thank you, God!

The End

(There's a little more on the next page.)

53

Aftermath & Other Neat Stuff

It's time to tie up some loose ends and let you know about other stuff that's happened since I started *Land of the Morning Calm*. This is my first book and I must say, writing it has been a true adventure. When I started, I wasn't quite sure exactly how to do it, but writing it just like I was telling someone the story seemed about right. Hedy was my writing inspiration; she gave me the encouragement, the time to do it and she brought me lots of cups of coffee.

So, who's Hedy? She's my second wife and we've been married for going on twelve years now. When I got out of the Army in 1990 I went to work at the Kennedy Space Center. Joyce took a job working for a doctor, who owned a clinic, and somehow, romance bloomed between them. I was emotionally crushed when I found out! No one can tell me now you can't die of a broken heart because I nearly did. I lost over seventy pounds and developed a frightening stomach ulcer which nearly did me in. After being alone for close to two years, Hedy came into my life through a mutual friend. We started slowly, as friends but, over time, we became much more. We were married in 1996 and I now have a whole new life and the unconditional love of this wonderful woman whom I literally owe my life to. She was the person who made me whole again.

Twenty-four of my twenty-five years with Joyce were wonderful and I treasure that time and all the adventures we had together. She is the mother of my three children and, for that alone; I will always love her at some level deep down inside.

I never thought I would ever again feel the same about another woman and I was right. Hedy has given me so much more. Joyce was the love of my youth and Hedy is the love of my life. Without her unselfishness, love and understanding, this book would never have been written. She said it was a beautiful story and I needed to tell it.

Bob & Ray: About a third of the way through writing this book, something happened which made me decide what I was doing was meant to be done. Mike

McCabe, a close friend who works with me called and said, "I've got something to tell you you're just not going to believe; I'll be right up." Mike walked in to my office and told me he'd been up north to Canada on vacation and ended up playing a solo round of golf on his last afternoon. In short order, he ended up behind a foursome of elderly women who were poking along. Now Mike could have approached the old dolls and asked if he could play through but something told him to wait his turn. As the afternoon progressed, at a *Valium* pace, two large men, maybe in their late fifties, came up from behind Mike. They too had caught up with the gals. They all introduced themselves and, as guys will do on a golf course, started to quickly get aquainted. Bob, the taller of the two, had recently retired from Chrysler and bought a vacation home on the golf course. Ray, the other big guy, was from Minnesota and was visiting Bob. Mike asked how the two had met. Bob said they were two old Army Military Police buddies who get together one weekend a year just to play golf and catch up; they had been doing so every summer since 1970. To keep the conversation going Mike offered, "One of the guys I work with used to be in the Military Police; either of you know a Herb Royce?" The two looked dumbfounded at each other and then, in shock, exclaimed, "You've got to be kidding; he was our MP Lieutenant in Korea!"

When Mike told me this, the little hairs on the back of my neck stood up straight. I had just finished a chapter talking about Bob and Ray the night before and I couldn't believe it! Being in some form of law enforcement for over thirty years, I tend not to believe in coincidence, but this was way too far out there for me to just blow off. Go figure the odds: A buddy of mine from work is playing a round of golf a couple hundred miles from home and he bumps into two guys who only play golf together once a year, on the very same golf course. These two guys were not only in the same unit with me in Korea in 1968 but I had just finished writing about them. I don't know what the odds are of that sort of thing happening, but it has to be right up there with winning the lottery, getting hit by lightening or shark bit in Kansas. The only thing I can think of is somebody wanted Bob and Ray to reconnect with me.

On the golf course, telephone numbers were exchanged. Mike, a really smart and cautious man, did not give these guys my number but promised them he'd get their names and numbers to me. When Mike told me who he had bumped into I thought he was pulling my leg, but then I knew he couldn't have just made this up because I've never told him about Bob & Ray.

I got to talk to Bob first, and when I heard his voice over the phone, it seemed as if he hadn't changed in the nearly thirty-nine years since I last saw or heard from him. We reminisced and played catch-up for the better part on an hour, then made plans. He invited Hedy and I to visit he and his wife, Nancy, at their place up north. They'd been married since shortly after he got back from Korea.

The visit was amazing. He was still this giant of a man and he looked great. Bob and his wife have this wonderful retirement home in a beautiful location and during our visit we took a trip back in time. I brought photos and about fifty pages from my book. We stayed up that night until nearly 3 AM just talking. I read some of the book to Bob and Nancy and there was both laughter, and then, a few tears in Bob's eyes. Bob started talking about some things I had totally forgotten about and he refreshed my memory about some of the guys. He had a better handle concerning when he and some of the others had arrived and left. I mentioned the great egg sandwiches and Nancy exclaimed, "It's true then! Bob's talked about those silly egg sandwiches for years."

A few days, later Ray called me because he had talked to Bob and the same thing happened when we started talking. Ray was still the same fun-loving guy I remembered from oh so long ago. He too filled in more missing pieces from his perspective. We ended the phone call with intentions of all getting together for a weekend sometime soon.

If writing this had anything to do with these two wonderful guys magically appearing out of the cosmos, then the monumental effort of putting this book together was well worth it.

Jin Hee & Paul: Other than those initial conversations with Jin Hee and Paul, the two of them just sort of faded into the sunset. That's really too bad because, Paul was the kinda' guy I figured would be one of those life-long, old Army buddies you hear so much about. I've also got a couple of dozen questions Jin Hee may have the answers to. Maybe this book can work its magic once more and they will see it on a bookstore shelf and get in touch because, so far, I've been unsuccessful.

Kuska: He's still the same enigma he always was. How do you track down a shadow, with no real name, who worked for maybe some unnamed agency of our government, in some capacity? He was considerably older than me at the time, so I would guess he's somewhere in his late seventies or maybe even his eighties, if he's still around. In his line of work, that's probably unlikely. He was an amazing person and one of those unforgettable people very few ever get a chance to meet. After the telegram, if it was really from him, and I have no proof it was, I never heard from anyone I even thought might be him again.

Over the years while traveling, or being stationed in Vietnam, Germany and The Netherlands there were a few times I thought I saw him. I dismiss this because, as I said, Kuska is a guy who looks like everybody and nobody at the same time. The summer of 2005, I saw an old man get off a tour bus at Winston Churchill's home in England. I almost went up to the old man but that would have been too weird. The old guy was in the company of an attractive Asian woman. I think it best all around that my old friend Kuska stay lost in time. If you are out there Kuska, now you know, I really did write something about you, and you're right, it is unbelievable.

ROK Army Captain Lee: In between Mindy's fourth birthday and the day I met the Southern flight in Dothan, I did do a tour in Vietnam as commander of the 66th Military Police Company. Most of my operation was in and around our base at Tuy Hoa. My unit had the job of keeping 210 miles of road open. Even in Nam, there was a Korea connection. I was rolling south down QL-1 (Main Supply Route One) along the coast in my V-100 Commando armored car when I bumped into a Korean, White Horse Division, Military Police check point. There, by the side of the road, was the same Captain Lee I knew from Chunchon. He was a Major now and was carrying a CAR-15 carbine. I yelled over, "Major Lee"! He turned and looked at me and his face broke out into a big smile. "Well look who finally showed up at the party, and you're a Captain now! War sure is good for rapid promotions ain't it?" At that point I started affecting a southern accent. "*Well I show nuff thank so too Major. Ya'll been heah in Vee-eight-nam a spell?*"

"What the hell you doing, Captain Royce?"

"Well, last time I was standing next to you at a checkpoint and you were carrying a sub-machine gun, you shot up a bunch of guys in a Jeep just because they sounded like they were from the North. I was talking southern just in case you're still shooting people based on the way they talk." That got a big laugh out of the Major.

It was about noon, so he invited me for lunch at his base camp. At the beginning of the meal he stood up and introduced me to all his junior officers as being from his home town of Chunchon. During my tour in Vietnam I had the opportunity to see Major Lee several times and to even go on a combined mission with him. In my opinion, the South Korean Army is one of the finest fighting forces in the world; they sure got results in Vietnam, but then they understood our enemy in ways we westerners never could.

The Rest: I've checked many websites and every other thing I could think of. Just about every person I knew in Korea at that time has faded away, but that's pretty much how it was in the days before the Internet and e-mails. There were always those few who made it a mission to keep in touch, but no matter how well-meaning, most others just seemed to fade away like old soldiers. I suspect many of them gave their all in the Vietnam War because it was not uncommon to go home from Korea for a short time and then come down on orders for Southeast Asia like I did.

Last but not least—Baby Mindy: I do have a daughter who's in her thirties now and currently lives just about twenty-two miles from us. She has blessed us with three energetic grandsons. She just so happens to be a naturalized American citizen of Korean heritage. She also has a younger sister and brother who were not adopted. They currently live in Florida and North Carolina.

We were always afraid something would come up which would somehow cause problems, so we held our breaths until Mindy's forth birthday when we could petition for her American Citizenship.

I was stationed at Fort Leonard Wood, Missouri when Mindy had her fourth birthday. With all her citizenship paperwork in hand, we traveled to the Federal Courthouse in Kansas City. There, Mindy was sworn in along with dozens of others. It was one of the proudest moments of my life. She had this little American Flag clutched in her left hand and, standing on a chair, she put her tiny little right hand over her heart. Everyone in the court house then recited what she called *"The Prege Areegence."* After the ceremony, there happened to be a "Kansas City Star" reporter at the courthouse covering another story. He took a fascination with Mindy and asked if he could take a picture for this story he was writing for the Sunday edition. We told him about Mindy and, when the paper came out, the reporter sent us some *cut sheets* with the story and photos. After that, we often referred to Mindy as our "Kansas City Star" after the newspaper and Roger Miller's comic song, "Kansas City Star, that's what I are!"

I sometimes think back to the day I found Mindy and I still wonder what it all means. Why, out of everyone in that village, was she the only survivor and why was I the one to find her? Sid said it's because I was the only one with a wife/nurse in the same grid square; so, I was automatically chosen to find her. Joyce was chosen because she had the skills to bring Mindy back to life and the deep love to be her mother.

All this still doesn't answer the "Why?" part. The only thing I can come up with is that God just did not want this one to die. Maybe she's destined to do His bidding in some important way or maybe she was saved to give birth to those three little grandsons of ours? Maybe one of them has some special mission in life none of us knows yet. I wonder a lot about it but I simply don't know. I hope to find out sometime during my time left here on Earth because I hate an unsolved mystery.

978-0-595-46939-
0-595-46939-6

CPSIA information can be obtained at www.ICGtesting.com
Printed in the USA
BVOW031811311011

274951BV00003B/16/A